FOREST OF LIES

FOREST OF LIES

CHRIS SPEYER

Xlibris
WRITE YOUR OWN SUCCESS

This is a work of fiction. Names, characters, places and incidents either
are the product of the author's imagination or are used fictitiously, and
any resemblance to any actual persons, living or dead, events, or locales is
entirely coincidental.

This book was printed in the United States of America.

Rev. date: 10/03/2013

To order additional copies of this book, contact:
Xlibris LLC
0-800-056-3182
www.xlibrispublishing.co.uk
Orders@xlibrispublishing.co.uk
305561

In memory of Roman
Surviving Auschwitz, he brought us light out of darkness

CHAPTER 1

'Mark?'

'Dad?'

'Mark, listen carefully.'

'What?… It's the middle of the night! I was asleep…'

'Mark, you have to listen. There's a flood. Don't try to leave the building. Do you understand? … Mark?'

'What?'

'There's a flood.'

'A flood?'

'The City – London. There was a huge surge. Mark, are you listening?'

'Yes.'

'The rescue services know where you are, and they are on their way. Don't try to leave the building. You'll be fine, but you'll need to get up on to the roof terrace. OK, Mark?'

'Dad, can't you come?'

'There's a flood, Mark. You have to get on to the roof!'

'The roof terrace?'

'That's right. For the helicopter.'

'But, Dad! When are they coming?'

'As soon as they can. Mark, we're going to get you out. Don't worry. We're going to get you out. You're safe so long as you don't leave the building. Get up to the roof and then call me… fifteen minutes. OK?'

'Dad … ?'

'Yes?'

'I'm scared.'

'Of course you are… but listen… You're going to be fine. OK? You're going to be fine.'

'Can't you stay on the phone?'

'No, Mark… No, it's difficult here. We're coordinating everything.'

'Please, Dad?'

'I'm sorry, Mark… It's important you just do what I say… And I'm sorry I'm not there… But you'll be fine. Just get to the roof and call me. If I haven't heard in fifteen minutes, I'll call you. OK?'

'OK.'

'Good lad. You'll be fine. Are you going now?'

'Yes, I'm going!'

'Good lad.'

Then my dad hangs up. Just like that!

A flood. I had to get on to the roof. It was the middle of the night. I tried to force my brain to connect these pieces of information. I stared at my glowing G-Port in the darkness. Then I let it drop on to the Chinese rug beside my bed. Slowly the sleep that was gumming up my brain began to trickle away.

I could hear a slurping, sucking noise, as though some monstrous, slobbering creature was feeding on the outer walls of the building. The flood! I could actually hear the flood! It was all around me!

'We're going to get you out.' That's what my dad said. *Yeah, it's going to be all right. It's going to be all right.* I took deep breaths and tried to think about what I should be doing. But when the bedside light didn't work, I was gripped by the fear of being trapped in the darkness by the unseen floodwater.

Mum! Where was Mum? Neither parent had come home before I went to bed, but that wasn't unusual; work came first, for both of them. Was Mum home now? No. Dad would have called her instead of me. Unless… Had he tried to call her? He'd called my G-Port. The house phones couldn't be working – maybe her Port was off. No, he would have told me to get her, to wake her up… Wouldn't he?

I couldn't think straight!

I was across the living room and at my parents' bedroom door in a matter of seconds. Flinging the door open, I called, 'Mum? Are you there?' I flipped the light switch, but of course, there was no power. Next I checked my mother's study. Also empty. I was definitely alone. Was Mum with my dad, or was she at the hospital where she worked?

It flashed into my mind that St Thomas was right by the river! I should call Dad back. Why hadn't he told me where she was? Not knowing was making me feel sick. I picked up the phone in the study, but there was no dial tone. No electricity and no phones. The sick, panicky feeling was growing worse. I went back to the living room, where there was more space, more air to breath.

Outside, it was very black. Obviously, a major power cut, even Bermondsey over the river was in darkness. I crossed to the tall floor-to-ceiling glass doors that made up most of the river-facing wall of the room, with its multi-million-pound view of the Thames. The double-glazing cut out most of the sound, but when I pressed my face against the glass, I could see what appeared to be a vast, undulating sheet of black silk, spreading out from a level just below the window. I slid the glass doors open. Rain spattered in on to the polished floor. I imagined my mother's voice shouting, *Shut those wretched doors before the floor gets completely ruined.* I left them open and stepped out on to the balcony.

Terror made me freeze. Water! It was like the sea. A nightmare, monstrous sea. Black. Coiling. Sucking and dragging at the old stone walls of the building. The churning water was less than a metre below my bare feet. The balcony trembled and shook as the water swept around the converted warehouse. In secret, in the night, the river had swollen up, climbed over the new levees, bloated itself out, and engulfed what should have been dry land. I could just make out the shapes of bits and pieces of debris that the distended river had dragged out of the back streets downstream – wheelie bins, furniture, lengths of timber, bolts of fabric, shoes – loads of shoes – a front door, a gas cylinder, great rafts of unidentifiable rubbish. The debris was moving upriver. This was tidal water, the sea had come to London, and the level was still rising!

Get to the roof! Get to the roof! I had to get to the roof. I leapt back through the doors and slammed the sliding glass shut – as though those brittle glass sheets could hold back the weight of the North Sea!

I ran to my bedroom, grabbed my G-Port off the floor, and dashed from the apartment into the dark stairwell. Seven or eight steps down, the stairs disappeared into filthy black water. Even if I wanted to leave the building, I couldn't. The flat below must be full of water. The Reynolds – their two little kids! Had they got out? In my mind I saw their flat full, like a fish tank, their floating, lifeless bodies pressed against the ceiling.

Upstairs! Get to the roof! I took the steps two at a time. As I passed the two apartments above ours, I hammered on their doors. No reply.

The door to the roof terrace had a crash bar. It was an emergency exit, so it couldn't be locked. You just pushed against the bar and the door opened. Only it didn't! It wouldn't open! Why wasn't it opening?! Something outside must be leaning against it. Something heavy must be blocking it! 'LET ME OUT!' I pushed; I threw all my weight against it. For a few minutes, I completely lost all control and lashed out, kicking and screaming at the door. It was no use. I was trapped. But I mustn't stay here. Once our apartment flooded, there'd be no escape from the stairwell.

I leapt back down the stairs, missed the last step in the darkness, and landed flat on my face. As my right arm hit the ground, my G-Port shot from my hand and skidded across the floor, and I heard the *click* as it ricocheted off the wall and then the *splash* as it hit the water in the flooded stairwell. I scrambled to my feet in time to see the glowing G-Port slowly sink out of sight. My heart sank with it. Without it, I had no way of telling my father that I couldn't get on to the roof. No way of calling for help. And there was no way anyone could reach me.

I went back to my bedroom. I wanted to hide. I wanted it all to be a dream. But as I stepped through the door of my room, I was stopped dead by a deep, creaking groan from the living room, as if a giant had set his foot on an enormous loose floorboard. My mouth was open, but no air would go in or out as I waited – knowing – dreading what would happen next. There was a rending crash like an explosion, and within seconds, the rug under my feet was wet.

It was inside. It was no longer prowling around licking the outside of the building. It had broken in. It was going to get me! The water had risen above the balcony – the glass doors had given way – the flood was in the flat!

I forced down the panic and made myself think. The fire-escape. Outside my mum's study window, the steep metal steps zigzagged from the top-floor flat, past our apartment, to the ground. I could get on the fire-escape and climb up to the roof – out of reach of the water. I was shivering – with fear more than cold. I needed to find something warm to wear before I set out. Yesterday's clothes were, as usual, in a heap on the floor; they'd be soaked. I stepped off the bed. The freezing water was already up to my ankles. How long did I have? How much higher would it get?

I pulled open draws and flung clothes on the bed; then climbed back on to it, dried my feet with the duvet, and started to dress. Jeans, T-shirt, sweatshirt. I rolled the jeans up as far as I could. Shoes? I stepped back into the water. It was getting higher. Everything at the bottom of the wardrobe was wet. There were shoes floating about. I remembered all the shoes floating past the balcony. Dead people's shoes. The flood broke into people's houses, drowned the occupants, and took their shoes. *Come on! Get a grip! They were just shoes!* Probably from a shoe shop or somewhere. Forget about shoes, my feet are going to be wet anyway! My leather jacket? – On the chair – I shrugged it on. *Go! Go! Go! Get out! Time to get out!* My breath was coming in short gasps. The water was almost up to my knees, and it was freezing cold.

Back in the living room, it was flowing like a river; I could hear it cascading down into the stairwell. I had to force myself to leave the seeming safety of my bedroom. The division between inside and outside had gone. Floating rubbish had already caught around the legs of the table and chairs. Black water extended out, through the shattered windows and blended with night. I clung, for a minute, to the doorframe willing myself to cross to the study, but in my mind, there was no longer a floor, and I imagined myself sinking down into the Reynolds' flat below – sinking past their drowned bodies.

Something nudged my leg, and I screamed in horror, imagining some creature swimming in the water, but it was a carved Korean coffee table, now adrift in the knee-deep water.

Get out! Get out! What was I doing? I shouldn't just stand here waiting to be swallowed up by the flood! Why couldn't I move? Something held me back – I needed to rescue something. I don't know why; I just couldn't leave empty-handed – I had to take something with me – something that was mine – something that mattered. I turned back into my room. I had loads of things. Even in the dark, I knew where most of them were – cameras, games, computer, and clothes. Then I saw my saxophone case on top of my chest-of-draws. I hadn't played it in over a year, not since it stopped mattering to anyone whether I practised or not. The case had straps like a rucksack. I slung it on my back. There! Now I was ready to leave. It didn't make much sense; a flat full of priceless art, and I took a not-very-good saxophone that I no longer played!

I waded as quickly as I could, across the living room, trying not to look out through the shattered windows at the expanse of water beyond. My mother's study was no longer in total darkness. A cold shimmer of moonlight silhouetted the objects on the window ledge. Sheets of computer paper floated, in pale rafts, on the surface of the water and clung to my legs as I waded through them.

Try not to think about what's outside – One step at a time. One step at a time.

Perhaps I should stay – wait in the flat until the last minute – but if the water rises above the level of the window, will I be able to get out?

The study window opens inwards. I move the objects off the window ledge and on to my mother's desk. On the desk, I see a small photo of the three of us – Mum, Dad, me – taken on a sailing holiday two years ago – Mum and I have our arms around each other – Dad is behind Mum, with one arm round her shoulders – We all look very happy. I un-sling my saxophone case, open it, and squeeze the little picture into the sheet-music pocket inside the lid, then sling the case back on my shoulders, open the window, and climb out on to the fire escape's rusted steel platform. All around are the sounds of water, and the current flowing through the lower sections of the steel stairway makes the metal of the fire escape hum and vibrate under my bare feet. Where the water is not in shadow, it glints, black, oily, evil – sudden eddies twisting and distorting its surface. Then the moon slides back behind clouds, plunging everything into total darkness, and the rain returns, driven by a violent gust that flings it, hissing across the water. It's hard to know which is more terrifying: seeing the swirling, coiling water that sweeps between the buildings, or clinging to the stairs in total darkness.

I begin to climb.

I have only gone a few steps when a deep, hollow, booming – like a great gong being struck – reverberates through the darkness. I freeze, and gripping the handrail, I peer about. What now? What was that? The rain stings my face as I turn in the direction that the sound seems to have come from. Then it comes again – BOOM! BOOOOM! – Louder. Closer. I scramble up a few more steps and wait. The next moment, I'm almost thrown from the fire escape as some massive, floating thing slams into it, shaking the whole, crumbling, rusted structure. I can feel that the section I'm on is no longer firmly anchored to the wall; it's moving far more than before the impact. It's going to come off! The whole thing's going to come off the wall! It's going to come off, and I'm going to go with it! Me and tons of metal are going to fall, sink, drown in that black water! Climb down! Try to get back into the flat! I take a step and then think, *No I can't go back. Back inside, I'll be trapped by the rising water.* Maybe higher up the fire escape is still sound. Paralysed by fear, I hang where I am, expecting at any minute to feel the structure give way. A sobbing cry of helplessness rises in my throat but, before it can burst out, the moon returns, and I see what struck the fire escape – an empty rubbish skip, like a small barge, is wedged by the pressure of water against the steel steps – I watch, mesmerised, as the force of the current heaps black water up behind the jammed skip, then pours over its rim, filling it in an instant and dragging it under. The rim of the sinking skip catches on the metalwork and with a scream of twisting steel, the platform that I had first stepped on to disappears with the skip below the swirling surface.

The steps on which I stand are now hanging in space, with nothing below them. There is no way back.

Although I haven't moved in several minutes, I am breathing as if I have just run a marathon. Up – I have to climb up. Gingerly, I begin to move. The steps sway as I shift my weight. I'm terrified that my movements will be enough to tear the remaining fixings from the wall. I manage to climb two more steps before fear locks every joint and sinew, and I can move no further.

I don't know how long I spent clinging to the fire escape but, as I clung there, I became aware of the shrieking sirens in those parts of the city that were still above water and of the approaching and retreating clatter of rotor blades. Other people were being rescued. Why weren't they coming for me? 'You promised!' I yelled at my father through the driving rain, 'You promised they'd come!' Eventually, on hands and knees, I begin to crawl up the shaking steps. At last, I reach the platform that gives access to the fire escape from the third floor. This section seems more stable. I'm wet through and shivering so much I can hardly hold on. The wind drives the rain up my jacket sleeves and down my neck. Should I smash a window, breaking into the top floor flat? Surely, the water wouldn't rise this high, and I could get out of the wind and rain. But how would they know I was there? If I want to be sure, they'll find me – if I want to be rescued, I need to stay in the open. I huddle against the low parapet that surrounds the roof. Once I climb over it, there will be no protection from the driving rain. I count to five, then slither on my belly over the parapet. The force of the wind across the flat roof is unbelievable! When I try to stand, it threatens to hurl me back over the edge and in to the flood. I drop to my hands and knees and crawl across to shelter by the side of the doorway to the internal stairs. Now I can see what had prevented me opening the door from the inside; the storm has piled the roof terrace furniture against it.

I was considering whether it would be worth clearing the doorway to shelter inside, when the air around me began to throb. As the throbbing became a deafening roar, I saw the helicopter, black against the moon-lit clouds, as it edged, huge, over the building and then, in the middle of the roaring beat, the darkness was driven back, and I was bathed in blinding light. As I squinted up into the glare I saw a figure, like a miracle descending slowly through the dazzling brightness. 'Nothing broken?' he shouted in my ear, as he landed beside me. I shook my head. 'Anyone else in the building?' I shook my head again. He hauled me to my feet, slipped the straps of the saxophone case off my shoulders, and slid a harness up under my arms. Then we were going up, turning in the air. Waiting hands helped me through the door of the helicopter, and my rescuer followed, swinging himself inside. I saw that he was holding out my dripping saxophone case. He grinned, but the noise of the aircraft's engines drowned out his cheery remark as he passed it to me.

I was wrapped in a blanket and strapped in as the helicopter tilted and rose up above the buildings. The cabin was packed with survivors – all ages, all colours, all wrapped, like me, in blankets. Couples clung together – parents clung to crying babies. Kids my own age, whose frightened eyes made them look much younger than they really were, stared at me as if I had arrived with some answer, some explanation. A blast of wind caught the helicopter, lifting it, then letting it drop in a sickening sea-sawing plunge. Screams filled the fuselage.

The winchman leant towards me, 'We've got instructions to drop you first. Bloody waste of precious time, if you ask me. Should be dropping you at the muster station with all the others. Must be useful to know the Prime Minister! Eh?'

'Shit,' I thought, 'it's not my fault who my father is!' I stared past the pilot, through the front windscreen of the aircraft. The unmistakeable shape of the Global Solutions building loomed ahead of us, towering majestically above the other tall buildings of the City; my dad's building, both the hub of the European carbon exchange and the nerve-centre of the global communication system; here they bought and sold every carbon quota this side of the Atlantic as well as controlling the GRID. Even through the driving rain it had an awesome beauty, like a perfectly proportioned leaf, narrow at the base, swelling in the centre, and tapering to its skyscraping tip. The vast, gently curved, polished surface with its coating of solar-voltaic cells glistened like an iridescent skin. The city's first truly carbon-neutral building, it generated all its own power, collected it's own water and released no emissions. I could never see it without feeling a surge of pride for my father whose brainchild it had been.

We landed on the building's suspended helipad. As the winchman bundled me out and hurried me through the downdraft of the rotor blades, I peered through the rain that swirled in the floodlights, expecting to see my father and hoping that my mother would be there too, anxiously waiting for me. But it was my father's personal assistant, not my father, who stood holding the door open. I turned to call my thanks to the winchman, but he was already running, head bent, back towards the aircraft, and as soon as he had scrambled aboard, it was off. 'Glad to be rid of me,' I thought.

CHAPTER 2

Abbie-the-all-knowing, as my dad called his PA, led me to the lift and made a great fuss over me as we dropped fifty floors to the centre of the building where my dad had his suite of offices. 'We were really, really worried, Mark! They had instructions to find you first and bring you straight back here! We're very, very annoyed with the rescue services.' Abbie is one of those women who talk like they're about twenty even though they're actually much older. Abbie had to be at least thirty-five because she'd been working for my dad for over ten years. 'Don't be fooled by the way she sounds,' my dad would say, 'she's got a first-class degree in economics.'

As the lift hummed down, I inspected myself in its mirrored walls. I didn't look as heroic as I'd hoped – A skinny wet boy with bruised shins and a pale face stared back at me – a puddle of water was forming around the boy's feet.

I followed Abbie out of the lift at floor number forty. Here, the polished grey granite of the rest of the building gave way to white marble in the corridors and public reception areas and then, once you passed through the security doors, to deep, sound-absorbing carpet that you could actually feel your feet sinking into. Each set of doors we approached gave a discreet sigh of recognition and opened to let us pass when Abbie pressed her hand on the print recognition pad, then sighed shut behind us.

Of course, Abbie-the-all-knowing knew I'd need dry clothes. 'I had to guess your size, so I had them send over a few of everything. Just choose the ones that suit you, and we'll send the rest back. Probably not your style, Mark. I'm afraid I'm not up on what's dead trendy for teenagers.' Only Abbie, I thought, could get clothes 'sent over' in the middle of major disaster and then apologise for the style!

She led me into an empty conference room where she'd laid out an assortment of new clothing. On a side table, I could see there were also sandwiches, bars of chocolate, and juices. 'You're probably starving, you poor thing. That's just to keep you going until I can organise something better,' she said as she left me to change.

Left alone in the softly lit, air-conditioned silence of the empty conference room, I felt totally spaced. The sort of feeling you get when you've flown half the night and they make you change planes in some strange-smelling airport in the middle of the desert. You know what I mean – you wonder about like the living-dead, staring at things but not really seeing what they are. What I really wanted to do was lie down on that nice spongy carpet and go to sleep, but I knew Abbie would be back pretty soon. Maybe if I ate some chocolate, I'd be able to cope. I ate a whole Fruit an' Nut and then another. How did Abbie know they were my favourite, had she asked my dad? And where the hell was my dad? The sugar and sudden surge of anger at my parents completely not caring what had happened to me got me going again. I changed into the least nerdish-looking things Abbie had found, scoffed a couple of sandwiches, and set off for my dad's office.

I'd have to go through the central control office for the GRID; pretty much everyone in the place knew who I was, but I felt a bit self-conscious in my new clothes. Then I thought, *The place'll be half empty. It's the middle of the night!* So it was a shock to enter and find every desk manned and mostly manned by people I'd never seen before. Some were in uniform, and all appeared to know exactly what they were doing. They were talking urgently into telephones or staring at maps on screens. As I passed through the maze of workstations, hardly anyone looked up – phones rang as soon as they were put down. *Of course!* I thought, *they'll be using the GRID to coordinate the search and rescue operation.*

The glass doors on the other side of the office led into Abbie's domain, where she controlled access to my father's suite. No one got passed Abbie without an appointment. As I entered, Abbie jumped up from her desk. 'Oh, Mark! I didn't think you'd be ready yet! Did you find everything you needed?'

'I'm going to see Dad,' I said.

'I don't think that's possible right now.' She stepped between me and the tall, brushed-metal doors.

'I'm his son! I'm going to see him!' My voice sounded as squeaky as a little kid's. I dodged past her and pressed my hand to the print-recognition pad.

'No, Mark. Just wait... !'

The doors swung open. My dad had programmed my handprint into the system for fun when I was ten.

'I'm very sorry, Sir Robert... But Mark's here,' I heard Abbie's embarrassed apology behind me.

My father spun round and glared at his PA. 'I thought I told you... ,' he thundered. Then he took a deep breath, sucking air in through his flared nostrils. His face relaxed – 'It's all right, Mark – Come on – come on, in.' He turned to the others in the room. 'As you know, my son had to be rescued from our apartment. He's had a bit of an adventure.'

A bit of an adventure! I thought, *You have absolutely no idea!* I looked at the others in the room. The Prime Minister, Mrs Grist, skinny as a dry stick, was surrounded by at least half the ministers in her cabinet, and there was the Mayor of London (the incredibly fat Ronald Parker, or Roll-over-Ron as my dad liked to call him). Sir Patrick Kelly, the chief of the Metropolitan Police was in heated conversation with the tall, blond Tristram Rainer – head of FIST (Force for Inland Security and counter-Terrorism). There were a number of other people that I didn't recognise but all looked either important or rich or both. Many of them had obviously been dragged from their beds – there were plenty of unshaven faces and bleary eyes.

Fortunately, my dad's office is the size of your average tennis court, because there was quite a crowd! They were sitting or standing around the screen that takes up most of one wall of his office. On the screen, multiple images of a devastated London kept flashing up – every CCTV camera in the capital is connected to the GRID, and everything on the GRID can be controlled from my dad's office. St Paul's cathedral appeared like an island in a raging river. Big Ben rose like a lighthouse from the water beside the inundated Houses of Parliament. People frantically waved from upper floors and rooftops – a lifeboat battled the current in the Strand. In flooded parks, people clung to the branches of trees and a desperate rescue attempt was underway at Victoria Station: each scene dramatically lit by the sweeping beams of searchlights and the blue flashing lights of emergency vehicles. A groan went up as the huge Ferris wheel of the London Eye twisted under the pressure of water on its lower gondolas, buckled, and collapsed into the river.

The atmosphere in the room was tense; Mrs Grist was looking daggers at Roll-over-Ron and Sir Patrick, who was now pacing up and down, looked like he was about to lose it completely. Only my father, standing slightly apart from the others, immaculately dressed as usual, appeared calm.

'If your government had given us the money to replace the Thames Barrier, this could have been avoided,' whined the fat little Mayor.

'My government!' snapped the Prime Minister, 'My government is completely blameless! Sufficient funds were made available for flood prevention, but you chose to spend it on the "Greening of London" Festival – on cycle paths, airhead celebrities, and rock bands! You fiddled while London sank!'

'This is wasting time!' cut in Sir Patrick. 'A quarter of London is under water. We need a coordinated strategy!'

'We have one, Sir Patrick,' my father said, 'and it's being implemented.'

'And what about security?'

'That's FIST's department.'

'FIST cannot be held responsible for the city's security now the Ring has been opened!' said Rainer.

'Now, Tristram,' my father said gently, turning to the head of the security service, 'we could hardly let the good people of Stepney drown! We had to open the Ring to provide extra escape routes.'

'There'll be looting. People will take advantage.'

'Perhaps Sir Patrick could lend you some officers.'

'You know how I feel about private police forces,' growled the head of the Met., who hated the fact that national security had been given to a private company. 'Anyway we're overstretched already.'

'Speak to the Defence Minister, there's always the army. Now, if you'll excuse me a moment...' My father led me to the other end of the room, where he sat on the edge of his huge, antique desk. I often think my dad would be happier in another century; he loves old-fashioned things. Would you believe, he even writes with a fountain pen? So on his desk, there is the latest touch screen to control all the gadgets in the room, but he actually works on sheets of paper!

'I would have come, but they are incapable of doing anything unless someone tells them what they need to do.' He picked up his large glass paperweight and stared into it as if it were a crystal ball.

'Dad! The flat's wrecked! Everything! Everything's gone – your paintings, Dad – everything! The water came right in! It smashed through the windows! And, Dad – downstairs... downstairs – I think they drowned!' The image of the floating bodies pressed up against the ceiling filled my head – suddenly I was sobbing like a four-year-old.

He put an arm round my shoulders. 'But we're all safe, Mark. That's what matters. We're all safe. I spoke to Mum half and hour ago – she's fine. You know what she's like! She's got everyone organised, evacuating the hospital.'

'Dad! I almost didn't get out!' – I didn't want reassurance; I wanted someone to understand what I'd been through. I could have died! Didn't he understand that?

'Mark, I know it was bad – but I have to get back. We've got thousands trapped in their houses... maybe thousands already dead. We've had to seal people in the underground. We don't know how to get them out.'

I looked up at the big screen. A grainy, closed circuit TV picture showed a group of people on a tube platform, their faces contorted by screams we couldn't hear.

The Prime Minister had detached herself from the rest of her party and was advancing on my father. The eyes of every government minister followed her.

'Sir Robert...'

'Prime Minister,' he put down the paperweight and swung his leg off the edge of his desk.

'How could this have happened?' the Prime Minister spat out each word like she was spitting pips.

'The Thames Barrier collapsed. It released a virtual tidal wave.'

'But this storm surge, why wasn't it forecast? What happened to the warning systems?'

'It was forecast, Angela,' my father replied.

'When? I received no warning.'

'In 2025, when the Ross Ice Shelf began to disintegrate.'

'I'm talking about tonight, not some vague predictions you made five years ago based on melting Antarctic ice!'

'There's nothing vague about a one-metre rise in sea levels.'

'You know what I'm talking about!'

'And you know what I'm talking about, Prime Minister! You ignored the warnings. South London has effectively been below sea level every high tide for the last two years! The Thames Barrier should have been replaced. Storms in the North Sea have been increasing in severity every year; this storm was off the scale. It pushed a mountain of water down the Channel.'

'I know all this!'

'But you did nothing!'

'Sir Robert...' Mrs Grist glared at my father, drawing herself up to her full, skinny, height.

'Prime Minister,' he responded, coldly.

'We pay Global Solutions a great deal of money to manage and deliver the government's environmental policy...'

'You're not suggesting my company's responsible for London being flooded, surely?'

'I know! I know – rising sea levels – factors beyond our control. But that's not how the electorate will see it. People will say that the government has failed, that we have wasted taxpayers' money, and that we should have invested more in flood prevention and not poured millions into expensive environmental experiments.'

'The Great West Forest.'

'Yes! The Great West Forest, for example.'

'The Great West Forest is not an experiment. It's the sort of long-term environmental solution that only the private sector can deliver.'

'Thank you, Robert – I don't need a lecture!'

'Perhaps I might remind you, Angela, that since Global Solutions took over the Great West Forest, London has become the carbon-trading centre of the world. The British economy depends on it.'

'Well, you've certainly done very well out of it, Robert!'

I saw my father's jaw tighten. He glanced down, but when he looked up again to meet the Prime Minister's stare, his face was calm.

'Don't you think we should be saving lives rather than debating government policy, Prime Minister?' Just like that, he said it so coolly – like he was the king, and she was some underling who was out of line.

'You don't have the world's press to face in half an hour! There are going to be a lot of very awkward questions. They'll want my head!'

'Then you need to get your message across first. Go on the GRID now. We can broadcast from this room to every news channel in every home and every G-Port in the country. Tell the people that everything is being done that can be done. Talk about the rescue operation – show that you are in control. The public loves a strong leader in a crisis. Play it right, Angela, it can be your finest hour. Explain that we planned for this and that, with the Houses of Parliament and Whitehall under water, the rescue operation is being coordinated through the GRID from the Global Solutions building – give them a human-interest story. I'll have my public relations people find you a family that's been reunited – with luck, a family with a pet. Those press people love animals.'

'What about an interview with your son – his escape – your apartment?'

'Absolutely not! Anyway, Mark has to leave for his aunt's house very shortly.'

My aunt's house?! This was the first I knew of a plan to ship me off to the countryside. I didn't want to be sent away. I wanted to stay with my dad. It was amazing watching him. It was amazing how people (it didn't matter who they were) just did whatever he told them. He made you believe in him. With my dad there, the flood stopped being a nightmare and became an adventure. He would save everyone, and I would be right there beside him.

'What about Mum?' I blurted out, 'I haven't seen Mum yet!'

'You'll be safe on the farm,' my father said, in a matter-of-fact voice. 'We need to know you're safe, then your mother, and I can concentrate on what we have to do.'

'But I want to stay with you!'

'This is not a time when we should be thinking about ourselves, Mark.' His look hardened. 'Even after the water has gone, South London will be uninhabitable; thousands will need to be evacuated. At least, you have somewhere to go.'

I knew it was pointless to argue. I was to be banished and forgotten about so that they could do exciting and important things.

Just then a cry went up in the room as the screen filled with the scene of a huge conflagration. A sea of fire was spreading from a burning oil terminal. Carried up river by the flood, the flames were engulfing everything in their path. The ashen faces in the room glowed orange in the fiery glare from the screen as a giant oil tanker, moored mid-river, exploded.

My father turned back to me, 'Jerzy will drive you. Tell Abbie if there is anything you need.'

I nodded. I'd been dismissed.

'I think it's time you spoke to the nation, Prime Minister. Calm people down – a steady hand at the helm and all that.' He tapped the touch screen on his desk; a ceiling panel slid back and a camera smoothly descended. 'Let me show you where to stand.' He took the Prime Minister by the arm and began to steer her towards the raised platform in front of the big screens. 'When the red light comes on, you will be speaking live to the country.'

'Prime Minister...' Rainer blocked their path.

'Tristram?'

'Perhaps I could have a word about security before you make any sort of statement.'

'Certainly.'

'Excuse me, Robert, I think I should speak to the Prime Minister in private.'

'Fine,' my father said. 'As soon as you are ready, Angela, we'll start the broadcast.'

Rainer drew Mrs Grist aside. Since she had made Rainer her security adviser, she hardly went anywhere without him.

Looking at them, I could see that in some ways Rainer and my dad were similar: both tall, both fit for their age, both tanned, and both very ambitious, but my dad was dark and Rainer was fair, and for all his drive, my dad could be quite laid-back, whereas Rainer never relaxed: his pale, blue eyes were constantly vigilant, and even when he was still, he had a habit of scratching his index finger with his thumbnail that was like the flick of the tip of a cat's tail that gives away its impatience as it watches its prey and waits to pounce.

I didn't like Rainer, but my dad knew about people, and my dad seemed to trust him; they did business together, even travelled together, and they were on the boards of each other's companies.

A moment later, Abbie arrived to escort me down to the parking bays. She was carrying my leather jacket and the saxophone case.

'We've dried these out as best we can. I don't think there's much damage.'

'I don't really know why I brought that,' I said, taking the sax from her. What a useless thing to save! – I was suddenly cold and shaking, and I had to put the case down and lean against the wall. The flooded apartment, the rusted fire escape – it all came back.

Abbie looked at me anxiously, 'Are you all right?'

'In a minute – Be all right in a minute,' I muttered. But the shocked faces of the other survivors in the helicopter were floating in front of my eyes and I could taste the chocolate I'd eaten too quickly and I thought I was going to be sick all over the plush carpet.

I could hear Abbie saying, 'Mark?... Mark?... Do you want to sit down?'

I took some deep breaths. The air in the room seemed stale, like too many people had been breathing it. I needed to get out.

'Come on,' I said, 'I'm OK.' But I could tell by the way that Abbie looked at me that she didn't really believe me.

We didn't need to go back out through the general office. My dad had what he called his 'escape route', a private lift that went direct from a lobby behind his office to the underground car park. That way, he could come and go as he liked without other people in the building knowing if he were in or out.

CHAPTER 3

Jerzy, my dad's Polish driver, was waiting for us in the parking bay at the bottom of the building. 'Ah, good – you finally here,' he grunted as soon as the lift door opened. 'You got luggage?' (Not, you will notice, 'Hello, Mark – Really sorry to hear you just lost your home and everything'.)

'Just this,' I said, holding out the saxophone case.

'Good. We take Porsche. Good car for quick travelling.'

'Mark will need to stop and buy himself some clothes and overnight things,' Abbie said in her best 'these are your instructions' voice.

'No problem. We stop at a Motorway Village when we need a fill up.'

I wasn't sorry we were going in the Porsche. If you're going to be banished to the boredom of the countryside, you may as well go in style, and Jerzy was a fantastic driver, which was why we all put up with his manner, which was verging on the rude.

The Porsche had pride of place in the centre of the bay between the Mercedes SUV and the Lamborghini. It was my dad's favourite as well as being Jerzy's. My mum said we should sell them all and get a Pneumat, but my dad wasn't having it. 'What's the point of running a carbon trading company if you can't drive a decent car?' he would say.

Jerzy dumped the sax in the small luggage compartment in the front of the car, slammed it shut, and climbed into the driver's seat.

'Here's your new G-Port,' Abbie said. I was disappointed. It looked pretty much the same as the GX2 I'd lost.

'Couldn't you get me a SoftPortal?' I said.

'These are tougher. You're going to be on farm, remember. And this one's completely waterproof.'

'Yeah, but it's not like I'm going to use my Port to muck-out the cows, or whatever!'

'Just call if you need anything.'

'When do I get to come back?'

'That depends on your dad.'

Yeah – stupid question, I thought.

Just then, Jerzy started the motor, and the throaty howl set every molecule of air in the concrete bay, vibrating.

'I think Jerzy's trying to tell us something,' I shouted over the din. Abbie gave me a quick hug and retreated to the lift while I climbed into the passenger seat.

'You finished kissy-kissy?' asked Jerzy.

'Oh stop it! Just drive!' I said.

Jerzy grinned, and I was immediately thrown back into the firm grip of the leather sports seat as he accelerated up the exit ramp and out into the grey morning.

The stench hit us as soon as we emerged. It filled the car – nauseating, like rotting cabbage – the air so thick you could taste it the moment you opened your mouth.

'Sheezus! That is filthy!' Jerzy exclaimed through clenched teeth.

'It's the sewage. They were talking about it upstairs. It's coming up everywhere. The sewers are running backwards.'

Jerzy muttered something in Polish as he took a right into Moorgate, and as we turned, I saw how close we were to the water. It had reached the steps of the Bank of England, where a crowd of people were sheltering under the portico.

Jerzy leant on the horn as he edged us into the barely moving traffic. Marshals from FIST in luminous stab-vests were attempting to clear a path for a fleet of ambulances headed south while an endless river of people flowed in from the flooded East End – people on foot, on bicycles, in cars, and on the backs of lorries, poor people, rich people, street people, washed out of their railway arches and underpasses – families with all their possessions loaded on to anything they could wheel, even a street market stall piled high with furniture and appliances. The scene, like pictures I'd seen on the news of Bangladesh in the monsoon, appeared and disappeared with every flick of the wiper blades.

At London Wall, more marshals directed those on foot towards the Barbican, where they'd set up a temporary refuge. As we ground to a halt for the umpteenth time a group of kids surrounded the car thumping on the roof, banging on the windows and waving bottles of vodka. The looting had obviously started and the booze shops been the first to be ransacked. Jerzy ignored the contorted faces pressed against the windows and stared straight ahead, but I saw his hands tighten on the steering wheel. It was the one problem with the Porsche: with so few emission vehicles on the roads, it always attracted attention. Eventually, they grew tired of us and moved on, whooping and yelling, to pick on a more satisfying target.

The whole of London seemed to be on the move, and all we could do was inch forward with the slowly moving mass. Down a side road, I saw that looting was well under way. The shattered glass from shopfronts glittered on the wet pavement amongst the discarded heaps of soggy packaging. The looters were all ages, some working on their own, with nothing better than shopping trolleys for transport, others in well-organised gangs, loading goods into the backs of vans. The piercing screams of burglar alarms filled the air. A FIST mini-bus disgorged an armed response unit in riot gear and a battle broke out between the officers and the looters. Then we lurched forward, and all I could see was the side of a coach.

After two hours of almost no progress, we were able to exit the Ring, where Farringdon Street meets Charterhouse. It was weird to see the great bombproof barriers standing open. The truck bombings that destroyed so much of the city and triggered the building of the Ring happened before I was born, so I had lived my whole life within its protection. Up until the age of five, I honestly believed that it was my dad shouting 'Open sesame!' that made the towering, metre-thick glass walls slide noiselessly aside to let us pass. When Kevin Butler in reception found out, he told the whole class, and for a week, I had to put up with kids dancing around me in the playground, shouting 'Open sesame! Open sesame!' I kicked Kevin Butler in the leg and made him cry, but I hated my dad for fooling me.

Of course, we often left the city – visits, school trips, holidays – but whenever we returned and the Ring slid shut behind us, I felt I was home and safe.

Normally, we would have taken the A4 to the motorway, but Hammersmith and Shepherds Bush were under water, and there was no option but to continue on with the endless queue of traffic through Harrow and then skirt around the flood to join the motorway well clear of London. I struggled to stay awake, but the warmth of the car, our slow progress through the crowded streets, and the exhaustion of the night before caught up with me, and I fell asleep to the sound of Jerzy's voice as he traded information with a couple in a Pneumat stuck in the queue beside us.

CHAPTER 4

When I woke up, we were travelling at speed in the toll lane, the radio was on and Jerzy was singing.

'Good morning, sleeping beauty!' Jerzy grinned when he saw my eyes were open.

'Oh – it was you singing. I wondered what that awful noise was,' I said as I wriggled up in the seat. 'I thought I was having a nightmare.' I tried to ease the crick out of my neck. 'Where are we?'

'How should I know? The navigator, he's asleep!'

'Oh for heaven's sake!' I leant over to look at the GRIDmap on the dashboard screen. I was surprised to find we were already past Bristol. I must have slept for over two hours. The almost empty road, Jerzy's cheeriness – for a moment it felt like a holiday jaunt, then I remembered what we had left behind. 'What's the news?' I asked.

Jerzy's cheery mask slipped. He shook his head, 'Very bad, very bad. Many dead.'

'How many?'

'They don't say. Probably they don't know. Now they are talking and talking and talking who is to blame.' He turned off the radio, and we drove on for a while with neither of us speaking. I found I was shivering, although it wasn't cold. The flooded flat, the swaying fire-escape. 'Can we stop soon?' I asked. 'I could do with getting out for a bit.'

'Yes, yes, we stop soon to make a fill up – And you need to make some shopping?'

'Oh yeah – I guess.' I hated shopping for clothes, especially in shops I didn't know, and I could just imagine what the shops were going to be like out here in the sticks. I needed shoes too; that was going to be a real disaster.

'We stop at New Bridgewater Village.'

There was nothing much to look at for the next half an hour. Some road works where they were digging up the remains of an electrified lane – Now those were a brilliant idea... until the uranium ran out and electricity prices went through the roof! On either side of the raised-up road, salt marshes stretched away into the distance. In some places, there were islands of firm ground fringed by reed beds, and in other places, there was nothing but water. This area had only recently become part of the Great West Forest. The little hummocky islands bristled with newly planted trees still in their protective tubes, making the islands look like giant, upside-down scrubbing brushes. When, to the right of the road, the conical island of Brent Knoll rose like a miniature volcano from the marshes; I turned to look inland, hoping to see Glastonbury Tor across the water, but it was lost in the mist and rain.

I could remember travelling through the Somerset Levels on the way to family holidays on the farm when I was younger, before Aunt Megan and my dad stopped speaking to each other, before the Levels were flooded by the rising sea and Glastonbury went back to being an island like they reckon it was when King Arthur was around. Then, flat fields were full of grazing sheep and cows and sometimes horses that would suddenly flick their tails and gallop about wildly, like they wanted to show off to us as we drove past. Now flocks of wading birds had taken over from the grazing animals.

I should explain that Aunt Megan is not really my aunt. She and Dad were at university together and, because they were both serious environment geeks, they started doing stuff together like setting up *SPACE* (that's the Social Partnership Against Carbon Emissions – in case you're wondering). At first, they were into direct action – sit-ins at airports to try to stop new runways from being built, chaining themselves to trees to block the path of new bypasses, that sort of thing. But then... I suppose they just grew up, and Aunt Megan got into organic farming, while Dad went to work for Friends of the Earth – and that's where he met my mum – Then Dad set up Global Solutions. Anyway, as I said, when I was younger, Dad and Mum and I used to go to stay on Aunt Megan's farm for holidays. She'd got together with Umi more or less the same time that Mum and Dad got married, and they had a daughter – well, have a daughter, who is the same age as I am. Umi's from some place in Africa, but I can't remember exactly where. Their daughter (the one who's my age) is called Ashanti. They've got a little girl as well now, but I haven't met her because she was born after *the big argument* – she's called Dilly, which sounds like it's short for something or other.

Nobody's ever told me what *the big argument* was about, either. It must have been about something pretty important because nothing Mum or Umi could do would get Dad and Aunt Megan to talk to each other again. Which makes me think it must have been Mum, and not Dad, who fixed it up for me to go to the farm after our flat was flooded.

I used to get on really well with Ashanti when we were little. As the Porsche howled down the toll lane of the M5 and I gazed out at the marshy countryside whizzing past, I wondered what Ashanti would be like now. She used to have masses of curly hair that Aunt Megan sometimes tied into little pigtails that stuck out all over her head. When I last saw her, she was missing a front tooth, and if she put her tongue against the gap, she could whistle. I'd been looking forward to seeing her, but I suddenly felt nervous. She wouldn't be missing any teeth now. She'd be as grown up as me. She had probably given up climbing trees and taken up nail varnish! What do teenage girls do when they're stuck in the middle of nowhere?

I was brought back to the present by Jerzy braking hard as we came up behind a prison convoy, a FIST security van accompanied by two patrol cars with flashing blue lights.

'What are they doing down here?' I asked.

'FIST have got a place for refugee people in this nook of the woods.'

'Neck,' I corrected him.

'What is neck?'

'It's "neck of the woods."'

'How can woods have a neck?'

'It's what people say.'

'Nook is better.'

'It might be better, but it's not good English.'

'Good English! There is no good English. English is stupid language!'

Jerzy swerved into the inside lane to pass the convoy.

'Why do they drive in the toll lane?' Jerzy grumbled. 'There are two other perfect very good lanes!'

It was true; there wasn't much traffic. A few road trains and empty timber jinkers rumbled along in the slow lane, but in the middle lane, there was only the occasional Pneumat, a sales rep, or a family off West for the Easter break. Although, of course, now that the big storms have swept away all the beaches, not many people holiday in the south west and if they do, they mostly use the high-speed hover-trains. There were a few other emission vehicles using the toll lane, a handful of big German saloons, and expensive sports EVs carrying the rich and famous to their forest hide-aways or to ritzy hunting lodges. I wondered how many of them, like me, had left behind a flooded London apartment.

We passed the abandoned ruins of a motorway service station with its rows of rusting petrol pumps. Amazing that there were once so may EVs on the roads that they needed all those pumps.

'How much longer 'till we stop?'

'Few minutes.' Jerzy turned up the radio and started to sing again, making up his own, unlikely version of the lyrics. I groaned as loudly as I could and slid down in my seat.

'Hey! You like my singing? I take you to Polish Karaoke night!' Jerzy offered. It was a pretty scary thought. 'Thanks, but maybe not.'

Luckily, just then, we reached the slip road for New Bridgewater Village. New Bridgewater turned out to be the thatched variety, all twisty streets and cobbled pedestrian areas with shop signs written in 'Ye Olde' writing. Of course, all the shops were really owned by English Villages, but they were made to look like each one was run by a little-olde-English shopkeeper. Even the filling station looked like some sort of barn. There were short queues of Pneumats waiting to use the air compressors but, as ours was the only EV on the forecourt, there was no competition for the single petrol pump.

We followed signs to the Village car park, which was sealed in some sort of green tarmac to make it look like the Village Green. There was even a fake cricket scoreboard with a score that never changed: New Bridgewater was always winning. The rain had stopped, but there were big puddles, where there were dips in the green.

'I need strong coffee,' Jerzy announced.

As we got out of the Porsche, the prison convoy we had overtaken on the motorway pulled into the car park and drew up by the fake score board. The doors of the patrol cars were flung open; armed FIST officers sprang out and surrounded the van in a military style manoeuvre. Jerzy and I waited to see what would happen next. The doors of the van were opened, and one of the officers helped the occupants to climb down. They stumbled and bumped into each other as they shuffled into a line. They were hooded and handcuffed. Eight adults and four children; the youngest, judging by height, couldn't have been more than six.

'Toilet stop,' Jerzy grunted. And then I realised that the fake score board disguised the public loos.

Refugees were getting to be a big problem. With so many countries flooded and all the food shortages, they were trying to get in from everywhere. But, as Mrs Grist said, we couldn't look after them all – Britain had its own problems. Her government had a zero immigration policy. Still, I felt sorry for them, especially the kids.

'Come on.' Jerzy headed off across the too-bright green tarmac towards a thatched building that claimed to be the 'Village Tea Shoppe'.

The menu was the same as every menu in every English Village eatery. There were the family chicken banquets, the rustic burgers, the Tudor tea cakes – I decided to risk a rustic burger – Jerzy went for an Old English egg and bacon sandwich but asked the waitress to make sure it was 'Ye Freshe Bread.' To which she said 'Oh, ha-bloody-ha' and flounced off.

When she returned with our food, I noticed the little tattoo on her forehead that said 'English Villages'.

'What?' she asked, when she caught me staring at it.

'Nothing. I was just wondering… if I could have some ketchup.'

'It's on the table.'

'How much they pay for yours?' Jerzy asked, pointing straight at the tattoo.

'Why? You want one? 'Cause you have to work here to have one.'

'I got one. Look.' Jerzy pushed up his sleeve to reveal a Michelin Man on his right bicep. He tensed his arm making the jolly little man of tyres swell up. 'Five thousand quid.'

'Nice,' said the waitress approvingly.

'You?' asked Jerzy.

'Bonus every month if we advertise. You don't get nothing much for your arm and that, but if it's on your forehead – it pays for me holidays.'

'Here,' Jerzy turned to me, 'Don't go tell your dad. My contract is written no advertising. But my little friend only comes out on weekends, so no problem, no advertising in company time.'

'What about now?' I asked, hoping to wind him up.

'I'm on my lunch break.'

'Where you going, then?' asked the waitress; friendly now, she and Jerzy had found they had something in common.

'Got to take the kid to his auntie's.'

'Where's that, then?'

'Little farm in the middle of Devon.'

'Farm?! He don't look like a farm boy!'

'I'm not,' I said.

'Didn't think there was that many farms left in Devon.'

'Yeah, well there are some,' I said, wishing she would go away and feeling totally fed up with Jerzy for getting her chatting.

'What way you thinking of going? You're not going up the old link road, are you?'

'Why? What's wrong with the link road?' asked Jerzy.

'Ferals.'

'Yeah?'

'Yeah. Lot of Ferals. They been causing no end of trouble. Been robbing cars and that.'

'I can handle Ferals,' Jerzy rocked his chair back and put on his best tough-guy expression.

'I wouldn't be too sure.'

'Just let them try their funny businesses with me. I got something that will mend their wagons.'

'Fix-their-wagon,' I corrected. Jerzy and the waitress ignored me. I was dying to ask what Ferals were, but I didn't want to look stupid in front of the waitress. I'd ask Jerzy as soon as we got back in the car.

'Well, you be careful, won't you?'

'You see that Porsche?' Jerzy pointed to our car through the window.

'Cool! That yours?'

'How is a bunch of Ferals going to catch up with that?'

'Well, you be careful,' she repeated.

'Don't you worry. I'll come and see you on my way back, no problem'

'Yeah, well – if you want. You finished with these?' She collected up the empty plates.

'We need to buy Mark some clothing. Is there a good shop?' asked Jerzy.

'Kids' clothes? Yeah, in the market place.'

'Come on,' I said, keen to get out of there. Even buying clothes would be better than watching Jerzy trying to chat up the waitress.

The choice of clothing available in New Bridgewater was about as bad as I had thought it would be, but I forced myself to buy some stuff anyway, and there was a sports shop where I managed to buy some better trainers than the ones Abbie had found me. Jerzy kept going on about walking boots, but I couldn't see the point as I had no intention of walking anywhere, and anyway, you can walk in trainers. But in the end, I let him buy me the boots just to shut him up. The guy in the sports store had 'English Villages recommends Trackman Shoes' tattooed down his right arm and the Trackman logo right in the middle of his forehead. Which probably meant he could afford more expensive holidays than the waitress. As I didn't have any kind of suitcase, I bought a small backpack at the sports store and stuffed everything except the walking boots (which wouldn't fit) into it.

Jerzy went a bit wild when he discovered that the supermarket next door to the sports store had a Polish food section, and he bought what looked like enough sausages, bread, and cheese to feed the entire Polish army! 'So I don't get starving on my way back to London,' he explained.

'With that lot, you wouldn't get starving on your way to Mars!' I said.

'It's good, this English Village,' Jerzy said, looking around at the triple-glazed, mock Tudor buildings with their artificial thatch. 'Maybe when I retire, I move to English Village. Better than London.'

I am most definitely a city kid, I thought. I could never be at home anywhere else. Then I thought about home, and I wondered what was happening now in London. What about our apartment? Would we ever go back to it? What would happen when the Easter break finished? For the first time, it occurred to me that my school would also have been flooded. Would I be sent to another school, or would we just stay on holiday until everything got back to normal?

My train of thought was interrupted by Jerzy asking, 'You going to stand there all day, or maybe get into the car?' He took the backpack of clothes from me and dumped it into the front with his bag of food. I tossed the walking boots behind my seat and got in.

It was a relief to be back in the Porsche and heading out on to the motorway. There was no sign of the prison convoy on the Village Green and no sign of it on the road. I kept expecting us to catch up with it, but we never did, so it must have turned off somewhere and taken a different route.

I got out my G-Port and clicked on GRIDnews to see the latest from London. Even in the pictures on the Port's little screen you could see the extent of the damage. Buildings had collapsed, there were sections missing from bridges, rescue teams were everywhere. An aerial view showed large areas still flooded. A mass evacuation was underway.

I switched to GRIDVid. My mum, looking really tired, smiled at me and told me she and Dad were both fine and then went on about stuff like what clothes I ought to buy and could I pass on her love to Aunt Megan, Umi, Ashanti, and Dilly, etc., etc. I switched to *Natter*. The site was jammed with desperate messages from friends wanting to know who was alive, who was missing. I scrolled through page after page of 'Has anyone heard from Nick?... Devi, please call Sanjay... Jan, are you OK?' and so on. I switched back to GRIDVid. and watched the pictures stream across the little screen. Some were the 'Look-at-me-being-rescued – This-is-so-cool!' type, but others were of bodies and people in trees. I posted a message on the *Natter board* saying I was OK and spammed everyone in my contact file, then I put the Port away because looking at the screen was beginning to make me feel car-sick. I kept remembering the people trapped in the tube. Could any of my friends have been down there? I tried not to think about it.

'So what's all this about Ferals?' I asked casually, hoping I sounded like I knew what Ferals were but hadn't heard the news about these particular ones.

'Just some kids. Nothing to worry about.'

'I'm not worried – just interested.'

Jerzy made not further comment but, instead, concentrated on accelerating the Porsche up to 120 mph.

'So, who are they? Where do they come from?' I shouted over the noise of engine, wind, and road.

'They live in the woods. Running wild. Like animals.'

I absorbed this information, picturing kids running around in animal skins. Maybe not. Probably more like a country version of the city gangs – now the kids in my head were wearing hillbilly bib-and-brace overalls and straw hats.

'What do they live on?' I shouted.

'Nothing to worry about. In glove box I have protection, OK?'

I flipped open the glove box. Seeing the gun was a bit of shock. Actually, up to then, I hadn't been worried.

'Does my dad know you've got this?'

Jerzy gave me a look that seemed to say 'Oh please!'

'What?!'

'Sometimes I have to look after him, you know? Sometimes I'm not only driver. Man like your father is big target. Many terrorists think "We have him, make nice ransom".'

This was even bigger news than the gun in the glove box. My dad needed a bodyguard! I looked at Jerzy, hoping for more information, but he was staring straight ahead through the windscreen and appeared to be working on breaking the land-speed record.

Neither of us said anything else until we reached the turnoff for the link road, but my head was full of questions like 'Have you ever had to use the gun?' – I mean, had Jerzy ever actually shot anyone? Of course, every country seemed to have its own terrorist group now, and you often heard about people like my dad, important people, people with money, being kidnapped. It did explain why Dad took a driver on overseas trips – I'd never really thought about that before.

The sudden deceleration on the exit ramp brought me back to where we were.

'Is this the link road?'

'Yes, link road,' Jerzy nodded.

So this was where the Ferals hung out. I wondered if we would actually see any. I half hoped we would – Jerzy said they were just kids… But that gun. You don't need a gun against a bunch of kids – unless – Did they have guns?

We passed the outskirts of what once must have been a large market town. There were rows and rows of boarded-up houses: the sort of cheap, badly made houses that they built at the beginning of the century when the population was still growing, before they limited families to two kids, before they stopped allowing immigrants into the country. The houses were beginning to fall apart. Their rotting fences had been blown over or were propped up at drunken angles by overgrown garden plants.

It was raining again, and in places, sheets of water stretched out across the road from drains that were blocked with last winter's fallen leaves. Jerzy was enjoying hitting the pools at speed, sending plumes of water jetting high into the air. Whenever the wheels lost traction, he coolly brought the skidding sports car back on course. Anyone else and I would have been petrified, but I had total faith in Jerzy's driving.

Past the town, the forest, which crowded right up to the hard shoulder, was older; the trees already twenty or more feet tall, but I could tell by their thin trunks that they had been planted in the last thirty years. I might not know much about the countryside, but I do know about trees. The Great West Forest was my dad's obsession, and he made sure Mum and I could tell an ash from a beech, a blackthorn from a hawthorn. When Global Solutions took over the Great West Forest, Dad insisted we went on tree planting holidays. He even dragged us off to lectures on 'Woodland Management'! Can you imagine anything more boring? But, although I was doing my best not to listen, a lot of that stuff seeped in – yeah, I could be a real woodland nerd if I wanted to be.

The forest here, beside the link road, could do with a bit of woodland management, I thought as I watched it flash past. It was in serious need of thinning out, and all the spaces between the trees were taken up by thick, tangly undergrowth. Branches reached out across the road. It was only April, and the trees were still bare, but once the trees came into leaf, this road would become like a long green tunnel.

The further we went, the worse the road became. Now the surface was broken and rutted, forcing Jerzy slow to what seemed a snail's pace after the crazy slipping and sliding of the earlier section. Although it had once been dual carriageway, only one lane in each direction had been maintained and, in places, quite large bushes grew from the cracks in the unused lanes. The low-slung Porsche bucked and rocked, and there was the occasional worrying bang when we hit a larger-than-usual pothole. The only other vehicles we met were timber jinkers loaded with logs heading for some sawmill or woodchip factory.

The road was following a valley. The ground on one side rose steeply, climbing up to a range of hills; the slope on the other side was more gentle. The trees themselves now changed from the bare oaks and ashes that we had been passing through to dark, evergreen pines. The low, grey sky and the tall, almost black trees that marched down the hill and overhung the road cut out so much light that it felt like late evening rather than the middle of the day.

The fallen tree was just beyond a decaying concrete overhead bridge. We weren't travelling fast, and Jerzy had plenty of time to stop, but he said some rude things in Polish as we slowed to a standstill half under the bridge, half out. Just as he opened the door to get out, the second tree came down with a splintering crash, missing the back of the Porsche by inches and sending Jerzy diving back into the car for cover.

'Can you see them?' He was twisting about, ducking up and down, trying to see in every direction at once.

'See who?' I was still thinking about the tree and how lucky it was it missed us. I hadn't twigged what was going on.

'Ferals!'

'Ferals?'

'I should have reversed! As soon as I saw the tree, I should have reversed! It is oldest trick! What was I thinking?'

Then I understood. We were in a trap.

'What should we do?'

'Keep your head down.'

I slid down in my seat. Jerzy reached across and took the pistol from the glove box. Now I was frightened. If he thought he needed the gun, this was scary.

He slowly opened the driver door, then waited. With my head pressed back into the seat so that I could look up and out the windows, I searched the forest – Nothing moved –The only sound was the beat of rain on the car's roof and bonnet. Jerzy eased himself out of the door and waited again, crouched, his back against the car. Still not a movement or sound from the surrounding trees. Jerzy slowly stood up and swung his whole body from side to side, sweeping the forest with the gun held at arm's length in front of him.

'Throw the gun off the road!' A boy's voice, but commanding.

Jerzy jerked around, as if yanked by a string, to face the direction he thought the order had come from.

'Don't play with me, kids! You come out and nobody will get hurt.'

'Throw away the gun!'

'You kids think I am an idiot? You think I give you my gun?'

'Last chance!'

'And then what? You going to come and take it?'

'Look up.'

Slowly, Jerzy raised his eyes to look at the bridge above us. His eyes widened, and he mouthed something silently.

'I will begin counting. You have until 5... 1...'

Jerzy hesitated. When he glanced back towards me, I saw the fear on his face.

'. . . 2...'

Jerzy reluctantly lowered the gun.

'. . . 3! Throw away the gun!'

I could see Jerzy was still trying to find the source of the voice.

'I mean it!... 4! You have one more second!'

Jerzy made up his mind and flung the gun towards the trees on the opposite side of the road from the voice, where it landed, still in sight but out of reach. He spun round and screamed at me, 'Get out of the car! Now!'

I scrambled from the passenger door and ran around the front of the car. Cowering in the rain beside Jerzy, I looked up to see what had frightened him into throwing away the gun. A section of the crumbling bridge's railings had been removed and a huge slab of concrete teetered on the edge of the bridge directly above the car. If it had fallen, I would have been crushed. Behind the slab, I could just see the heads of a group of children.

'What we do now? Play hide-and-seek?' Jerzy yelled.

'Please don't annoy them! They can still smash the car!' I whispered, horrified.

Jerzy grunted angrily.

Dark shapes moved in the forest on either side of the road. A tall, skinny boy stepped out on to the hard shoulder. Thumbs hooked into the back pockets of a pair of ragged jeans, he sauntered towards us. One by one, others slipped out from between the trees. Girls, boys – a mix of ages and, it seemed, of every race; their clothes dirty and either too big or too small for the kid inside. They waved and grinned at their friends on the bridge. They were all soaked to the skin with dripping rats' tails of hair hanging down over grimy faces. They made a rough circle around us but kept their distance, the younger ones hopping from one foot to the other in their excitement. A small boy in an overcoat so large it came down to his feet picked up the gun, aimed it at us and went 'Pi-ow! Pi-ow!'

'Abuja!' one of the older girls snapped. The small boy's face fell, and he dropped the gun. A heavily built boy with dark almond eyes and a mouth that was set in a mocking sneer pick it up and thrust it into the waistband of his trousers.

'No need to get wet. We can stand under the bridge,' the tall boy spoke with only a slight trace of an accent, but he spoke slowly with a rehearsed precision.

'Why? Have you got something else you want to drop on us?' inquired Jerzy, with heavy irony.

'You are quite safe now; you have my word. But your car... Well, please do not try anything.'

'Your word! Foreign brat!' Jerzy spat on the ground.

The boy smiled slightly and moved under the shelter of the bridge, indicating with a little sideways flick of his head that we should do the same. Although I could see that Jerzy hated to do what the kid told him, there wasn't much point getting any wetter, so we followed.

'Now we can talk.'

'I do not want talk! You move the tree and we go.'

'We are only children. We cannot move such a big tree. I am sorry, but you will have to wait for the timber lorry to come.'

Jerzy let fly a string of Polish curses. There was obviously nothing I could do, so I studied the boy. Chinese perhaps, or Korean; a lot of Koreans had tried to get in since the famine. His hair was cropped short, and his thinness made his high cheekbones stick out. His face was calm and serious, but all the time there seemed to be a teasing smile just below the surface. As I waited for his next move, the girl who had made the little boy drop the gun walked over, slipped her arm through the boy's, and leant gently against him. *Girlfriend,* I thought. Then I saw how alike they were, the same prominent cheekbones, the same steady eyes, and the strong mouth that seemed on the verge of smiling, and I changed my mind – brother and sister – almost certainly brother and sister.

'Hey, Yongjo Pa, what you want us to do?' called out the heavily built boy who I guessed was about the same age as the leader.

The tall boy turned to Jerzy, 'Your son goes back to the car and takes everything out. He puts everything on the road. Either of you do anything stupid, and the car is scrap metal.'

'My boss's son, not mine. And I go to the car, not him.'

'I prefer you stay here.'

'I don't give a… !'

'It's OK,' I cut in quickly, 'I'll go.' I thought Jerzy might be crazy enough to try something, and I was sure that Yongjo, or whatever he was called, was serious about the scrap metal.

'If anything happens…' began Jerzy.

'Nothing will happen… if you are sensible. Now, you boy… You go to the car with Yongjo Ma and my friend Casablanca and take everything out. You put it on the road, and we will see if there is anything we would like. You understand?'

I nodded. They were in for a disappointment, unless they were desperate for a saxophone.

'Come,' the girl ordered.

'If anything happens to him, I will kill you with my naked hands,' I heard Jerzy growl. *Bare hands, you mean bare hands*, I couldn't help thinking to myself as I followed the girl.

The one he called Casablanca, the one who had picked up the gun, fell in with us as we approached the car. 'Hey, rich boy, you look a little pale!' he mocked, and I instantly hated him. 'You know how heavy that little bit of concrete up there is? Maybe one ton, maybe two! You ever been this scared before?'

Yeah, I thought, *on that fire escape. This seems to be my week for being terrified. What do you know?!*

'Rich boy going to have smelly pants!'

'Rich boy! Rich boy!' chorused the younger kids who were nearest to us.

'Stop it!' snapped the girl.

Casablanca leered at me. 'One day', I thought, 'one day…' I prayed another car would come. I prayed the FIST convoy would turn up and the armed guards would round up the whole rag-tag lot of them – especially Casablanca. Maybe Casablanca would try to escape, and they'd have to shoot him.

'Everything out of the car,' the girl ordered. 'We stay here. And no more guns.'

So I'll be the only one to get squashed if they drop the concrete. I could see how this worked.

The Porsche, of course, had a rear engine. The luggage went in the front. I leant into the car and opened the bonnet. All that was in there was my backpack of new clothes, the saxophone in its case, and Jerzy's bag of Polish goodies. I took them out one at a time, carried them over, and placed them on the road by the girl and Casablanca.

'That's it,' I said as I put down the bag of food.

Casablanca stood on tiptoe and craned his neck to see into the luggage compartment. 'Yeah. Look empty.'

'Now, you sit in the car,' the girl said.

She obviously didn't trust Jerzy, and she was making sure he didn't try anything. As I climbed back into the car, I was very aware of the precariously balanced block of concrete above my head. What if those kids up there started messing about? What if they just thought it would be funny to kill the rich boy in the flash car?

The girl shook the contents of my backpack on to the road. She held up a T-shirt and called 'Abuja!' The little boy in the oversized coat shouted 'Here! Ma!' She tossed him the shirt, which he scrumpled up and stuffed into a pocket of the coat. She continued, holding up one garment at a time – 'Sarayova!… Chittagong!… Bucharest!…' – 'Here Ma!'… 'Here Ma!'… 'Here Ma!' Clothes flew through the air. 'Owando!' 'Here Ma!' A little hand shot up. All the fingers were missing.

Soon the role call was finished, and all my new purchases had been given away. Next it was the turn of Jerzy's food bag. She called over three of the older kids, divided the bread, sausages, and cheeses between them and sent them off to feed the rest of the gang. Scuffling and shouting scrums quickly formed, and the food was torn up and devoured in a few frenzied seconds. All that was left was my saxophone.

Casablanca opened the case. He looked up at me and grinned. He took the instrument out, struck a pose like a jazz player, put the mouthpiece to his lips, and blew. A raucous squawk blasted the stillness making all the younger kids laugh and clap. Casablanca, looking pleased, put the sax back in the case. 'I keep this one.' The girl shrugged. As she turned to look at her brother, who was still standing with Jerzy, a shrill whistle sounded somewhere high up on the hill. In a matter of seconds, all but Casablanca, the girl who had distributed my clothes, and the leader had vanished. The girl stepped into Casablanca's path. 'The gun,' she said and held out her hand.

Casablanca glanced at the leader. 'You know the rules,' the leader said. Casablanca's dark eyes flashed with annoyance, but he handed the girl the gun, who inspect it expertly, removing the magazine as if it were something she did all the time, emptied out the shells, and put them into her pocket. She checked the breach was empty, then walked across to Jerzy, and handed him his empty pistol before following her brother and Casablanca into the trees.

'You won't get away with this!' Jerzy shouted after them. 'You don't know who you are dealing at! I will have you all rounded up. Just you wait!' There was no reply. Nothing moved. For a few minutes, all we could hear was the hiss of wind and rain through pine trees; then came the 'Dee-daa' of a twin-tone truck horn and an empty timber jinker growled around the corner and juddered to a halt with a great sneezing of air brakes.

'Not again!' laughed the driver as she jumped down from her cab. Since I was expecting a six-foot lumberjack, the fact that she was about five-foot-nothing and a female was a bit of a surprise. It obviously surprised Jerzy too, because, for once, he said nothing.

'Don't worry, we'll soon get these trees moved. They take much?'

'My saxophone,' I said, getting out of the car again.

'Saxophone! That's got to be a first! Maybe they're starting a band.' She seemed to find the idea very funny.

'Little brats, they took my dinner,' complained a very disgruntled Jerzy.

'Oh food! Well, what do you expect? They must be half starved.'

'And my clothes,' I added.

'Yep, that figures,' said the truck driver.

'No credit cards, no money, no watches! What sort of bandits are they?' Jerzy wanted to know.

'Well, think about it. What are they going to do with credit cards in the middle of a blinkin' forest?'

She had a point.

'If you don't mind giving me a hand with the cable, we can start moving these trees.'

The driver pulled a chainsaw from her cab and soon had the first tree cut into manageable-sized logs. Like the Feral kids, the rain didn't seem to bother her. I guessed people who lived down here just got used to it. We dragged the cable over from the truck's winch and after half an hour's work, the sections of the first tree were loaded on to the truck. The operation was repeated on the second tree, and we were free to go. Jerzy wanted to pay the driver, but she wouldn't take anything.

'I've got the logs', she said, 'and the story of the saxophone's got to be worth a few drinks when I meet the Truckers after work! – Saxophone! What do they want with a saxophone?!' She laughed and shook her head as she climbed back into her truck. We got into the Porsche, and after the truck driver had given us a cheery goodbye 'dee-daa', we were on our way again.

Jerzy was uncharacteristically quiet. He put on the car heater to dry our clothes, but soon it was like a steam bath, and he had to put the AC on to get the mist off the windows.

'Did you notice their names?' I asked after a few very grumpy miles.

'What about them?'

'Bucharest, Abuja, Casablanca – they're places, aren't they?'

'So?'

'Can you remember any of the other names?'

'I don't give a damn what they're called.'

'Just try to remember.'

'Sarayova – There was a girl called Sarayova – Happy now?'

I got out my G-Port, called up GRIDmaps, and typed Sarayova into the search bar. A map of Turkey appeared with an arrow pointing to a small town. I closed my eyes and pictured the girl handing out my clothes. What other names did she call out?... That little African boy with the missing fingers, what was his name? I should be able to remember him – Owandi – Owando – something like that. I typed Owando into the search and got a map of the Congo with another small town arrowed.

'Yes!' I said, punching the air. 'They're all place names!'

'So? What does that prove?'

'It's obvious. It tells us where they come from.'

'Who gives a damn where they come from?! The problem is they're here!'

I clearly wasn't going to interest Jerzy in my theory and, in a way, he was right – What did it matter where they originally came from? What mattered was that they were running wild in the Great West Forest, causing all kinds of trouble – And! And they had my saxophone! OK, big deal – It wasn't like I was going to play my sax for Aunt Megan's cows or goats or whatever she had now – but it was mine... It was the only thing from the home I had left. I'd saved it. I'd risked my life to save it! OK, maybe that was an exaggeration, but suddenly, the saxophone was the most precious thing I'd ever owned – And they'd stolen it! The more I thought about it, the more it mattered. And the picture! The picture of me and Mum and Dad, it was in the saxophone case! That bastard Casablanca! I spent the next few miles thinking of all the things I'd like to do to him, most of which involved inflicting serious pain.

We turned north off the link road and began to climb into the hills. The road narrowed to a single-track lane with occasional passing places – not that we met any other vehicles to pass. The beech hedges on either side hadn't been cut for years and had grown into trees that arched over the lane, the brown leaves of the previous summer still clinging to the lower branches. Winding our way upward, we passed through areas of old forest, mature oaks, and ashes that were here before the Great West Forest was even thought of. Then, as we swung round a bend, there was a break in the trees, and I caught a glimpse of a hilltop covered in heather, a little bit of old Exmoor.

'It should be here. You think you recognise it?' Jerzy asked.

'Check the map.'

'Map's gone.'

'That's odd.' It was true; the dashboard display was blank except for an error message, saying 'No satellites found'.

'I'll try my portal.'

The message on my G-Port said 'No GRID'.

'Nowhere's off the GRID. The GRID is global!'

'Probably temporary hitch,' suggested Jerzy. 'See if you recognise anything.'

I tried to remember if there were any prominent landmarks near the farm entrance. What was it Ashanti and I used to sit on when we'd ridden our bikes down to the bottom gate? – An old stone platform in the hedge that made a sunny seat where we two used to sit and chatter away for hours like little kids do. Or we'd pick targets in the hedge on the other side of the lane to throw pebbles at. Aunt Megan said the platform was for milk churns in the really old days.

We came to a stretch of hedge that had been recently laid, and beyond the hedge, there were fields instead of forest, and then, there it was – our seat in the hedge, almost covered now by a tangle of brambles.

'It's here!' I shouted. 'There'll be a gate on the left with "Higher Heathcombe" on it.' And there was. Jerzy swung the car into the gateway, and I jumped out to open the gate but, instead of driving through, Jerzy also got out and came to stand beside me in the rain.

'Never get the Porsche up there,' he said, looking at the farm track. He was right. It had been worn into two deep, water-filled ruts with a high mound in the middle. 'Sorry kid, you have to walk.'

'Walk! But it's pouring and it's miles! Have you at least got an umbrella or something in the car?'

Jerzy shook his head.

'Well, they'll just have to come and get me. I'm not walking in this!'

I got back into the car and pulled my portal from my pocket. I had had quite enough of being wet. I was certainly not trudging around the blooming countryside in the pouring rain – and I was hungry – and why did my stupid parents dump me in this mess – and why couldn't Aunt Megan and Umi look after their stupid track?

I looked down at my portal – 'No GRID' – No GRID! – I was sorely tempted to hurl the stupid thing out the car window!

We spent the next five minutes (but it seemed more like half and hour) sitting in the car – me sulking and Jerzy humming and drumming on the steering wheel until I couldn't stand it any longer.

'All right! All right,' I said, 'I'm going.'

'Better put the boots on,' said Jerzy, continuing his infuriating drumming on the steering wheel.

The walking boots – I'd forgotten, we still had them. They were behind my seat where I'd chucked them. I wished I'd bought myself something else waterproof in New Bridgewater, and then it occurred to me that it wouldn't have helped because the Ferals would have stolen whatever I'd bought. At that moment, I hated the Ferals, I hated Jerzy, and most of all, I hated the countryside.

Muttering bitterly, I changed my trainers for the boots. Of course, I had to listen to Jerzy going on about how 'he knew I'd need them' and 'what did he tell me?' and 'when he was a boy in Poland they all had boots, etc., etc., etc...'

Wondering what to do with the trainers I'd taken off reminded me of the floating shoes in the flat and that reminded me of the flood and that actually I had a perfect right to feel miserable because I'd just lost my home and everything in it except for my saxophone, which some bastard had just stolen!

I put the trainers in the bag that the boots had come in – and I was ready. When we stood in the rain to say goodbye, Jerzy gave me a big Polish pat on the back and told me 'Hey! It's not so bad! Soon hot soup with auntie! Think of me – No dinner!' then he got back into the warmth of the car, turned the Porsche round, gave me a wave, and was gone.

'I hope the Ferals get you!' I shouted after him.

It must be a mile from the bottom gate to the farmhouse, but that day, in the rain and the mud and the wind, it seemed like three. This was not how I had hoped to arrive. I was meant to be the smart kid from the city, and now I was going to turn up looking like, I don't know what, the creature from the swamp, or something. I was not well pleased, I can tell you!

At first, I tried to find ways of avoiding the really deep mud, jumping from one side of the track to the other or balancing along the hummock in the middle, but it wasn't easy because the track ran between two high banks topped with hedges, and in places the mud had been so churned up by animals' feet that the hummock disappeared completely, and it was just one big bog from one bank to the other. In the end, I gave up and just sludged through it.

Everything was dripping: my nose, my hair, my ears, the hedges, the trees, and the sky. Water was falling, trickling, oozing, running everywhere. Nowhere could be wetter than this. Whenever the mud gave way to rock, the track went from being a bog to a running stream. The air seemed so full of water, it's surprising I didn't drown! Why would anyone choose to live in a place like this, and what were my parents thinking of sending me here? What would have been wrong with a five-star hotel in Hampstead or somewhere else civilised?!

CHAPTER 5

It was very nearly dark by the time I reached the farm buildings. I wanted desperately to be inside, to be dry and warm. Most of all, I wanted to eat and then go to bed. The only sleep I'd had in the last two days had been in the car on the way down, and the rustic burger from the Village Tea Shoppe had been digested long ago.

The sound of the big farmyard gate opening set the dogs barking, and a young sheepdog I didn't recognise came bounding over to wriggle and bark and jump around me. It was followed by an older dog that I guessed must be Tess, although she was much stiffer and slower than the dog which would always accompany me and Ashanti on picnics and help to eat our sandwiches.

''Ere! Stop yer noise!' Old Harlan came stumping out of the barn after the dogs. Harlan was as much a part of the farm as the mossy cobbles in the yard. Nobody knew how old he was and, as far as I know, nobody knew if Harlan was his first name or his surname. He was just Harlan, and it was as if he had always been there. 'He came with the farm,' Aunt Megan once explained.

'Is that you?' he now asked, peering at me.

'Yes, it's me, Harlan,' I said, supposing I couldn't very well get that wrong.

'Megan!' he bellowed, 'The boy's 'ere!' Then he stood nodding a little and smiling and looking at the dogs and looking at his feet and occasionally looking, not quite at me, but at a point just above my left shoulder in that strange, shy way he always had. 'You's growed into a gert big boy,' he said, more to the dogs than to me. 'We's been 'spectin' you some hours befoe now.'

'We had a bit of trouble,' I explained, hoping we could now head for the shelter of the house.

Harlan thought for a bit and then said, 'I had a feelin' you 'ad. Did you lose the directions?'

'No, it wasn't that.' I wondered if Harlan knew about the Ferals. I didn't want to get into any lengthy explanations because he was obviously quite happy to stand in the rain and chat for hours. *Probably hasn't even noticed it's raining*, I thought.

'Look, I'm a bit wet,' I said.

Harlan nodded, 'We've 'ad a perty good drop o' rain today.'

'Bit more than a drop!' I said.

'Dry drizzle us calls it.' Harlan went back to nodding and smiling and showing no sign of moving towards the house.

'Are you here for yer holidays or is it for makin' yourself useful?' he asked, eventually.

'We had a flood in London. Our flat got wrecked.'

'I thought you was lookin' a bit worse for wear,' he said in the general direction of the old sheep dog.

Luckily, at that point, the door of the farmhouse opened, and Aunt Megan stepped out into the little covered porch. 'Mark!' she shouted, 'Come out of the rain! You'll catch your death!'

'Got to go,' I told Harlan and hurried off before the old boy had time to say anything else. I glanced back as Aunt Megan led me inside and saw that he was still standing in the middle of the yard.

'Mark, you're soaked!' exclaimed Aunt Megan. 'Better put some dry things on straight away! – But where's your bag? Has Harlan got it for you?'

'Stolen,' I said. 'Everything – All I've got's a pair of trainers.'

'Stolen? When? – No, don't tell me – Tell me later – Umi! Ashanti!' she shouted, 'Come and find something dry for Mark to wear!'

We were standing in the entrance hall. In my memory, it had seemed like the entrance to a great Tudor manor house, the massive, worn flagstones, the dark oak panelling, but now it seemed smaller, just an old house with a stone floor that smelt a bit damp. Aunt Megan's movements were as quick and energetic as I remembered them and her grey, smiling eyes were just as warm, but she'd got a bit bigger around the hips, as though her weight was settling. Next to arrive was Umi. There were touches of white in his wiry hair, but nothing else about him seemed to have changed, not even the thick, knitted sweater that I swear was the same one he'd been wearing the last time I'd seen him!

'Oh my Lord!' he declared, 'Oh my Lord! I have never seen anything that wet! – Dilly! Dilly sweetheart – Come and see what your mum has found!'

A little girl peeped around the kitchen door and then came to stand behind her dad's legs. Clinging to his trouser leg, she examined me with big, serious eyes for a long time as though trying to decide what I was, before turning to her mother and pointing a small finger at me – 'Boy's all wet,' she announced and even I had to laugh.

'What's so funny?' It was Ashanti. She came down the stairs and stopped on the bottom step. Because she was looking down at me, I couldn't tell which of us was taller. I had been wrong about the nail varnish. Whatever Ashanti was into now, it certainly wouldn't be cosmetics. Her hair, that had been long and wild, was cut short and clung to her head in tight, no nonsense curls, and there was nothing fashionable about her old sweatshirt and jeans.

'Hi!' I said. I suddenly, desperately wanted to see the big, gap-toothed grin, but all I got was the twitch of a polite smile. 'Hi,' she replied, flatly. Then to her mum, 'I've probably got some stuff that will fit him. I'll put it in the spare room, yeah?' and she was back up the stairs. 'The spare room', it sounded so odd, so cold. It had always been 'Mark's room', my room, when we were frequent visitors.

'Umi – boxer shorts!' said Aunt Megan.

'You'd get two of him in my boxers,' Umi laughed.

'Your old ones. Before you grew that big belly.'

'Come on, Mark. We'll sort something out.' Umi transferred little Dilly's clutching hand from his trouser leg to the hem of Aunt Megan's skirt and took me upstairs.

Half an hour later, wearing an odd assortment of clothes, I was sitting with the whole family in the warmth of the farmhouse kitchen, tucking into something sort of African that Umi had cooked, which was really tasty. Mind you, he could have given me stewed snake and I would have thought it was delicious, I was that hungry! And by the time I'd finished telling them about the London flood and my escape from the flat, I'd almost forgotten that I must look pretty weird in Ashanti's jeans and one of Umi's big sweaters, and I was beginning to positively enjoy myself. It was nice to be the centre of attention after being thoroughly ignored by my loving parents. If only Ashanti would loosen up. It was as though she resented me being there. *Perhaps,* I thought, *it's just because she's a teenager stuck in the middle of the country with nothing to do, and she resents the fact that I live somewhere interesting.* And she scowled at little Dilly when she climbed on to my knee and snuggled into my borrowed sweater.

'But what's this about your clothes being stolen?' asked Aunt Megan. So I told them how the Ferals had trapped us under the bridge with the fallen trees – and that Jerzy had a gun, but they'd made him give it up – and that they'd taken my clothes and that the one called Casablanca had taken my saxophone, which was the only thing, besides the picture of my parents, that I managed to save from our flat.

'Casablanca?' Ashanti looked up from fiddling with her knife and fork, 'That's the name of a place. Are you absolutely certain it was Casablanca?'

'That's the thing,' I said, 'They all had place names.'

'Like what?' asked Ashanti. So I told them the ones I could remember.

'If these trees were so big, how did the two of you move them?' Ashanti asked. She obviously thought I was making it all up. So I told them about the little woman with the big lorry, thinking *she's never going to believe that either!*

'That'll be Ruby!' said Aunt Megan.

'Do you know her?'

'Everyone left around here knows Ruby. Bit of a character,' said Umi.

Then I went on to tell them about how the GRID was down, and I couldn't phone them to tell them I had arrived.

'There's no GRID,' said Ashanti, as though I was an idiot not to know that.

'What do you mean?' I asked. 'There's GRID everywhere. That's why it's called GRID – Global Reach Information Distributor – It works off satellites.'

'Not here,' said Ashanti. 'They've turned it off.'

I looked at Umi to see if this could be true. He nodded. 'Ashanti's right. We can't get the GRID here any more. We didn't even know about London being under water until your mum phoned us. The old landline is our only contact with the outside world.'

Oh boy! I thought. *How do they survive? No GRIDmail, no GRIDnews no GRIDVid, what do they find to talk about? No wonder Ashanti's so moody!* But, of course, I didn't say that.

'Something to do with security and the Refugee Centre up by the north coast,' said Aunt Megan.

Then it was time for Dilly to go to bed, and when Aunt Megan took Dilly upstairs, Umi went out to do farm stuff like putting chickens away for the night, which left me on my own with moody Ashanti.

'Look,' I said when I couldn't take the atmosphere any more, 'is there something wrong, or what? Because I thought we were friends once.'

'Yeah, of course, there's something wrong. And you know very well what it is.'

Well, I didn't. I hadn't a clue what she was talking about, and I was too tired to play mind games so I said, 'What do you mean? I honestly have no idea what the problem is.'

She gave me a very long, hard look, as if she were trying to read my mind to see if I were telling the truth. At last, she said, 'I think your mother had a real cheek asking us to take you in.'

'What! We've just lost our home! I very nearly lost my life! You sit here in the country with your stupid cows and chickens! You don't know what's going on in the world! If anything happened to your home, I bet my parents would take you in!'

'Yeah, they took us in all right.'

'What are you talking about?'

Ashanti gave me another one of her searching looks.

'It's about your dad, OK? About him refusing to sell us the farm?'

'Wait a minute,' I said. 'You just said my dad wouldn't sell you the farm. Right?'

'Yeah. That's right.'

'But... I'm not getting this. He doesn't own your farm. How can he sell it to you?'

'Yes, he does. Or he did. Perhaps he doesn't any more.'

Then she looked at me a bit differently. Like maybe she didn't really hate me, but she couldn't believe anyone could be so ignorant.

'You really don't know about any of this, do you?'

'No, I don't!'

Ashanti got up from the table and walked about the kitchen a bit. 'My mum and dad had a couple of really bad years. When most of the farms around here were turned into forest, it was as if all the pests from all the other farms moved into our place. Everything we tried to grow got eaten or it got some disease. We couldn't grow anything, we couldn't sell anything, and we couldn't make any money. And because we're organic, it took several years to get the pests under control. Mum and Dad couldn't keep up the payments on the farm – we were going to lose everything, so Mum went to your dad for help.'

'And he helped you, right? Because that's the sort of guy he is.'

'We thought he was helping us. He paid off the debts and bought the farm.'

'Well, you could hardly ask more than that.'

'But now my parents are doing better, and they want to buy the farm back.'

'And?'

'And your father says he can't sell it to them because he's done some deal or other.'

'But you can still stay here, can't you? You can still work the farm?'

'We don't know.'

'Oh, come on! Dad wouldn't do something like that! He knows what the farm means to your mum – and to you – and to Umi.'

Ashanti sat down on the chair opposite me across the table. She picked at her thumbnail for a few seconds, then she looked up, and her eyes were brimming with tears – 'Mum and Dad are worried because the guy your dad's done the deal with is the same guy who is buying up the only other farms that are left around here, and he's turning them all into forest.'

'Forest? But Global Solutions owns the forest.'

Ashanti sniffed and went back to worrying her thumbnail.

'What's this guy's name?'

'Tristram something or other.'

'Not Tristram Rainer?'

'That's him. What? Do you know something about him?'

'A bit.'

I was about to tell Ashanti what I knew about Tristram Rainer – which wasn't much – just that he was the boss of FIST – when Aunt Megan came back into the kitchen. Ashanti got up quickly, rubbing her eyes on the sleeve of her sweatshirt, 'I'm going to see to Starlight,' she announce and almost ran out of the room. Aunt Megan's eyes followed her daughter out and then came back to rest on me with a look that asked, 'Is everything all right?'

'If it's OK with you, I think I'll go to bed. I'm pretty tired,' I said, and I was, it was true, but also I wanted to think about the conversation I just had. At least, I knew what the *big argument* had been about now. But what was my dad up to?

'There's a new toothbrush for you in the bathroom,' she said, and I remembered coming here when I was younger and being amazed they didn't have electric ones.

I lay down on the bed to think and was asleep within minutes. I woke to find myself still dressed and the room in total darkness; it was just after eleven. I went over the conversation I'd had with Ashanti. My father had never said anything about Aunt Megan and Umi having money problems or about buying the farm. Maybe he didn't want to embarrass them. Adults often had secrets and secret reasons for keeping things secret.

Eleven o'clock; it wasn't late. Maybe Ashanti would still be awake. I could go across to her room, and we could finish the conversation.

We used to talk all night, practically, but then we used to do a lot of things, like looking for toads in the hedgerows after rain and sitting down by the edge of the woods with a torch, sharing pockets full of broken biscuits, waiting for the badgers to come out. Ashanti even knew where you could see water vole when all the experts said that the frequent floods and higher temperatures had wiped them all out. That was the last time we fell out; the water voles were her big secret. She said if she told the rest of us where they were, we'd go barging down there and frighten them away. For ages, she wouldn't tell me, she'd just disappear off before anyone else was awake and come back at breakfast time with her sketchbook, full of drawings. I got so jealous I stopped speaking to her until, very early one morning; she came and woke me up. She was hopping with excitement and her eyes were full of wonder – 'You have to come now!' she said, frantically shaking me, 'My water vole have had babies!'

I lay on the bed and pretended the *big argument* hadn't happened, and I could go to her room to talk to her whenever I liked and she'd be pleased to see me.

Maybe she was still awake. Maybe if we finished this conversation, we could still be friends. I sat on the edge of the bed, listening. The house was quiet; all I could hear was the steady hush of the rain outside. I made up my mind, tiptoed down the passage, and tapped softly on Ashanti's door. When there was no answer, I opened the door a crack and whispered, 'Ashanti!' Still nothing.

Oh well, I've come this far, I thought. I opened the door enough to slide in. Even in the darkness, I could see the room was empty. The bedclothes were rumpled, but Ashanti had never been big on making beds, so that didn't tell me anything. Surely she couldn't still be out in the stables with Starlight? I wandered around the room using the glow from my G-Port as a torch. Her room hadn't changed much – The same collections of found objects arranged on all the surfaces: strangely shaped pebbles, the tiny skeletons of birds and rodents, and feathers of every size and texture. There were shelves full of books and a clutter of text books (which must have been well out of date, seeing as no one had used text books since God knows when!), exercise books, sketch books, pencils, paints, and brushes on the old table that she used as her desk. A papery wasps' nest, like a tiny Chinese lantern, was hung by a fine cotton thread over her bed.

Ashanti didn't go to school. Her parents taught her at home, although mostly she seemed to teach herself. There was no computer. How did she manage without a computer? I was thinking about this when I noticed a draught was blowing one of the window curtains in and out. I pulled the curtain back and found the window wide open. I knew at once she had climbed out of it. It was our old, favourite route in and out of her room. A thick, knobbly wisteria grew up the wall below the window, providing plenty of hand and footholds. Of course, we were smaller and lighter when we used to climb up and down it, but I was pretty sure it would still take our weight, particularly one at a time.

Did she climb out the window to avoid me when I tapped on her door, or was she already outside? Perhaps she was crouching at the bottom of the creeper, waiting for me to go away. No, that wasn't like her. She must still be going off on her secret missions. Probably found a family of owls or a colony of rare bats that needed keeping an eye on.

I knelt on the wide window ledge and peered down. It wasn't far – no more than ten feet. You could almost jump it if the ground was soft. Nothing moved down below. I thought about climbing out after her, but what was the point? She could have gone anywhere. Also, it was still raining, and I'd been wet too many times recently to want to get soaked again. I thought I'd wait for half an hour to see if she would come back. I sat on a chair by the window, but even with the cold draught from the open window, I had to fight to keep my eyes open, and after about twenty minutes, I gave up and decided to go back to my room and go to bed.

CHAPTER 6

News from London continued to be bad. It would be months, my parents said, before I could even think about returning home. New levees were being built to protect the business centre, the City (Square Mile), but there was a cholera outbreak in South London spread by polluted water supplies and huge areas remained uninhabitable. I was doomed to weeks of boredom in soggy Devon.

I was always the last up in the morning and the last down to breakfast. Each evening, I made the same resolution, 'Tomorrow I'm getting up early.' But each grey morning, hearing the rain beating down outside and the wind rattling the window, I'd burrow deeper into the bedclothes and think, *Just another half an hour – it doesn't matter – after all, it's not as if they need me for anything.* Half and hour, an hour, two hours would go by as I drifted in and out of sleep. Finally, I would force myself to get up, splash some water on my face, pull on several layers of borrowed clothes, and go downstairs.

Sometimes, if they had had urgent farming things to do that morning, the table would still be littered with the remains of the family's breakfast. More often, everything would have been cleared away, and there would be a note saying something like, 'Morning, Mark! Help yourself to muesli,' or 'Fresh bread in the breadbin and eggs in the larder.' Well, I didn't know much about cooking, and I'd never cooked anything on a wood-burning stove, so I never bothered with the eggs, but the home-made bread was as good as I remembered it, a thick, dark crust on the outside, moist and a bit chewy inside, but not soggy like shop-bought bread, and the taste, a little sour, that was just right with loads of Aunt Megan's raspberry jam. After I'd eaten, I'd go back up to my room.

Umi has this obsession with old books. Printed books. The sort you'd find in antique shops. Maybe it's because the farm's no longer on the GRID – but, now I come to think about it, I think they always had them. On my way back to my room, I'd pass all these shelves stuffed with books. You wouldn't believe the amount of space those books took up! They were mostly things like *The Organic Herb Garden*, or *Successful Composting*, or *An Introduction to Microgeneration*. There were novels, but they were the old-fashioned sort, written by people like Charles Dickens. One morning I flipped through *The Tale of Two Cities,* but the hundreds of pages full of words put me off. I'd never read a novel on paper. Anyway, I couldn't work up much interest in reading, so I'd play one of the games stored on my portal until I had beaten my previous best score and then watch the rooks.

Rooks are a sort of crow (maybe you know that). They live in big groups and build their nests in the tops of very tall trees. From the window of my room, I had a perfect view of the trees where they were nesting. I'd found a pair of binoculars in the living room, so I'd brought those upstairs, and I'd moved a comfy cane armchair in front of the window. I'd sit with my elbows on the window ledge to steady the binoculars, and I'd train them on the tops of the trees. If there was a half-decent gale blowing, the birds would spend the whole day playing in the wind. A big, ragged bunch of them would battle their way upwind. They've got a funny way of flying, like they're rowing through the air – their wings go forward a little bit on the down stroke and then back and up. Anyway, they'd all sort of row upwind, and I could see it was hard work, and then they'd all fling themselves downwind, like they were surfing on the air. They must have been doing fifty miles an hour by the time they passed the house. They'd turn when they reached the trees and then beat their way upwind again. It was a game. You could see it was a game. There was no other reason for them to do it.

When it wasn't windy, I'd watch them building their crazy nests, which are just a great pile of sticks, but somehow they get them to stay put in the tops of the trees. Actually, it's amazing they ever get to finish their nests because when one rook isn't looking, another one will come along and steal its sticks to build its own nest, so they're always fighting and half the sticks get dropped on the ground.

About a week after I arrived at the farm, I was watching the rooks as usual, and I was just lowering the binoculars to rest my arms and let the blood flow back to my hands that had started to get pins-and-needles, when I noticed little Dilly toddling about all on her own by the duck pond. She was wearing her little red rain hat and raincoat and wellies. As I watched, she squatted down, plucked a handful of grass, and tossed it in the direction of a few ducks that ignored her. I guessed that Aunt Megan couldn't be far away as Dilly mostly trailed after her mother.

Once I'd restored the circulation in my fingers, I picked up the binoculars again to train them back on the treetops, but there was something red floating in the duck pond. I focused the binoculars on it to see what it was. It was Dilly's little rain hat. Where was Dilly? I swept the binoculars all around the pond. There was no sign of her. I flung the window open and shouted 'Dilly!' Nothing moved except the little, red hat that was being blown slowly towards the reeds at the far end of the pond. 'Dilly!' I shouted again. No answer. It could only mean one thing. I knew immediately it could only mean one thing! Dilly must be in the pond!

I was down the stairs and out the kitchen door in seconds. I screamed for the others as I pounded, barefoot, across the yard and around the corner of the farmhouse. There was the pond. The gate in the fence that surrounded the pond hung open. There was the red hat caught amongst the reeds. I could see Dilly's little footprints in the soft mud at the water's edge. Her raincoat! Surely, even if she were under the water, I'd see her red raincoat. But the water was muddy and green, floating weed covered the surface, and I'd no idea how deep the water was. I hesitated a second, and then I went in. The water was cold, but I hardly noticed it. My feet sank into the soft, clinging mud at the bottom that oozed up between my toes. I groped about desperately with my hands under the weed, hoping, fearing any moment I'd feel the little body. How long had she been under the water? How long does it take to drown? I kept shouting 'Dilly! Dilly!' as though my voice could draw her to the surface. I waded deeper and deeper into the filthy water, the nightmare grip of the mud holding me back as I struggled towards the centre of the pond.

'Mark!... Mark!' It was Aunt Megan standing at the water's edge.

'Help me!' I shouted back. 'Help me! Dilly's in here!'

'Mark!' came Aunt Megan's voice, firm and steady. But I was too frantic, too certain to hear the rest of her words.

'Mark! Stop!' this time it was Umi. Defeated – suddenly exhausted, I looked up. A little, hatless figure stood between Aunt Megan and Umi, her eyes wide with amazement.

We stood staring at each other, the group on the bank, me up to my chest in the green water, the rain steadily falling. 'I saw her hat... I thought...' – Then I found I was laughing hysterically with relief. With the weed dripping from my arms, I must have looked completely mad.

Next to arrive was Ashanti, ashen faced and out of breath – 'What's happened?... Where's Dilly?... I heard the shouting...'

'It's all right – it's all right. False alarm. Everything's all right,' her mother calmed her.

'I thought there's been an accident! What's going on?'

'Just a lost hat. Nothing to worry about.'

I retrieved the little red hat from reeds and waded to the edge where Umi reached down and hauled me up the slippery bank.

'Boy's all wet again!' Dilly exclaimed as I stood, dripping beside her.

I wiped the remains of the pondweed from the hat and handed it to Dilly, who solemnly examined it and then put it back on her head.

Ashanti looked from her sister to me, and I could see that she was mentally working back through the chain of events that had led to me and the little red hat being in the pond, and as she worked it out her face thawed. For the first time since I had arrived at the farm, she didn't look at me as if I were some sort of insect that ought to be trodden on. Then, miracle of miracles, she actually laughed! 'You look a bit muddy. Do you want me to hose you down?'

'You're so kind,' I said.

'Well, we can hardly have you in the house like that!'

'I don't suppose you'd consider throwing a bucket of warm water over me instead?'

'All right, it's a deal. Come on.'

Dilly was allowed to fetch her little plastic bucket and help. I sat in the old horse trough in the yard while she and Ashanti poured not-very-warm water over me. It was obvious that Dilly thought this was the best game ever invented, and she was very disappointed when I was finally judged clean enough to go into the utility room, strip off, and head upstairs for a proper hot bath.

That evening I helped Ashanti chase the chickens into the chicken coop. You'd think chickens would have the brains to know they're safer inside at night, but then chickens' heads are pretty small.

'Get inside, you pea-brain!' Ashanti yelled at the last one as it ducked between us, doubled back and ran clucking off around the shed for the umpteenth time. Finally cornered, Ashanti passed the bird to me so that she could open the coop. It was surprisingly light, as though made of nothing but feathers.

As we crossed the field that everyone called the horse paddock (although it was occupied by five goats), the rain stopped and a little colour crept into the landscape. I looked up as Ashanti opened the last gate. The blanket of grey cloud that had hung low overhead ever since my arrival was drawing back from the horizon.

'What are you waiting for?'

'Look,' I said.

Ashanti also looked up. Now a gap had opened all along the western skyline revealing a clear sky that looked just created and shone with a soft golden light. As we watched, the gap grew bigger and bigger, the grey blanket sliding slowly, steadily east, the golden light from the brand-new sky spreading down from the high moorland, catching the top branches of the bare trees, the roofs of the farm buildings, the reeds in the duck pond, and finally us.

'Hungry?'

'Starving!' I said.

We ran, neck-and-neck the rest of the way. No one said it was a race, but it got to be one anyway. Reaching the utility room, we leapt about in a wild dance, trying to be the first to kick off both wellies and then pushed and shoved as we skidded and slid in our socked feet battling to beat each other into the kitchen, where we arrived laughing and panting.

'Hands,' said Aunt Megan, as if we were six-year-olds, hardly glancing up from her cooking.

We washed together at the sink, the soap passing backwards and forwards between four hands under the cold tap.

'That gate ought to have something to keep it shut,' I said once there was enough baked potato in my stomach to allow my brain to begin operating again.

'What gate would that be?' asked Umi.

'The one to the duck pond. To stop Dilly falling in.'

'We don't do locks here,' said Aunt Megan.

'It has a latch,' said Umi.

'I mean something that closes it,' I said.

'Mark's right,' said Ashanti. 'Half the time it's left open.'

'What about a sign that says, "Shut the bloody gate"?' suggested Umi.

'I'll make something,' I said. 'I've got an idea how to do it.'

'Fine,' said Umi. 'What do you need?'

'A length of chain, a few long bolts, something to act as a weight. Not much.'

'There's plenty of that sort of things in the workshop,' Umi said. 'We'll sort it out in the morning.'

In my room that night, I drew the design for my patent gate-closer: A loop of chain with a weight in the middle, bolted halfway along the top rail of the gate. The other end of the chain bolted to the top of a post in the fence that ran at right angles to the gate. When the gate opened, the chain would straighten. As soon as the gate was released, the weight would pull the chain down, closing the gate.

There was a tap on the door, and Ashanti let herself in.

'Might work,' she said, looking over my shoulder.

'What are you doing tomorrow?' I asked.

'Thought I'd go for a ride in the morning. You could help me and Harlan in the afternoon if you get this contraption of yours finished.'

'OK. See you at breakfast.'

'What! You're not thinking of getting up in the morning, are you?!'

'I just might.' (I'd already set the alarm on my G-Port for six thirty, but I wasn't telling Ashanti that).

CHAPTER 7

I didn't see Ashanti at breakfast. Although I was up early, she was up even earlier and off seeing to her pony. I was beginning work on my contraption in the workshop when I saw her ride out of the farmyard on Starlight. A pair of saddlebags made it look as if she and her pony were setting off on a journey, but she had said she would meet me after lunch, so she couldn't have been going all that far. She was always collecting things, so I guessed the bags were to hold anything that interested her, or that needed bringing home for identification: wild flowers, toadstools, bugs, and unusual rocks, whatever.

Umi had helped me find the bits and pieces I need and then had left me to it. The workshop was a converted barn in which most of the space was taken up with the various alternative technology projects that Aunt Megan and Umi were working on. There was an ancient 4 x 4 that Aunt Megan was converting to run on methane, its bonnet propped open and half its engine in bits spread out on a bench. There were wind turbines with different-shaped propellers, and one entire end of the workshop was taken up by the heavy, new water wheel that Umi was building for the hydro plant that supplied most of the farm's power. The ever-increasing heavy rains meant the turbine was frequently shut down and the water diverted to protect the old wheel from being damaged by the sudden torrents the storms sent down the millrace.

Later that morning, Harlan dropped in to check on my progress.

'Never see'd one like that before,' the old man said, examining my handiwork.

'I need to bolt it to the gate, but I don't know what to drill the holes with.'

'I'll fetch me ol' brace. What size bolts you reckon on usin'?'

I showed Harlan the ones I'd chosen. They were a bit on the large size, but I wanted to be sure they were strong enough to support the rusty flywheel from some long-dead piece of farm machinery that I'd found to hang in the middle of the chain as a counter weight.

'Don't know 'bout Dilly, but should keep the hellifants out!' said Harlan, trying the weight of the flywheel. 'Course, the fence might fall over when you hang that lot on it. I'll meet you by the pond. You fetch over yer bits 'n' bobs an' I'll fetch me brace.'

I met Harlan by the duck pond. The old man showed me how to use the brace and bit to drill holes for the bolts in the gate and the fence post. I was drilling the last hole when sounds from the other side of the valley made Harlan look up. He took the brace from my hand and laid it on the ground. 'Fetch Umi,' he said. 'Tell him they're back.'

'Who's back? What's going on?'

'Listen.'

It was an eerie sound – an echoing cry – 'Dogs?'

'Hounds. It's the hunt. Where's Ashanti to?'

'Went off on Starlight this morning.'

'That's what I was feared of. Now hurry!'

'But why? What will they do?'

'Get goin'!' the old man barked.

I hesitated another moment, but Harlan was already lumbering off around the pond. The baying of the hounds was getting louder, then a shot was fired. That did it. I set off at a run back towards the farm buildings. As I reached the gate to the yard, I met Umi coming the other way. He was carrying a stick the size of a baseball bat.

'The hunters – Harlan sent me to get you!' I panted.

'I know. I heard them. You better stay here.'

I watched as Umi strode down the track that led to a wooden bridge across the stream at the bottom of the valley. Harlan was already almost at the bridge. He too had picked up a large stick. On the other side of the stream, there was a strip of rough meadow and then the dark wall of the forest. As the two men reached the bridge, I made up my mind to join them. I looked around for a weapon but couldn't see anything suitable, so I set off empty-handed, feeling anything but brave. Half way down the hill, I stopped and wondered if it wouldn't be more sensible to go back. I had no idea what was going on, and I might just be in the way.

Harlan and Umi had crossed the bridge and were now standing guard on the other side.

A horse and rider burst out of the darkness of the forest into the sunlight. It was Ashanti. She was looking over her shoulder as she rode and dragging something on a rope behind the horse. She galloped Starlight across the meadow and then pulled her round to face the forest. The horse's coat glistened with sweat; she stamped and snorted, jiggering from side to side, and Ashanti had to work to keep her steady. I wondered what it was on the end of the rope but, whatever it was, it was hidden by the long grass. What if Ashanti looked round and saw me lurking like a coward half way up the hill? Reluctantly, I continued on down. Then the hounds began to pour out of the forest, their baying much louder now that it wasn't muffled by the trees. As soon as they broke from cover, they spread out, ranging over the meadow, searching for the scent they had been following. There must have been fifty or more of them, big, powerful dogs, tongues hanging out, their pale, mottled fur covered in mud from the chase. Soon they were all around Ashanti.

'Get across the bridge!' shouted Umi.

'No!' came Ashanti's defiant reply.

A moment later, the meadow was full of riders, their big horses dwarfing Ashanti on her pony. Some of the hunters were dressed in traditional black and white, others in camouflage jackets. A single red-coated rider urged his horse through to the front of the pack. There was the roar and sputter of emission engines, and four uniformed figures on track-bikes emerged to flank the group, two on each side. If there was going to be some sort of showdown, we were severely outnumbered! I noticed the bike riders were armed. Had one of them fired the shot?

'I warned you!' screamed the red-coated leader.

'Ha!' laughed Ashanti.

'I could have the forest guard arrest you!'

'You leave her alone!' thundered Umi, advancing and beating his stick into palm of his free hand.

'And you ought to teach your brat of a half-cast daughter not to break the law!'

By now, I had reached the bridge but decided that this was far enough.

Umi took a breath and seemed to grow broader and taller. 'You're on my land!' He pointed his stick, threateningly, up at Red-coat's face.

'This is a public right-of-way.'

'There is no hunting on my property.'

'We wouldn't be on your property if it hadn't been for her!'

The man on the horse and the man on the ground stared at each other.

Umi squared his shoulders, 'You, and all your crew have five minutes to get off my land.'

'And then what? Are you going to call FIST?'

This brought a loud, jeering laugh and shouts of 'Call FIST! – Go on, call FIST!' from the other riders.

'Anyway,' continued Red-coat, nastily, 'It won't be your land much longer.'

'You bastard! What do you mean, it won't be ours?' Exploded Ashanti as she drove her heels into Starlight's flanks and sent the pony leaping forward. Umi managed to catch hold of Starlight's bridle. 'Easy... easy,' he soothed.

There were more taunting shouts and laughter.

'What does he mean? What does he mean?' Ashanti kept shouting, half to the crowd and half to her father.

Umi, talking gently all the time to the spooked pony, led her on to the bridge. Harlan stepped aside to let them pass and then resumed his post.

'And you, old man – you ought to know better. You're one of us. You belong here,' sneered the Red-coat, pointing his riding crop at Harlan before turning his horse towards his followers. 'Ladies and gents – Let's get back to business!'

'Yeah! Back to business!' they shouted. The hounds were called in, and horses and motorbike outriders headed back into the trees.

Ashanti gathered in her rope. Tied to the end was an old sack. She stuffed the sack and rope into one of the saddlebags. So that's what she'd been doing – she'd been dragging a sent to lure the hounds away from whatever they had been hunting. Deer probably. I knew they were allowed to hunt deer in the forest.

'You can let go now,' Ashanti said to Umi.

'Don't even think about going after them,' said her father as he let go the bridle but kept a calming hand on the pony's neck.

'I've done what I needed to do,' Ashanti replied and then rode off up the hill. She didn't even glance in my direction as she passed me. Her head was up and on her face was an expression of grim triumph.

Ashanti didn't join the rest of us for lunch, and nobody mentioned the morning's events by the bridge, but it was clear from the heavy silence that hung over the farm kitchen that was usually full of easy chatter that the morning's events were on everybody's mind.

In the afternoon, I went to help Harlan who was rebuilding the dry-stone wall that ran up the hill behind the farmhouse. I expected Ashanti to come and help, like she'd said she would the evening before, but she didn't.

The walling was slow but satisfying work and soon all I was thinking about was finding exactly the right-shaped stone to fit each space. Harlan showed me how the two sides of the wall must slope in towards the top so that the wall is held together by its own weight and, foot by foot, the piles of tumbled-down stones grew back into a neat wall capped by a row of upright spines, like the serrated back of a dinosaur. By the end of the afternoon, my muscles ached and my hands were raw, and it was a relief when Harlan said he thought we'd done enough, but I couldn't help smiling proudly when the old man nodded approvingly after examining the side I'd been working on and said, gruffly, 'Yeah, reckon it'll do.'

'She's in the milking parlour, but I'd leave her be,' Aunt Megan told me much later when I went looking for Ashanti. I ignored the warning. We were friends again now, weren't we? Ashanti might not want to talk to the adults about what she'd been up to in the forest, but I was sure she'd talk to me. Besides, I wanted her to admire my handiwork on the self-closing gate.

I crossed the yard to the parlour. There was no door to the parlour, but a wooden gate closed off the entrance to the farmyard. There was a second entrance at the back that opened directly into a field. I leant on the gate and looked in. Tess got up stiffly from the floor and came to greet me. The old dog always helped to bring the cows in, not by chasing them, but by walking ahead, and they would follow her. There was a cow in each of the four stalls, and I could hear the rhythmic sound of milk hitting the side of the metal bucket. Ashanti was seated on a stool by the cow in the nearest stall, her head resting against the cow's flank. The cow shifted its weight from time to time and flicked its tail to chase away the occasional fly while Ashanti continued to milk. The air was heavy with the smell of hay and warm animal and milk. I slid back the bolt on the gate, the loud rattle disturbing the cow, which lifted a hind leg and stamped it down. But Ashanti didn't look round.

'Ashanti?' I said, quietly. 'Can I talk to you?'

She didn't answer immediately, but I knew she had heard me, so I waited. After a minute or so, she got up to empty the pail into a tall, metal milk churn. I could see the full pail was heavy, and it took all her strength to lift it and pour it steadily into the churn, but the way she ignored me told me I shouldn't offer to help. When the pail was empty, she turned to face me. 'Well? What is it?' she asked.

'I've finished the gate,' I said. 'I thought you might like to see it.'

'I'm milking,' she said.

She moved on to the next cow. She touched the cow gently on the hind leg. The cow lifted its head and blew out loudly through its nostrils, then tore off a mouthful of hay from the byre in front of it and returned to chewing. Ashanti settled herself, her head turned away from me, and began to milk.

'What happened in the forest?' I asked.

Four jets of milk hit the side of the bucket. 'I thought you saw,' she said.

'I only saw what happened after you rode out and the hunters followed you.'

The rhythmic beating of the milk against the bucket continued, but Ashanti's shoulders became more hunched, and the cow shifted restlessly.

'You're disturbing the cows,' she said, eventually.

'Do you want me to go out?'

She didn't reply, so I continued to wait. Perhaps Aunt Megan was right, and I shouldn't have come looking for her.

'Look,' she said at last, her face still turned away, 'I don't like hunters, OK? They kill things. So sometimes I do stuff.'

'Isn't it a bit dangerous?'

She seemed to ignore the question – But then, messing with the hunters, especially hunters with guns obviously was dangerous, so I supposed it was a silly thing to ask.

'I heard a shot. Were they shooting at you?'

She stopped milking and turned to me, 'Look, what I do in the forest is my business. OK? You don't live here. You don't know what goes on. You wouldn't understand.'

'I'm trying to understand! I'm trying to find out what goes on! That's why I came to talk to you,' I said – thinking, *She doesn't have to be so bloody prickly!*

'Well, I'd rather you didn't,' she said and turned away again.

'Fine!' I said. 'Fine, I'll go.'

But I didn't go. I wanted her to explain. It was like when we were younger and she wouldn't tell me where to find her water vole. I felt left out.

'Hunting's not illegal, right?' I said at last. 'If there are too many deer, they damage the forest. You may not like what these guys are doing, but if they didn't hunt the deer, the deer would have to be culled.'

That did it. It was like I'd dropped a match into a box of fireworks. She turned on me, her eyes shining; 'Get out! Just get out! You're like your stupid father! You think you know everything! That you can fix everything! That you're so big and clever because you live in the city. Well, you're not! You know nothing! Now get out and leave me alone!'

I was angry. I wanted to shout back at her, but I knew she'd only accuse me of ruining the milking. Why was she being like this? I was doing my best, wasn't I? I was helping around the place, for goodness sake! And it wasn't like I'd asked to be here! There was obviously no point trying to talk to her. She was just in some stupid mood about her precious animals, so I left her to her milking and went off up the hill, thinking I might put a few more stones on the wall.

By the time I reached the point where Harlan and I had been working, the idea of heaving more rocks about had lost its appeal, and I decided to keep going to the top of the hill. I followed the line of the old wall. Parts of it were still standing and other parts broken down by the weather or by animals scrambling over it. Near the top of the hill, another wall crossed at right angles. I climbed it by a stone style and jumped down on the other side. Now the fields gave way to heather and gorse, the remains of what had once been the open heathland of Exmoor.

At the very top of the hill was a cairn, a large pyramid of loose stones that Ashanti and I had added to every time we climbed the hill together. From here, I could look down on the farm and the surrounding forest, a forest that stretched away in all directions as far as I could see. The Great West Forest, that now covered most of Devon, half of Cornwall, and half of Somerset. My dad's forest! The lungs of England – breathing in the carbon dioxide and breathing out oxygen. Ashanti was wrong about my dad. He did fix things. But he fixed things on a big scale! Not like Aunt Megan and Umi fiddling about on their little farm. They weren't going to save the world – but my dad might! My dad, and people like him. Right now, he was working to get every country in Europe to plant a forest like this. Europe's forest would replace the lost forests of the Amazon, Africa, and Asia. It really was possible to live in a modern world and control the climate. People like Ashanti just couldn't see that.

The valley was already in shadow, but the tops of the trees were still caught in the late-evening sunlight, and I could see that they were losing the monotonous grey of winter and turning shades of green and red as the new buds and leaves appeared. It was as if the trees were drawing colour up from the ground. Here and there, amongst the trees, the roofs of abandoned farm buildings were visible and, in the distance, the steeple of a church rose out of the forest. Like the city of Atlantis, a lost civilisation, swallowed by the sea, I knew there were whole abandoned towns, roads, and canals down there. Above the trees, a pair of buzzards circled, soaring higher and higher without once beating their huge wings.

Then I remembered that Ashanti and I had hidden two toys at the base of the cairn. Were they still there? I worked my way around the cairn, shifting stones and peering into crevasses. I was about half way round, on the far side from the farm, when Ashanti surprised me.

'They're under the round stone. Remember? Where we used to leave messages. The stone I carried up from the river.'

'Where did you appear from?' I said, trying to sound like I wasn't pleased to see her.

'Forest path,' she said, nodding to a place where the trees climbed one side of the hill. She had the two dogs with her, and they greeted me, tongues hanging out, tails wagging, pushing against me, and asking to have their ears scratched. It was hard to make a fuss of the dogs and stay angry with Ashanti.

She was right, of course. The round river stone was still there. I remembered her struggling up the hill with it when we were about six, refusing to let me help her. I lifted the stone, and there was her small plastic horse and my aeroplane. I'd forgotten about the messages. It was a game that only lasted one summer. One of us would climb the hill and leave a message under the stone giving a secret meeting place and time. The other of us would then 'find' the message, and we'd meet at the secret rendezvous. By the following summer, we'd grown out of secret messages and codes.

I gave Ashanti her toy horse, and we sat for a while, leaning back against the cairn, not saying anything, watching the sunset while the dogs hunted for interesting smells amongst the gorse bushes.

'I'm sorry about earlier,' Ashanti said at last.

I didn't say anything. She wasn't getting off that easily.

'They upset me, you know? I really hate what they do!'

'No need to take it out on me!' I said.

'I know. But this is between me and them. You won't be here that much longer.'

'I wouldn't count on it,' I said.

We were silent again and then I said, 'I could help you. We could drag two scents! That would be fun! That would really confuse their dogs!'

But she turned on me again, 'No! This is not fun, Mark! This is not a game!'

'You mean this is your game, and I'm not allowed to play it!'

She got up quickly.

'Sorry!' I said. 'Sorry I spoke – OK? I'll keep out of it. I don't get why you don't want to talk to me about all this hunting stuff, but I'll stay out of it. OK?'

Ashanti lifted the round stone and put her horse back under it. I handed her the plane.

'OK?' I asked again.

'OK,' she said.

We walked back down the hill together, the young dog, Scat, running ahead, and old Tess, who had to be helped over the style, keeping at our heels.

CHAPTER 8

'Ah ha!' said Umi, when we entered the kitchen. Umi, Dilly, Aunt Megan, and Harlan were already seated around the table, eating. I was surprised to see Harlan, who usually ate on his own in his cottage in the evening.

Aunt Megan's face lit in a big smile, obviously happy to see us together. I even wondered if she'd sent Ashanti up the hill to apologise.

'What?' said Ashanti.

'Just please to see you two are still speaking.'

'Sit down, sit down,' said Umi. 'You're missing an important meeting.'

We sat and when the large plate of roast chicken, roast potatoes, crispy roast parsnips, and carrots was placed in front of me, I forgot about everything except that I was absolutely starving! I did briefly wonder which of the chickens I was eating, but I didn't really care. Whichever it was, it was delicious. I noticed Ashanti was tucking in as enthusiastically as I was, so saving our furry and feathered friends didn't extend to farm animals!

Umi allowed us to get a few mouthfuls in before saying, 'Right – Tomorrow, I am going to need everybody to help me.'

Ashanti and I looked up from shovelling food into our mouths.

'I've finished that monster water wheel!'

'Congratulations,' said Ashanti, through potato and gravy.

'Thank you, kind daughter. Now, the problem is, how to get it down to the turbine.'

'Shouldn't you have thought about that before you made it so big?' asked Ashanti.

'There is an old African saying: The man who thinks only of the problems never catches the antelope.'

'You just made that up,' said Ashanti.

'Well? I am an old African.'

'Roll it?' I suggested.

'That's what we all thought, but the problem is, we'll never hold it on the downhill. Now, if my wife hadn't taken the four-wheel-drive apart, we could have used the winch, but Harlan thinks we can use the two work horses and a series of pulleys.'

Everyone looked at Harlan, who nodded slowly, 'Reckon we could.'

'Ashanti and Harlan are best with the horses,' continued Umi. 'The rest of us will try to keep the wheel on the track and stop it from falling over.'

'And crushing us,' added Aunt Megan.

'That's the plan,' said Umi. 'Any thoughts?'

'Well, Harlan and I should survive. Don't know about the rest of you,' said Ashanti.

We were washing the dishes, when the phone rang. Amazingly the ringtone was still the same as it had been when I had first stayed on the farm! It had to be the oldest phone in the country!

It was my mother. I took the phone into the living room for a bit of privacy.

'You could call us now and again,' she complained.

'My G-Port's not working, remember? There's no GRID here.'

Of course, I could have called them on the phone, but they were the ones who had sent me away. They could call me. Anyway, I hated calling either of them at work, because there was always something in their voices that told me that they were only half listening to me while they were actually doing something else. And I couldn't very well call them at home, because we didn't have a home.

'But you could have used the landline,' she sounded tired.

'How's everything in London?' I asked, beginning to feel guilty about not calling.

'It's...' she took a deep breath, '. . . well, it's terrible. You're much better off where you are. They're still finding bodies. And now with the cholera – We're turning schools into hospitals.'

'How's Dad?'

There was another pause. 'I suppose you ought to know...'

My heart missed a beat. What had happened?

'He's not ill, or something?!'

'No… But he's lost Global Solutions. Well, he's still there, he's still on the board, but he's not running it any more.' There was silence again at the other end of the line, but I could feel that my mother was holding something back – trying to think how she could tell me something awful.

'How? But it's Dad's company,' I said.

'After the flood… people started to blame him… There always has to be someone to blame, you know… The newspapers attacked him – began calling him "Mr Disaster" instead of "Mr Environment". The banks took their money out of the company. Global would have collapsed if FIST hadn't bought it. Tristram Rainer is the new chairman.'

'Tristram Rainer is running Global Solutions!?'

'That's right.'

I couldn't believe it. Global was Dad. Dad was Global. And Tristram Rainer… ! 'But why FIST? Why Tristram Rainer?' I demanded. I hated the thought of Tristram Rainer being my dad's boss.

'Dad sold FIST most of the Great West Forest ages ago to raise capital – when Global Solutions bought the GRID and to pay for the Global building. But they kept the deal quiet. Rainer only needed a few more shares to get total control of the company.'

'I can't believe Dad sold the forest!'

'It's what big companies do, darling. They buy and sell bits of themselves to raise money to do other things.'

Now it made sense – *the big argument*! 'Is that why… ?'

'The farm?' said my mother. 'Yes, that's why Dad couldn't sell the farm back to Aunt Megan. He bought it as part of the Great West Forest – some scheme to avoid tax – but once FIST got the Forest, it belonged to FIST. Dad's been trying to get it back, but Rainer won't part with it. He'll never part with it now he's got everything.'

'Does Aunt Megan know FIST owns her farm?'

'No – and please don't tell her. You know how proud your dad is. Who knows, maybe something can still be done.'

The rest of the conversation was mostly mum asking what I'd been doing. She tried to be chatty and cheerful, but the tiredness kept creeping back into her voice. I asked about our apartment. They hadn't been to see it. No one was allowed into the areas of London that had been flooded while the search for bodies continued, and nothing could be rebuilt until the Thames Barrier was replaced. 'It's gone,' she said. 'We won't live there any more. When you come back, we'll find somewhere new. Somewhere with a garden – Would you like that? Somewhere on a big hill without a river view!' I could tell she meant the bit about the hill as a joke, but neither of us laughed.

Later in my room, I lay on my bed. I hadn't undressed yet. I didn't feel like going to sleep, but I didn't want to be with the others. I felt guilty. Embarrassed. I was ashamed to face them. My dad – the one we all counted on – had sold out to Rainer! That's all I could think about. How could he do that? He'd sold the forest, his forest! his BIG PROJECT! He'd begun planting the forest before I was born, a forest that would join up all the old small forests of the West Country. I pictured the giant map on the big screen in his office – dark green for forest, light green for fields, and purple for moorland. Year by year the dark green areas grew, spreading out, merging with each other, millions upon millions of new trees until almost the entire map was dark green. Whenever I visited the office, I'd bring the map up on the screen, and I'd search for the little dot of light green that was Aunt Megan's farm. 'That's one bit that will never go dark green,' he'd say.

Of course he'd been forced to sell Global – London had flooded – that wasn't his fault – It wasn't! Whatever people were saying. But then, I remembered what my mother had just told me; he sold most of the Forest to Rainer *long before* London flooded – so that he could be the boss of the GRID and to pay for the new Global Solutions building. It was like he had to show off, the forest wasn't enough, he had to have the biggest fanciest, Look-what-I've-got! building in the whole of London – maybe the world!

I thought about facing Ashanti, knowing what I now knew, knowing that her family would probably never be able to buy back their farm. That their farm – everything they'd worked for – belonged to Rainer – to FIST. It was worse than that. I knew Rainer – He wasn't going to let them keep it. No way.

What do you do if you know something like that? Something that's maybe going to ruin someone's life when you tell them – if you tell them – but it's happened already? You can't change it. It's not something you've done, but you know, and they don't know, and they ought to know because it's important. But it's also really bad. What do you do?

If I tell Ashanti – that's it. That's our friendship over. But she'll find out sooner or later anyway and then she'll hate me for not telling her.

I ought to go and talk to Aunt Megan, I thought. Maybe she knows already. Yeah, she must know! But what if she doesn't? I really didn't want to be the one who told her, so I kept lying on the bed.

What, I kept asking myself, *does a security organisation like FIST want with a little farm?… Or with a big forest, for that matter?*

As I lay on my bed, twilight faded into darkness. I stared up at the dark ceiling, not bothering to put on the light. At last, I got up and crossed to the window to close the curtains. There was no moon. Over the valley, the tops of the forest trees stood out black against a slightly lighter, clear night sky. Here in the country, when it was dark, it was really and truly dark, not like in the city, where there is always the glow of street lighting and light spilling out of windows or from passing cars' headlights.

I was about to draw the curtains, when a flickering light in the blackness of the forest wall caught my attention. I peered through the glass, but it had gone. I waited. Had I imagined it? Or maybe it had just been something reflected in the window. There it was again! Several quick flickers and then gone. Like something was swinging in front of a light. Or was it a light moving through the trees, disappearing behind the trunks? I kept my eyes on the spot where I had last seen it. About a minute later, I saw it again, but this time, a little further to the left, a series of quick flashes. Who was down there? I hadn't heard any movement in the house for some time, and I certainly hadn't heard any sounds of doors or gates.

Harlan, perhaps? More likely Ashanti gone out through her bedroom window on some night-time nature-watch. I decided to investigate. Anything was better than lying here in the darkness, thinking about that conversation with my mother.

What was the best way of leaving the house without disturbing anyone? My first thought was to go out through Ashanti's window. But what if it wasn't Ashanti down there? I decided to go out through the utility room. If I met anyone on the way to the kitchen, I could always say I was going to get a drink of water.

I eased open my bedroom door and crept along the corridor, trying to avoid those places where I knew the old floorboards tended to creak. The stairs were the worst, but by keeping close to the wall, where the boards moved the least, I managed to get down fairly quietly. In the hall and kitchen, the floors were all stone, so I only had to be careful not to bump into any furniture in the dark and avoid rattling the door handles.

I pulled my boots on in the utility room and then slipped out into the yard. I had a moment's panic, thinking the dogs would hear me and start barking. But they slept in the barn by the main gate at the far end of the yard, and my rubber boots made very little sound on the cobbles. I climbed the wooden fence rather than risking the noisy gate, and I was on the path down to the bridge. Once I was well away of the farm buildings, I stopped to take a few deep breaths. It was cold and still, and the stars! It was such a clear night, and they were so bright that they seemed to hang in empty darkness. I looked up at the arch of the Milky Way, and for a moment, it felt like the Earth might slide from under me, and I would fall into space. I looked down to regain my balance and then to the forest for any sign of the light. Nothing. Perhaps whoever it was had seen me, or perhaps they had moved further into the forest. I waited. Still nothing. Go back, or go on? Well, I'd come this far.

Down in the valley the darkness seemed thicker. I crossed the little bridge and stopped again. There, on the other side of the narrow meadow, was the forest. I knew a bridleway led into it, a gap in the trees through which the hunt had ridden.

The long, wet grass soaked my trouser legs above my boots as I pushed through it to get to the stone gateway in the remains of the hedge on the far side of the meadow. The darkness beneath the trees was almost total, and horses' hooves had churned up the black mud of the bridleway so that it seemed like my boots were sinking into an even thicker darkness that clung and held me back. I forced myself to go on for twenty metres, or so, then stopped and listened. Something moved to my right – a rustling in the dead leaves and undergrowth – then was quiet. It sounded quite close. A person or an animal? I strained to see into the dark spaces between the trees and imagined them, full of eyes, looking at me. I had heard there were wild boars in some parts of the forest. Were they dangerous?

'Ashanti?' I called. My voice came out trembly and small. There was no answer, but I heard a twig snap.

OK, I'm scared, I told myself, *and whoever or whatever that is, it knows the forest better than I do.*

Actually, I wanted to run, but I also didn't want to turn my back on those eyes I imagined in the darkness, so I edged sort of sideways back along the track. Once I was out of the trees, I plunged across the meadow, and I didn't look back until I was safely over the bridge.

Now I told myself I had been stupid to be frightened. It was probably a badger or something. But badgers don't go around flashing lights. I bet it was Ashanti. Why did she have to be so bloody secretive about everything?

I got back to my room without waking any dogs or people and then stood at my window for a long time willing the light to show itself again. But it didn't, and Ashanti didn't come back up the path. I was tempted to check her room to see if she was there, but it would be a bit difficult to explain what I was doing if she were there and she woke up. I gave up. I'd find a way of asking her in the morning.

CHAPTER 9

Getting the giant new water wheel from the workshop down to the turbine house at the bottom of the hill took all morning. By the time we had rolled it across the cobbled yard, it was obvious that the idea of rolling it all the way down the hill was a non-starter. Any dip in the cobbles and the wheel teetered over, threatening to squash us all flat. Harlan went off to inspect the track and came back shaking his head. 'Full o' bumps and gullies, besides bendin' this way and that.'

'Could we get it on the cart?' Umi wondered.

Harlan frowned, first at the wheel and then at the cart and then at the wheel again – 'Reckon we might, if we had some sort o' ramp.'

A ramp up to the back of the cart was improvised out of some long, sturdy planks supported in the middle by a pile of bricks, but we found there was no way we could push the wheel up the ramp.

'What about using the horses to get the wheel on to the cart?' said Ashanti.

'Worth a try,' said Harlan, and he and Ashanti, with Dilly running after them, went off to fetch the horses while the rest of us waited by the cart.

'A sensible person would have made it in pieces and put it together down there,' said Aunt Megan, crisply.

'A sensible person would buy their electricity from the national grid,' said Umi.

'You know you don't mean that,' said Aunt Megan.

'I never said *I* was a sensible person,' said Umi, with a grin.

'Well, I'd never have married you if you were,' said Aunt Megan, putting her arm around his waist.

Those two were so happy together, it made you smile just watching them tease each other. And then it hit me like an electric shock, like someone had just fired a bolt of electricity into my chest:

They shouldn't be happy – not if they knew what I knew. All this was a waste of time. All this was going to be taken away from them. I should tell them about Rainer. I knew I should, but I just couldn't bring myself to do it. They looked so happy.

Harlan and Ashanti returned leading the two chestnut workhorses, Big Red and Dora-Bella, with Dilly riding on Dora-Bella's back, holding firmly on to the horse's blond mane. She looked ridiculously small on the great, powerful creature's back, her little, brown legs sticking almost straight out on each side.

The horses waited patiently while they were harnessed up, tossing their heads occasionally, as if to say, 'Well, really! Why didn't they ask us to help in the first place?'

A chain was passed through the middle of the wheel, run across the cart, and the ends made fast to the harnesses.

'You lead 'em, girl,' said Harlan to Ashanti. 'They listens best to you.'

Umi issued us each with a long pole with which to steady the wheel as it went up the ramp, and Dilly was made to stand at a safe distance. 'If it starts to fall, run like hell!' he instructed the rest of us.

'Walk on,' Ashanti said quietly to the horses after a signal from Umi. They planted their large feet, arched their necks, and leant their shoulders into their harnesses. They were obviously used to pulling much bigger weights than this, and the wheel immediately began to move.

'Steady! Steady, Bella,' Ashanti slowed the younger horse.

The wheel climbed up the ramp, rocked dangerously as it reached the top, and rolled on to the cart. Dilly jumped up and down and gave a little cheer, and Umi, wiping some nervous sweat from his forehead, said, 'Well, at least that worked, OK.'

The wheel was lashed upright on the cart with a web of ropes while Ashanti unhitched Big Red and Dora-Bella from the chain and hitched them to the cart.

I was hoping that at some point we'd take a break so that I could talk to Ashanti about the light I'd seen in the forest, but she was completely focused on the horses, her hand always resting on one or the other, talking to them clearly and calmly as they bent their big, intelligent faces down to listen to her.

'She has a way with 'em,' said Harlan, seeing me watching her.

'I suppose you taught her,' I said.

'Me? No.' He gave a little snort. 'More like her taught me. Always been a tractor man m'self, but your Aunt Megan won't hear of usin' 'em. You just try an' imagine what it's like ploughin' with horses. By the end of the day, you'll 'ave walked twenty miles up an' down, up an' down a slopin' great muddy field. No, give me a nice warm tractor cab any day. You can listen to the radio in a tractor, you don't get that with a horse, neither.'

'There was a tractor, wasn't there?' I said, remembering when I was younger.

'Still there. Locked up, it is. In the shed by my cottage.'

'So we could have used it today?'

''Gainst her principles,' Harlan said, nodding towards Aunt Megan, then stared at the ground for a bit, and I wondered if the conversation was over. 'Beautiful creatures, though, them Suffolks,' he added, as if he thought he might have gone too far. 'Plenty of heart. Work 'till they drop, if you ask 'em to.'

When Umi was happy with his ropes, we set off down the hill, Ashanti leading the horses, Dilly riding on Dora-Bella, and everyone else following the cart.

Umi had already diverted the water from the millrace and removed the old mill wheel, but it took over an hour, a lot of head scratching, and quite a bit of shouting before we safely manoeuvred the new wheel off the cart and into the place so that it could be connected up to the turbine.

'Moment of truth!' said Umi at last. We all waited, Dilly hopping about in excitement, as Umi went off to release the water. He came running back, racing the water that poured down its narrow channel and shot out over the wheel. At first, the water ran over the wheel and nothing seemed to happen.

'Not working!' declared Dilly.

'Wait,' said Umi.

We waited.

Gradually the wheel began to turn, slowly at first, but getting faster and faster and faster. This time, everyone, even Harlan cheered.

'No more power cuts,' said Umi.

'Better wait for the next big storm before you say that,' said Aunt Megan.

'Always the pessimist!' said Umi. 'Come on. This calls for a celebration.'

The horses were turned out into their field, and we all gathered in the kitchen. Everyone was hungry, so when Aunt Megan asked, 'How should we celebrate?' Umi said, 'Loads of food!' and we all agreed.

Dilly had just announced, 'I'm full up to my neck!' and Umi was sitting back patting his stomach, when there was the throbbing sound of a large engine approaching and then the loud 'dee-daa' of a truck horn.

'Must be Ruby,' said Aunt Megan.

Sure enough, the shiny, red side of Ruby's truck cab filled the kitchen window and I was surprised to see that Ashanti was the first to the door. Since this Ruby character had had to rescue me from a bunch of weird kids last time we met, I felt a bit embarrassed about meeting her again, but I followed the rest of the family outside. There was no trailer on the truck but, with its waving aerials and chrome exhaust pipes, it still looked monumental in the farmyard. The cab door opened, and Ruby bounced out.

'Hi, Meg! Hi, Umi!' She hugged Aunt Megan and Ashanti, pumped Umi's hand and swung a giggling Dilly round and round. Ashanti was all smiles, for once, and the dogs, tails wagging like mad, pushed their way between their owners' legs to be close to Ruby, who worried their ears and made a great fuss of them. She was obviously a popular visitor. I lurked on the edge of the gathering, but Ruby strode over to me. 'Don't think I ever found out your name, kiddo.'

'Mark,' I said.

'Mark! Pleased to meet you again, Mark. Where's your bodyguard?'

'Jerzy? Gone back to London.'

'Probably better off there. He didn't seem to like the countryside much! Well, what's new down on the farm?'

'Dad's got his water wheel working,' said Ashanti.

'Already?! Congratulations, Umi. It's only taken... what?... a year and a half?'

'Never rush a genius,' said Umi, good-naturedly.

'And what about the fart-cart, Meg? Or should we call it the poo-mobile? Is methane the fuel of the future?'

'Actually, I'd like you to have a look at it. The digester is working fine. We're getting loads of methane from the cow dung, but when I use the gas to run the four-wheel-drive, I get a white coating in the engine. I've taken it to bits again.'

'Happy to take a look at it, but I dunno if I'll be able to help. Didn't do cow dung at college. Now, Mark – I've got a surprise for you!' She climbed back into her cab. *What*, I wondered, *could she possibly have for me?*

'Guess what it is!' she called, sticking her head out.

'I've no idea,' I said.

'Daa-daa!' she held out the saxophone case. It looked dirty and a bit battered, but it didn't look completely wrecked.

'Well? Aren't you going to say thank you?'

'Thank you,' I said. 'But how did you get it back?'

'Found it under that same bridge. Ferals must have dumped it. Got sick of carting it round, probably. Well? Let's have a tune then!'

'Oh,' I said, wishing she'd never found the thing. 'No, you wouldn't want to listen to me playing. It's been ages.'

'If you play your sax, I'll play my horn,' she said and dived back into the cab. It was one of those trucks that has a sort of bed behind the seats so that the driver, on a long trip, can pull over and have a sleep. I thought she was talking about the truck's horn, but she knelt on the driver's seat and pulled another instrument case from the sleeping compartment. She opened the case and took out a trumpet.

'You must know "When the saints go marching in",' she said, as she fitted the mouthpiece to the trumpet. Well, as it happened, I did know it. In fact, I'd played a solo in it with the school jazz band in a concert. But that was over a year ago.

'I'm a bit out of practice,' I said.

'Tell you what. I'll go and have a look at Meg's fart-cart – see what's clogging up her engine – while you have a bit of a warm up. Then we'll have a jam – see how good you are.'

'More like, how bad I am,' I said.

Ruby, Aunt Megan, Dilly, and Ashanti – all headed off to the workshop, leaving me standing by the truck with my saxophone case and Umi and Harlan both grinning at me.

'You won't get away with not playing,' said Umi. 'Not with Ruby. When she says something's going to happen, it happens!'

'I'll be complete rubbish,' I said.

'Harlan and I have to go repair a gate. Don't we, Harlan?' said Umi.

'Do we?' said Harlan. Then I caught Umi winking at him. 'Oh yeah!' said Harlan, 'I was forgettin'. We'd best be off then, hadn't we?'

'So we'll leave you to practise,' said Umi, and off they went, but I caught them both looking back over their shoulders, checking to see if I was getting the saxophone out.

As the house was empty, I decided to go into the kitchen, where no one would hear me. The sax, when I got it out, was also rather dirty, and the reed was split and looked a bit chewed. I fitted a new one. The first noises I made were truly awful, but once I'd settled down and the reed had softened up, I got a bit more confident and soon I thought I was sounding pretty cool. *Yeah,* I told myself, *you're really quite good.*

I checked in the case for any sheet music. There was a scrumpled sheet for a tune called 'Body and Soul' but shoved in; with it was the family photograph that I'd taken from Mum's desk the day of the flood. There we were: me, Mum... Dad. My dad – He looked relaxed – happy. Pleased with himself! That was it, he looked pleased with himself.

The holiday when that picture was taken was just after the opening of the Global Solutions building. No wonder he looked pleased with himself, he'd got pretty much everything he wanted. He'd got his beautiful new building, he'd just been given a knighthood, he was the government's environmental adviser – He'd be *Lord* Robert soon, he had said. Had he already sold the Forest to FIST? Had he already lost Aunt Megan and Umi and Ashanti and Dilly their farm? If he had, he didn't look like he cared. I stared at the picture. Seeing him, even in a picture, had the same effect on me that seeing him always did; I was little and he was big, and he could do anything and he always knew what to do. But I used to think he always did the right thing, now I wasn't so sure.

Ruby stuck her head round the door. 'Ah! So that's where you're hiding! You won't get away, you know.'

She came in and picked up the sheet of music.

'You know this? I'm impressed!'

'It was a favourite of my dad's. I was trying to learn it to surprise him.' (*Not as though Dad ever managed to make it to any of the school concerts,* I thought to myself) 'He had an old recording by Colman Hawkins. But I can't play it like Hawkins.'

'I won't hold that against you, kiddo! He was one of the greatest sax players of all time! Now come on out. We've got an audience waiting.'

An audience was exactly what I didn't want. I followed Ruby out into the yard. Sure enough, the others were all there, and they gave us a round of applause, just like we were a band coming on stage. Ruby pulled her trumpet out of the truck, and we tuned up.

'Ladies and gentlemen,' announced Ruby, 'guesting today with Ruby's Truckers is Mark on tenor sax! A big hand for *Mark*!' There was more clapping. 'Just follow me,' she said, out of the corner of her mouth and launched into the opening of 'When the Saints…'

At first, we passed the tune backwards and forwards; she'd play a bit, then I'd echo it back, then she'd play the next bit, and I'd echo that. But soon, we loosened up, and we were bouncing the tune all over the place, turning it inside out and generally messing it about.

Our little audience started laughing and clapping along, and Dilly was dancing, and I could even see Harlan's foot tapping. Just as I thought we'd come up with every possible variation, and I was wondering where we could take the tune next, Ruby gave me the nod, and we joined together for the big finale; '. . . when the saints go marching iiiiiiiiiiiiiiiiiiiiiiiin!' sang the sax and the trumpet together, followed by much whistling and stamping of feet.

Ruby shook me by the hand. 'What are you doing next Saturday, Mark?' she asked.

'Mm,' I said, 'I'd have to check my diary. I could be chasing a runaway goat, or, if I'm lucky, mucking out the cowshed.'

'That's a shame', she said, 'because Ruby's Truckers have got a concert, and we could use a sax player.' She climbed back into the truck, put away her trumpet, and jumped back down clutching a scruffy cardboard binder. 'Here! Have a look. This is some of the stuff the Truckers play. You probably know one or two of these. Anyway, you've got a week to get the others together. What do you think, kiddo?'

I flipped through the file. 'Tiger Rag' I knew, and 'Honeysuckle Rose', but most of the tunes were new to me. They had names like 'Struttin' with Some Barbecue' and 'Muskrat Ramble'.

'Old jazz standards,' she said. 'Of course, you wouldn't have to play on all of them, and we do some of our own stuff. What do you think? Or just come along and have a jam with the band.' She glanced at Ashanti, who gave me an encouraging smile. What did she know that I didn't? Had Ashanti put Ruby up to this? But Ashanti couldn't have known that I was going to get my saxophone back.

'OK.' I said. 'Yeah, why not? I can always chase goats another day.'

'Marvellous!' said Ruby, thumping me on the back. 'Welcome to Ruby's Truckers! We'll run through a few numbers before the gig, and we'll busk the rest. It's jazz after all, so the punters don't know when we get it wrong!' She turned to Ashanti, 'Well, we better get going. We'll see you all at the gig.'

'Are you sure you can spare me?' Ashanti asked Aunt Megan.

'Of course we can, pet. Anyway, we've got Mark.'

Ashanti gave her mother a hug and scrambled into the truck's passenger seat.

What was going on? This was the first I knew about Ashanti going off with Ruby. Did this often happen?

'How will I get to the concert?' I asked, suddenly feeling like I could do with a bit more information.

'Don't worry,' Ruby called over her shoulder, as she too climbed aboard. 'Umi and Meg'll bring you after they do the market. Try to be early, and you'll get a bit of rehearsal.' She started up the truck, neatly turned it around, gave us a 'dee-daa' on the horn, and then the huge, red vehicle lumbered off down the farm track, its aerials waving like the feelers on some giant insect.

I still hadn't managed to say anything to Ashanti about the phone conversation I'd had with my mother the night before. I looked at Aunt Megan and Umi waving happily at the retreating truck, at the barking dogs chasing after it down the lane, and at old Harlan leaning on the gate he'd just shut. They all so obviously belonged here. What had my dad done?

CHAPTER 10

Not having Ashanti around was strange. Everything went on as usual, and Umi and Aunt Megan made sure I had plenty to do, but... and it wasn't as if we got on all the time, Ashanti and me... but there were loads of times most days when we just chatted about nothing in particular, over a meal or while we were putting the chickens in, or whatever really, and I missed that.

I wondered what Ashanti did when she went to stay with Ruby. I supposed it was a change from being on the farm, but I couldn't see that riding around in a timber truck would be Ashanti's sort of thing. Maybe I was even a bit angry that riding around with Ruby was more fun than doing stuff with me. I guess, to be honest, I felt a bit left out.

It kept on being sunny and dry. 'Just like a proper spring. Just like we used to have,' Umi said. And, as Harlan was busy ploughing with Big Red and Dora-Bella, I decided to make repairing the stone wall up the hill my personal project. When Aunt Megan didn't need help cheese-making in the dairy, or Umi hadn't got me weeding the herbs and vegetables, I'd take my saxophone and spend the morning, or afternoon, arranging stones and, in the breaks I allowed myself, I'd practise the tunes Ruby had left with me. Sometimes, at the end of the day, I'd climb on up to the top of the hill and sit at the bottom of the cairn, playing, as the sun set.

Looking down from there, through the tops of trees, the carpet of bluebells that covered the forest floor made it look as if the trees were growing out of a purple sea. On the other side of the hill, the field that Harlan was ploughing was changing from brown to red as the plough turned over the red earth. The beech hedges, which had held on to their dead leaves all winter, were now an almost painful green. The colours all around me got into the music, and I found a new way of playing, more like painting the air than playing notes on a scale.

The day before the concert, I finished wall-building early and went up to the top of the hill to run through all the tunes I had learnt. I was in the middle of 'St Louis Blues' when I noticed a thin column of smoke rising from the chimney of one of the abandoned farms in the forest. Somebody was using the building. Hunters having a picnic? Forest guards? I supposed they might use the old buildings as handy shelters on their patrols. *Maybe,* I thought, *whoever it was, was the same person who had been flashing that light about the other night.* I went back to practising, but the column of smoke kept catching my eye. Who was down there? Perhaps it was because of the saxophone, and it being the Ferals who had taken it, but the more I saw the smoke, the more convinced I became that there was a group of Ferals in that old farm. Were they living there? I hadn't seen the smoke before.

I began to make a plan. I could leave the saxophone in the turbine shed, then cross the bridge, and enter the forest by the bridleway. The column of smoke was pretty much due west of the bridge. The forest trees were not yet in full-leaf, so even if I had to leave the bridleway, I should be able to see enough of the sky for the setting sun to tell me which way was west. It was hard to judge the distance, but I guessed the old farm was a mile into the forest. Even going slowly, I should be able to find it in half an hour. If I hadn't found it in three-quarters of an hour, I'd turn back. That way, I'd be sure of getting out of the forest before dark.

I wondered if I should say anything to Aunt Megan or Umi, but, I figured, *I'll be back before tea, so why bother?* And, anyway, I'd waste time by going back to the farmhouse.

I hesitated when I reached the old stone gateway at the beginning of the bridleway. At night, I hadn't noticed the sign on a post just past the gateway that said, 'Private Property – Permits must be obtained from Great West Forests before entering' – and a GRIDsite address. A week ago, it was 'our' forest and the sign wouldn't have bothered me. But now – now it was different. Well, if I met a forest guard, I'd say one of the goats had run off, and I was looking for it.

The fine weather had given the track a chance to dry out and, if I kept to the edge, it wasn't too muddy. At first, the track took me west, but soon it began to swing off to the north. I kept going, hoping it would swing west again, but the setting sun was getting further and further to my left, and I knew I would have to leave the path and make my way through the trees. Luckily, being spring, apart from the sea of bluebells, the undergrowth hadn't really got going yet, and the trees here were old and big with plenty of space between them. The forest on the western side of Higher Heathcombe existed before the new forest was planted.

After about a quarter of an hour, I saw there was a gap in the forest ahead. When I reached it, I found the gap was a road, one of the many old roads that ran through the forest, and nobody used any more, except, perhaps the forest patrols and hunters. The tarmac was broken and potholed and lifted here and there by the roots of trees. On the other side of the road, the trees were younger and closer together, growing in what once would have been a field.

Somewhere, I thought, *there must be a lane that leads to the old farm and that lane probably runs off this road.* The problem was knowing whether the lane joined the road to the left or right of where I was now standing. I guessed left, since right would take me further north.

I was about to head off along the road when it occurred to me I would need some sort of mark to tell me to leave the road again at this point on my way back. I stood on the road and looked at the trees I'd just left. There was nothing special about them, nothing that stood out. I found three dead sticks that were fairly straight and laid them in an arrow shape on the side of the road. Would I see them if it were getting dark when I came back? I bent down a small tree branch at eye level until it snapped. The freshly broken wood was easy to spot even when I walked a few metres down the road. *Hey!* I thought, *a few weeks in the country and I'm turning into a Boy Scout!*

The road dropped down into a valley and crossed a stream at the bottom. A little way up the hill on the other side of the stream a lane led off to the right. This had to be the lane to the farm, unless I was well off course.

There must have been half a metre of last autumn's leaves in the bottom of the lane. It was obvious no vehicle, or even horses, had been up here for a long time. If this did lead to the farm, then, whoever was there had come on foot, unless there was another way in. The uncut hedges on either side of the lane had grown into trees that met overhead and, with the sun now down below the hills, it was quite dark in the lane and eerily quiet, the thick carpet of dead leaves soaking up all the sound except the sound of my feet brushing through the layer of dry leaves on the top. I began to hurry. It had been OK in the forest and on the old road, with the last of the sunlight filtering down through the trees, but in this dark lane, the idea of coming here didn't seem so clever. After all, if the people in the house were Ferals, they wouldn't exactly welcome me dropping in on them, would they?

The hedges came to an end. The farm gate was off its hinges and lying across the lane, buried in leaves. I edged forward, keeping in the deepest shadows until I could see the house. It was a two-storey stone building, heavy and square, the windows covered by sheets of corrugated iron to keep out squatters. Slates had slipped from the roof and lay broken around the walls. Plants had grown in the clogged gutters that sagged away from the eaves. The front steps were green with moss, but the door was half open, the heavy padlock that had been used to secure it still locked on the hasp that had been levered out of the doorframe by whoever first broke in. Smoke, thin and wispy, was rising from one of the chimneys. To the left of the house, a barn with a tree growing through its roof contained rusting farm machinery.

I had imagined that I'd be able to creep up to a window and see who was inside without being seen, but I hadn't reckoned on the corrugated iron. Thinking it over, there were only three things I could do: give up (obviously the most sensible), hide in the barn and see if anyone came out, or (and this would be totally insane) I could go into the house. I decided on the barn option and made a dash for the shelter of a rusting tractor. From my new vantage point, I saw something that I hadn't been able to see from the lane: one of the sheets of corrugated iron was loose, curling away from the wall, and the window behind it was open. If I got close enough, I might be able to hear, or even see, who was in the house.

I was getting cold, crouched behind the tractor, and it was getting quite dark. I should be starting back if I wanted to get out of the forest in daylight. I decided to give it another five minutes and, if nobody came out, to try the window.

The minutes dragged by, and the damp cold in the barn made my shoulders ache. It was pointless to wait any longer. I straightened up, checked the front door one last time for movement, then quickly, and as quietly as I could, crossed to the wall by the open window. Even pressed against the wall, I was in sight of the door. Anyone coming out would be able to see me. Slowly, I slid my head and shoulders behind the corrugated iron, taking care not to move it in case it rattled. The room I found myself looking into was dark but obviously unoccupied. It must have been a storeroom; the walls were lined with shelves that were empty, apart from some soggy-looking cardboard boxes. I leant further in to listen. There was a strong smell of things rotting. I held my breath, partly because of the smell, partly because my breathing seemed very loud in the empty room.

I could hear a voice. I strained to catch some words, but the voice was muffled by the closed door of the storeroom. There only seemed to be one person speaking. Then I heard a door opening and closing, and footsteps went past the door to the storeroom. Now the voice began again, but louder, angry – a boy's voice. Was that English? He had a strong accent. These were Ferals. Definitely Ferals! As I listened, another sound caught my attention – the groan of rusty hinges – the front door! Somebody was coming out! If I stayed where I was, I'd be seen for certain! I was about to wriggle out and run for the barn when I realised that that would be even worse. There was only one thing to do! I hauled myself over the window ledge and dropped into the room, landing on my hands and knees. The floor was covered in bits of bark and twigs. Stuff that had found its way in through the open window, I supposed.

There were footsteps outside – They went past the window and kept going. I hadn't been seen. Whoever it was, was going to the barn.

Good thing I wasn't still crouching behind the tractor! But now what? A new sound started outside... *chunk... chunk... chunk*. Someone was chopping wood. *Chunk... chunk... chunk...* on and on. Stopping occasionally and then starting up again. How much firewood did they need?! Must be chopping enough to last the night.

I risked a peek out the window but, although I could see the old tractor I had hidden behind, I couldn't see the person cutting the firewood. *Must be at the other end of the barn,* I figured. It really was getting quite dark out there. If I waited much longer, I didn't fancy my chances of finding my way back to Aunt Megan's.

I crept across the room, trying to avoid the sticks and twigs that littered the floor, and carefully eased the door open a few centimetres. Perhaps I could find another way out of the house without being seen. I pushed the door a little further open. I was looking into a corridor that was in almost total darkness. At the far end, a line of orange light flickered under a closed door, and it looked like there was a split in one of the door panels because I could occasionally see another flicker of orange higher up. Just before the door, there was an opening to the left that I guessed led to the back of the house, or maybe to the stairs up to the next floor. *There must be a back door,* I told myself. *That's your best bet. Go out the front, or climb out the window, and whoever it is outside will see you.*

I was trying to work up enough courage to step into the corridor when a heavy *thud* by the window almost made me jump out of my skin. What on earth?!... The person outside was lobbing firewood through the window. So that's why there were sticks all over the floor; this was how they brought the logs into the house! At any moment, someone could come to take the firewood into the main room and, with Ferals inside and outside, I'd be caught for certain, and who knew what these crazy kids did to spies! *Back door! I have to find the back door!*

I stepped into the corridor and crept towards the turning that I hoped led to the back. As I got near to the door with the light under it, I began to be able to make out what the people in the room were saying – 'I don't come here to live like an animal. And you, eh? Is that why you come here?' That voice! I had heard that voice before – one of the Ferals who hijacked our car. Would I be able to see who it was through the crack in the door panel?

I tiptoed past the turning in the corridor and put my eye to the crack. There was a good blaze burning in the fireplace, and there were at least a dozen of them sitting in a rough semicircle around the fire, some on the floor and others, on an assortment of chairs that they must have dragged there from around the house. Most of them had their backs to me, but seated beside the fire in a tattered sofa, with an Asian-looking girl beside him, was the boy they called Casablanca. He had his arm around the girl, and her head rested on his muscular shoulder. His other arm rested on the arm of the sofa, and there was something in his hand that he was toying with, but I couldn't make it out. A couple of kids squatted by the fire, cooking bits of food on the ends of sticks, and there was a smell of burning fat. Long staves with sharpened ends were propped against the wall. Had they been hunting? Is that how they lived?

'What you want, eh? Stay in this forest your whole life?' Casablanca was saying. 'Eat berries, kill rabbit when you are old mens? That what you want?'

'But Yongjo Pa says this life is not forever – just for now – One day, we all free,' objected a younger voice.

'Yongjo Pa!' spat Casablanca. 'Yongjo Pa run out of ideas! You stay with Yongjo Pa, you die in the forest!'

'How can we leave the forest? If we leave the forest, they catch us.'

'First we need money. With money you can do anything.'

'Yongjo Pa says we don't take money.'

'Hey! You don't listen!' Casablanca was on his feet. 'I told you – Yongjo Pa is finished! We have this! Soon we have more.' He raised his hand, and I saw now what he had been playing with – It was a gun. 'Then we take what we want!' He stepped in amongst the kids seated around him, bent down, and lifted a boy to his feet by the front of his clothing. He pressed the gun to the boy's head. 'Maybe you spy for Yongjo Pa?'

'No!' squealed the boy.

'Maybe you lie!'

'No! No, please! No! I only... I only...'

The girl got up from the sofa and spoke softly to Casablanca who threw the boy back down on the floor. 'I'm watching you, Gabura – Remember that – I'm watching you.'

I was so mesmerised by what I could see through the crack in the door that I forgot, for a moment, the danger I was in. As the girl led Casablanca back to the sofa, I realised that the sound of the logs being tossed into the storeroom had stopped. Did that mean that whoever was out there would soon be coming back in? I listened for other sounds. The chopping hadn't started again. Probably time for me to get out. But as I started towards the entrance to the other passage, the front door grated open and a large figure holding an axe stood in the doorway. Had he seen me? It was dark in the corridor. If I stood still I might be invisible. What would he do? Surely he'd go to the storeroom to collect some of the wood he'd thrown through the window. I froze. He pulled the front door closed and began to walk towards me. *Go into the room! Go into the room!* He stopped by the storeroom door and leant the axe against the wall. Yes! He was going to go in! – But that's when I heard the door open behind me!

'Hey!'

I heard the shout and spun round. Kids in the room were already scrambling to their feet; two had grabbed sharpened staves; the girl who had opened the door made a grab for me, but I dodged and began to run. It was like my boots were full of cement, but I willed my legs to move. The boy by the storeroom picked up the axe and charged at me just as I turned the corner and dashed down the side passage. In the darkness, I blundered full speed into the foot of the stairs, managed to catch hold of the banisters to stop myself from falling; pushed off, and careered on down what might easily be a dead end with the gang behind me screaming instructions to each other.

A way out! Please let there be a way out! A crack of grey light told me the back door was ajar. As I reached it and pulled it open, I allowed myself one quick glance back over my shoulder. They were pushing and shoving each other to get at me. Out the door, I slipped on the mossy steps and almost fell, staggered for a moment, then got my balance and sprinted around the house for the gateway in the dim twilight.

As soon as I was in the lane, the deep layer of dead leaves slowed me down, and I heard the leader shouting 'Get him! Get him!' to the pack on my heels. I was trapped! I had a head start, but they'd run me down before I reached the road unless I got out of this lane. Desperately, as I ran, I looked right and left for a gap in the hedge. Then I saw it! – A place where deer crossing the lane had broken through. I scrambled up the bank and plunged into the forest. The trees here were close together. I stumbled on roots, twigs whipped my face, and brambles tore at my ankles. It was impossible to move quietly.

'There!' a girl's voice screamed.

'Spread out!' came the order from the leader.

They're going to get me! They're going to get me! I kept thinking – and then I tripped and fell. The fall knocked the wind out of me, and I lay breathless in the undergrowth, hearing my pursuers crashing about amongst the trees and calling to each other.

There was a sort of tunnel made by the arching branches of the tangle of brambles that had tripped me up. Carefully, trying not to get snagged, I dragged myself on my stomach into the hollow. Several times I had to stop to disentangle my clothes from thorns, but eventually, I was completely inside the mound. Time after time, I heard feet pass less than a metre from my hiding place, and each time I held my breath, but the thorny tangle stopped them getting any closer.

Gradually, the sounds of searching faded as the Ferals moved further and further off, but I lay, not daring to move, long after they had gone. I was about to drag myself out from under the brambles, when I heard them returning along the lane. I could make out some English words, but there were other languages as well. *Probably discussing what they'd have done to me if they'd caught me,* I thought. The voices passed on.

I gave them plenty of time to get back inside the house before creeping out and stealthily making my way back to the lane. But what if they left one of the kids to watch the gap in the hedge? I decided to stay on the forest side of the hedge until I reached the old road.

It was now really, really dark, and I didn't dare make a sound in case one of them had stayed in the lane, so it took an age to reach the corner where the lane met the road, but I got there eventually.

On the road, in the darkness, every bush pretended to be a figure lurking amongst the trees, waiting to jump on me. I was so busy looking out for ambushes that I almost missed the broken branch I had used to mark the place where I should leave the road and cut through the forest to the farm. The arrow I had made out of twigs on the ground was still there. I kicked it apart. Not that anyone would see it in the dark, but I didn't want to tell the Ferals exactly where I came from if they should come along the road in the daylight.

Of course, once I left the road and got back into the forest, I got completely lost and probably would have ended up wandering around all night if the moon hadn't come up. There was a ghostly glow in the tops of the trees and then there it was, bright as anything, and I realised I'd been going north instead of east for at least half an hour.

I sat down on a fallen tree, feeling exhausted and miserable. I guess it was knowing I now had to trudge all the way back the way I'd come and that it was going to be at least another half an hour before I could hope to find the bridleway – and I was hungry – and now that I wasn't worrying about being jumped on at any moment, I noticed that my hands and face and legs were scratched to pieces and stinging and sore. In the moonlight, I could see the dark lines of blood on the backs of my hands and when I rubbed my face, I found blood on my fingertips.

I began to think what a stupid idea this had been in the first place, and then how useless the Forest Guards were that they allowed a bunch of semi-wild kids, who were most probably illegal immigrants anyway, to run around in the forest causing everybody grief. Then, for the first time, I thought about Aunt Megan and Umi. What would they be thinking? They would have been expecting me to be back at the farmhouse hours ago! As far as they knew, I'd gone up the hill to mend the wall. They were probably out searching for me, thinking I'd fallen down a cliff, or something; maybe even called out the rescue services! That got me to my feet again. I had to get back as quickly as I could, or there'd be no end of fuss.

It took more than half an hour to find the bridleway, but once I was on it, it was only a few more minutes before I was at the edge of the forest. As soon as I came out of the trees, I could see the lights moving on the hill, and I knew they were up there looking for me. I shouted, 'I'm here!' but they were too far away. I forced my legs into a tired jog – over the bridge and up the track and past the turbine house. I stopped and shouted again. This time one of the dogs barked, and one of the lights began to move down the hill. 'It's me! Mark! I'm here!' I yelled. Now both dogs were barking, and three lights were coming down towards me.

The dogs reached me first and then Aunt Megan, who put her arms around me and said, 'Thank God! Thank God! Thank God!' and I knew instantly how worried she'd been. Umi arrived next with Harlan close behind, but I couldn't see any of their faces properly because all their torches were directed at me.

'Megan, he's bleeding,' said Umi.

'I'm OK', I said, 'they're just scratches.'

'What's happened to you?' asked Aunt Megan, stepping back so that she could get a good look at me.

'I got lost', I said, 'in the forest.'

'Well, thank God you're safe,' said Aunt Megan. 'We thought you'd fallen down one of the old quarries.'

'Better get him inside and patch him up,' said Umi.

'Well, now the excitement's over, if you 'ave no objection, I'll be getting back to my tea!' said Harlan. 'G'night all.' And he marched off down the hill towards his cottage.

Clearly, nobody had eaten. There were plates on the table and an untouched loaf of bread. A large pot of soup sat cooling by the stove. Aunt Megan cleaned up my cuts and scratches while Umi warmed up the food.

'I'm really sorry... ,' I began to say. But Aunt Megan hushed me, 'It's easy to get lost in the forest. Especially once it's dark. You're safe, that's all that matters. Oh dear!... (She closed her eyes as if picturing all the terrible things that might have happened)... I kept thinking of your poor mother.'

It was quite obvious that it was enough for Aunt Megan and Umi that they'd found me and that all the dreadful things they'd imagined hadn't happened. They didn't want any further explanation; they just wanted to be able to eat and relax. I had thought I would tell them all about the Ferals and get them to call out the forest guard, but now I felt like I'd cause everyone enough trouble. And anyway, to be honest, I'd had enough too. I decided that the best person to talk to about the Ferals was Ashanti. Well, I could do that tomorrow. The concert! Tomorrow night was the concert with Ruby's Truckers! But I was too tired to even get properly nervous about it.

Tomorrow, I said to myself as I got into bed. *I'll worry about the concert tomorrow.* Bed was heaven, and the sheets, as I slid between them, were cool and soothing on my torn skin.

CHAPTER 11

I got a bit of a shock when I saw my face the next morning in the mirror. There was this big scratch that went right across my forehead, with dots of dried blood all along it – like I should have had 'Cut along dotted line' printed on one side of my head! My cheeks looked like someone has whipped them with a stick, which, I suppose, was pretty much what had happened, and there was even a scratch on my nose. The backs of my hands were just as bad.

I didn't think I'd overslept, but when I got downstairs, Umi and Aunt Megan were already outside (which was lucky in a way because I could have breakfast on my own instead of having people commenting on the way I looked). Then, when I got out, I found the trailer loaded up with everything for the market and a working fart-cart hitched to it, and Dilly chasing one of the farm cats across the yard with a stick, which wasn't like Dilly because she usually loved animals.

'Ready to go?' Umi shouted, as he and Harlan finish tying a tarpaulin over the load on the trailer.

I'd remembered the concert, but I'd forgotten that we were doing the Saturday Farmers' Market first.

'Got your sax?' he asked.

For a moment I couldn't think where it was; then I remembered it was in the turbine house. 'I'll get it. Can you wait five minutes?'

'Quick as you can. We ought to get going.' And Umi was off, shouting for Aunt Megan.

When I got back, Umi and Aunt Megan were already in the fart-cart and the engine was running, but Dilly was standing in front of it brandishing her stick.

'OK, Dilly, get in now,' called Umi.

'No! You can't bring that stick!' shouted Aunt Megan as Dilly tried to get in, still clutching it.

'It's all right. Cats have gone. You don't need the stick,' Umi soothed.

Harlan was standing by to open and close the gate, so I climbed in the back beside Dilly.

'Are there cats at the market?' Dilly wanted to know, as we bumped down the lane.

'What's all this about cats, anyway?' I asked Dilly after I've done the gate at the bottom of the lane, and we were on the road.

'Silly cats get in the engine and break it,' she said.

'Really?'

Dilly nodded solemnly. 'Ruby said so.'

'Could somebody explain?' I asked.

'Silicates,' said Aunt Megan. 'Ruby reckons when we run the engine on methane, we get a build-up of silicates. That's what's been choking it up.'

'Silly-cats. You see?' said Umi.

'Silly cats,' repeated Dilly, looking at me very seriously, as if I'm the one who is really too young to understand.

'I see,' I said. 'Good thing you had the stick.'

The Farmers' Market is in New Molton. The standard English Villages sign welcomed us to a town which looks pretty much the same as New Bridgewater and, probably, a hundred other towns built by English Villages, except that on the outskirts, there's the biggest FIST base you could imagine with a giant car park full of patrol cars, rows and rows of security vehicles, and at least, twenty of those grey buses with the black tinted windows so you can't see who's inside them.

'Why's FIST got such a big place here?' I wanted to know.

'Holdstone Refugee Centre,' Aunt Megan explained. Most of the guards live in New Molton, plus they service all FIST's vehicles here.

In the centre of the town, there's a 'Market Square', all paved in very new looking bricks, with a covered area that's called The Pannier Market. I asked Aunt Megan what a pannier was, and she said it was a big basket you put on a horse or donkey to take your things to market.

There weren't any horses or donkeys in New Molton Pannier Market, but there were a number of pretty shaky-looking vans and four-by-fours parked by the market and people setting up stalls selling cakes, bread, house plants, eggs, tools that were sure to break when you tried to use them, furry slippers, manky-looking clothes, second-hand furniture, and a good deal of other junk. Turned out we had one of the biggest stalls because we were selling vegetables, herbs, and eggs, plus Aunt Megan's cheeses. Aunt Megan was all excited because she was trying out a goats' cheese for the first time and kept fussing about the best place to put it on the stand so that everyone would see it, which almost led to an argument with Umi, who was trying to get everything else set up, until Dilly made them both laugh by saying it didn't matter where it went because goat's cheese was so pooy everyone could smell it.

The stall owners all knew each other, and the ones that got set up first offered to fetch teas and coffees from the van for the late arrivals. It was all really friendly. And then it got busy. There was a constant queue at our stall, and I was rubbish at adding up the money and doing the right change.

'Don't you have a calculator?'

'Don't need one,' Umi says. 'You'll get the hang of it.'

I couldn't believe the way Umi and Aunt Megan could do all the figures in their heads *and* talk to people at the same time! I got out my G-Port and turned on the calculator app.

'I wouldn't use that,' says Umi, a bit snappy.

'Why not? It's got a calculator.'

'Yeah, I know. But FIST patrols get twitchy about GRIDs. We're still in the exclusion zone here, even though you can get a signal. Those terrorists used GRIDs to set off the London truck bombs, remember. With their big base here in town, FIST are paranoid about bombs.'

I put the phone away and went back to adding up figures on a paper bag. I did get quicker, but couldn't do it in my head like Umi and Aunt Megan.

The market got quiet after three, and Aunt Megan suggested I take Dilly off to the play-park for a go on the swings, which I didn't mind doing, especially after the man from the dodgy tool stand came over to chat. At first, it was just 'Ratchet screwdriver this' and 'Socket wrench that', blah, blah, blah... But then he got on to foreigners and how there weren't any English people left in Bristol, and he kept saying 'No offence, mate,' to Umi (who is obviously African), and Umi kept really cool, but I could see that Aunt Megan was dying to throttle the guy, so I told Dilly I'd give her piggy-back to the playground.

New Molton is all pedestrianised in the middle and super-clean. There were smiley people in bright T-shirts with hearts on them collecting for a charity, but otherwise, there wasn't a lot going on, and Dilly knew exactly where the play-park was, which left me free to start worrying about the concert that evening and whether I'd be good enough.

The sign at the entrance to the park said as follows:

Property of English Villages
Children must be supervised by an adult
No anti-social behaviour
No ball games
No cycling
No skateboards
No loitering
No alcohol
No food
No music
No dogs
Anyone defacing equipment will be prosecuted
Regular FIST patrols

Which sounded pretty welcoming.

A knot of older kids had taken over the shelter in the corner of play-park. They had their backs to me and looked like they were doing one or more of the things that the sign on the gate said they shouldn't, so I sat on one of the swings while Dilly made friends with a little girl about her own age, who was playing in some dirt under the slide. I could hear Dilly chattering away – 'Pretend I'm a princess and you're this mummy who gives me this apple', and stuff like that. But the other little girl wasn't saying anything at all. Still, they seemed happy enough, and it was probably nice for Dilly to have someone her own age for a change. I wondered where Dilly's little friend's mum was. Maybe one of the big kids was her brother or sister. I glanced over at them. Several of them had dark skin and dark hair like the little girl.

There must be a rough part of New Molton, I thought. They don't look like they'd live in one of those new houses off the high street with the neat little railings and shiny front doors. Come to think of it, the little girl looked like she could do with a hot bath and a change of clothes, and when she stood up, I could see she was terribly skinny.

Anyway, Dilly and her friend are taking turns at going up the ladder and sliding down the slide when there's a shrill whistle from somewhere, and it's just as if someone has pushed the fast-forward button. The kids in the shelter are suddenly on their feet and sprinting across the playground. They reach up and snatch the little girl off the ladder, and Dilly starts screaming, and in two seconds, the group is out through the gate with two of the bigger kids carrying the little girl between them! *What?!* I'm thinking! *What is going on?* Had I just watched a child being abducted, or what? 'Hey!' I shout. I put my hand in my jacket pocket, pull out my G-port to dial 911, remember it mightn't work, start to dial it anyway but stop, because a FIST patrol vehicle with lights flashing has just screeched to a halt by the gate, and armed officers are running in all directions.

I scooped Dilly up and did my best to comfort her as one of the officers clocked us and headed in our direction. I just had time to notice the torn bread packets and the bits of sliced bread scattered in the shelter before he reached us. The kids had been eating! That's what they'd been doing. They'd been eating sliced white bread!

'Speak English?' this guy barks, and he looks huge in his stab-vest and uniform, and I'm so surprised by the question that my mouth sort of hangs open with nothing coming out.

'English?' he repeats even louder.

'Yeah… English… of course. Yeah, I can speak… Yeah, of course.'

'OK.' His automatic weapon is slung over his shoulder, but one hand rests on it all the time, and the barrel is pointed straight at my chest. 'OK, son. Put the portal down. Nice and gentle – Put... the port... down.'

I had Dilly balanced on my left hip with my arm around her. But my G-Port was still in my right hand.

'On the ground, son. Portal on the ground,' he spoke slowly, never taking his eyes off me. Umi was right! These guys are paranoid about the GRID. I did what I was told. It was hard to keep my balance while squatting and holding Dilly, but when I tried to let her slip down on to the ground, she clung on like a little octopus and sobbed, 'Mummy, I want Mummy.'

'I saw where they went, if that's a help,' I say.

'Oh yes? Well, let's just find out who you are first, shall we? Any ID?'

'Yeah, sure. I've got my card.' I slide my free hand into my jacket for my ID card.

'Slowly! S-l-o-w-l-y!'

I held the card out for him to take. He reached for it, keeping as big a distance between us as possible; then his eyes flicked forward and back between the photograph and my face. He unhooked a card-reader from his belt, slotted my card into it, and held it out so that I could press my fingers on the print-recognition screen. The card-reader gave a little bleep, and he checked the screen. 'Right-oh – so it's Mark, is it?' his voice less challenging, but still suspicious. 'And who's this we have here? Can't be your sister, can she?'

Suddenly I saw it from his point of view, a white kid holding a little black kid. And me with my face all scratched up. If it wasn't for the fact that our clothes were fairly clean, we could easily have fitted into the group that had just run from the park.

'Cousin,' I said. 'Well... sort of.'

'Meaning?'

'Her mum and dad have a stall at the market. Friends of my parents. I'm just looking after her. Her name's Dilly.'

The officer seemed to lose interest in us. He handed back my ID card. 'Right-oh son, on your way. You can pick up your GRID, but don't let us catch you trying to use it in the exclusion zone again.'

Dilly had stopped crying, and she allowed me to put her down, although she kept a firm grip on one leg of my jeans.

'What's going on? I mean, what did they do?' I ask as I retrieve my G-Port.

'Ferals. They've been thieving things from the bins behind the supermarket again. Don't worry, we'll soon round them up. But I wouldn't hang around here just at the moment.'

Dilly was pretty keen to get back to her mum, so we headed off.

By the time we were back at the Pannier Market, Umi and Aunt Megan had the stand packed away and loaded back on to the trailer. They seemed pleased with the way the market had gone and, apparently, goat's cheese was a winner.

While Aunt Megan was driving us to the concert, I told them all about the bit of excitement with the Ferals and how Dilly and I almost got arrested.

CHAPTER 12

About a mile out of New Molton, we came to a FIST checkpoint. A patrol vehicle was parked so that it blocked half the road, and two more were parked off to the side. The shiny new Pneumat in front of us was waved through, but apparently, we looked suspicious because they made us stop, and we all had to show out ID cards while one of the officers poked about in the trailer.

'Don't stop for strangers and don't pick up any hitchhikers,' we were told as our IDs were handed back. 'Been some illegals in town. Best to be careful.' Then the guy pulls a face and says, 'What are you running that thing on?'

'Cow poo,' says Aunt Megan, without even cracking a smile.

'Yeah! Smells like it!' He fans his nose and then says, 'Go on. Get out of here. You're stinking the place out!' And we're on our way again, with Dilly in uncontrollable giggles.

After winding through the forest for an hour or so, we passed a sign that said 'Buckland', and we came into a little village – maybe twelve houses along the road and a church, and there are chickens running around in the street. The houses are genuinely old, but there are clearly still people living in them. Which is strange, because I didn't think there were any villages like that left in the forest.

We pulled up outside a long low building that I guessed was the village hall.

'Is this where the gig is?' I asked.

'Were you expecting the Albert Hall?' asked Umi, and we all piled out.

I don't know what I was expecting, but I wasn't expecting this! There are families arriving on horse-drawn carts, there are ancient cars, trucks, and tractors that look and smell like they've been converted to run on everything from chip fat to woodchip, there's a double-decker bus painted to look like a stately mansion with curtains in the windows, there are people on foot and people on bicycles, and there are dogs and kids running around in all directions and a hand-painted banner over the doorway that says 'Ruby's Truckers Benefit Concert'. Some of the kids have their faces painted, and a lot of the adults look like they're in fancy dress, but I'm thinking, *Whoa! Maybe that's just how they dress around here!* when a girl, whose clothes are almost normal, comes up and says, 'Hi. I'm Bethan. You must be Mark. Come and meet the band.' Umi and Aunt Megan are talking to a bunch of people they know, so I follow the girl into the hall.

By this point, I'd already noticed that Ruby's truck was not parked outside, and when we got in, there were people setting up a bar at one end of the hall and another group on a little stage that had to be the band, but no sign of Ruby.

The band gives me a big cheer, and there are shouts of 'Hey!' – 'Hi, Mark!' and 'Come on up!' and then I'm shaking hands with everyone – Mick, the drummer (but everyone calls him Monkey on account of his long arms), the twins – Cara on trombone and Tony on clarinet, and Trigger on guitar, bass, banjo, and anything else with strings. I found out later that Trigger is really called Martin, but they call him Trigger because he's always happy. Trigger-happy? You see? No, I didn't get it straight away. Bethan plays keyboard, but she's also the band's sound engineer, so she was running around, setting up mikes and doing sound checks.

Eventually, I get a chance to ask where Ruby is. Seems she's running late and we're to start the gig without her, which does nothing for my confidence. But after we've run through a few practice numbers, I feel a bit better, and Tony the clarinet player says, 'If in doubt, just follow me,' and Cara says, 'Well, that'll be the blind leading the blind, then!' and everyone laughs, and I start to relax.

Soon after that, the doors opened, and in a matter of minutes, the hall was heaving with people.

Half way through the second number, which happens to be 'Oh When the Saints', there's an outburst of whistling and cheering around the door, and Ruby comes in, dressed in bib-and-brace overalls that are edged in sparkling sequins, playing her trumpet. She marches through the crowd, like she's leading a carnival, and up on to the stage. At which point, the rest of the band takes a step back, and I find myself at the front of the stage, jamming with Ruby; then the rest of the band comes back in, and the hall simply erupts in cheering and stamping. Seems like Ruby's a big favourite around here.

I scanned the hall between numbers to see if I could spot Ashanti. Umi was dancing with Dilly on his shoulders, Aunt Megan was with a group of women by the bar, but it wasn't until almost the break that I saw Ashanti come in and stand at the back near the door. I gave her wave, and she waved back, but the next time I looked she had gone again. I guess I was hoping she'd stay to watch. Hoping to show her that I wasn't just some little kid she used to muck about with, that there was actually something I was quite good at!

By the end of the first set, it was pretty hot and sweaty in the hall, and while most of the band headed for the bar, I went outside for a bit of fresh air and to cool off. I wasn't exactly looking for Ashanti, but it crossed my mind I might bump into her. But I didn't. Instead, this guy comes up to me, and he's got this big friendly smile even if he does have some scary-looking tattoos all over one arm and up his neck, and he says, 'Hey, Mark, love the saxophone! You're good!'

Naturally, I was pretty pleased. Of course, I know now what he was up to, but I didn't then. And this is the point – How could I?

Anyway, we get chatting. And then he says, 'I heard a story about your saxophone being stolen by Ferals.'

I was a bit surprised the story had got around, but then, small towns and all that. So, I told him what happened with the bridge and the concrete block and everything. And naturally he wanted to know how I got it back. 'Ruby', I told him, 'she found it.'

Then he got really interested! Wanted to know if Ruby had said anything about the Ferals. Had she seen them? Did she think there were any still in the district? So I told him about the house in the forest near the farm and about my narrow escape.

'Yeah,' he nodded, 'I wondered what happened to your face.'

At this point, Tony the clarinet player came out of the hall to tell me that it was time for the next set. I see Tony and the guy I'm talking to look at each other, and I get the distinct impression that they're not best friends.

The guy with the tattoos says, 'Good meeting you, Mark. Sorry I can't stay for the second half, but I've got things to do.' And disappears off through the shambles of parked tractors, vans, and carts. Tony grabs me by the arm. Tony is big. I don't mean he's tall, he's sort of square and so's his twin sister, Cara, and as he marches me back on to the stage, he growls, 'You don't want to go talking to that bloke,' leaving me thinking, *What the hell was that all about?*

I was pleased to see that Ashanti was back in the hall for the second half of the concert. She even danced with Dilly, and she looked like she was enjoying herself, but she had that same look that she had the day of the hunt. That look of triumph. Like, in her mind, she was still somewhere else, somewhere where something much more important had happened.

Ruby's Truckers played several of their own numbers in the second half. I didn't know the tunes, so I took the chance to have another break outside. It was dark out and starting to spit with rain. There was a big bunch of the face-painted kids over by the double-decker bus, where someone had set up a barbecue. Seemed like they were having a private party. Some kid's birthday, I guessed, so I didn't go over. Anyway, I didn't fancy getting wet, and I soon went back in.

The evening finished with a big conga dance that wound around the hall, out the side door, and back in through the main entrance. Ruby took up a collection for victims of climate change, which, it turns out, was whom the benefit was in aid of; then Cara and Tony told me how well I'd played, which was nice, and Monkey said, 'Hey, man, yeah... yeah, really good, man – yeah?' And Trigger gave me a high five. Bethan asked if I'd like to play with them again and, of course, I said yes. And then we were back in the four-by-four, heading home through the rain. Ashanti came back with us, but she and Dilly fell asleep when we'd only gone about half a mile, and I dozed off not long after.

CHAPTER 13

I woke up to hear the rain drumming down on the metal roof of the four-by-four. Ashanti and Dilly were still asleep next to me in the back seat, but Umi and Aunt Megan were no longer in the vehicle. All around, there were the blue and red flashing lights of emergency vehicles, the lights splintering and refracting through the rain water that poured down the windows. My first thought was that there had been an accident. I used my sleeve to wipe the fog from the side window and found we were in the farmyard, the familiar walls and buildings pulsing with the flashing lights.

'What's happened?' Ashanti asked, opening her eyes and stretching.

'I don't know,' I said. 'We're back at the farm, but… I don't know.'

'At our farm?' Ashanti was wide-awake, and the next second had the door open.

'Hey!' I called after her. 'It's pouring out there!' But she was gone.

Rather reluctantly, I decided I should find out what was going on. I didn't have a waterproof, so I zipped my jacket up to the collar and stepped out into the downpour. Dilly was still sound asleep, so I left her where she was.

There were no less than three FIST patrol cars plus a couple of vans. Everyone was by the gate to the track that led down to the bridge. *Perhaps the valley's flooded*, I thought. I wondered if the river ever rose as high as Harlan's cottage. Then I saw Ashanti push her way into the knot of people by the gate and heard her shout, 'You can't do this! You can't do this! Dad! Tell them they can't come through here! Tell them they have to get off our farm!'

As I got closer to the gate, I could see that there were powerful lights coming up the hill. Two large four-by-fours, rocking and bouncing over the uneven track, were climbing up out of the valley. Umi and Aunt Megan appeared to be restraining Ashanti, who kept repeating, 'No! No! They can't!'

I was still thinking there had been some sort of natural disaster when a voice at my side said, 'Hi, Mark. Thanks for the tip-off.' It was the man with the tattoos, the man who had talked to me at the concert. 'Might even be a reward in it for us if they catch any of the ringleaders,' he continued with a wink. I saw Ashanti look round quickly. Then she tore herself free from Umi and stepped towards us. 'What did he just say to you?' she demanded.

The man had answered before I had a chance to get a word out. 'Between me and Mark, sweetheart, I was just thanking him for the information,' he said, smoothly.

'Information?' Ashanti's eyes bored into me, 'What does he mean?'

'I don't know,' I said. 'I don't even know what's going on.'

'Your music-loving friends – the ones who took your sax? I reckon we've got 'em,' the man said.

Then Ashanti was at me, 'You idiot! You creep! What have you done? What have you been saying? Who have you been talking to? Did you speak to him?' She jabbed her finger in the man's direction. 'Did you?... *Well, did you?*'

'Ashanti! For God's sake!' Umi moved in again to restrain her as the first of the four-by-fours came through the gate, its headlights throwing the waiting FIST officers into sharp silhouette and sending their giant shadows marching across the walls of the farm buildings as they hurried to meet the approaching vehicles.

The second four-by-four followed the first, and they pulled up by the waiting vans as the FIST officers, guns at the ready, made a cordon around the four vehicles. The back doors of the four-by-fours opened, and eight very frightened-looking children were hauled out, their wet clothes clinging to their thin bodies, their hands fastened tightly together with plastic cable ties, their terrified faces drained of colour in the glare of the headlights.

'Look what you've done! Look! Look at them! I hope you're proud of yourself! They're kids! They're just kids like us!' Ashanti screamed at me.

None of them looked over twelve years old. There was no sign of Casablanca.

Now I saw. Now I understood. Now I knew why Ashanti slipped off at night. The light signalling to her. In some way, Ashanti was involved with the Ferals.

The children were bundled into one of the waiting vans; the armed guards climbed into the other, doors slammed, engines revved, and the convoy began to move off, leaving only one patrol vehicle in the farmyard. The remaining officer strode over to us. 'Nice work, Jake,' he said to the man with the tattoos. 'Is this the young man we have to thank?'

'Yeah, this is Mark,' the man, who I now knew was Jake, replied.

'Well done, Mark. I'm Commander Fraser. If you have any more information, come straight to me. We need more citizens like you.' He turned to Umi. 'I have reason to believe that you and your family have been assisting illegals. Might I remind you that helping illegals is a criminal offence and could result in the termination of your tenancy and your eviction from this farm?'

'We're not your tenants,' said Umi.

'Really?' said the officer. 'That's not what I understand.' He turned to Tattoos. 'Give you a lift, Jake?'

'I think a drink might be in order, don't you, Collin?'

'Yeah,' the commander replied. 'Let's get out of this rain. Bloody climate! Pity we didn't get any of the big fish.'

The car drove off, its blue and red flashing lights receding down the lane, leaving us in the darkness; the only sounds now, the sounds of the rain beating down on the cobbles and the gurgling water draining from the downpipes.

I stood apart from the others, waiting for Ashanti to turn on me again. She had become very quiet. Then I saw her shoulders shaking and realised she was crying. Aunt Megan put an arm around Ashanti and steered her towards the house, but I stayed where I was. How could I go in with them? For Ashanti, I was a traitor, an informer. Without knowing it, I had betrayed her. But why couldn't she have said something? Why didn't she tell me what she was doing? If she had trusted me, this would never have happened. The rain was running in rivulets down through my hair, it had soaked through my jacket and was filling up my shoes. Aunt Megan returned and carried a sleeping Dilly from the car into the house.

'Mark...' I hadn't noticed that Umi was still standing a few feet away from me. 'This wasn't your fault.'

I looked up at him. What was he talking about? Of course it was my fault!

'Ashanti should have spoken to you.'

'But you knew! You could have told me!' I blurted out. 'Aunt Megan could have told me!'

'We didn't think you would be here very long...' Umi sounded uncomfortable. 'What Ashanti is doing is dangerous. It's against the law. Megan and I didn't want you involved. If you didn't know... well, no one could accuse you of anything. God knows, we'd rather Ashanti wasn't involved. But... How do you stop your child doing what you know is right?'

'But... They're illegals... aren't they? These kids, they're not meant to be here! They go round stealing things – robbing people!'

'It's complicated.'

Yeah, I thought, *that's what adults always say when they can't answer your question.*

'Look,' said Umi, 'there's not much difference between them and me. I wasn't born in this country.'

'Yeah, but you're married to Aunt Megan. Anyway, you came here before they closed the borders.'

'OK, the difference is I was lucky. But if I hadn't married Megan, I couldn't have stayed. Or, if I had stayed, I'd be an illegal... just like them.'

'So... ? So what are you saying? Everyone should be allowed into the country?'

'Come on. Come inside.' Umi turned and began to walk towards the house, but I still hesitated. I could picture Ashanti sitting in the kitchen, the look she would give me as I came in. I felt the anger rising inside me. She was to blame for this as much as I was.

Umi waited by the door. 'Come on, Mark.'

I couldn't very well stand in the rain all night, so I followed him in and hoped that Ashanti had gone up to her room already. It seemed like she had, because she wasn't in the kitchen. Perhaps she was as keen to avoid me as I was to avoid her. Aunt Megan offered me a hot drink, but I said I just wanted to get out of my wet things, and I headed for my room.

I didn't go downstairs again that night, but instead, lay awake listening to rain beating on the slate roof. Soon the wind got up, driving the rain against the windows so hard it sounded like the glass was being pelted with handfuls of gravel.

So Ashanti was mixed up with the Ferals. But how? What was she doing? Then it struck me that Ruby must have something to do with this. That would explain why Ashanti went off with her. It would also explain how Ruby had got my saxophone back. She hadn't found it under the bridge, like she'd said, they had given it to her! Did that mean... when the Ferals ambushed me and Jerzy... Did that mean Ruby knew it was gong to happen? Was she part of the plot? And the concert... Those kids with painted faces that were having the barbeque by the double-decker bus... Were they Ferals?

I ought to call my dad in the morning. Get Jerzy to pick me up and take me back to London before Ashanti, Ruby, and their friends got us all arrested!

CHAPTER 14

I didn't call my dad in the morning. I didn't really get a chance. Things started happening rather too fast.

I'd waited until the time when Ashanti was usually out, doing the morning milking, then I'd gone down to the kitchen. I'd just started on the porridge Aunt Megan had given me when Harlan stomps in to say the storm's washed half the top soil from the field he's been ploughing into the mill race and that Umi's up to his knees in mud trying to clear it, and hadn't somebody better give him a hand – And Harlan's looking at me in a meaningful sort of way.

'I'll go,' says Aunt Megan. 'No, It's all right, I'll go,' I say, and I burn my mouth trying to gulp down a few more spoonfuls of porridge.

'Good,' says Harlan, ''cause I've got to fetch them blimmin' goats in for milkin', and he marshes out again.

I follow Harlan to the door. It's still raining, but not so heavily as during the night, and I'm in the doorway pulling my coat on when I see a FIST patrol car and a FIST van pull into the farmyard.

Commander Fraser climbs out of the patrol car, and six officers pile out of the van. 'Spread out! Search every building!' he shouts.

'Hey!' screams Aunt Megan, pushing past me, 'What do you think gives you the right to march in here and start throwing your weight around?' The officers all stop and look at her and then at Fraser.

'This warrant,' says Fraser waving a piece of paper. 'Move it!' he shouts at his officers, and they start running in all directions.

For a moment Aunt Megan hesitates. She looks desperately at Harlan who is at the other side of the yard.

'Not so fast!' Harlan steps in front of a young officer who's heading for the milking parlour. 'There's milkin' goin' on. You'll upset the cows.'

Commander Fraser turns to see what the problem is, but Aunt Megan strides up to him, Dilly balanced on her hip. 'Let me see that warrant!' she demands.

'Out of my way!' says the officer, trying to push Harlan aside, but Harlan grabs him by the jacket. 'Look 'ere, boy,' he says, 'this 'ere's a workin' farm. You got to respect that.'

'We've got a warrant,' the officer says.

'I don't care what you got, Tom Batton, you was raised on a farm, you ought to know better.'

'And you ought to know farming's dead round here, Harlan!'

Harlan catches my eye and motions with a jerk of his head towards the milking parlour.

The last thing I want to do after last night is to disturb Ashanti while she's milking, in fact, she's about the last person I want to see right now. But it's obvious that Aunt Megan and Harlan are worried about FIST seeing something in the milking parlour, and I don't reckon it's the cows. So I quickly skirt around the building and in through the back where they bring the cows in. Tess is there as usual, waiting to lead the cows out. She wags her tail but doesn't bother to get up. The cows are in their stalls, but it looks like Ashanti has finished milking because she's not sitting by any of them. *Perhaps*, I think, *she's already gone out.* But she would have let the cows out. Then I hear something move up in the hayloft. Quickly, I climb up the old wooden ladder. As my head comes level with the loft floor, I whisper, 'Ashanti!' There's not much light. A bit of pale daylight that filters through two small, dirty skylights. Then I see them. Ashanti is kneeing by a girl who is lying in the hay. So that's it! That's what going on! A Feral. Must have got away last night. Are there others? And Harlan knew she was here! Maybe brought her here – He never showed up last night.

'Get out!' Ashanti hisses.

'No. Ashanti, listen...'

'Thought you'd spy on us, did you?'

'Ashanti! FIST! They're back! They're searching the buildings.'

Ashanti stiffens and the girl sits up, her eyes wide with fear. Her dark hair straggles out over a bandage wrapped around her forehead. I catch my breath – I can't be certain, but I am pretty sure this is the same girl I saw sitting with Casablanca in the old house.

'We have to get her out, now!' I say.

'How? Where are they? They'll see her!'

'They'll find her if she stays here.'

'Please! No!' Suddenly the girl grabs hold of Ashanti. 'They take me! They take me! Don't let them find! Please!' Her eyes seem to grow even bigger.

'The cows! Take her out with the cows!' I say. Then I have a better idea. 'No. I'll take her out with the cows. You get out the front and start an argument.'

'Why you?' Ashanti demands.

'Because Fraser thinks I'm the good guy, and you're good at starting fights. But hurry!'

For once, Ashanti doesn't argue, she puts an arm around the girl and helps her to her feet. 'Hatiya, listen. You must go with Mark. Go with this boy.'

'No. I stay with you,' the girl pleads.

'You'll be safer with Mark. Come on, Hatiya. We have to hurry.'

Together, we get the girl down the ladder. She seems unsteady on her feet, but perhaps it's just that she's terrified; I feel her shaking as I hold her. She's so thin, so light that, although she is almost as tall as I am, I actually lift her down the last few steps. All I feel through her clothes are bones.

'They beat her,' Ashanti says through clenched teeth. 'But she fell in a ditch and managed to crawl away.'

Tess gets up and comes over to us. The old dog senses something is wrong and licks the girl's hand. Ashanti brings the cows out of their stalls, and they stand by the gate, heads down, watching Tess, waiting for her to lead them out.

Ashanti takes both the girl's hands. 'Hatiya, listen, you must hide amongst the cows. Do you understand? Stay in the middle so you can't be seen. OK?'

The girl nods but doesn't move. Fear seems to have rooted her to the spot; perhaps she's also afraid of the cows. We lead her over to them, and the cows move aside to allow us into the centre.

'Keep going through the first field. After you get through the next gate, Hatiya can slip behind the hedge. That hedge runs right down to the bottom of the valley. Have FIST brought dogs?'

'I didn't see any.'

'Thank God for that.'

The girl bends over so that she is hidden by the cows' bodies. With her skirt hitched up, her thin, brown legs are almost invisible amongst all the legs of the cows. *Maybe,* I say to myself, *this will actually work*, and I mentally cross my fingers.

Ashanti opens the back gate. 'Slowly, Tess. Slowly,' she tells the dog. 'Keep just behind them, and they'll stay together,' she says to me, and then she picks up the milking pail and strides back towards the gate to the farmyard.

'Oh! It's you, Tom Batton!' I hear her sneer at the FIST officer, and then, 'All right, all right, you can come in. I've finished now. And make yourself useful! Muck the stalls out while you're in there!'

Tess does what she's been told and takes her time crossing the first field. The rain has eased to a gentle drizzle. I stay close behind the cows, keeping them in a bunch and not letting them straggle out into a line as they usually do, all the time expecting to hear a shout, a command to stop. My back is stiff with anticipation, but I don't dare look round.

'Hey! Mark!'

My joints go ridged. It's Commander Fraser's voice. I look over my shoulder but keep going. He is coming across the field. I turn. 'I'll come back to you!' I shout. 'Stay there! This field is really muddy!' He slows and then stops and looks at the ground in front of him. It's true about the mud. 'Just got to get 'em through this gate,' I call.

At last, we reach the other side of the field. I move around the cows and open the gate. 'Go! Go!' I tell the girl. She ducks around the cows and off behind the hedge.

'Come on, Tess!' I call loudly to the dog. I close the gate and walk back across the field, trying to look casual. Commander Fraser is holding out a colourful length of fabric for me to see.

'Know anything about this?' he asks.

The fabric looks foreign. Maybe a headscarf. I know immediately it belongs to the girl.

'Oh, that's Aunt Megan's,' I lie. 'I'll give it back to her. She'll be wondering where that's got to. I'll bet Ashanti borrowed it.' And I hold out my hand, but he doesn't give it to me.

'You certain?' Fraser is clearly not convinced. 'Batton found it when he searched that barn.'

'Sure. Well, at least, it looks like one of hers. Yeah, I think she brought it back from some holiday. Bit of a favourite, as a matter of fact. She'll be pleased you found it,' I rattle on, rather pleased with my story.

'There's blood on it.'

Shit! I think.

'So, how does your aunt's scarf come to have blood on it?' His eyes have gone cold and accusing.

'I've no idea. Why don't we ask her?' I suggest and I hold out my hand again for the scarf. All the time I'm conscious of the girl hidden behind the hedge. I just pray she's had the sense to get down to the bottom of the valley.

'I don't think so,' says Fraser. 'I'll tell you what we are going to do. We're going to keep it. We're going to keep it because it may be evidence. Evidence that someone has been hiding illegal immigrants on this farm. Blood. DNA. Easy enough to find out whose it is. And, sonny Jim, if I find out you're mixed up in this, don't think your famous father will keep you out of trouble.'

'My dad?'

'Oh yes. We've been doing a bit of checking. We know all about you.'

Then Fraser turns and goes back up the field taking the scarf with him.

Shit! I think again. *I really should have called my dad this morning and got him to get me out of here!* Then I remember the girl. The terror in her eyes – eyes that seemed too big in her thin face; her body shaking with fear. Whose side was I on? But what about Casablanca and the gun?

Nothing else was found, but Commander Fraser's parting words to us were, 'We'll be back. You can count on it.'

We were all in the yard as they drove out. Harlan closed the gate and walked slowly back to join us. 'Where's that young maid to?' he asked.

'She's probably down the valley,' I said.

'She'd best stay in the cottage. Closer to the woods in case they comes back.'

'We can't ask you to break the law,' said Umi.

'You didn't ask, I offered, and some laws should be broke,' replied Harlan. 'Come on, girl. We better go and find her.' He and Ashanti set off down the hill.

'Well... ,' said Aunt Megan, and she looked at Umi, who met her eyes and shook his head gently. Dilly reached up and took her mother's hand. 'Was the man angry with us?' she asked.

'Not with you, sweetheart. No one's angry with you.' And she lifted Dilly up and carried her into the house.

'Millrace is still full of mud. Fancy giving me a hand?' asked Umi.

'Sure,' I said.

And we spent the rest of the day shovelling mud in the rain.

CHAPTER 15

That evening Ashanti didn't show up for tea, so she must have stayed at Harlan's to look after the girl. It was a very quiet meal. Even Dilly wasn't her normal chirpy self. It was like everybody was waiting for somebody else to say something, like the air was full of questions that none of us wanted to ask because none of us really wanted to face up to the answers.

When we'd finished eating, Umi took Dilly up to bed. I stood up to help clear the table, but Aunt Megan said, 'Sit down a minute, Mark. We need to talk.' I pulled a chair out and sat across the table from her.

'I think I should call your dad. Ask him if you could go back to London, or if there is somewhere else you could stay.'

I should have guessed that was coming, and just a few hours ago, I'd been thinking pretty much the same thing – that I shouldn't get mixed up in whatever this family was up to. But this morning had changed everything. Seeing the girl. Feeling the way her body shook with fear.

'Mark?'

I realised Aunt Megan was waiting for me to say something.

'I can't go. Not now,' I said.

'Yes, you can. And I think you should.'

'But...'

'I know. You feel responsible. But how could you know... any of this? We should have warned you. What you said to Jake you said in all innocence. How could you know that he was an informer? That he would go straight to FIST? No, Mark, it's not you who's responsible, it's us, Umi and I. We've allowed Ashanti to get involved... Of course, we didn't know, to begin with. You know how she is, always off on her own. Then we found she was taking them food. Stuff kept disappearing from the kitchen. God knows! They're only children, and they're half starved! You can't blame her for wanting to help them. Then she got Ruby to help her collect things – things to give them, old clothes, bedding… But she's never brought any of them here before.'

'Aunt Megan?' I cut in.

'Yes?'

'How many of them are there?'

'I've no idea. They escape from the refugee centre and when the patrols catch them, they take them back.'

'I want to stay here,' I said firmly.

'No, Mark. We crossed a line today. In the eyes of the law, we are now criminals.'

'I don't care,' I said. 'I'm staying.'

Aunt Megan looked far from happy. She took a deep breath and then sighed. 'We'll talk about it again tomorrow,' she said.

I cleared the table as Aunt Megan filled the sink.

'If Ashanti is going to stop down at Harlan's, might she need some things?' I asked.

'I've put some clothes in a bag for her. It's by the door.'

'I'll take it down,' I said.

As if there weren't enough vegetables growing on the farm, Harlan had his own patch in front of his cottage. The light from my torch caught on the neat rows of onions and the feathery leaves of carrots. The curtains were drawn in the small windows, shutting the light and warmth in and me out. I'd never been inside Harlan's cottage, and I wasn't sure what sort of reception I'd get. I knocked, rather too lightly, on the heavy door and waited, wondering if anyone had heard and whether I should knock again, but the door swung open, and Harlan's bulk filled the small lobby.

'I've brought some things for Ashanti,' I said, holding out the bag, half expecting Harlan to take it and close the door on me. But instead, he said, 'Her's in the front room,' and went off down the little passage to the back.

I kicked my boots off and hung up my coat in the lobby and half opened the door to the small front room. Ashanti was curled into an old armchair, her legs tucked up under her. 'I brought you some things,' I said, like it was a password.

'Thanks.'

'Where do you want them?'

'You can come in,' she said.

The room was small, the low ceiling sagging slightly in the middle. Apart from Ashanti's armchair, there was an old two-seater settee covered with a tartan blanket and a table by the window, with four straight-backed, wooden chairs. The fire was lit, and air in the room was very warm. There were pictures on the walls of flowers and landscapes that might have come from calendars and made me wonder if there was once a Mrs Harlan.

Seeing me looking around the room, Ashanti said, 'She's asleep... upstairs.'

'Oh,' I said. 'Yeah, I wondered.'

'You can sit down, if you want.'

I perched on the edge of the settee and put Ashanti's bag by my feet.

'Thanks,' Ashanti said again.

'Aunt Megan packed it for you.'

'No,' she said. 'Thanks for what you did today.'

'What happens now?' I asked. 'You can't keep her here, can you? I mean, FIST'll come back.'

'Probably the less you know the better,' said Ashanti.

'That hasn't worked very well so far,' I said bitterly.

'OK. If she's well enough tomorrow, I'll take her back to the others.'

'What? To that house in the forest?'

'No, not there. They should never have been there. That house was only used as a drop-off. They shouldn't have been staying there. To the main group.'

'And you're not going to tell me where that is, are you?'

Ashanti didn't reply.

'Well, you could at least tell me what this is all about! Who are they? What's going on? You could try to trust me a little!'

'Most of them are from Holdstone Refugee Centre.'

'So they're illegal immigrants.'

'According to the government.'

'And according to you?'

'Oh Jesus!'

'What?'

'Look – I don't care about any of that! You saw her! Do you have any idea what she's been through? She's been smuggled across Europe from Bangladesh. Her little brother and her two sisters drowned in a cyclone that hit their town. Her home is under water. Her parents sold everything they had left to get her here, and what happens? We lock her up in a stinking prison! And now she's been beaten up by some thug in a uniform! Jesus, Mark! How can you talk about legal and illegal? What happened to moral and immoral? What happened to right and wrong?!'

What could I say? Neither of us said anything for a while. We both stared into the fire.

'Do you know her real name?' I asked, at last, without looking at Ashanti. 'I mean, Hatiya's where she's from, isn't it? Like, her town, or something. Do any of them tell you their real names?'

'Some of them do…. Yes, I know hers.'

I waited, watching the small flames. I knew she didn't trust me enough to tell me.

'It's Shahana,' Ashanti said quietly. 'She says it means patience.'

One of the logs must have been wet because a little jet of steam escaped from it with a soft hiss as it burned.

'There must be thousands… no, millions like her,' Ashanti said. 'They've got nothing and we've got everything and we won't share any of it.'

'Isn't that the problem?'

'Meaning?'

'There are too many.'

'There's a disaster going on, Mark! And we're in a lifeboat! It's our duty to pick up survivors.'

'And what happens when the lifeboat's full?'

'Oh shit, Mark! Just bugger off! You've got all the answer, haven't you?!'

'No!' I said. 'No! That's not fair! I'm just trying to get my head around all of this!'

'No, you're not. You're not! You're just doing what everyone does. You're saying it's too big, it's impossible, so we won't do anything.'

'So? Then? What is the answer?'

'So... so I do what I can.'

'I'd better get back,' I said. She seemed to have made up her mind that I was one of the bad guys. I stood up. But as I reached the door, Ashanti suddenly asked, 'Why were you in the old house?'

'I saw smoke,' I said. 'I was curious. Yeah, OK, I guessed it was Ferals, and I wanted to know what they were up to.'

'And what were they up to?'

'Shahana didn't tell you?'

'Don't use her real name.'

'OK, Hatiya.'

Ashanti shook her head.

'I think there's a split in the group. Looks like the one that calls himself Casablanca is trying to take over. Could be Hatiya's on his side.'

'I see.' Ashanti looked thoughtful. 'OK, thanks.' She turned back to the fire.

I went out into the little entrance lobby. There was no sign of Harlan. Maybe he had gone to bed. I put my boots and coat on and let myself out into the rain.

CHAPTER 16

I was up on the hill with Umi and Harlan, digging a drainage ditch to stop any more of the field from being washed away when we saw the patrol car coming up the lane. Umi flung his shovel aside. 'Get down the cottage quick! Get the girl out and get her hidden! And pray they don't bring dogs.' He and Harlan headed for the farmyard while I ran as fast as the rough ground would let me around the edge of the field and down the track to Harlan's cottage. I arrived out of breath, the blood pounding in my ears. The front of the cottage was visible from the farm, so I ran round the back and opened the back door.

'Ashanti! They're here! We have to get out!' I screamed.

Ashanti and Hatiya were with me in a matter of seconds. Hatiya, dressed in some of Ashanti's clothes, looked a little stronger, but the hunted look was back in her eyes, and she seemed to crumple as she left the shelter of the cottage. With Ashanti on one side of her and me on the other, we half carried, half dragged her down the hill.

From the back of the cottage, it was a short distance to the stream, but to cross it and reach the forest, we would have to use the bridge and that would put us in full view. We looked around desperately for a hiding place.

'Under the bridge!' Ashanti plunged down the bank into the swollen stream, pulling me and the girl with her. Even at the edge, the current was strong and the water was cold. Holding each other up as we slipped and stumbled on the loose stones of the riverbed, we forced our way upstream until we were hidden under the bridge.

It was impossible to know what was happening up the hill; the noise of the rushing stream drowned out all other sounds. They could have been right above us and we wouldn't have known. We crouched there, clinging on to each other, the water up to our thighs and the cold creeping up our bodies until we were all shivering and shaking.

No one came. My legs grew numb. At last, we heard Umi shouting our names. We crept out from our hiding place, but we were too frozen to shout back. When Umi saw us, he hurried down to help us up the bank.

'They've gone,' he said. 'You can take her back inside.'

I left Hatiya with Ashanti at the cottage and went back up to the farmhouse with Umi, or rather, after Umi. He strode up the hill, his head down, as if he was walking into a strong wind, and I had to almost run to keep up with him. He had hardly said anything to us, and now he seemed to be trying to get away from us, like he had something much more important to do than hiding illegal immigrants. It wasn't at all like Umi, usually so patient and calm. What had happened while we were under the bridge? It had to have something to do with the latest visit from FIST.

I went up to my room and changed out of my wet clothes. When I came back down, I found Umi, Aunt Megan, and Harlan in the kitchen standing in total silence, as though under some spell; Aunt Megan by the stove, Umi by the dresser, and Harlan leaning back against the edge of the sink. They were all staring at a sheet of paper in the middle of the table. The only sounds came from Dilly, who was playing in a corner, chatting quietly to herself.

I looked from one to the other. Eventually, Aunt Megan took in a big breath and let it out slowly. She shifted her gaze from the piece of paper to me. 'Read it for yourself, Mark. You might as well. It'll tell you all you need to know.'

Conscious that everybody was watching me, I reached for the sheet of paper and began to read. It was written in the sort language that lawyers use, and I didn't understand all of it, but the meaning was clear enough. '. . . Possession Order... two months to vacate the property known as Higher Heathcombe... warrant for eviction.' I put the piece of paper back on the table.

'What I don't understand', said Harlan, 'is how FIST can throw you out. They don't own this property.'

Umi shook his head. Aunt Megan shrugged. I stared at the piece of paper, trying to gather the courage to say what had to be said.

'They do own it,' I almost whispered.

Aunt Megan gave a little groan, as if something had hurt her.

'Excuse me?... How?' demanded Umi.

'Dad sold the Great West Forest to Tristram Rainer to raise money for the Global Building.'

'But the farm... !' Umi began to protest. Aunt Megan held up a hand to shush him.

'It's awful!' I said. 'I'm really sorry.'

'We're not blaming you, Mark,' said Aunt Megan. 'But, just please explain about the farm.'

'Dad did some deal when he bought the farm that meant it became part of the forest. So when he sold the forest, he sold the farm.'

'How could he do that?!' shouted Umi. 'He knows what it means to us! He was meant to be helping us!'

'Umi... please,' said Aunt Megan.

In the corner, Dilly stopped playing and looked at her father.

'Mum says it was a mistake, and he's been trying to get it back.'

'Well, it's a bit late now!' roared Umi. 'I told you, Megan! I told you we should never have trusted him. Robert's a businessman! He's a wheeler-dealer! All he's interested in, and all he's ever been interested in, is power and money!'

'He was my friend,' said Aunt Megan.

'Well, your *friend* just lost us everything!'

'No,' said Aunt Megan. 'We're going to fight this. FIST may act like they're the law, but they're not the law. They may police half the country, but they're just a jumped-up private security firm, and they have no right to evict us!'

'What about the girl? What if they bring charges?' asked Umi.

'They never saw 'er,' said Harlan.

'Harlan's right. They have to prove we've broken the law.'

'You can bet your life they'll be watching the place now,' said Umi.

'Then we mustn't let them see anything,' said Aunt Megan.

'Try explaining that to Ashanti,' said Umi.

'Come on, Umi! Ashanti's fighting for what she believes in, and we need to do the same.'

Umi sat down heavily on a chair by the table and put his head in his hands. 'Everything,' he said. 'Everything! So much work, and they take everything! And what about the animals? What happens to them?'

'Nobody's taking anything! We've got two months. We're going to fight! I'm going to call Robert.'

'Oh! Wonderful! He's the one that got us into this!'

'Then he can get us out of it!'

Aunt Megan strode out of the room.

Dilly quietly came over and stood by Umi. She put a small hand on his broad back. 'Dada,' she said, 'don't cry, Dada. It's OK. I'll look after the animals.'

'Thank you, little one,' said Umi. He raised his head and put an arm around her.

'Best you and I get on,' Harlan said looking at me. 'There's that ol' drain to finish.'

I trailed up the hill after Harlan and reluctantly picked up my spade as he started to dig. There didn't seem much point digging ditches to protect a field that was now never going to be planted with anything. But the old man worked steadily on as though today was the same as any day. *Always been here,* I thought. Probably can't imagine being anywhere else. Where will he end up if they take his cottage? I couldn't see Harlan in some old people's home. Then I thought about Ashanti. She was still with Hatiya. She didn't know yet. What was she going to be like when she heard that my dad had lost them the farm? She had every right to hate me! That was all I could think as I heaved another shovel full of wet, red earth out of the trench. It was me that brought this bad luck on the farm, me and my bloody family! The anger swelled up inside me. I stopped digging and watched Harlan toiling away like some dumb animal. I threw my spade down. 'What's the point!' I shouted at Harlan's back. 'What's bloody the point of doing this?!'

Harlan turned slowly, rested on his spade, and regarded my spade lying in the mud. Then, for once, he looked me straight in the eye, 'Best to finish what you start, boy,' he said, and returned to digging.

CHAPTER 17

My father promised Aunt Megan to do everything he could to stop Tristram Rainer throwing them off the farm, but it was decided that Aunt Megan and Umi should go to London to fight the eviction. Dilly would go with them, and Harlan, Ashanti, and I would look after the farm while they were away. My dad insisted on sending Jerzy to pick them up. Seemed like Rainer had allowed my dad to keep a few little luxuries, and Jerzy was one of them.

Jerzy pulled into the farmyard two days later, driving the Merc. 'Very superior for country roads,' he explained. 'And more legs room for passengers.' He'd even found a baby seat for Dilly. There'd been no trouble with Ferals this time. I wondered if Ashanti had got the word out to them, but I couldn't think how she would have done that.

Jerzy was an instant hit with Dilly. While Aunt Megan and Umi packed, Jerzy interrogated her about the farm animals. 'Do you have any tigers on this farm?... No? No tigers!' He sounded truly shocked. 'Then what about giraffes?... No? No giraffes either! Then you must be having hippopotamuses! No? Then what animals are you having on this strange farm with no tigers?'

'Goats!' Dilly shrieked, obviously delighted to have found such a stupid adult. 'Goats and cows and chickens and ducks and sometimes we have pigs and eggs.'

'Goats and cows and chickens and ducks are much better than hippopotamuses!' Jerzy said. 'Will you show them to me?'

'Of course,' said Dilly. And they went off hand in hand to inspect the animals.

'I particularly like to see pigs' eggs,' Jerzy said as they left. And I could hear Dilly's giggles right across the farmyard.

Harlan, Ashanti, and I watched as the Merc bounced down the lane; Dilly, twisting around in her car seat, waved and waved through the back window. The two dogs ran after the car, barking, then gave up and trotted back to sit at our feet and look at us, their heads cocked to one side as if to ask, 'Well, what happens now?'

'Harlan, do think you can manage all the milking if I'm not here?' asked Ashanti.

'Four cows and few goats? Reckon I could just about manage.'

'Because I think I should get Hatiya out of here. FIST are sure to have seen mum and dad leave, and they might get suspicious and come snooping around.'

'She fit?'

'Fit enough.'

'You be careful,' Harlan said, almost gently. 'Just be careful.'

'Don't worry. I will.'

Harlan nodded. Studied the ground by his feet for a moment or two, nodded again, and said, 'Well, standin' here dith'n stop the weeds growin',' and went off to hoe the herb garden. The dogs ran after him.

I walked down the hill with Ashanti. I wanted her to say something to show that she didn't blame me for everything that had happened, but she didn't; she walked quickly with a brutal determination that made me feel invisible.

'Ashanti! Stop! Please,' I said. 'I really need to talk to you.'

She stopped and turned. 'About what?' she asked, impatiently.

'I want to help.'

'OK, then help.'

'How?'

'That's up to you, isn't it?'

'But these kids… ,' I began.

'There isn't time to go into all this now. You help Harlan, OK? That's the most useful thing you can do at the moment.'

She was probably right, but it wasn't what I wanted to hear.

'This isn't about you, Mark,' she said.

'So – how long will you be?' I asked.

'Two days – maybe three. I don't know. Listen – there is one thing you can do.'

'Anything.'

'If I have to stay longer, I'll try to get a message to you.'

'How?'

She thought for a second, then almost smiled. 'Like we used to, remember?'

'Under the stone!' And for a moment we were just two kids, with a secret hiding place.

'Exactly. FIST will be watching the farmyard – they won't be watching up on the moor.'

'But how will you get it there?'

'Owando – the little kid with the missing fingers? He never gets caught. He's our messenger.'

'I'll check every day.'

'Check first thing in the morning. If we have to send him, it'll be at night. There are fewer forest patrols at night.'

'Right,' I said.'. . . And... good luck, Ashanti.'

'Thanks.' She turned to go, but stopped and turned back. 'Mark – I'm really not blaming you – OK?'

'Yeah... OK.'

She went on to the cottage, and I went back to help Harlan.

CHAPTER 18

When I woke up, I expected to be alone in the farmhouse, so I was surprised to hear noises downstairs. I guess I was getting a bit paranoid after the business with FIST and the Hatiya, so I crept down to see who it was. The noises were coming from the kitchen. I opened the door as quietly as I could.

'There's a drop o' tea, if you want one,' said Harlan. 'And your eggs'll be ready directly. I've fetched a bit o' bacon over from the cottage. I can't abide eggs with no bacon.'

'You don't have do this!' I said.

'I always comes in for a cup o' tea after the milkin' and seeing as you wasn't up, I thought I'd make myself useful.'

It was really only then that I noticed Harlan was wearing one of Aunt Megan's aprons. I had to have a violent coughing fit to cover the laugh that became a snort when I tried to keep it in.

'Come on, please. Let me do that,' I said when I'd finished coughing and snorting.

'No, no. You stop where you're to. I'll fetch it over when it's ready.'

So I sat at the table, and Harlan delivered a plate piled with eggs, bacon, tomatoes, mushrooms, and fried bread. He stood over me while I ate and threatened to make more if I was still hungry. I decided I'd better set my alarm for an hour earlier so that Harlan wouldn't think he had to cook for me every morning, although, I have to admit, it was one of the best breakfasts I'd ever eaten.

Ashanti and Hatiya had gone in the night, Harlan told me. I wondered how far they'd had to go and how they knew where in the forest they'd find the main group. Harlan didn't say anything else, but I could see that Ashanti going off worried him.

Ashanti didn't come back that night, nor the next, or the next. Each morning, I took the dogs so that if FIST were watching the farm, it would just look as if we were going for a walk and climbed up the hill to the cairn, but there was no message under the stone. Aunt Megan phoned to see how we were, and I told her that Ashanti had gone off with Hatiya. I thought she should know. There was a silence at the other end of the line and then Aunt Megan said, 'Call me if she's not back tomorrow.'

Next morning, I climbed the hill as usual. For a change, it wasn't raining, and a lark was singing somewhere high above the moor; the first one I'd heard since I arrived. I'd thought they must be all gone. It made me happy and sad to hear it; like there was hope for the world, but not much. Like everything was held in place by that tiny bird and its song. What if it was the last one? What if it sang and sang and never found a mate? I searched the bright sky for a black speck. When we were little, lying on our backs with the smell of the heather and the gorse all around us, Ashanti was always the first to see them. I could hear her saying, 'There! There! Can't you see it? It's there, stupid! Look! There!' Then I found it, high, high up in the blue.

After the dazzle of the sky, it took a moment for my eyes to adjust, so that, at first when I lifted the stone, I only saw our two old toys. Then I saw that tucked underneath them was a crumpled piece of paper. I looked quickly over my shoulder. Was I being watched? I pulled out the piece of paper and replaced the stone. Then I read Ashanti's brief message:

Owando will wait in the forest near bridge. Meet tonight at midnight. Bring food and water for Owando.

What had happened? Why didn't she say more? *Bring food and water.* Was Owando going to take me somewhere? I called the dogs and went back down to the farm. What should I say to Harlan, if anything? In the end, I said nothing, but I worried about it all through a day that seemed to creep by ever so slowly.

In the late afternoon, Ruby called by, as arranged with Umi, to collect eggs and vegetables for the shops the farm supplied in New Molton and Buckland. She came in one of those old, electric pickups you hardly see these days, now the uranium's run out and electricity's got so pricy – but Ruby's sure to have her own turbine like Umi – She's that sort.

'Yeah, bit of wreck,' she said with a grin, seeing me inspecting the pickup. 'Belonged to my dear dead granddad.'

When we had finished loading boxes of vegetables and Harlan had gone off for the eggs, she said, 'OK, kiddo, what's happening? Where's Ashanti? Umi says you got raided.'

I knew that Ashanti and Ruby were friends and probably Ruby was more mixed up in the Feral stuff than just collecting old clothes for them, but would Ashanti want me to tell her about the note?

'It's all right', she said, 'you can tell me.'

When I still hesitated, she put one hand on my shoulder. 'Yeah – fair enough. Why should you know who to trust? And for the record, I'm really sorry about the business with that bastard Jake. That was our fault, not yours. Listen – I know you're cool – OK? And because I know that, I'm going to tell you something that doesn't go past here – Right? – The members of the band are all in this. We're the ones that get the kids out of Holdstone. Tony and Cara, they're foresters in the daytime, so they look out for the kids once they're in the forest. Trigger, he's got a smasher-repair business, so he adapted my truck – put a hidey-hole in the sleeping compartment big enough to get two kids in. Pete and Monkey haul skips out of Holdstone, and we sometimes use the skip truck to get kids out. And Bethan – if we need anything technical, like how to disable an alarm system, she's the one – Then there's the travellers in that painted bus. They help from time to time.'

She grinned at my astonished expression. 'Yeah, I know – Probably you'd guessed something, but you weren't quite expecting that! So now – What's happening?'

What I actually wanted to do straight away was ask Ruby loads of questions. What did she mean 'get the kids out of Holdstone'? How? Why? But she was looking at me like she was expecting an answer, and she didn't want to wait for ever.

I told her about the old house in the forest and that FIST had caught eight of the younger children. I told her about Hatiya – that Ashanti had taken her back to the main group, and then I told her about the note.

Ruby listened carefully. 'Maybe I should go to meet Owando,' she said when I'd finished.

'No. I'm going. Definitely,' I said.

'Well – OK. You seem very certain.'

'I am certain,' I said. It seemed like this was my chance to redeem myself. Yeah, everyone kept telling me none of this was my fault, but that didn't stop me feeling like it was, and I was sure the farm wouldn't have been raided if I hadn't talked to Jake.

'Two things to watch out for in the forest: Rangers and FIST patrols. Often they go around together.'

'I could always pretend I got lost.' I said.

'Yeah, but you can't pretend you're alive after they've shot you,' said Ruby. 'If you go into the forest, just be really careful, OK? Find out what's happened to Ashanti and let Harlan and me know. Then we'll work out what's best to do.'

'What should I say to Harlan?' I asked.

Don't say anything to him today. He'll only fret. He seems as hard as rock, but he's an old mother hen. I'll come by in the morning. You will have had the news from Owando. We'll know what to tell him when we know what's going on.

'Thanks.'

'You're welcome, kiddo. Now, where is Harlan? Don't tell me he's waiting for the chickens to lay those eggs!'

Later that evening, when Harlan had checked for the third time that I didn't want him to make me some tea, he went off to his cottage. I was pretty much living on cheese omelettes and mashed potato, seeing as I wasn't a great cook, but I branched out that night and made cheese with jacket potatoes.

I packed a small rucksack of food for Owando – bread, cheese, biscuits, carrots, and two bars of chocolate that I found in the store cupboard, plus I took a torch, and I filled a water bottle. At ten thirty, I turned the lights out to make anyone watching think I had gone to bed. The hour of waiting in the darkness seemed more like three. At eleven thirty, I crept out of the house wearing an old waxed coat of Umi's that was waterproof and a sort of mucky green, so good camouflage. I stopped outside the door, my hand still on the door handle, and thought, *What the hell am I doing getting mixed up in this? This is total madness!*

It wasn't raining, but the sky had begun to cloud over – the moon coming and going. I walked quickly in the periods of darkness and skulked in shadows each time the moon reappeared. There were no lights on in Harlan's cottage, but I passed it as quietly as possible, then over the bridge, through the river meadow, and I was in the darkness of the forest. Where would Owando be? Should I turn my torch on so he could see me? I stood still and listened. There were scurrying sounds that were too small to be made by a human. A twig falling when a gust of wind sighed through the upper branches. I took a few more steps then almost screamed when a dark shape dropped from a tree and landed with a dull thud in front of me.

'Shh!' the shape said, as it unfolded and became a small boy. 'You follow,' and beckoned with a fingerless hand.

'Where... ?' I began, but he had already turned off the bridleway and into the forest, and I had to hurry after him not to lose him.

We reached a small clearing where a tree had fallen. Owando motioned for me to stop. He stood still, listening. When he was satisfied that there were only the usual forest sounds, he said, 'OK, we talk.'

'What's happened? Where's Ashanti?' I demanded at once.

'Big trouble.'

'What trouble? FIST?'

'No, not FIST. Casablanca make himself chief. He declares war on FIST. He say we must have guns and become guerrillas. Rob for moneys.'

'But your old leaders? What do they say?'

'Yongjo Ma and Yongjo Pa against him, of course.'

'Then can't they stop him?'

'How? Casablanca have guns already. Guns he took from ship. Now he lock up everyone not want to make war. Lock up Ashanti, lock up Yongjo Ma, lock up Yongjo Pa. Only Owando escape. I go back in the night. Talk to Ashanti. She say I tell you message.'

'Guns from ship? What ship?'

'Broken ship Yongjo Pa find.'

'In the forest?!'

He made an impatient 'Tst!' and said, 'By the sea!'

'So, what do we do?'

'Too dangerous for you. Owando must go back.'

'You! On your own? Don't be crazy. We have friends. Come up to the farm and wait 'till the morning. We'll get help and go together. Ruby – you know – the woman with the truck. She'll help us.'

'Better I go alone. Better I go now, before Casablanca start war.'

'Ashanti wouldn't have sent you to me if she meant you to do this on your own.'

'Rich boy doesn't know forest. Only Owando know forest. I give you Ashanti's message, now I go back.'

Rich boy! That did it! No way was this little kid with no fingers going back without me. How did I know he was even telling the truth? What if he was one of Casablanca's gang?

'Listen!' I said, 'Ashanti is my friend, OK? You're not going anywhere unless I go with you. Understand?'

It was too dark to see the expression on his face, but I saw the shrug of the shoulders before he turned and began to walk out of the clearing.

'Hey!' I called.... 'Hey, I've got food! Hey, wait!' But he just kept going, and all I could do was follow.

Owando moved as silently as a shadow, while I stumbled along behind him, tripping over tree roots and snapping dead branches.

At first, we seemed to take the route that I'd taken when I went to the old house, leaving the bridleway and cutting through the forest to the old road. When we reached the road, he signalled for me to stop and then to crouch down. He crept forward and listened, then beckoned me on.

'Easier for you on the road. But we must be listening. All the time listening,' he said.

'Where are we going?' I asked.

'Better to walk now,' he said, and off we went again.

We passed the lane to the old house and kept going. Although he was a lot smaller than me and, I noticed with a sudden shock, barefooted, I was almost jogging to keep up with him. *Just how long are we going to have to keep this up?* I wondered.

We came to a crossroads and turned right. There was an old signpost, but I couldn't read it in the dark. At the bottom of the next valley, we entered an abandoned village: a pub, a few shops, houses that crowded right up to the pavement. Most of the windows were broken, and some of the houses were burnt out. Window boxes still stood on windowsills, and the pub had plant pots by the front door, but they were all overflowing with weeds. The sign on the village notice board said, 'Best Kept Village 2015.' As we left the village, we passed a dark, overgrown churchyard, its yew trees rising like plumes of denser blackness amongst the graves. I shuddered at the thought of the dead lying forgotten in that dead churchyard and was glad when we were out of the village and back in the arching tunnel of trees that overhung the road.

It was after two o'clock in the morning, and we had been walking fast along the forest road for over two hours. I could feel a blister forming on my left heel. Owando stopped and held up his hand. He turned his head one way, then the other, listening, his head cocked like a dog. I could hear nothing.

'We hide – Quick!'

But there was no way through the old, grow-out hedges on each side of the road. Owando turned and began to sprint back the way we had come, and I ran after him, dropping further and further behind. *How could that little kid move so fast!?* Reaching an open gateway, Owando dived off the road and disappeared. Now I could hear the sound of the approaching vehicle. I glanced back as its headlights swept around the bend behind me. In a few seconds, I'd be caught like a rabbit! I willed my legs to go faster, then plunged after Owando, who grabbed me and dragged me to the ground. I lay, gasping for breath as the patrol passed; an open truck with four armed guards lounging in the back while a fifth stood, operating a powerful searchlight on the truck's roof. Owando pushed my face into the mud as its beam raked through the undergrowth around us.

'Will they come back?' I asked, after spitting out a mouthful dirt.

'No, no. These go to Holdstone.'

'Can we rest a bit?'

Owando shook his head, 'Keep going. After, we rest.'

'After what?'

'After we pass the camp.'

'Is that far?'

Owando gave a little giggle. 'I think, maybe far for you.'

He got up and stepped back on to the road.

I took off my left trainer, adjusted my sock and then put the shoe back on, pulling the laces tight to try to stop it rubbing. It didn't help much. Maybe boots would have been better, but I hadn't reckoned on walking all night.

Four o'clock came and went, and we still hadn't passed Holdstone; my legs ached, and I was sure my left heel was bleeding.

For the first few hours, I had been trying to memorise our route, but the road branched and branched again. We joined a bigger road complete with roundabouts that had become mini jungles, and I looked for road signs, but then Owando took us overland through the forest, and I realised I would have no hope of finding my way back on my own.

At last, Owando stopped and waited for me to catch up.

'Now we must be careful,' he said. 'Look. You see? Big road to Holdstone.'

Through the trees, there were lights. Another hundred metres and we were at the edge of the road. This road was unlike anything else in the forest. Its surface was smooth and well maintained; it was lit by the orange glare of streetlights, and the forest had been cut back for twenty metres on each side. This was what Owando had been keen to cross in the night, before it got busy.

'We must cross quickly. When I say run, you run, run, run!' Owando urged.

'OK. I've got that. What if anyone comes?'

'You run faster!'

Owando stepped out cautiously, listened, then slid back beside me. 'Down, down! Something coming.'

We lay in the undergrowth. Soon, there were headlights and then a convoy like the one Jerzy and I had seen on our way down from London, a prison van, accompanied by two patrol vehicles.

'All the time, all the time. More, more, more!' Owando muttered. He let the convoy pass and, when it was out of sight, stepped out and listened again. He turned and beckoned frantically and, as soon as I was beside him, ordered, 'Run!'

The few seconds it took to cross the brightly lit road seemed stretched into minutes. Owando was gone in a flash, and when I crashed down next him on the other side of the road, he was laughing uncontrollably. 'You run so funny!... Legs go everywhere!... Up and down like ant on hot frying pan!'

'All right,' I said, feeling rather stung. 'Where to now?'

'Uphill,' Owando replied and, still breaking into little cascades of giggles, led the way.

Half an hour or so of hard climbing brought us out by a rocky tor, a tumble of huge boulders that crowned the hill.

'We rest here,' Owando said. He scrambled up the tor and jumped lightly from boulder to boulder until he came to a sort of natural seat where he could rest his back against one of the stones. I climbed up and sat next to him. We'd been up all night, and, if you didn't count when we were hiding, we hadn't stopped. I was exhausted.

'You have some food?' Owando asked.

'Oh yeah. Sure.' I opened my rucksack and dumped the contents on the rock between us. 'Help yourself.' For the moment, I was too tired to eat, but I drank some water. Owando broke off lumps of bread and cheese and ate hungrily. I caught myself staring at the way he used the hand with the missing fingers and looked away. 'Sorry, should have brought a knife,' I said. He shrugged and continued eating. I remembered how they had devoured Jerzy's food when they ambushed the car and wondered when Owando had last eaten.

The sky was beginning to grow lighter, turning a pearly, pinkish grey. I could feel my legs growing stiff, sitting on the cold rock, so I got up to stretch, but Owando caught hold of my coat before I could straighten up. 'Stay down, or maybe they see,' he said. I sat and shuffled forward until I could look over the edge of the boulder. The bottom of the valley was a web of lights. I could see where the road we had crossed arrived at a floodlit checkpoint and then continued on to a bare, floodlit square, like a parade ground. From here, strings of lights marked where smaller roads lead off in all directions. As it grew a little lighter, I could make out rows and rows of long low buildings. Down the valley, there was a complex of much larger buildings, giant hangers, or warehouses and what might have been a factory with chimneys from which smoke or steam was billowing. At the higher end of the valley, a glitter of water – a small canal approached the perimeter and disappeared. I guessed it was connected in some way to the reservoir I could see inside the camp.

Owando crawled forward and sat next to me. 'Holdstone,' he said.

I nodded, amazed at the size of the place, it filled the entire valley.

'Fence,' he said, sweeping his hand around in a big circle. 'Guards,' he jabbed the air as he made the circle again. I searched the edge of the camp. I couldn't see the fence in the grey morning light, but I found a few of the watchtowers. I pointed to one to show I had seen it. Owando nodded and mimed aiming a gun and firing.

Bloody hell! I thought.

'Better you eat,' Owando said.

I was more tired than hungry, but I ate some of the bread and drank some more water.

'Your parents, your mother, your father – are they here?' I asked, pointing at the camp.

Owando shook his head.

'At home?... Where you come from?'

He shook his head again. 'I am looking for my mother when they catch me.'

'You're looking for her – What, here in England?'

'Of course in England!' he says, as though I've got to be the stupidest person he's ever met.

'So you were here together, but she went off or something?'

'Two years ago, she leave us and come to England.'

'I don't quite get it. Why did she leave you?'

He actually groans now at my stupidity and holds his head. When he takes his hands away from his face he leans towards me, 'She-come-to-England-for-working! No rain! Everything dead! No food! No money!'

'OK,' I say. 'OK, I've got the picture. There was a drought, and your mum came here to work. And then you came to look for her. But when they caught you, did you tell them you were looking for your mother?'

'Tell?'

'Yes. They could help you find her.'

'Ow!' he says, and raises his hands up as if praying for patience. 'I tell them my mother is here, they find her and lock her up!'

Oh yeah, of course. He's right. I really am stupid! She's illegal. Like you'd go to the authorities and tell them your mother's an illegal immigrant!

'Yeah, right. I get it,' I say. Then it occurs to me that this kid can't be more than ten years old. How old was he when he left Africa? Seven? Eight? How the hell did he get to England? So I ask him, 'Did you come on your own?'

He looks down, and when he looks at me again, he's crying.

'What?' I say. 'Oh God! Look, I'm sorry.'

He wipes his nose on his sleeve and his eyes are wet and they are full of so much pain that I have to look away and he just says, 'With my sister,' and sniffs and I'm not going to ask him what happened, but I know she's dead.

Neither of us says anything until Owando, keeping low, climbs down off the tor.

'We go,' he says.

CHAPTER 19

It rains on and off throughout the morning, and even when it doesn't rain, the forest drips. Occasionally the clouds are thin enough for me to see where the sun is, and I know we are heading north-west, towards the coast. Mostly my mind is blank, and I just concentrate on putting one foot in front of the other. Now it's daylight, we avoid the roads, but we're following a muddy lane downhill between fern-covered stone walls. I'm pleased when Owando stops, and I'm about to ask how much further when I notice his face. It's the first time I've seen him look scared.

'Dogs!' is all he says. Then he starts running. I know I should run after him, but there's nothing left. I've had no sleep for over twenty-four hours, my head's muzzy, and my feet are stuck to the ground.

Owando looks around, sees me standing there, races back towards me, grabs hold of my arm, and forces me to run. 'Dogs,' he keeps saying, 'Dogs!' Mud flies from our feet as we pound down the lane. I slip but Owando keeps me from falling. At the bottom of the hill, the lane fords a stream. Instead of crossing, Owando steers us into the water and downstream, then up the bank, where the low branches of a tree overhang the water. He swings himself on to the bottom branch, then, quick as a cat, climbs up. I follow, but much more clumsily, my wet trainers sliding on the mossy bark. I can hear the dogs now – that same wild baying I heard the day Ashanti led the hunters out of the forest, and they're getting closer. We cling to the branches, looking down through the leaves. Nothing has prepared me for what happens next.

A girl and a small boy dash into sight. The boy is wearing an overcoat that is much too big and flies like a cape behind him. They reach the stream and hesitate. In that moment, the hounds are on them. But the girl seizes a stick, pulls the boy close to her, and lashes out wildly in all directions as together they back into the water. They get to the middle of the stream with the hounds all around them. The water is churned to foam as the dogs leap and plunge, trying to get past the girl's stick. The valley echoes with their barking. It's obvious that the children cannot hold the hounds off for long even though the water is making it harder for the dogs to attack. Owando begins to slither down the tree.

'No!' I scream, making a grab for his collar, but he's too quick for me, dropping from branch to branch and on to the ground. Now Owando is also brandishing a stick and throws himself into the fight. He beats his way through the pack to stand back to back with the girl. One of the hounds manages to get a hold of the drifting hem of the small boy's oversized coat and begins to pull, hackles raised and growling. The boy cries out and clings to the girl, but other dogs join the tug-of-war. The girl is beating at the hounds with her stick – Owando trying to defend her back. I know I should go to help, but I'm certain the dogs will kill us, and I watch in horror as the small boy slips and disappears under the water.

There is the thudding of hooves and the hunters canter down the lane and halt their horses at the water's edge. It's a big crowd, and their horses push and jostle around the hunt master in his red coat. But instead of calling the dogs off, they shout encouragement, laughing and pointing. As the girl bends to pull the little boy to his feet, a hound leaps on her back, another has Owando by the arm, four are tugging and shaking the little boy's coat. *Oh shit! Oh shit!* I'm thinking, *They're going to be torn to pieces, and those bastards are going to watch!* But the master of the hunt urges his horse in to the water, calling to the dogs and laying about with his whip. Other riders follow, and after a good deal of shouting and cursing, the hounds leave the water and trot about, tongues hanging out, tails wagging as if they are a bunch of harmless pets.

The children stumble out of the stream, supporting each other. There are wounds on the girl's neck and face, and Owando's sleeve is torn and bloody. I'm almost certain the girl is the one they called Sarayova, and the little boy is definitely the one who played with Jerzy's pistol. Is this the same group of hunters that Ashanti confronted that day by the bridge? Red Coat could easily be the same bully who called Ashanti a half-cast. And she wasn't stopping them from hunting deer that day; she was stopping them from hunting children! No wonder she was in such a state. Then, with a shock, I realise I recognise one of the other riders. It's Tristram Rainer! He sits, quietly on his horse, just watching, as the children's wrists are fastened behind their backs, and they are roped together and led off behind one of the horses. Rainer falls in beside the last rider and, as they turn to ride back up the lane, I see Rainer's companion has a tattoo that runs up the side of his neck. Jake!

I stay in the tree a long time, feeling sick and faint. When I climb down, I'm shaking. What do I do now? I have no idea where I am. Owando's been captured. I have no idea where Ashanti is, and if I hang around here much longer, the hunters are going to get me as well.

I'm fairly certain we have been heading roughly north-east. I could probably find my way back to Holdstone. What would happen if I just walked in there and said I was lost? After all, I'm not an illegal immigrant. I'm a British citizen. I have rights. They'd call my father and someone would come and get me. All right, it might be a bit tricky explaining what I was doing in the forest, but what can they do to me?

I tell myself, *There is nothing else I can do. I shouldn't have got mixed up in this in the first place – this is not my battle – it has nothing to do with me.* And I start walking back up the lane.

CHAPTER 20

I reached the point where I thought Owando and I had first come on to the lane. It was hard to tell; our footprints were now lost under the churned-up mud and hoof prints of all the horses. Well, if I kept going in a general south-easterly direction, I should hit the road that led to Holdstone. I left the lane and headed through the forest.

So this is what I'm going to do – I'm going to get to Holdstone and then I'm going to get hold of my dad and then I'm clearing off out of here. Yeah. It's the only sensible thing to do. Bugger off back to London…. back to my mates… back to normal life. Well, maybe it won't be quite normal, what with half of London being destroyed and people dying of cholera and us not having a proper home and that – but it will be more normal than this!… And what do I say to Aunt Megan and Umi? Dear Aunt Megan, I've left your daughter somewhere in the forest with a load of mad hunters and illegal immigrants? Yeah, well, my dad can speak to them. He'll sort it out. Organise a search party or something…. What if something happens to her? What if something has already happened to her? Why the hell didn't I get more information out of Owando? I just followed him like an idiot! Well, it's a bit late now. Bit late for Owando, come to that.

I stopped walking. *He was bloody brave. The way he just waded in there with that stick amongst all those dogs. I wonder how he lost his fingers – I never asked him that. Never asked him a lot of things. Too late now. Oh hell! Oh shit! Oh crap!*

I turned around and walked back the way I had just come. It wasn't going to be hard to track them, even for a city boy like me.

The hunting party's tracks led along the lane and off on to a bridleway that joined another lane that joined one of the old roads by a bridge and a cluster of abandoned houses. *Well, there we go – That's it!* I thought, *I can't track them on a sealed road. Sorry. I tried. But, quite honestly, from here they could have gone either way. Have to give up.*

Then I saw that a recent flood had left a layer of mud on the road by the bridge, and in the mud, there were clear hoof prints, and amongst the hoof prints, the bare foot prints of three children. *Damn!* I thought.

Now I knew which way they were heading, all I needed to do was keep going until I saw where they turned off. Apart from the houses near the bridge, the forest continued, unbroken, on each side of the road. If the horses left the road, they'd leave prints in the soft mud at the edge, unless, of course, they turned off on to another sealed road.

I'd been going less than an hour when I came to the turn-off, and it was much more obvious than I had thought it would be. The forest to the left of the road stopped and was replaced by a high stone wall. The wall continued for some way and then was interrupted by a big pair of fancy, iron gates. Beyond the gates, a gravel drive led gently uphill to a large, white mansion. On either side of the drive was well-kept parkland, where horses grazed amongst ornamental trees. It was like a picture out of a history book, but I knew what it was. It was one of the old National Trust properties that had been taken over by the Great West Forest and turned into hunting lodges for celebrities, city types, and rich overseas visitors. One of my dad's ideas. They have swimming pools and helipads. Some even have their own golf courses. 'Perfect for the super-rich,' Dad says. 'They can fly in, have a luxury holiday, and know all the money they spend goes towards planting trees. No need to worry about carbon footprints. They get a clear conscience included in the price.' I wondered if my dad knew they had added children-hunting to their range of attractions.

Keeping well clear of the gates, which would be sure to be fitted with security cameras, I crossed the road and hid in the forest on the other side. Unless they had already been taken back to Holdstone, Owando and his friends were somewhere in that building. As there'd be no chance of rescuing them once they were taken back to the refugee camp, I needed to find them, and find them before they were moved.

The trick was going to be getting in without getting caught. It would be easier to do it after dark, but that might already be too late. I had once stayed in one of these places with my dad and mum, so I knew the layout. They didn't have perimeter fences, but cameras covered every millimetre of their grounds, so there was no way I could walk up to that building from any direction without being seen. What I needed was somebody to give me a lift in. Pity Jerzy wasn't here, he could blag his way past anyone! I studied the building and what I could see of the grounds through the iron gates. There had to be a way. But, as the front gates didn't offer an answer, I decided to skirt around to the back.

I recrossed the road well away from the gates and, staying hidden in the trees, made my way around the property. The back of the property was an even worse prospect than the front! An immaculate golf course spread out into the forest, the close-cropped fairways like wide inlets winding between islands of trees and shrubs with sand traps full of impossibly clean white sand and little flags fluttering on the smooth greens. There was even an artificial lake with a boathouse. A couple of players, having finished their game, were returning to the lodge in an electric golf buggy.

Crossing the golf course, I'd be as visible as beetle on a billiard table! This was looking hopeless.

The golf buggy reached the lodge. The players got out and went inside. *Probably got some under-paid teenager to take the buggies back,* I thought. I looked around to see where they parked them and saw a dozen or so down by the first tee and some more by the far side of the lodge.

Just a minute! The first tee is right on the edge of the course, and the buggy park is between the first tee and the start of the forest. If I can get into one of those buggies, I can drive it up to the back door of the lodge. The security cameras will see the golf buggy, but they won't be able to tell who's inside it! Do I know how to drive a golf buggy? No, I don't. But they're electric – how hard can it be?

I cut around through the forest to get as close to the buggy park as possible, without leaving the cover of the trees. There's a little out-building by the buggies, and I can see a security camera up on the corner of it. But if I keep low, the buggies will be between me and the camera. Once I'm in a buggy, I'll be hidden from the camera by the buggy's roof. There's no one left on the golf course and no one around the back of the lodge.

I get down as low as I can, without actually being on my hands and knees, and do this frantic sort of chimpanzee gallop across to the nearest buggy. Right, I'm in, and I'm waiting for the alarms to start going off… but nothing happens. I strain my ears, but all I can hear is some hounds barking. Now, where's the on switch? Oh yeah, right in front of my nose. And I'm about to switch it on when alarms really do start going off! Shit! They must have seen me! People come running out of the lodge and half of them are carrying guns!

So I'm out of the buggy in a split second, and I crawl around behind the out-building. There's a door. I try the handle, and it opens. It's some sort of storeroom or changing room; there are uniforms and umbrellas, golf carts and bags of clubs. But I don't have time to take much in before I hear a roaring clatter overhead. There's a window at the front. I go and look out, and I realise it's not me they're interested in. The cause of all the excitement is a helicopter that's coming in to land. It touches down on the lawn behind the lodge, and whoever it's got in it must be hyper-important because they've now got a small army of gorillas in suits and sunglasses up there on guard. The helicopter's door opens as soon as the rotor blades stop turning, and the steps fold down. Then I see Tristram Rainer is in the welcoming party, and he moves forward to greet the VIP, and then there she is! Skinny as a stick, handbag over her arm – Mrs Grist, the prime minister! Rainer and Grist! What are they up to out here in the Forest? Mrs Grist doesn't look like she's dressed for hunting!

The Prime Minister and her welcoming party quickly make their way inside, followed shortly after by the crew from the helicopter. This could be my chance. With everyone's attention on the Prime Minister, they might not look too closely at a golf buggy coming off the golf course.

Now I realise what this little building is. It's the place where the golf caddies keep all their stuff – the guys who look after the players, who carry their bags, hold their umbrellas, and all that. And these are their uniforms. They're like a white overall with a green baseball cap. I take Umi's waxed coat off, find an overall that looks about my size, and I pull it on over my clothes. Next, I find a green cap that fits me and, Hey presto! I'm a golf caddy! I roll up Umi's coat and stuff it in an empty sports bag. Then I take a deep breath and walk outside, carrying the bag, as if I'm meant to be here.

I get back into the buggy, turn the thing on, and press the accelerator down. The buggy lurches forward. I instinctively pull my foot off the pedal, making the buggy stop, so suddenly I almost bash my nose on the steering wheel. Got to do better than that! This time, I press the pedal more gently, and the buggy gradually gathers speed. That's more like it! I go down and around the first tee and then up a little path that I saw the other buggy take, past the practice putting green, towards the lawn where the helicopter is standing. Where should I end up? I decide to go around to the side where the other buggies are parked and hope there is a service entrance of some kind.

I'm just beginning to believe that this might work, when there's a shout. 'Hey! Caddy! You boy!'

I stop. One of the gorillas in shades is standing by the helicopter, pointing at me. I try to look casual, like I belong here.

'When you've parked that one, get this buggy out of here! This area's meant to be kept clear. Do you understand?!'

'Yes, sir!' I say.

'Don't let it happen again!'

'No, sir!'

He turns and marches back to the building.

Whew!

I figure these guys in shades don't work here. Probably not even local. They're extra security for the Prime Minister, and I see the one who shouted at me is now standing guard by the rear entrance, like a bouncer outside a nightclub.

I drive my buggy around the side of the lodge and park it with the ones already there. The noise of the hounds is louder here. Their kennels must be nearby. I wonder it they always bark like that? Surprised the posh visitors don't complain!

I walk back to get the other buggy, like I've been told. When I'm in, I give Mr Shades a cheery wave and, would you believe, he actually waves back!

Next problem, how to get into the building? As I get out of the buggy, I see there is a side entrance, but there's another gorilla guarding it, and I'm prepared to bet it's the same story at all the other doors. But if I stand here much longer, one of these heavies is going to get suspicious. And, yep! Sure enough, I'm being shouted at again. I look round. It's the guy by the back door, and now the other guard is looking at me as well. Do I make a run for it? He's obviously figured out there's something wrong. But if I run, I won't get far and, more to the point, I might get shot. This is not good. In fact, this is very, very bad. Now the first guy's beckoning to me to come over. What do I do? Oh God. Look's like he's getting impatient.

'Hey! Kid! Get your arse over here!'

Better do what he says… Think of a story… Think of a story!… And stop looking so scared!… Smile, you're a caddy… just doing your job.

'Can I help?' I ask politely.

'What's so funny?'

'Nothing,' I say, realising I'm trying so hard not to look petrified I'm grinning like an imbecile.

'Listen, kid, I'm stuck guarding this bleedin' door, and I'm gaspin' for a fag. You work here. They got a machine in there?'

'Yeah, sure they have,' I say, like I know everything about this place.

'Do us a favour. Here's some money, duck in there and get us some. Yeah?'

'I'm meant to be on the golf course,' I say.

'Won't take you long. I'll watch your back,' he says.

'Any particular brand,' I ask, trying to stop my hand from shaking as I hold it out to take the money.

'Whatever they got. I'm dying here.'

'OK.'

Then he hesitates, still holding the money. 'You look kind'a young.'

'Holiday job,' I say, quickly.

'Well, if anyone catches you buying the fags, just blame me.' He hands me the change and has a look around inside the door. 'Coast's clear, kid. Off you go.'

And I'm in the building! Brilliant!

CHAPTER 21

But now what? If I don't go back with the security guard's cigarettes, he'll come looking for me. Or maybe not – he can't leave his post. The important thing is to find where they're holding Owando and the other two as quickly as possible. What do I say if I meet someone? Are golf caddies allowed in the building? Are there cameras in here?

Footsteps! Someone just around the corner! Coming along the corridor! There's a stairway on the right. Up or down? I choose up. The stairs are carpeted, and I take them two at a time.

I find myself on a mezzanine, a sort of indoor balcony off which doors open to – I'm guessing – bedrooms or guest suites. On the balcony is a sitting area with big leather sofas and low tables. I can hear voices so I dive behind one of the big sofas and I'm between the back of the sofa and the heavy, wooden balustrade that runs along the edge of the balcony.

Now I can hear that the voices are coming from below me, and I know immediately who those voices belong to. The strident tones of Mrs Grist, demanding, accusing, bullying interspersed with Tristram Rainer's calm, almost lazy replies. I lie on my stomach and wriggle over so that I can see through one of the gaps in the balustrade and down into the room below. The room looks like a baronial hall – Maybe it was one once, all wood panelled with stags' heads on the walls and big, dark oil paintings of hunting scenes. A fire is burning in an enormous stone fireplace at the far end of the room, and the flames are reflected and multiplied in the leaded panes of a tall trophy cabinet, full of stuffed birds, most of which are probably now extinct.

I'm lying on my G-Port, and it's sticking into my thigh. I have a sudden panic that pressing on it will set the thing off. I get my hand inside my overall and mange to pull the port out of my trouser pocket. Seeing it gives me an idea. I start the video record function and place the port in a gap in the balustrade. Now I can watch what Grist and Rainer are doing on the G-Port's little screen while keeping my head down and out of sight.

Tristram Rainer is lounging in a throne-like chair. Mrs Grist is pacing up and down in front of the fireplace.

'If there were an election now, we would lose. The public still blames us for the flooding of London. The opposition have tabled a vote of no confidence. I don't know how much longer we can hold on to power.'

'If yours were the only party, there'd be no opposition, and there'd be no need for elections.'

'What are you saying?'

'Get rid of the opposition.'

'How? The courts would never allow it!'

'The courts need the police. You begin by giving the policing of the country to FIST.'

'Abolish every police force in Britain? Is that what you're suggesting?'

'I wouldn't use the word "abolish".'

'What word would you use?' She stops pacing and looks at him.

Rainer smiles. 'Call it "restructuring", Prime Minister.'

'Restructuring?'

'Exactly.'

Mrs Grist goes back to pacing. 'And then FIST would police the whole country?'

'We already police the City of London and the entire West Country.'

'And just how do you think I am going to convince parliament, let alone the general population?'

'Frighten them. The terrorist threat. Tell them the truth. Tell them Britain is going to be overrun by foreigners. Every year there are more droughts in Africa, more hurricanes in America, crop failures in Spain, Italy, Greece, Turkey, floods in India, famines in China and Korea...'

'Yes, yes! I know all that!'

'There are millions of refugees on the move. Soon, there will be millions more. Britain is under siege. This is a war we are fighting,

Angela. This is not a time for democracy and elections and votes of no confidence. This is a time for action! For every true Briton to stand up for the motherland! We are fighting for our survival against a foreign invasion.'

'And FIST can keep them out?'

'Most of them. With a big enough force.'

'And the ones that get in?'

'We round them up... and... you know our solution.'

'More slave camps like Holdstone?'

'Refugee Centres, Prime Minister.'

'That's not what the press is going to call them once they find out what's really going on in places like Holdstone.'

'Then the press mustn't find out.'

'You make that sound very simple.'

'Once FIST becomes the police force, we can begin closing down the press. You declare a state of emergency, and journalists who make trouble can be arrested for supporting terrorism. Then we get rid of the opposition.'

'A state of emergency! And what possible reason do I give for declaring a state of emergency?'

'The sabotaging of the Thames Barrier.'

'But the barrier wasn't sabotaged!'

'Wasn't it? What if we found out that it was? That terrorists, illegal immigrants, with support from dissident members of the opposition, sabotaged the barrier allowing London to flood, killing thousands of innocent people?'

'Well, naturally, in that case... But, wouldn't we need evidence?'

'Oh, FIST could provide you with evidence... even a few suspects who, given enough... persuasion, will admit that they did it.'

'And if I agree to all this, how soon do we need to act?'

'In the next few weeks. As soon as possible. While the country is still in shock over the flooding of London.'

'What about Sir Robert Blyth? He knows what really happened. Won't he make trouble?'

'Ha! Sir Robert? Not if we pay him well enough. We could even let him have his forest back, then, if anyone finds out what's happening in the camps, we blame him. Of course, if he won't cooperate, then we "discover" that he has links with terrorists.'

'And what do I gain from all of this?'

'You? How does 'president for life' sound? The woman who saved Britain – the new Churchill. And you'll never have to face another election.'

'I see. There is just one flaw.'

'What's that?'

'These escapes from your slave camp.'

'A few children. We're on top of it.'

'Really?'

'Absolutely. As a matter of fact, we caught three today. We're holding them here... and soon they're going tell us where their leaders are.'

'How can you be so sure?'

'They seemed to be quite frightened of the hounds, so we've shut them in the kennels with some of our fiercer guard dogs.'

'But won't the dogs kill them before they talk?'

'Oh no. The dogs are chained up. We just let them have a bit more chain every half an hour. Eventually they will be able to reach the children. But I'm sure the little brats will have talked by then.'

The kennels! So that's where they were holding them. I had a pretty good idea where the kennels were, but now I had to get out of this building. The only thing to do was to buy the guard his cigarettes and go back out the way I had come in.

I retrieved my G-Port, turned it to 'sleep', wriggled from behind the sofa, and crept over to the top of the stairs. No one coming that I could hear, so I made my way carefully down. As I stepped into the corridor, I almost collided with a large West-Indian housemaid carrying a great pile of fresh bath towels.

'What you doing in here?' she demanded.

Panic!

Then I remembered I worked here, I was a golf caddy, and I had an excuse.

'One of those security guys sent me in to buy him some cigarettes,' I said. 'But I can't find a machine.'

'Well, you don't ought to be in here anyhow!' she scowled at me over the top of her towels. 'In the basement, by the toilets. And don't let nobody else catch you!'

'Thanks,' I said. 'Thank you very much.'

She sailed off along the corridor while I returned to the stairs and, this time, went down. Sure enough, there was a machine by the toilets. I fed in the money, grabbed the packet the machine spat out, ran up the stairs, and reached the rear door without encountering anyone else. The security guard's broad, black-suited back was towards me. I could see the curly wire that ran up beside his thick, muscular neck to the earpiece of his two-way radio.

'Got your cigarettes,' I said. 'Sorry I took so long.'

He turned.

'What you talking about?' he said.

It was a different guy! They'd gone and changed while I was inside! I could see my shocked expression reflected in the mirrored surface of his dark glasses.

'But... ,' I began.

'But what?'

'The guy... the one who was here before... He wanted some cigarettes. He gave me some money. Look!' I said. 'Here's his change and everything.'

'No one's allowed in the building without a pass.'

'No, of course. I know. But your mate asked me... as a favour.'

The guard stared down at my hand holding the cigarettes and the change. I could feel my hand beginning to shake, and the sweat breaking out under my clothes.

'Yeah, well,' said the new guard, 'he shouldn't have, should he?'

'I know – I know. But...'

'So where's your pass?'

'No, you see, the other guy...'

'WHERE'S YOUR BLOODY PASS?!'

'I don't have one.'

'You don't have a pass?'

'No.'

'YOU'VE BEEN IN THE BUILDING WITHOUT A PASS?'

'Yes, but...'

'BUT NOTHING! SONNY! You need a pass to go in there! OK! O-BLOODY-K?'

'Yes, OK, OK.'

'No. It's not OK! You're not hearing me, are you!? You don't have a pass, you've been in that building – you're dead!'

'I'm sorry... !'

'You're going to be more than sorry!'

'But?'

'But what?!'

'The cigarettes?'

'Cigarettes.'

'Yes.'

'You went in to buy some cigarettes.'

'For the guy who was here before.'

'OK. So let's have a think,' he said. 'Let's have a bloody think. If my superiors were to hear about this, I could be in deep, deep dodo. You understand? Letting kids wander in and out of a space that's strictly off limits, don't look good, do it? Eh? Don't look good. Do you know who's in there, sonny?'

'No idea,' I lied.

'Well, if you did, I'd probably have to shoot you!'

I could see he was beginning to enjoy himself.

'Look,' I said. 'I don't suppose you could give these to your mate.'

'What makes you think he's my mate? Eh?'

'Nothing. I just meant...'

'WHAT? YOU JUST MEANT WHAT?'

'You know...'

'No. I don't know. Suppose you tell me.'

'Look, I'm sorry. I didn't mean... You know... the other guy. I just meant the guy that was here before.'

He just stood sucking his bottom lip in and out and rocking slightly. Then suddenly he said, 'Here, give me the bloody things. Right, now piss off. Piss of out of here and don't go doing nobody any more bloody favours!'

'Thanks,' I said. 'Thanks.' And I hurried off to where I'd parked the buggies, collected the sports bag with the coat in it, and kept going. I could hear the baying of the hounds, but what were my chances of reaching the kennels without being stopped again?

CHAPTER 22

Between the golf course at the back of the lodge and the open parkland at the front, there were gardens that were sort of Japanese-y, flowering shrubs and maples with soft feathery leaves – reds, yellows, and greens. Little gravel paths ran between the bushes. I chose a path that I guessed would take me towards the kennels, and as soon as I was in amongst the shrubbery and out of view of the guards by the lodge, I broke into a run, my feet scrunching on the deep gravel. The paths weren't straight but wound around like paths in a maze, meeting and crossing other paths, forcing me to stop frequently to listen for the sound of the dogs.

The paths led to a gateway in the centre of a high conifer hedge that hid everything that lay beyond the bottom of the garden. Guessing that the gateway would be covered by a security camera, I squeezed through the hedge where the foliage had died back and thinned. On the other side of the hedge was a chain-link fence enclosing some open ground and a long, low, concrete block building. There were no doors or windows on this side of the building, so I followed the fence around to the other side. Now I could see that the building was divided into a series of cages each with a wire mesh door that opened into the surrounding exercise area.

There were five or six big, long-legged deerhounds in all but the last two cages. The second last cage seemed to be empty. The last cage contained three Alsatians. These three huge dogs were going crazy, barking and snarling, jerking at their chains, the ends of which were somehow tethered in the empty cage. Every so often one of the dogs would hurl itself, with all its weight, towards the back corner of the cage, only to be brought up short by its chain that sprung, taut and quivering, into the air, making the whole cage jangle. Each time this happened, it would set all that other dogs in the kennels barking.

There was too little light to see to the back of the cage, but I didn't need to see to know that it was the three children that the dogs were trying to reach.

Above a gate in the outer fence was a camera that faced inwards towards the kennels. The camera panned slowly backwards and forwards along the entire length of the building.

From the kennels to the edge of the forest was no more than twenty metres. I quickly crossed the open space and hid in the undergrowth where I could watch the kennels and think what to do next. My white caddy's overall now seemed rather conspicuous. I stripped it off, put the green, waxed coat from the bag back on, and tucked the overall and bag out of sight.

I had hidden only just in time. Two men came around the fence and entered the enclosure. One of them was Jake; the other was a uniformed FIST officer. They stopped in front of the last cage. The dogs seemed to become even more incensed and their barking, louder and as rapid as machine-gun fire as they leapt about at the ends of their chains. I could hear the men laughing.

Then the men went into the empty cage. They bent over something on the floor. A moment later, a piercing shriek ripped through the noise of the barking dogs. A chill nausea flushed through my whole body. I waited for more cries, but no more came. The two men left the cage and sauntered back towards me.

'If they still insist on not talking, what do you reckon, we shut one of them in with the dogs and let the other two watch?' asked Jake.

'What? Take the chains off?'

'Yeah. Let the dogs have a go at one of them. That'd get the others talking.'

'Which do you reckon? The girl or the little kid?'

'Now, that's an interesting question.... Yeah, interesting.... I favour the girl.'

'Nah. I reckon the little kid. The girl would talk to save the little kid. That's what girls are like'.

'You could be right. Yeah, you could be right. Maybe you should have been a psychologist.'

'Maybe I should!'

They went off around the fence, laughing.

I wanted to kill. I hated them. The anger that boiled in my head made it impossible to think. I gripped the ground, digging my fingers into the mud, forcing myself to calm down.

Right. How long did I have before they came back? No way of knowing. I'd just have to work as fast as possible. I unclipped the shoulder strap from the carryall; then crossed to the gate and, scrambling up the wire mesh, got a leg over the top. Balanced on top of the gate, gripping with my knees, I slipped the loop at one end of the shoulder strap over the end of the camera, taking care not to obscure the lens. I allowed the motor drive to complete one pan of the building and then clipped the free end of the belt to the mesh so that the camera could no longer pan beyond half way along. I figured that so long as the camera was still showing the kennels, the guards might take a while to notice that there was anything wrong. What they mustn't see for the next few minutes were the end two cages.

I dropped down on the inside of the fence and ran to the kennels. The three children were huddled in the back of the last cage, pressed together into a corner to keep just beyond the reach of the snapping, slathering mouths of the enormous dogs.

The wire mesh doors on the fronts of the cages were bolted, but they weren't locked. My first thought was to slide back the bolt on the cage and let the children out, but I quickly saw they'd never get past the dogs. Instead, I opened the cage next to them and stepped in. As soon as the dogs heard the rattle of the door, they threw themselves at the wire that separated the cages. Standing on their hind legs, their heads were level with mine. Black lips drawn back, ears flat against their skulls, they tore with their teeth at the mesh between us. The dogs' chains ran through the mesh wall to a ring fastened to the floor of the cage I was in. A short steel bar pushed through the links of the chains secured them to the ring. Jake and his vicious mate could adjust the length of the chains by pulling out the bar, letting more chain run through the ring and then sticking the bar back through the chain links.

Quickly, I seized the chains. With the dogs trying to get at me, the chains were slack. I yanked them through the ring, pulled out the steel bar, and thrust it back through the links closest to the ring. Now the dogs found themselves held tightly against the wire. They twisted and turned, jerking back against their collars, trying to get their heads free. Owando, the girl and small boy still cowered in the corner, clinging to each other, eyes wide, not daring for a moment to shift their attention from the dogs. I ran from the cage. I pulled back the bolt on the last cage and flung the door open.

'Come on!' I screamed. 'Run! *Run!*' Still they clung together in the corner, eyes wild with fear and disbelief. '*Run!* You can get past the dogs!' But they didn't move. Next moment I was in the cage, grabbing Owando by the wrist. His wrists, I noticed, were no longer fastened together. Then I saw the chewed remains of the plastic cable ties on the ground. Like captive animals, they'd gnawed through each other's bonds. 'Run!' I ordered, 'Run!' as I pulled with all my strength. He cried out in pain. I was pulling him by the arm that the hound had bitten. The blood was dry and black on his sleeve, but I didn't let go. At last, they began to move, clumsy and stumbling, tripping over their own feet – but we were past the dogs, out of the cage, staggering across the enclosure. 'Come on!' I kept urging, 'Come on!'

The outer gate was locked, but we climbed over it. When Owando's feet hit the ground on the other side, he seemed to come to life. He looked left and right, like someone who has just woken up, wondering where he was. 'This way!' he called and plunged into the forest.

As we pounded after Owando, the certainty of what would happen next hit me. Jake and friend would find the kids had escaped and would let out the hounds. Even with a head start, there was no way we could outrun the dogs. Owando must know that too. Had he got a plan? Where was he leading us? I could hear the dogs' mad barking, but so far it didn't seem to be getting nearer. Then there was another sound. The unmistakeable clatter and roar of a helicopter taking off. The Prime Minister must be leaving. The attention of everyone up at the lodge would be distracted for the next few minutes. It would give us a bit of time. Not much. But a bit.

By now, it was late in the afternoon and quite dark under the trees. We ran with our hands up, trying to guard our faces from the branches that whipped past. Roots caught at our feet as we jumped and ducked and dodged – Owando running ahead, then the girl, and the small boy, with me bringing up the rear.

Suddenly, Owando stopped. We halted, panting, beside him.

'You swim?' he asked, looking at me.

'Swim? Yes,' I said.

He turned and pushed aside the low branches, and I saw rushing water.

'Quick. Give me his coat.'

The girl stripped the long coat off the small boy and handed it, without a word, to Owando.

'We all hold the coat. Stay together. No one drown.'

I looked down at the black, roiling water of the swollen stream and shuddered. Now I could see Owando's plan. It was either this, or be torn apart by the dogs.

'Everyone hold!' Owando commanded.

We each gripped the coat. I was between Owando and the girl. Her teeth were clenched and her hands were shaking, her face and neck bloody and bruised from the dog bites.

'We count three!... One...' he started.

'Two,' we joined in. 'Three!' And we threw ourselves into the stream. Immediately, we were in the grip of the current. The water, deep and cold. Each clung to the coat with one hand, legs kicking and free hand paddling madly to keep heads above water as we were swept downstream.

Occasionally, our feet touched the stony bottom, we crashed into boulders, and our clothes snagged on the branches of sunken logs, but we stayed together, pulling each other free and tumbling together down cataracts clinging to the sodden coat. As the stream swung round a bend, we staggered out on to a gravely spit on the opposite side of the water from the one that we had entered. The dogs would track us to the stream, but they wouldn't know where we had left it, and it would take them time to pick up our scent. It was almost totally dark now. Perhaps they'd even give up looking for us until the morning, but that was probably wishful thinking.

The small boy crumpled in a heap on the gravelly ground. The girl dropped down beside him. 'Abuja? Are you hurt?'

The only reply was a muffled sob. The terror of the past twelve hours, the cold, the river, and the fear of being caught again – it was all too much for him.

'Abuja,' the girl urged, 'get up. You have to get up.' She tugged at him, but he pulled away from her and rolled into a tight ball.

'We must go,' Owando said firmly.

'He won't. I tell him, but he won't.'

'Abuja, get up!' ordered Owando. But the boy didn't move except to curl even more tightly as though trying to disappear into himself.

Owando turned and walked into the darkness.

I could hear the baying of the hounds, and now the sound was definitely getting nearer. I prayed they were still on the other side of the water.

The girl bent and tried again to haul Abuja to his feet. She looked up desperately and in the darkness her eyes shone, pleading. I squatted beside Abuja and got one arm under his. Together the girl and I forced Abuja up on to his feet and, half carrying him, we followed Owando.

CHAPTER 23

At first, that night, we followed a smaller watercourse, walking in the water as much as we could to make it difficult for the dogs to pick up our scent and to leave no footprints. Our clothes were wet and heavy. I was cold and very hungry, and my many bruises from the boulders in the stream were beginning to stiffen. I was sure the others must feel the same, but Owando never slowed his pace except when we came to fallen trees with piles of driftwood caught in their branches that had been washed down the gully we were climbing in the frequent storms when this little stream must become a raging torrent. We clambered over or round these obstacles and continued on and up.

No one spoke; we needed all our energy to keep going, except once, when Owando was scouting a way around a big pile of debris, the girl asked, 'Why do you help us?'

'I'm looking for my friend – for Ashanti,' I said.

'We rob you in the car.'

'Yes,' I said.

'And now you save us,' she said it as if it were a puzzle she couldn't figure out.

'You're the one they call Sarayova,' I said.

'Yes.'

'From Turkey.'

'Yes.'

Neither of us said anything else, and soon Owando was beckoning to us to follow.

Near the top of the hill, we reached the source of the stream, an area of boggy peat that sucked our feet down into its black ooze. Owando turned off on to drier ground and led us around the rocky crown of the hill, keeping below the skyline.

How Owando knew where he was going was a mystery to me. We followed no paths and whenever we came to an old road or lane we crossed it as quickly as possible. Maybe he navigated by the pale glow of the moon that showed from time to time through the trees. It was as though he held a map of all of North Devon in his head.

Sometime after midnight, we scrambled over a moss-covered stone wall and dropped down into long grass. In front of us, half buried in tangles of brambles and weeds, were rows mobile homes. An abandoned caravan park.

'We can rest here,' Owando announced.

We made our way between the rows. Many of the windows were smashed and doors hung open. Here and there, amongst the weeds, were plastic buckets and spades, and concrete gnomes still grinned stupidly by the steps to several cabins.

Sites like this were usually near the sea, so I figured we must be close to the North Devon coast.

Orange gas cylinders stood beside many of the trailers, and as we passed them, Owando rocked them to test their weight.

'Here,' he said, 'this one is good.' He turned on the gas tap on the top of the cylinder and then went into the trailer, and we all followed. We stood shivering in our damp clothes, listening to the rattle of draws being opened and searched in the dark and then the click, click of a lighter. Suddenly, Owando's face appeared like a glowing blue mask over a gas flame. He lit all four burners on the cooker, then opened the oven and lit that as well, leaving the oven door open. The rest of us crowded around the cooker, trying to draw the warmth from the flames into our tired bodies.

'Maybe some food,' Owando said, and he was gone.

How does he do that? How does he keep going? I'm ready to drop and this half-starved ten year-old (well, that's what I'm guessing his age is) keeps on going. Not only keeps going, he's taking care of the rest of us.

I looked around the trailer in the light from the gas flames. The part we are in was a sort of kitchen, dining, and living room. There were kitchen units and cupboards, a couple of kitchen stools, a table with padded bench seats on each side, and then a sitting area with a small settee, two armchairs, and a sunlounger. There was a partition with doors in it that I guessed led to bedrooms and the bathroom. Sarayova opened one of these doors and went through. She returned moments later with a blanket, and Abuja allowed her to peal off his wet clothes and wrap him in it; then she led him over to the settee, where he lay down and seemed to fall asleep immediately. She went back to the bedroom and was gone a little longer. When she returned, she too was wrapped in a blanket and carrying her wet clothes.

'Better to be dry,' she said. She stood holding the clothes, looking for somewhere to hang them. I stared at her moronically; then it occurred to my exhausted brain that perhaps I should help her.

'Just a minute,' I said, 'I'll see if I can find some string or something.' I searched the draws and cupboards and found a length of cord. Climbing on the furniture, I managed to tie it to a window catch on one side of the room and a coat hook on the other. I took the clothes from her and hung hers and Abuja's over my improvised clothesline.

'You too?' she asked.

'Yeah, 'spose I should.'

'There are blankets,' she pointed to the other room.

'Yeah – Thanks – I'll go and look.'

There were two bedrooms, one with a double bed and one with bunk beds. The beds were damp and looked like various things had nested on them, but when I felt around in a cupboard in the double room, I found some blankets that were pretty dry and only a bit smelly. I was suddenly embarrassed by the idea of taking my clothes off, but I told myself not to be stupid. Still, I kept my boxers on. And I had to admit that the musty blanket was a lot warmer than my wet clothes.

On the way back to the living room, I checked out the little bathroom. It was very dark and stank of mould. In the cupboard under the basin, there were toilet rolls that had swollen up to twice their size with the damp. I pushed them aside and reached behind them. There was a box, and it felt the right size. 'Yeah! Good people!' I thought. I pulled the box out and took it next door to examine in the light from the cooker. Green with a white cross on the lid, one of those standard issue first-aid kits. I placed it proudly on the table. Sarayova looked at it, nodded approvingly, and gave me a smile that her damaged cheek made lopsided.

Owando came back while I was hanging up my clothes.

'You start a laundry!' he said, looking up. Then dumped a box full of tins on the table. 'Now we eat!'

Many of the tins had lost their labels, and we had no idea what was in them until we opened them, but we found beans, tomatoes, sausages, pears, something that might have been steak and kidney or possibly pet food, peas, and tinned pineapple. We mixed together the tomatoes, the beans, and sausages in a big saucepan and put it on the cooker to heat up. I persuaded Owando not to include the meat in case it was dog food, but he ate it anyway straight from the tin and declared it 'first quality!' Meanwhile, Sarayova and I ate the fruit and drank the juice.

Owando showed no interest in changing out of his wet clothes until after we had eaten. He stood by the cooker, a thin steam rising from whichever side of his body he turned towards the heat so that he looked like a pint-sized magician in a halo of smoke, stirring the bubbling pot, his dark skin shining in the blue gaslight. Sarayova found some candles, lit them, and stood them in saucers on the table. I drew the drooping, stained curtains across the windows so that the light wouldn't show from the outside. Then, when the food was hot, Sarayova woke Abuja and brought him to the table. She did it very gently, kneeling beside the settee, talking to him softly, and letting the little boy lean his head against her as they crossed the room. *Perhaps*, I thought, *she has a little brother or sister of her own somewhere.* I guessed she was about the same age as me, and Abuja no more than six, but these kids were all so skinny it was hard to tell.

We found bowls and spoons, ladled out the food and ate with silent determination. No food had ever tasted so good! If I burnt my mouth, I didn't care. It heated my body from the inside like I'd lit a fire in my belly, and it was warming my blood. I could feel it coursing up through my chest and down through my legs like a golden glow, driving out the chill and spreading a contented happiness.

When we had eaten all we could, we just sat and stared into space, no one even had the energy to speak. Abuja curled up on the bench seat beside Sarayova, his head resting in her lap, and she combed her fingers through his tangled mat of hair, teasing out bits of twig and burrs.

'Do you think it's safe to stay here?' I asked, after the question had been circling in my head for five or ten minutes.

Owando shrugged, 'They never come here before.'

'Will the dogs track us?'

He shook his head. 'No. Or they come already.'

We went back to staring into space. The first-aid kit was lying on the table. I knew we needed to treat the dog bites on Sarayova's neck and Owando's arm, but I didn't know how bad they were, and I really wasn't keen to look. I felt my eyes starting to close. We could leave it 'till the morning. Weren't we all too tired? But what if they became infected? What if they got sick? Better to face it now. I opened the box. It looked like it had never been used. There were sealed packets containing disposable gloves, sterile dressings, antiseptic wipes, bandages, plasters, a roll of tape, a tube of ointment, and a pair of scissors.

I looked at the dark crusted blood on Owando's sleeve. 'Let me see your arm,' I said.

'It isn't bad.'

'Owando,' said Sarayova, 'show him your arm.'

For a moment, the tough street-kid was gone, and I saw a nervous little boy who refuses to go to the doctor. He didn't want to know how bad his wound was any more than I did. He stood up and reluctantly took off his grubby nylon jacket. Under it was a sweatshirt. He pulled it over his head and got his left arm out of its sleeve, but the right sleeve had stuck to the open wound.

'We'll need some water,' I said. His arm was a mess, and looking at it made me feel sick. I was glad to have an excuse to turn to the sink. But the sink tap only produced a rusty trickle. I took a candle and a small saucepan and went into the bathroom. The bathroom taps didn't work either. The water supply must have been turned off. I took the lid off the toilet cistern. It was still full of water, but it would need to be boiled. I dipped the saucepan and filled it and, returning to the living room, put it on the stove. Then I fetched another blanket and gave it to Owando to wrap himself in while we waited for the water to boil and cool. I could dress Sarayova's wounds in the meantime.

I glanced at Sarayova, and she dropped her eyes. Dealing with Owando's arm might make me feel faint, but the thought of touching Sarayova's neck made me embarrassed and awkward.

'Your turn for the doctor,' I said, trying to sound nonchalant. She looked up and then easing Abuja's head off her lap, slid to the end of the bench seat, tipped her head to one side and pushed her long, dark hair out of the way. I moved the candle closer to get better light and sat on a stool next to her. The dog's mouth had closed over the back of her neck, its front teeth biting into her jaw, but the hunters had driven it off before if had a chance to shake its head. There were puncture marks, some gouging and a lot of bruising. I watched the pulsing of the artery, so near the surface, and forced myself not to think what would have happened if the dog's teeth had torn deeper through the soft skin. I put on the gloves, took a deep breath, opened the wipes, and began to clean up the lines of bloody holes. She winced occasionally, but didn't make a sound. The deepest wounds were on her neck. I dressed these with the sterile dressings and taped them into place. I put antiseptic ointment on the ones on her face and left them uncovered.

There was a small, recently healed wound on her upper left arm, just below the shoulder that looked like it might be infected. I'd noticed an identical one on Owando's arm.

'What happened here?' I asked.

'The guards, they put a microchip in our arm for identity. We cut them out when we escape.'

'Bloody hell! Isn't that what they do to animals?'

'That's what they think we are.'

I put some ointment on the little cut. 'Best I can do,' I said.

'Thank you,' she said, easing her neck and then rearranging her hair. 'You are a good doctor.'

'I wish,' I said.

I checked the temperature of the water. It was cool enough to use. Owando and Sarayova changed places, and Owando laid his damaged arm on the table. He didn't look at me.

Sarayova stood beside me as I worked, moving the candles when I needed more light, soaking swabs and passing them to me and helping to ease the bits of fabric out of the wound. Her being there and the need to concentrate steadied me, but it was a huge relief when we had the arm dressed and bandaged, and I no longer had to look at the ugly, torn flesh.

I went outside to empty the saucepan and retched. I stayed to breathe the cool air and wait for my nausea to pass.

When I came back, Abuja was asleep on the bench on one side of the table, and Owando was rolled in his blanket lying on the other. His eyes were closed, but I wasn't sure if he was actually asleep. It was still warm in the room, though someone had turned off the cooker. Sarayova was on the settee, so that left me with the sunlounger.

'Do you mind?' she asked as I tested it.

'No. I could sleep anywhere,' I said.

I blew out the candles and shifted about, trying to find a position that didn't press on a bruise. There was rather too much furniture in the room for the limited space, so the lounger was only about a foot from the settee, and I was dead certain I was disturbing Sarayova every time I turned over. But soon I drifted off.

I was woken by screams and shouts. I thought *Oh my God! They've found us! The dogs are in the room! Someone's being attacked!*

But when I sat up, all I saw was Sarayova crouching by Abuja. Again I heard her talking to him gently, soothing, calming. His cries died down, and she returned to the settee.

'Is he OK?'

'He has nightmares… Many of us do.'

'You?'

'Yes.'

After a short silence, she said, 'They catch him twice.'

'Abuja? How do you mean?'

'Once when they take his parents away. Then we get him out and find people who will look after him. But they are arrested, and he is back in Holdstone. Now we get him out again, but you see how he is. I think something is broken... inside... you know what I mean.'

'It's hardly surprising. He seems... well... He's much too little for all of this.'

'Is anyone big enough?'

I waited, but when she didn't say anything else, I asked, 'Why did you come here, to England?'

'I thought it would be safe.'

'From what?'

'First there were droughts, then the fires came. Everything burnt. Everything. The forests, our house, the animals – everything. There was not a leaf left.'

There was a long pause, then she said, 'And it used to be so beautiful.'

She was quiet for a while, and I thought maybe she'd gone to sleep, but then she said, 'There was a stream.... When I was little, there was a stream near our house. We used to go – all of us – my family, our neighbours – down the mountain. We used to take food and play by the stream... Our stream. Then the stream dried up.... Then the fires.... Then the fighting.'

She was quiet again.

'And now this,' I said.

'And now this.'

I reached over and found her hand in the little gap between the lounger and the settee. Perhaps she reached out at the same moment. Anyway, we stayed like that for a few minutes; then she let my hand go and drew hers in under her blanket.

'Owando says you are called Mark.'

'That's right. But I suppose you ought to call me London.'

'London?'

'It's where I come from – You know – like they call you Sarayova because that's the name of your town.' Then I had to laugh.

'What's funny?' she asked.

'Well, you could call me Wapping!'

'Wapping?'

'I'm sorry. I'm being silly. It's the bit of London where our flat was – before the flood.'

'You had a flood?'

'You didn't know?'

'No.'

'Wow! That's amazing! I thought everyone knew. Yeah, half of London was flooded. Lots of people died. We lost our flat – all our stuff. It was really bad.'

'So – you are like us – No home.'

'Yeah.' Then I thought about it. 'No. It's different. We had places we could go. Friends to stay with. People who would look after us.'

'You were lucky.'

'Yeah.'

'My name is Rana. That's my real name. But, only when no one listens. You understand?'

'Yeah. Sure.'

'We should sleep.'

'I guess so.'

'Goodnight, Dr London.'

Then I thought there was a muffled giggle.

'Goodnight, Rana.'

But I don't go to sleep straight away.

She's so close I can hear her breathing. *Rana.* I say her name in my head, trying to remember how she said it. I picture the way she tilted her head and swept her heavy, black hair aside. I want to reach out again and find her hand. But I don't. And there are loads of things I want to ask, like what's happening with Casablanca? And how come she and Abuja aren't with the others? And where are they keeping Ashanti?

But I must have fallen asleep in the end, and when I woke, it was broad daylight, and the other three were up and dressed.

CHAPTER 24

'Good morning, Dr London,' Owando was standing over me with a big grin on his face, holding a steaming mug of something. 'Real English tea?' he asked.

'Tea? Yeah! Thanks!' – 'But where did you get the water?' I asked, as I sat up and took the mug.

'Big water tank by one of these places.'

I looked around the trailer. Sarayova was sorting through a pile of clothes on the floor. There was a second first-aid kit on the table, more tins of food had appeared, plus a few jars, packets, and bottles and a collection of bags and carryalls.

'You've been busy!' I said.

'Owando and I, we look in all the other places,' explained Sarayova. 'Now we must choose what we take. Everything left, we hide here for when we are back.'

The tea was hot, black, very sweet, and just what I needed.

'Look, Abuja! For you!' Sarayova held up a small, hooded anorak. Abuja, at the table, looked up and then went back to spooning honey out of a jar into his mouth and sucking the spoon, his face worryingly blank, like something inside him had shut down.

Owando, who was making breakfast, had found a replacement for his torn and bloodstained jacket amongst the scavenged clothes, and Sarayova was now wearing a yellow sweatshirt that said 'University of East Anglia' across the back. It was a little big, and she had rolled up the sleeves revealing the words 'English Villages' tattooed on her left forearm.

'You worked here,' I said.

She looked up to meet my stare and glanced down at her arm. 'Yes, I had papers when I come – Forged – But they catch me.' She continued sorting through the clothes.

Over a breakfast of more tinned sausages and beans, I asked what the plan was. Turned out we hadn't far to go. Casablanca had made his base in a wrecked ship in Combe Martin, about five kilometres from where we were now. Owando suggested that he and Sarayova scout out the situation while Abuja and I wait in the trailer park. But Abuja set up a little moaning noise, rocking backwards and forwards until Sarayova put her arms around him and told him it was all right and she wasn't going to leave him. So although Owando was clearly not happy about it, it was decided that we would all go.

In my new role of doctor, I re-dressed Owando's arm and Sarayova's neck. I found it helped to think about Rainer and Jake as I swabbed and bandaged. Hating those two scumbags distracted me from feeling queasy. When I was done with the others, I strapped up the broken blisters on my own feet, then packed the first-aid kits and some bottles of water into a shoulder bag that had held someone's fishing tackle in the days when there were still fish to catch. There was a roll of fishing line with a lead weight and a hook on one end and a fishing knife in the bag; I thought they might come in handy for something, so I left them in there.

Owando and Sarayova packed enough food for a day and some spare clothes, and we were ready to leave; the idea being that, once we had released Ashanti and the other leaders Casablanca was holding, we would come back to the trailer. Quite how we were going spring the prisoners from their gaol we weren't sure.

As we set off, the sun was shining and a blackbird was singing somewhere nearby. The events of the days before seemed like a long, bad dream that I'd just woken out of, or something that I heard about but had happened to a different bunch of kids. I found myself struggling to believe that the business with Casablanca was anything more than some sort of game. It was simply too nice a day for anything bad to happen. Owando was in the lead as usual, with Sarayova following holding Abuja's hand and, to see them, you might have thought they were off on a picnic.

The trees around the holiday park were old and tall with plenty of space between them, so the going was quite easy, but after the first half hour, the trees became more stunted and the undergrowth thicker so that we had to force our way through bushes that scratched our faces and caught our clothing. Another half an hour and the trees gave way to gorse, rough grass and bracken as we came out on to a high bluff that fell away steeply to the blue, wrinkled sea that stretched away into the hazy distance under a blue sky. With no wind, it was hot in the open, and the air was full of the coconut smell of gorse. To the west, the coast swung in and out of rocky bays with deep, forested valleys running back from little inlets into hills behind. We followed Owando through the tall bracken to the cliff edge, where we squatted and watched seagulls sail through the giddy space below us.

At first, the only sounds we heard were the calls of the gulls and the slow rhythm of the waves breaking on the rocks below. Then a new sound emerged, a hum that grew steadily louder. Owando glanced up and then he was pushing us back into the densest clump of bracken. 'Down! Keep down! No moving!'

The sound was definitely coming from high above us. Like someone was flying around in lawnmower! From where I lay, I peered up through the green fronds. I could only see small areas of blue sky. Slowly, across one of these patches, an oval shape, like a miniature airship was making its way. A drone! One of FIST's unmanned patrol aircraft. I knew there were loads of them over the south coast. They are like flying CCTV cameras, some armed with small missile launchers. They use them to spot the boats that the smugglers use to bring illegals into the country. But I never knew they had them up here!

Gradually, the sound receded and died away.

'OK. Safe now,' Owando said, and we all returned to the cliff edge.

'Are there many of those?' I asked.

'No, not here,' Owando said. 'I never see them here before.'

'Maybe they look for us,' Sarayova suggested in a worried voice.

'Surely they wouldn't waste the money,' I said, not wanting her to be right.

'Ba-da! Ba-da! Ba-da! Ba-da! Boooom!' Abuja mimed shooting the drone out of the sky.

'The ship is this way.' Owando pointed west. 'Casablanca will have lookouts, but they don't look out to sea, so we come from the water.'

'How?' I demanded.

'We go down.' He pointed over the cliff.

'That's mad!' I said. 'We can't get down there!'

'I know a way.'

'What about Abuja? Can he get down?' Sarayova asked.

Owando shrugged. 'He have to.'

Owando led us around a large boulder that seemed so precariously balanced that the slightest push should send it crashing down the cliff face. On the other side of the rock, a narrow ravine had been carved into the cliff by a stream that still ran down it. This slippery gully was Owando's idea of a way down.

'Are you serious?' I asked.

There were a few stunted and twisted trees in the gully, but apart from those, there didn't seem to be anything to hang on to.

'You don't like – you stay here,' he replied. 'I only got one and half hands. You got two.' (There were times when I could have kicked him!)

Without waiting for any further objections from the rest of us, Owando slithered down to the first tree root, and we had no alternative but to follow. Roots and protruding bits of stone acted like a sort of ladder. Below us, the sea rocked and swayed so that, if I looked down for even a second, the whole cliff seemed to be on the move, and I was forced to cling where I was until the world stopped swinging. Above me, Abuja dislodged a stone, and I felt the wind of it as it hurtled past my head and went bounding and crashing down the ravine until it ricocheted off a boulder, arced out into space and fell from sight.

The ravine ended on a ledge two-thirds of the way down the cliff but still a dizzying height above the sea. The ledge was two metres wide, certainly no more, and wet and slippery where the stream ran across it to trickle over the edge and be swept away in a rainbow of droplets by the wind.

Hugging the cliff, I followed Owando along the ledge, trying not to look at the waves rolling in and out below us. After a few metres, we came to a deep fissure in the rock face. Owando climbed into the crack and, pressing his back against the rock on one side and his feet against the other, he eased himself down. One by one, we copied him. The crack narrowed towards the bottom, but we were able to clamber the rest of the way down to the foot of the cliff over the tumbled slabs of an ancient rock-fall.

We stood at the bottom, rubbing our chafed elbows and looking up at the folded face of the cliff that we'd just climbed down.

'Now we must be careful,' said Owando.

'What the hell do you think I was doing up there?' I couldn't help asking. But Owando shhed me. 'Casablanca's ship around this headland. Maybe he has guards on the rocks. But there is a cave where we hide and look.'

Again, our little party set out in single file, jumping from rock to rock. Every now and then, we were doused by the spray of breaking waves, and I wondered if Owando knew whether the tide was coming in or going out. Were we going to come back this way? I hoped not.

The end of the headland looked as though it had split and a huge chunk of it slipped into the sea, leaving a V-shaped gap filled with a chaotic pile of stone slabs, each as big as a house. We climbed through this gap, going around and sometimes under the slabs, and then we saw the ship!

Owando had kept on mentioning Casablanca's ship. But knowing it was there didn't prepare me for the reality of seeing it! Ships out of the water look a lot bigger than ships in the water. Well, obviously there is a lot more to be seen when half of the ship isn't under the surface. But a ship sitting in the middle of a small town looks positively monstrous! And that's exactly what we were now looking at.

The village of Combe Martin had been abandoned long ago when the rising sea inundated the waterfront properties and the storms carried the beach up into the village, choking the lanes, caving in the doors and windows of shops and houses, and filling them full of sand and shingle. Then, in what must have been the mother of all storms, a ship had been driven ashore by the sea and dumped in the middle of what had probably been the high street! All right, it wasn't like a gigantic cruise liner, but it was a genuine, proper ship. Some sort of cargo boat with the cabins and the bridge-deck towards the back – And there it was, towering above the roofs of the shops and cottages, its huge propeller and rudder hanging over the edge of what remained of the seawall.

There must once have been a hotel down on the seafront, but the ship had ploughed through the middle of it, leaving a heap of rubble on each side, and other, smaller buildings that had stood in its path were now crushed beneath it.

It was hard to tell how long the ship had been sitting there in the middle of the town. Sand, driven by the wind and sea, had scoured most of the paint off ship's sides, leaving them streaked with orange rust, and her name, 'Pride of Oban', was only just readable across her stern. But she hadn't started to break up, perhaps, because she had been driven so far ashore when she first arrived, she was out of reach of all but the biggest storm waves.

Owando signalled that we should keep down amongst the boulders and to follow him into a small opening at the base of the cliff. Once inside, the cave opened out into a large cavern with a second cave mouth higher up, through which a shaft of light entered and reflected off a rock pool in the floor of the cave so that lines of light flickered across the walls.

'Wow!' I couldn't help exclaiming, and my voice echoed round the chamber.

'Ahhhh!' sang Abuja, trying out the echo for himself.

'Shh!' Owando scowled at us, placing the thumb of his fingerless right hand across his lips. 'We wait for night. But we can watch from there,' he pointed to the second opening.

I climbed on to the tumble of rocks below the second opening. Standing on the top of the pile, the lip of the cave mouth was level with my chest so that it was like looking out a natural window. Sarayova climbed up beside me. Leaning on the ledge below the opening, we had a good view of the ship, the houses around it, and the forested hill behind. Like the bluff that we had just climbed down from, the forest on the hill across the valley gave way to grass and bracken as it approached the sea cliff. For a moment, I thought I saw the silhouette of a figure break the skyline. I glanced at Sarayova. She nodded, 'I see him too,' she said. 'They are watching.'

I could feel the warmth of her shoulder and arm against mine, at first just touching, and then we each leant slightly against the other while pretending that nothing was happening.

I watched the ship, trying to see any sign of movement. Were they really there? I couldn't see anyone on board.

'They stay out of sight in the day time,' said Sarayova as if she had read my thoughts. 'It's the rule with us. Except for lookouts. At night we hunt for food, make journeys – unless we make hijacking – Sometimes we make hijacking in the daytime.'

'Yeah,' I said, 'I know.' Which made us both laugh. Weird, I thought. Not so long ago she just stood by while her friends threatened to drop a two-ton block of concrete on top of me, and now we're laughing about it as if it was nothing.

'You still got that T-shirt you stole off me?' I asked.

'Oh!... no. Sorry. I give it away.'

'It's OK. I didn't like it much either.'

'No, it was nice T-shirt!'

'No, it was rubbish. I'd just bought it because...' And then, whoa! I remembered the flat and the flood and everything that had happened in London and being on the road with Jerzy, and everything since – It all poured into my head, like I'd been travelling so fast, it had only just caught up with me.

'Are you OK?' Sarayova was holding my arm and trying to look into my face.

'Yeah,' I said, 'but maybe I ought to sit down for a bit.'

I climbed back down to the floor of the cave and Sarayova followed.

Abuja was dropping shells and pebbles into the rock pool, and Owando was lying on a patch of dry sand, his head cradled on one arm, resting.

Sarayova and I sat next to each other, our backs against the cave wall and watched Abuja trying to make an empty limpet shell float on the surface of the pool. He was completely absorbed in what he was doing. *Just a little kid playing at the seaside* I thought.

'Why didn't you join Casablanca and his lot?' I asked.

'He wants to be a gang leader. He wants to fight. He wants guns. He says the British need to be taught a lesson.'

'And you? You don't think that?'

'I've seen fighting.'

'At home, you mean.'

'At home.' And I heard the bitterness in her voice.

She breathed out and then breathed in quickly and her breath shook.

'I've seen what people do when they get guns.'

I didn't want her to say any more because now I could see the raw pain on her face, and I knew something awful was coming. She looked down and then said very quietly, 'They shot my parents.'

'Who did?' It was the shock. I didn't mean to ask.

When she answered, I could hardly hear her. There was disbelief, there was betrayal and grief – Like an awful secret, she whispered, 'Our neighbours.'

Then she looked at me like she wanted the horror of it explained. The colour had drained from her face.

'Our neighbours,' she said again.

I was staring at her, not knowing what to do or what to say when Abuja suddenly flung himself at me from across the cave, kicking, hitting, screaming, 'Get away! She doesn't want you! Get away! Get away! She doesn't want you!'

I scrambled sideways trying to dodge the flailing feet and fists, but he was on to me again like a deranged windmill, all flying arms and legs.

'Hey!' I said. 'Hey!... Hey! Stop!... It's OK! It's OK!'

Owando was on his feet. He tried to grab Abuja, but he ducked under his arm and threw himself at me again, lashing out furiously. Owando got a hand over Abuja's mouth to silence him, but Abuja bit him making Owando yelp and snatch his hand away. Then Sarayova was there, and she had her arms tightly around Abuja, pinning his own arms to his sides, and she was talking to him all the time in that quiet, gentle way. Gradually he stopped struggling. She knelt and drew him down into her, letting him bury his head in her chest as she burrowed her face into his hair, her words becoming a crooning song as she rocked the two of them back and forwards.

Owando looked at them and shook his head. He examined the red bite mark on his hand. Then climbed up to look out of the cave mouth and see if the noise had attracted anyone's attention.

I stood where I was, stunned and confused by the sudden attack. What had I done? The kid was obviously unbalanced, but why had he gone for me? Did he think I was upsetting Sarayova? I suppose, in a way, I was. Or maybe he just didn't like anyone else getting close to her.

'I think it's time we eat something,' Sarayova said when Owando returned from cave mouth.

'Yeah, maybe it is,' I agreed. But at the sound of my voice, Abuja twisted his face away from Sarayova and glared at me.

Owando set about opening more of our tinned supplies, and we ate in silence. After that it was a question of waiting for darkness. Owando and I took turns at climbing up to the cave mouth to make sure nobody was approaching the cave and to look out for any activity on the ship. When Owando and I were changing places, I asked him how you got on to the ship.

'Look – You see ropes?' he said, pointing.

Now I saw that there were ropes and a rope ladder that hung down and across to the flat roof of one of the taller buildings close the side of the ship.

'They'll have a guard at the top of that for sure,' I said.

'We don't go that way. We use the big chain.'

'What, the anchor chain?!'

'Anchor chain,' Owando nodded.

I couldn't see the bow of the boat but could imagine the big, rusty chain hanging down. How high was the side of that ship? I looked at the buildings around it. It was higher than a three-storey building!

And we were going to climb that in the dark! Owando seemed completely unfazed by the idea. But then, think what these kids had done already: crossed seas in leaky boats, escaped from wars, found their way across whole continents, hidden in lorries, and dodged border guards, and I'd heard stories of kids hanging under cross-channel trains. What was climbing an anchor chain at night to them?

'Do you know where on the ship they've got Ashanti and the others?' I asked.

Owando shook his head, 'We have to find them.'

And so we waited. I wanted the night to come quickly. I wanted to get on with it. I wanted to get that climb over with and to face whatever we were going to have to face on the ship. But the time crawled by as it does when you have nothing to do but wait. Until at last it was dark.

CHAPTER 25

I was scared. OK? I think it was the waiting. I had had the whole afternoon to get myself well and truly freaked out.

We left the bags we had brought from the caravan park in the cave. I put the fishing knife and the nylon line in my pocket – just in case – of what, I wasn't sure.

'No time to fish,' Owando joked.

'Yeah – very funny,' I said.

It had clouded over during the afternoon, and the moon wasn't up. This pleased Owando but, as we felt our way along the rocky foreshore, I could hear the invisible breakers and I could feel their spray and I expected any minute to be swept off the rocks into the blackness of the sea.

Once we got further into the bay, the waves grew quieter; then we left them behind completely as we entered the ruined town.

The great, dark bulk of the ship loomed above us. But, instead of making straight for it, Owando took us up a side street that ran parallel to it, in which sand and shingle were mixed with the rubble of partially collapsed buildings.

In one of the more intact buildings, we saw lights moving about and heard hammering, shouts, and then a crash. Kids from the ship out foraging, I guessed. We slipped past as quickly and quietly as we could. Twice, the shadowy shapes of feral cats ran silently across our path, making me catch my breath.

We turned into a narrow alleyway. Owando put his hand on my chest to stop me and the others pressed up behind.

'Wait!' he hissed.

We waited as Owando went on. We could see him stop in the slightly lighter gap between the buildings at the end of the alley. Keeping as close to a wall as possible, he cautiously looked around the corner. Then he was beckoning to us to come on.

The bow of the ship towered up into the darkness above us, a massive anchor chain descending from a big dark hawser hole like a sightless eye, high on the side of the bow. The chain ran back along the side of the ship, disappearing under the rubble. The crew must have dropped the anchor to try to stop the ship from being driven ashore, but the ship, lifted by the huge storm waves, had dragged the anchor from the seabed.

I felt my knees turning to jelly at the thought of climbing that chain, but Owando was already sprinting across the gap between the buildings and ship's side. Sarayova, then Abuja dashed after him, leaving me still hovering at the end of the lane. I could see the dark shapes of the others. They look so small at the bottom of that shear wall of metal. Arms were frantically signalling for me to follow them, but I remained rooted to the spot.

'You have to do it,' I lectured myself. 'You can't turn back now. What about Ashanti? She's counting on you.' But I still hesitated. Then I heard sounds behind me. Voices... Laughter... Things being dragged. And I ran.

As soon as I was across the open ground between the lane and the ship, hands pulled me down behind a pile of rubble. The sounds of voices grew louder, and now I could see the flickering orange light of burning torches sending shadows leaping across the walls in the lane that we had just left. A large group of laughing, chattering children emerged. It was the foraging party. They were carrying and dragging branches, bits of furniture, floorboards, broken window frames, even doors. Their torches were made from oil-soaked rags on the ends of sticks that burned with a thick smoke, lit up by the sputtering flames. They were obviously going to build a bonfire somewhere.

At first, they were coming straight towards us, but then they turned down beside the ship and made for the half-ruined building from the top of which ropes and the rope ladder were strung across to the ship's bulwarks. The leaders of the group disappeared into the building to emerge a few moments later on the flat roof. They dropped the ends of ropes down to those waiting below. Now, more children holding torches could be seen leaning over the railing high up on the ship's side deck. They called out to their friends on the rooftop. Slowly, the boards and bits of furniture and branches began to be hauled, first to the roof of the building and then up to the deck.

We watched from our hiding place until the final bundle of firewood was on-board and the last of the foraging party had emerged on the roof of the house, climbed the rope ladder, and dropped out of sight on to the ship's deck.

'We go now,' whispered Owando and, without waiting, began to climb the anchor chain. Each link of the enormous chain was over a metre long and wider than my body. It was so heavy that Owando's weight made no impression on it. Despite his missing fingers and injured arm, he seemed to almost run up it and was soon no more than a small, dark shape moving high above us. And then he disappeared through the hole into the ship's side.

'You next, Abuja,' Sarayova said.

The little boy climbed the first few links, then stopped. 'You come!' he demanded in an anxious voice.

'Yes, Abuja, I'm come too. Just behind you,' she reassured him and began to climb, keeping a just link's distance below him.

Their journey up the chain was much slower than Owando's, and there was a desperate moment when one of Abuja's feet slipped, and I heard his cry of fright. He seemed to cling there, refusing to go on. I saw Sarayova move up so that she was holding on to the chain with her arms around his body. They stayed like that for what seemed ages. My neck ached as I waited, staring up, expecting at any moment that Abuja would lose his grip and I'd see their two bodies hurtling towards the ground. But then they began to move again and, eventually, they too disappeared through the hole.

Now it was my turn. Big flakes of rust came away on my sweating hands and stuck between my fingers as I climbed the first links.

At the bottom of the chain, where it hung beside the ship's hull, I could lean my shoulder against the side of the ship for balance, but as I got higher, the angle of the chain grew steeper until it was hanging vertically in space. If I looked up, the flakes of rust I disturbed with my hands fell into my eyes; if I looked down, I felt sick. Each big link was at right angles to the one above and below it so that it was like climbing a twisting ladder, forcing me to feel around with my foot to find each new hole. I thought I could never reach the top. Each time I looked, the distance between me and the hole hardly seemed to have changed. *The others have done it. It must be possible – The others have done it. It must be possible,* I kept telling myself over and over and over.

To hold on, I had to hook my whole forearm through each link and grip with my knees. My arms were rubbed raw, my shoulders ached, and my legs were beginning to shake. There was no comfortable way to rest. I had to keep going.

I don't know how long it really took, but it seemed like eternity. I stopped when, at last, my head was level with the hole that gaped like a giant's mouth. Below me, the chain dropped away forever into the darkness. I needed a final push from my legs to get me on top of the chain, where it entered the hole, but my legs wouldn't do it. I just didn't have the strength left.

'I can't do it,' I muttered.

'Yes, you can. You're there. You've done it. I can almost reach you.' It was Sarayova, quietly, calmly – like she spoke to Abuja.

I focused on her voice. I gathered myself. I pushed – and I was on top of the chain! I felt her hand grip my shoulder, steadying, reassuring. Now I could pull myself along the top of the chain and through the hole. A moment later, I was kneeling, shaking beside Sarayova, 'Thank you!' I whispered. 'Thank you. I didn't think I could do it.'

She put her hand over my mouth to silence me. We were at the very front of the ship, in a gap between two decks. The deck over our heads extended back along the ship, maybe fifteen metres, like a roof to protect the heavy machinery that lifted the anchors. Back beyond this forward section was the main deck and the opening for the ship's cargo hold, and beyond that, like a four-storey building on the back of the ship, the bit with all the cabins for the crew and the bridge.

I peered around in the darkness, looking for Owando and Abuja. Sarayova gave a little tug at my sleeve and pointed. They were out on the deck crouched by the coaming that ran like a low steel wall around the edge of the ship's hold. She gave my sleeve another tug and indicated with a tilt of her head that we should join them, then scurried across the deck to crouch by Abuja, and I scuttled after her. Now I could hear laughter and voices from down in the hold. Cautiously, we rose up until we could look over the top of the coaming.

Down there, in the empty hold, it was like an alien world, or a glimpse of hell! Bonfires were burning on the floor of the hold, and two whole deer were roasting, skewered on metal poles that were being turned by children, stripped to the waist, their skins a strange powdery white streaked by dark lines of sweat. Other children with the same strange white coating crouched by the fires, grilling lumps of meat on long sticks held in the flames. Others fed the fires, throwing on more wood and sending swirling columns of sparks up through the opening into the night. Knots of smaller children danced and chased each other between the bonfires while the light from the flames made the vast empty belly of the ship glow and pulse.

At first, I thought all these kids had painted themselves white. Then I saw that a white powder lay on the floor and covered the walls of the hold. The ship had been used for carrying clay. The dry dust, stirred up by the children's feet, filled the air and stuck to their skins. Some of them had even made patterns in the dust by wiping their fingers across their chests or down their cheeks so that they look as if they were wearing war paint.

The smell of roasting meat rose up to us. A rich smell that seemed to thicken the air we breathed. My stomach rumbled, and I saw Abuja wipe the saliva from his mouth with sleeve.

While we were watching the cooking fires below us, we could hear bursts of cheering and stamping coming from further along the ship. Between the hold we were above and the crew's quarters was a second cargo hold, divided from this one by a steel wall. Owando signalled that he was going to take a look. I followed him in a crouching run, around the edge of the hold, down the side deck, to the coaming around hold number two. Again, we cautiously rose up to look over the edge.

Fires burned in the corners of this hold, and the same white clay dust covered the floor. There must have been over forty kids down there, and they were standing in a tight circle, eyes glittering in the light from the fires and from the flaming torches that some held above their heads. In the centre of the ring, two figures circled each other. They were coated in white from head to foot, even their hair was caked with the clay dust, but the white coating was stained crimson with streaks of blood, and their backs were smudged and striped with the marks of hands and fingers, where they had grappled and clawed each other. Blood streamed from a split eyebrow and from a swollen lip, and there were bloody footprints in the dust on the floor.

They held their hands up like boxers, but looking at the state they were in, I guessed this fight didn't have any rules. The stamping and shouting grew louder and louder, and each time one of the fighters threw a punch or lashed out with a kick, the crowd hooted and cheered, then the smaller of the two fighters dropped his head and charged, ramming into his opponent who staggered back, winded, was caught by the crowd, and flung back into the ring with so much force that he collided with the smaller boy, and that sent them both crashing to the ground. Now he sat on top of the smaller boy, raining punches on his face, cheered on by the spectators who closed in until the two on the ground were hidden from view.

Suddenly, the shouting stopped, and the crowd moved back to reveal the familiar figure of Casablanca standing over the fighters. The larger boy was still straddling his opponent, who lay motionless under him, his face a bloody mask. Casablanca hauled the winner to his feet and lifted his arm above his head.

'And the winner is Salamandaga of Mali!' he boomed to a great roar of approval from the crowd. 'Bad luck, Kiribati! First your island sink, now you sink!' Casablanca jeered, and there was an explosion of laughter and derisive whistling. 'Take him away, we don't want losers!'

The limp, battered body of the unfortunate islander was lifted and carried out through a big iron doorway that led towards the back of the ship.

'Salamandaga will be the new chief of my personal bodyguard,' Casablanca announced to more cheering. He threw his arm around the boy's shoulders. 'Enough of fun! Now it is time for feasting!' This produced the biggest cheer of all. The door to the forward hold was thrown open, and a procession entered, led by a girl beating a loud tattoo on an empty plastic barrel. She was followed by pairs of 'cooks' with the smoking carcasses of the deer slung between them. After them came others carrying boards piled high with charred chunks of meat and at the rear marched little kids with the roasted bodies of small animals skewered on sticks.

Wooden crates and some plastic chairs had been arranged near one of the fires for Casablanca and his bodyguards. On one of the crates was a large collection of bottles and cans. Booze! They'd found a supply of alcohol somewhere in the ruined town and, when Casablanca and his bodyguards had taken their places, they settled in to some serious drinking. The bodyguards were all armed. Three had guns – automatic weapons that they must have taken from the armoury that ships now carry to defend themselves against pirates. The rest were wielding machetes and clubs made out of hunks of wood. Since the bodyguards had obviously been picked for their size, it was no wonder the rest of the kids were in awe of them.

The girl, who had led the procession, put down her drum and went to sit beside Casablanca. She looked familiar... Hatiya! The Bangladeshi girl that Ashanti had sheltered in the barn; the one I'd help to escape. The one Ashanti had escorted back here. So, I was right, she was Casablanca's girlfriend. *If we hadn't helped her,* I thought bitterly, *Ashanti wouldn't be Casablanca's prisoner, and we wouldn't be here right now.*

The feasting got under way. Casablanca and his crew were served first, and took their pick of the best bits, then it was a case of every kid for himself or herself.

There was tug at my sleeve. Sarayova crouched down beside me.

'Where's Abuja?' she asked, urgently.

'Isn't he with you?' I asked.

'No! I think he follow you.'

I nudged Owando. 'Have you seen Abuja?'

'He's with Sarayova.'

'No,' I said, 'he's not.'

Owando muttered something that didn't sound polite.

'I must find him,' Sarayova said and began to go, but I pulled her back.

'Wait! We need to find where they're holding Ashanti and the others. We'll all go. We can look for Abuja at the same time.'

'Yes. Dr London is right. We all go,' said Owando.

Keeping low, we sped along the side deck. If Casablanca had set guards, they had all deserted their posts long ago to join the feasting, and we reached a door that led into the ship's accommodation without encountering anyone. Owando carefully swung the door open, and we stepped inside. It was pitch black. I could feel walls on each side, so I assumed we were in a corridor.

'There are four levels above the deck,' I whispered. 'I'll go to the top, Owando, you take the next level, Sarayova, you go to the one above this one. We meet back here. If no one finds them, we work our way down.'

'There are stairs here!' I heard Owando whisper. Holding on to each other, we felt our way up the metal stairway that rang out alarmingly any time one of us stumbled. Sarayova went off along the corridor on the first level we reached, and we could hear her tapping and whispering at doors. Owando left on the next level, and I continued to the top. Here a little light entered through windows, and I guessed the moon must have risen. None of the doors on the floor I was searching were locked. There was a radio operator's room, a room full of maps and stuff, three cabins that might have been for the captain and officers, but, judging by the mess, had been taken over by some of the kids and then I found myself on the bridge. I had been right about the moon; its silvery light caught the rooftops of the ruined town on either side that we seemed to be sailing through. Standing by the wheel and looking down through the windows that ran the width of the ship, I could see the fires burning in the open holds and the long deck stretching away to the bow.

There was nobody on this level. I might as well get back down and see if the others had had found anything.

I crept down the stairs, stopping to listen for Owando at the third level before continuing.

As I reached the second floor a hand gripped my arm in the darkness, and my heart missed a beat.

'I've found them! They're here!' It was Sarayova.

'No need to scare me half to death! Where's Owando?'

'He's by their door. But it's locked. Come on!'

She took my hand and towed me down the corridor, stopping when we reach Owando.

'How many in there?' I asked.

'Yongjo Ma, Yongjo Pa, and Ashanti,' he replied.

'How do we get them out? Can we bust the door open?'

'Steel door. No way!'

'Ashanti!' I whispered as loudly as I dared. 'It's me, Mark!'

'Mark? Thank God!'

'Is there a window?'

'No. It's some sort of storeroom.'

'Are you all OK?'

'No. Yongjo Pa's hurt. Bastards beat him up. We need to get him out.'

'OK. OK, wait. We'll think of something.' *But what? I'm wondering. We need the key, which Casablanca or one of his ugly friends will be carrying for sure.*

'Who do you think's got the key?' I asked.

'Casablanca,' said Owando. 'That boy trust nobody!'

Then Sarayava says, 'I'll get it.' Just like that! Like she's offered to pop out for the milk!

'How?' I ask.

'I live on the streets.'

'And?'

'I pick pockets.'

'Yeah – She the best,' says Owando, with obvious respect.

Shit! I'm way out of my depth here! These kids do things and know things I've never even thought of! That's what I'm thinking, but what I say is, 'Rana, no. They've got guns. You're not going in there. They'll recognise you.' And I don't know why, but I've used her real name.

'And what?' she asks angrily. 'We leave your friend here? We let Yongjo Pa die?'

'Let me think,' I say – and I'm desperately trying to find another plan.

'No,' she says firmly. 'Owando, you stay here by the door. Mark, go up and watch from top. If they catch me, you go quickly, tell Owando, and get off the ship.'

'Wait!'

'No!' and she's gone, and I can hear her footsteps on the steel stairway hurrying down into the guts of the vessel.

'What's going on?' Ashanti asks on the other side of the door.

'Sarayavo, she will get the key,' Owando says.

I don't wait to hear any more but rush back to the door and along the side deck to look down into the open hold, and I'm just in time to see Sarayavo enter through a door in the bulkhead. She's in the shadows, the only light in the hold is from the fires, which have burnt down, and everyone's attention is still on the food and drink. She quickly squats and coats her face in the white dust from the floor, then pulls up the hood of her sweatshirt. There is a drunken, singing crowd around Casablanca, where bottles and cans are being passed from hand to hand. Sarayavo makes her way to the back of the crowd and eases herself into the press of bodies. I'm hardly breathing, and I feel cold and I'm sweating. The bodyguards' guns and machetes have been dumped on the wooden crates amongst the empty bottles, but they could be snatched up in a moment. I lose sight of Sarayavo and then I see her right behind Casablanca. She's swaying and singing with the others. She seems to be there for much too long! What's she doing? Has she got the keys? Maybe Casablanca doesn't have them after all!

Go! I'm shouting in my head. *Get the keys and go! Get out before they recognise you!*

Yes! She's moving away! And I'm praying, *Please, God, don't let them catch her! Don't let them catch her!*

She slides down, and I imagine her crawling between people's legs and then I see her come out the back of the crowd.

She's heading for the door! She must have got them! God she's brilliant!

And then it happens.

A shout. A small boy's voice. 'Sarayova! Hey! Look what I got!'

It's Abuja. The little idiot! He's running towards her, waving a half-chewed bone!

She hesitates, not knowing what to do.

'I get you some! You want some?' he shouts.

Heads turn. And she's caught half way between Casablanca and the door. Will she run? If she does, they'll know something's up. She begins to walk briskly across the open space.

'Sarayova! Wait!' Abuja calls, running after her.

'*Sarayova!*' Casablanca's voice reverberates in the hollow space. He steps from the crowd. He has his arm around his girlfriend, Hatiya, and seems to lean on her. His other arm comes up. In his hand is a big, black pistol. 'Not leaving, are you?' His arm sways slightly. He is obviously drunk.

Sarayova stops and turns to face him. Abuja also stops and looks from one to the other.

'Welcome back, Sarayova. Glad you could come,' says Casablanca. 'And you bring your little friend, Abuja. How nice. We thought you don't want to be in Casablanca's army. Don't we, Hatiya? Eh?'

He pushes off from Hatiya, steadies himself, and then walks over to Abuja, locks his arm around the boy's head, and pulls the boy towards him in a rough hug. 'You like to be in my army, eh little Abuja? Look what big food we give you, eh? You are going to be one of my little soldiers!'

'Leave him alone!' Sarayavo takes a step towards them.

The gun comes up again.

'Did I speak to you? I don't think so. You stand over there by that wall! Maybe I shoot you later. That's what we do to deserters in the army!' He waves his pistol, waving Sarayova away from the door to stand almost directly under where I am crouching. She must know I'm here. She told me to watch. But she doesn't once look up.

'So, Abuja, why you come back, eh?'

'I was hungry!'

'He was hungry! You hear that? He was hungry!' Casablanca roars with laughter, and everyone but Sarayova joins in. 'You stay with Casablanca, you don't get hungry.' And he pinches Abuja's cheek hard between his thumb and first finger. 'Hey!' he shouts, pointing to the newly promoted Salamandaga, 'Bring him the best piece of meat.'

Casablanca tucks his pistol into the waistband of his trousers and marches Abuja back to join the bodyguard and hangers-on. He lifts Abuja up and stands him on one of the crates. 'Give him a beer!' he orders. Someone hands the little kid an opened bottle.

'To Casablanca's soldiers!' Casablanca bellows and lifts a bottle to ring against Abuja's.

'Drink! Drink! Drink!' All gather around Casablanca and Abuja, clapping and chanting.

For a moment Sarayova is forgotten. She doesn't risk looking up, but she knows I'm looking down. She turns over one of her hands so that I can see into it. In it are the keys.

She must think I can do something. Why else would she show me the keys? The fishing line! Is she thinking that too?

Quickly, my hands shaking, I get the reel of line out of my pocket. The hook jabs my finger as I work it loose from the reel. Mustn't get the line tangled! I begin to lower the hook over the edge of the coaming, the little lead fishing weight taking it down. The thin line is invisible in the dim light; only the hook catches the occasional glint from the fires. And still no one is looking towards Sarayova.

Down, down, down. It's hanging too far to her left. I move until the line brushes her face. Down a bit more until the hook is level with her hand. I'm having to lean out more than I like to see the end of the line. If anyone looks up... ! But nobody is, nobody is... keep calm, just keep calm... that's easy to say! There! Yes, there! I feel the weight of the keys on the line, like a fish taking the bait! Now... up... gently...

gently... up... pull the line up. Stop shaking! Up... up. No one look, please no one look! If the keys come off now... ! Don't think about it – keep pulling... up... Almost there. Oh no! What's happening? Casablanca is coming towards Sarayova!

I stop pulling. The keys hanging, twisting, three metres below the top of the hold, and I duck down to hide behind the coaming and continue slowly drawing in the line – one metre – another metre. They're stuck! They've caught on something! What do I do? Should I let the line out a bit? Try again? I'll have to look. I ease up and peep over the coaming. The hook has caught on something just below me. I could reach the keys if I leant over. No one's looking up. 'People never look up.' I remember my dad telling me that. Is it true? Wish that moon would go behind a cloud. Whatever! Go for it! I hold the line taut with my left hand and reach down with my right. Got them!

I'm back behind the coaming with the keys in my hand. We've done it! We've done it! My heart's trying to leap out of my throat.

But what about Sarayova? I've been concentrating so hard on the line and the keys... Now I strain to hear what's happening in the hold.

'Dr London, what happens?' It's Owando. He's right beside me. 'Does she have the keys? Why she doesn't she come?'

'I've got them,' I say, showing him.

'You?... How?'

'Look.' I show him the line.

'You fish them?!'

'Yes.'

'Sarayova?'

'They've got her. We have to do something.'

'Do what?'

'I don't know. Here. Take the keys. Get the others out.'

'And you?'

'Don't know. Go! Get the others out. I want to see what's going on. Go!'

'Yes. OK!' And he goes.

I have to know what's happening in the hold. Carefully, I look over the edge. I am looking almost straight down on Sarayova, so I move along until I can see her from the side. She looks so calm. The white dust has turned her face into a beautiful mask. The fires in the corners are now a mass of embers lighting the space, and everyone in it, with an eerie red glow. Casablanca is standing, feet apart, rocking slightly from heel to toe, in front of her. He has Abuja with him. He grips the back of the little boy's neck with his left hand and holds the pistol loosely in his right. He gives Abuja the occasional shake to emphasise what he is saying. The rest of the kids are standing or crouching in a semicircle well back from Casablanca, watching with wolfish interest.

'So, Abuja,' *shake*, 'she doesn't want to be in Casablanca's army. What do you think, eh, little brother?' *Shake*. 'You think she don't like us? Maybe she think she's too good to be in Casablanca's army!' *Shake*. 'Too proud!' *Shake*. 'Too clever!' *Shake*. 'Or maybe she's a coward! Not brave enough!' *Shake, shake*. 'Eh?... Eh? Is that it? Is that it, Sarayova? Too scared?! Too frightened?'

He raises the gun and strokes the barrel down the left side of her face, under her chin and up the right side, rests it in the middle of her forehead, and then lowers it again. I'm shivering all over, but she stands there and stares him in the eye.

'So, what shall we do with her? Eh, Abuja?' *Shake*. 'Eh, little brother? Do you know what we do with traitors? You know what we do with deserters? You know what we do with spies? Eh?' *Shake*. 'We shoot them! That's what we do. That's what we do, Sarayova. That's what we do, Mrs Too Good For The Rest Of Us! That's what we do! So tell me why I shouldn't shoot you?'

She says nothing.

Casablanca lets go of Abuja, who just stands there staring up, his eyes enormous, shining, terrified, tears making dark tracks through the white powder that has settled on his face. Sarayova reaches a hand out to Abuja, offering to take the little boy's hand, to comfort him, but Casablanca knocks her arm away. 'Don't touch him. He don't like you any more!'

Why doesn't she say something? Try to reason with him? Her silence is making him crazier. He's drunk. He's off his head! Then I realise. She's playing for time. She's drawing it out. She's giving us time to get the others away!

'Last chance, Sarayova. Last chance, Mrs Too Good For Us. Last chance to change your mind. You see Abuja? You see how kind I am? You see? I give her one more chance to join us.' He raises the gun and points it at her. 'Well, what do you say, Sarayova? You want to be a soldier now? Or you want to be dead?'

She takes a breath and seems to grow taller. I think she is going to say something, but after a long moment, she lets the breath out again and continues to stare silently at Casablanca. It is so quiet I hear her breathing out.

'I will count to five...' Casablanca uses his other hand to steady the hand that holds the gun. 'One... two...'

'*No!*' I scream. And my voice echoes around the vast metal chamber below. Every face turns upward, and Casablanca's pistol swings away from Sarayova to point in my direction.

'Who's there?' he calls.

'Leave her alone!' I call back.

I know he can't see me clearly. In the darkness, I must be just a silhouette. But he can see me well enough to shoot me, if his aim is any good. Maybe he doesn't trust his aim, because he swings the gun back on to Sarayova.

'If she matters so much to you, you come down here and save her.'

'You let her go!'

'. . . three... four...'

'Stop! How do I get down?'

'The ladder.' He indicates the far corner of the hold, and I see that there is a narrow, metal ladder welded to the inside of the coaming and running down to the floor of the hold.

'Just wait! I'm coming down!' I shout.

As I hurry around the edge of the hold, I see Owando, Ashanti, Yongjo Ma, and Yongjo Pa come out of the cabin door. Ashanti and Yongjo Ma are supporting Yongjo Pa. I signal to them to stay back from the edge of the hold and head towards them.

'What happens?' Owando asks.

'Get off the ship as fast as you can,' I say.

'Mark? What's going on?' Ashanti asks.

'Owando, take them to the caravan park.'

'OK, Dr London.'

'Mark, what are you doing?'

'Just get off the ship!' And I run to the corner with the ladder.

'I'm coming down!' I shout again, climbing over the coaming and on to the ladder, and I'm praying that he won't shoot me in the back as I climb down, waiting for the shot I probably won't even hear. It's a very long ladder and my back feels such an easy target. As soon as my feet are on the floor, I turn to face Casablanca. Maybe it's the dim red light, but he seems much bigger than when we last met.

'Rich boy!' He sounds truly surprised. 'You… ! Why?'

In two seconds he's going to guess the truth, so I get in first.

'I'm looking for Ashanti.'

'Ashanti? Ashanti? Do you see any Ashanti here?'

'You've got her locked up somewhere.'

'Who tell you that? Sarayova?'

'Never mind who told me. Just let her go.'

'Why? Why let her go? Because you tell me? You, rich boy? You don't give orders here. Nobody give Casablanca orders any more.' He advances towards me. 'You got give me respect. Everybody got to give me respect.' He shoves the gun in my face.

'I don't respect people just because they've got guns,' I say. And I know as soon as the words are out of my mouth that it's a stupid thing to say.

'Then maybe you need a lesson. Maybe you need to learn.' I can smell the alcohol on his breath. *Don't push him,* I tell myself, *Back off.*

'Listen, I'm sure you've got your reasons for what you're doing…'

'What do you know about my reasons, rich boy? What do you know about anything? You live in big house, ride in flashy car, live nice life. You know why you have nice life? Because you got slaves, that's why. Because you got slaves like the English always had slaves.'

'What are you talking about? Slaves? I don't have slaves!'

Casablanca turns to the semicircle of kids who are silently watching us. 'You see?' he says, 'Rich boy doesn't know shit!' There's a burst of mocking laughter. He turns back to me, and there's a triumphant grin on his face. 'Who made your jacket?'

'I don't know.'

'Slaves! Who made your jeans?'

'Look, this isn't…'

'Slaves! Who made your trainers?'

'OK, but…'

'Slaves!' all the other kids shout.

Casablanca has stopped swaying. He stands feet apart, in command. 'Your daddy, how did he get so rich?'

'He's not that rich.'

'Answer!'

'In business.'

'Business. What business? All business is bad business.'

'That's ridiculous! My father's business is a good business. Carbon trading. Managing this forest… so that people can fly – You know, so we can visit each other's countries.'

'You can visit my country, rich boy, but when we come to yours, you lock us up. This business is a lie. This forest is a lie. Once you have slaves in China, in India, in Bangladesh, in Africa, in Indonesia, in our factories, in our mines, now you hide them here in this forest.'

I need to steer him away from this stuff about slaves. I look at Sarayova. She still hasn't said anything.

'Listen,' I say, 'I know about the camps. That's why I'm here. We've got to stop them, but not with violence.'

'Hey! I was wrong about rich boy! He's come to save us!' There's more laughter. 'You come with guns to our countries, that's all right, eh? Rich countries rob poor countries, that's all right. You take everything, make us work for shit, that's all right. But now we got guns. You take from us, now we take from you.'

'You can't win this with guns!'

'Oh, I see, we should say to FIST, "Put down your guns, we all friends now!"'

'No…'

'Guns OK for FIST?'

'No!'

'So what are you saying?'

'I'm saying if you start a war with FIST, they'll win. You start shooting at them, they'll kill you. Do you want to die?'

'Casablanca is not afraid to die. You afraid of dying, rich boy? Better be dead than a slave. Better be dead than live without honour. I got my pride. I got to have respect. This country take everything from me. This country make me a slave. Now this country is going to learn a lesson. This country going to learn who it's dealing with. I'm going to get respect. Right? Respect! Respect is worth dying for, rich boy. Honour is worth dying for. Life's not worth shit if you don't have honour and life's not worth shit if you don't believe in something that's worth dying for!'

He's breathing hard, and his face is no more than a foot from mine. The red of the fires glows in his eyes, and he looks very, very dangerous.

'Look,' I say, 'I don't like FIST any more than you do.'

'Is that why you showed them where to find us?'

There's a murmur from the crowd, and it's like the ice just cracked under me and I'm about to fall through. He knows it was me that day at the old farmhouse. He knows I told Jake where they were.

'I made a mistake!'

'Yeah, a big mistake.' He levels the pistol at my head, and I know this is it. I have to hold on to the ladder to stop my legs from buckling.

'Casablanca, don't.' It's the first time Sarayova has said anything. But her voice is flat, without hope.

'Don't worry,' he says coldly, 'I'm going to shoot you too.'

Oh God, I think, and close my eyes.

It's completely silent. What's he waiting for? In the silence, I hear the soft pad of bare feet.

'Casablanca – please – he saved me.'

I open my eyes. It's Hatiya. She reaches out and gently pushed the pistol away from my head. 'He's not against us, Casablanca. Maybe he did make a mistake.'

'He saved you?' Casablanca looks puzzled.

'After the raid. When I hide in the barn and FIST come. He get me out.'

Casablanca looks from Hatiya to me. Maybe the moment has passed. Maybe he won't shoot me after all.

'So, if I don't shoot him, what should I do with him?'

'We take him as a hostage. His father is important man.'

'And?'

'We ask for a lot of money.'

'Hey! She is clever! Perhaps, rich boy, you are worth more alive than dead. What do you think? Your father pay to get you back?... What happened? You lost your tongue?'

'Yeah.' My throat is so tight that I have to force the words out. 'I think he would.'

I notice that Abuja has crept up to Sarayova and is holding her hand.

'Good! Then you got nothing to worry about.' He throws his arm round my shoulders and hugs me like we're best buddies.

'But you better say thank you to Hatiya, because she just saved your life.'

'Thank you, Hatiya.'

'You can do nicer than that.'

'Thank you very much for saving my life.'

'Yeah, that's good. You see? Now you even learning manners. Tonight you come with us. If FIST shoot at us, we use you as a shield. Salamandaga! You watch rich boy. If he tries anything, you kill him!'

He turns to Sarayova, 'And your girlfriend – this time I spare her – but she stays here with Hatiya to look after the little ones. I don't trust you two together. Casablanca is not a fool. You got something going on.'

He seems to lose interest in us. He tucks his pistol into the waist band of his trousers, takes a can of beer from one of his bodyguards, and drains it.

Now that I no longer have a gun pointing at my head, I begin to worry about what's going to happen when Casablanca discovers that

Ashanti, Yongjo Pa, and Yongjo Ma are missing. What if he puts his hand in his pocket and finds the keys are gone? I look at Sarayova, but I can't read her expression. It's like her spirit is somewhere else. Salamandaga ties one end of a long piece of rope around my neck and ties the other end around his wrist. He picks up an ugly looking home-made machete that's been beaten out of bit of old iron and had its jagged edge sharpened on a stone. He waves it under my nose.

'Yeah, OK. I'm not about to try anything,' I say.

Casablanca leaps up on one of the wooden crates.

'Are you ready?!' he shouts.

'*Yes!*' they all scream.

'Are we slaves?'

'*No!*'

'Are we animals to be hunted?'

'*No!*'

'Do we take what we want?'

'*Yes!*'

Even to me, at that moment, he looks like a leader, and I feel a mad surge of excitement that quickly turns to fear.

'Tonight,' Casablanca roars, 'I take only my big soldiers. But don't worry, my little soldiers, soon there will be guns for anyone strong enough to hold them.'

'*Casablanca! Casablanca!*' they chant, fists punching the air and a group of the smaller boys do a sort of war dance as members of the bodyguard pick up their weapons and gather around their leader. But I notice there are a few who join in with less enthusiasm.

'Where are we going?' I risk asking Salamandaga.

'Big house for hunters,' he says. 'Plenty of guns.'

The hunting lodge – Back to the hunting lodge! I look at Sarayova to see if she has heard. The white dust on her face makes her eyes look very big, very dark, and all I can read in them is sadness.

CHAPTER 26

Getting off the ship was easier than getting on but because my guard and I were tied to each other, we had to climb down the rope ladder together, which made it twist and sway and whenever my foot slipped the rope jerked tight around my neck, threatening to strangle me, so it was a relief when we reached the roof of the ruined house beside the ship and could use its stairway to get to the street.

We left Combe Martin by the old road that runs up the valley. The moon was still up as our ragged little army with its collection of assorted weapons jogged through the abandoned town and out into the beginnings of the forest. At the head of the valley there was a steep climb, but Casablanca never slackened the pace and soon I was struggling to keep up, and my neck was rubbed raw by the angry tugs that Salamandaga would give my rope each time I fell behind.

I wondered if Casablanca would keep to the road all the way to the hunting lodge. He didn't seem to be worried about patrols, so I guessed there must be fewer of them this far from Holdstone. I kept hoping he would cut off into the forest where the undergrowth and rougher ground would force him to slow down, but he didn't, and my captors swung along in an easy rhythm, hardly even breathing hard, as I gasped and panted on the end of my rope.

I have to escape, that's what I kept thinking. *Somehow, I've got to get away.* Crazy plans went through my head. Could I unbalance Salamandaga with a sudden jerk on the rope? Grab his machete? *You must be joking!* I told myself, *You saw him fight. These guys were chosen because they could beat the crap out of everyone else! And if you did get away, how long would it be before they ran you down? They're one hundred times fitter than you are!* But I knew that if I didn't escape, and we got back to the ship in one piece, and Casablanca discovered that we'd let his prisoners out, then he'd shoot me for sure. Also, I didn't fancy getting caught in the crossfire at the hunting lodge. And what side was I on, anyway? And what was he thinking? Did he know the place was bristling with security cameras? Yeah, they probably did keep loads of hunting guns there, but I couldn't imagine how he was planning to steal them.

We must have been running for over an hour, but I'd lost track of time and was just concentrating on keeping going. The moon had gone down, and it was so dark beneath the trees that arched over the road that I could hardly see the main group that had got well ahead despite Salamandaga's efforts to drag me along. The last of the runners ahead of us had just disappeared over a small rise when a dark shape dropped from an overhanging branch on to the shoulders of Salamandaga, knocking him to the ground. It happened so suddenly that I almost tripped over the struggling bodies. An arm rose and fell, a thud and a groan and Salamandaga lay still. A second figure leapt from the undergrowth, snatched up the machete, and I thought I was about to be sliced in two, but the falling blade neatly severed the rope.

'Quick, Dr London, get him off the road!'

My brain was in a whirl, but I managed to help drag Salamandaga off the road and behind some bushes.

'Run! Run!'

I was grabbed on either side and propelled through the trees for a hundred metres or more before being pulled to the ground.

'Lie still. No noise!'

I tried to quieten my breathing that was rushing in and out in great noisy gasps. Owando on my left and Ashanti on my right lay as still as stones. Soon there was the sound of voices on the road. They were calling softly for Salamandaga. Then I heard Casablanca say, 'How this can happen? Salamandaga is much stronger than rich boy! Search! Search! They must be near by!' Followed by the rustling of vegetation.

'Maybe they return to the ship,' one of the bodyguards suggested.

'Why? Why would they do that?' Casablanca demanded. 'Don't say stupid things. Just find them. Why? Why didn't I shoot him? I knew I should shoot him. Next time I see rich boy, I shoot him for certain.'

The searching continued but, in the almost total darkness, they missed the bushes where we had left the unconscious Salamandaga. Soon Casablanca grew impatient. He left one of his gang to search, while he and the rest of them ran on down the road.

'We go,' Owando whispered, 'Very quiet.' Like a shadow, he slid off through the trees, and we followed him as silently as we could.

No one spoke again until we had got well away from the road.

'You OK?' Ashanti asked.

'Thanks to you two,' I said.

'You don't think we leave you, Dr London?' Owando said.

'Well, I didn't expect you to drop out of the sky like that!'

Owando giggled.

'I owe Hatiya as well,' I said. 'He was going to shoot me, but she stopped him.'

'Hatiya!' Ashanti spat the name out. 'If I hadn't brought her back – conniving little... ! Well... and then she sides with her wretched boyfriend.'

'I did try to warn you back at the farm,' I said.

'Yeah, I suppose you did.'

'But how come Casablanca locked you up?'

'I tried to stop him taking over.'

'Surprised he didn't shoot you.'

'I got him out of Holdstone.'

'Right – so he owes you.'

'Without Ashanti and Ruby, none of us free,' Owando said. 'And then you, Dr London, you save us from the dogs.'

'I think you just made us even,' I said. 'But how come you knew we'd be coming along this road?'

'Not all the kids on the ship are on Casablanca's side,' Ashanti said. 'Most of them only go along with him because they're scared of him. Yongjo Pa's still got a lot of supporters, and they'd come and tell us all of Casablanca's plans. So we knew about tonight.'

'How long before Casablanca gets back to the ship?'

'If his plan works, twenty-four hours.'

'What is his plan? He's got to be crazy, doesn't he?'

'No. Don't underestimate him. He was our top hijack and break-in guy. The security guards at the hunting lodge change shift at one in the morning. They come up from New Molton in a minibus. His plan is to hijack the minibus and go into the lodge disguised as the late shift. Once he's got the guns, he'll hide them somewhere in the forest and then make his way back to the ship the following night.'

'Look, I've got to go back to the ship. I have to get Sarayova off before he gets back.'

'Mark, you've done enough. You've done more than enough. I shouldn't have got you into this.'

'You didn't get me into this! I got myself into it. And you're not the only person who cares about things! All right! And I'm not doing this for you... or to prove anything to you, so you can get that out of your head for a start! I'm doing it because it matters! It matters to me! All right? I'm doing because she... because Sarayova... because... God knows what he'll do to her when he finds out you're missing!... And she almost got killed for you. I hope you realise that.'

We walked on in silence for a little.

'I come with you,' Owando said.

Then Ashanti said, 'Mark, I'm sorry.'

'For what?'

'For thinking you'd be different.'

'You've known me long enough!'

'Yeah, but... I thought all the money would have changed you.'

'And you always were a judgemental, secretive little sod. Remember how you wouldn't show me the water voles?'

'I did show them to you!'

'Not until they had babies, you didn't.'

'OK... Look, we'll all go to the ship. But first we have to go to the caravan and tell Yongjo Ma what's happening. When did you last eat anything?'

'Can't remember.'

'That's what I thought,' said Ashanti.

CHAPTER 27

The first thing I noticed when I entered the caravan was that something smelt much better than tinned sausages and beans. The second thing was that the place was tidy, really tidy, like someone had actually cleaned it, not just shoved things out of the way. Yongjo Pa wasn't in the room, so I guessed they must have cleaned up one of the bedrooms for him.

Yongjo Ma greeted me politely as if I were a guest and this was her home, and she was about forty-something and not about seventeen or thereabouts. She asked if she should call me Mark or Dr London, and she asked in such a serious way that I almost laughed.

'Mark's fine', I said, 'but I've got quite used to Dr London.'

'He particular good at medicines,' Owando said, patting his own arm.

'A pity you are not a real doctor. It would be good for my brother.'

'Perhaps we should get him to hospital,' I said.

Yongjo Ma shook her head. 'They call him a terrorist. They will lock him up. Please, you are hungry. You must eat.'

The food tasted as good as it smelt. There was rice, that they must have found in one of the caravans, with some sort of Asian dish that seemed to be full of fresh vegetables, but I couldn't think where they could have got fresh vegetables from.

'This is amazing! What's in here?' I asked.

'I find things in the forest. I don't know the English names,' Yongjo Ma said.

'There's sorrel and wild garlic and some sort of fungi amongst other things,' said Ashanti. 'You should taste what she can do with seaweed.'

'My brother is a better cook,' she said.

'No, he isn't,' said Ashanti. But that's why the kids call them Ma and Pa, 'cause they feed everyone.

The talk about cooking and Yongjo Ma's rather proper, old-fashioned English made me feel even more like a guest at a polite dinner. But as I watched her serving out second helpings, I remembered the skilful way she emptied the shells out of Jerzy's pistol and wondered what she must have lived through to have learnt all about guns as well as surviving on wild food.

With my stomach full I could hardly keep awake, but Yongjo Ma said that her brother would like to speak to me.

'His name is Myung-Dae,' she said. 'Which means "right" in Korean, so he must always be right and always do the right thing. Casablanca said they must fight for the leadership. But Myung-Dae would not fight, so they beat him up. Now he is worried about what happens to all the small children.'

'What about you?' I asked.

'My name?'

'Yes.'

'It is Soon-Hi.'

'Soon-Hi,' I repeated. 'Does it have a meaning?'

'Some would say "goodness" some would say "joy". I don't feel much of either at the moment.' She opened the door to the bedroom. Her brother was lying on his back, his face so bruised and swollen that his eyes were almost shut, but he turned his head towards us when he saw the candle light.

'Ah, good. They found you. Are you all right?' he asked.

'Yeah, I'm fine. But you don't look too good,' I said.

'I think I live. A few broken ribs. Nothing more serious. First, I must thank you for what you did, although I don't understand how you did it. Owando tells me some nonsense about a fishing line.'

'It's Sarayova you need to thank, and she's still on the ship,' I said.

'Will you go back?'

'Yes.'

'What about Casablanca?'

'We don't think he will come back for a day or so.'

'Will Owando go with you?'

'He says he will.'

'Good. He knows which of the older ones are still loyal to me. Maybe they can help you. Perhaps you can even get some of them off the ship. The little ones, how did they seem?'

'They seemed like they were having a ball! But I hate to think what will happen if Casablanca starts handing out guns.'

'I wish I could come with you,' he said.

'You don't go anywhere!' his sister said.

'When will you go?'

'In an hour or two. After we've had a bit of a rest.'

'Does Ashanti go?'

'Yes.'

'Good. The three of you make a good team. Did you see any FIST patrols?'

'No. But there was an unmanned drone flying about before we went on the ship.'

'Here? In the north?'

'Yes.'

'They never send them here before. They know something. It's time we moved again. Casablanca likes it too much on that ship.'

He was silent for a moment. Maybe he was thinking or maybe talking was rather too painful.

'Will you come back here?' he asked.

'So long as no one is following us.'

'Good. Very good. When you do, we must plan what to do next.'

There didn't seem to be anything else to say, so I said I was going to go and lie down for a bit, and he wished us luck.

'He always needs to know everything. Always needs to be the boss,' his sister said when she had closed the door.

Owando and Ashanti were already asleep. I asked Yongjo Ma to wake us in two hours and lay down on the lounger.

I hardly seemed to have closed my eyes when she was gently shaking my shoulder.

CHAPTER 28

I hoped Owando would take us back to Combe Martin by the road. But he chose the same route we had used before. It was already light when we set out and I was glad that even Owando didn't think climbing down that cliff in the dark was a good idea. The wind had got up overnight, and it was beginning to spit with rain but once we were in the forest, the trees sheltered us.

On the way, I asked if there was a plan for getting Sarayova off the ship. Owando said he should go on alone because he was smaller and better at hiding than either of us, but Ashanti said no, that she would go aboard, and that she wasn't going to hide; she said she would speak to all of them and warn them that they should all leave the ship before FIST found them. Both their plans sounded dodgy to me, and I began to wish I'd come on my own. Not that I could think of a better plan, I just hated the idea of sitting in the cave with nothing to do, waiting for things to go wrong. Also, to be honest, I wanted to be the one who rescued Sarayova.

When we came out of the shelter of the trees on to the exposed bluff above Combe Martin, we found the wind had turned into a gale. It hissed through the bracken, and we had to lean into the gusts to make headway to the cliff edge. Below, the waves were exploding over the reef, the spray reaching as high as the rock ledge half way down. But Owando didn't hesitate; he went around the precariously balanced boulder and slid down into the gully that was now full of cascading water. The rock ledge, when we reached it, was slick with spray from below and falling water from above and the wind buffeted and tugged at our clothing, threatening one moment to throw us against the rock face and the next to drag us over the edge.

At the base of the cliff, the danger of falling was replaced by the danger of being swept off the rocks by the surf, and we had to wait, each time, for the sea to suck the water back before leaping from boulder to boulder. Fortunately, the waves hadn't reached as high as the entrance to the cave and inside it was dry and the thunder of the surf became a muffled roar.

'That was a bit hairy!' I said.

'Yeah,' said Ashanti, shaking the worst of the water off her clothes. 'I hope we can reach the ship.'

'Listen,' I said, 'how do we know Casablanca hasn't come back? I mean, what if something went wrong, or he changed his mind?'

Ashanti and Owando looked at each other.

'We don't,' Ashanti said.

'I go first,' Owando said.

'No,' Ashanti said.

'No guards in this weather,' Owando said. 'All inside. I go. I look. I come back and tell you. No one see me.'

I could see that Ashanti still didn't like the idea, but it would be a disaster if she went and walked straight into Casablanca, and he'd promised to shoot me the next time he saw me.

'OK,' Ashanti said. 'You go, but you stay hidden. You come back and you tell us who's on board and what's happening. Don't take any risks.'

We climbed up to the second cave mouth to watch as Owando dodged the waves on his way round the cove. It was unlikely that anyone else would notice the little figure ducking around the boulders in this weather.

'He doesn't seem to be scared of anything,' Ashanti said.

'Yes, he is. He's scared of being deported. He told me,' I said.

'They're all scared of that.'

'So, what do we do?'

'Meaning?'

'Well, even without this trouble with Casablanca, they can't hide in the forest forever.'

'That isn't the plan. We find families that will take them. We've got dozens out already.'

'How do you get them out of the forest?'

'The travellers. FIST think they're a bunch of stoned-out hippies who aren't capable of organising a picnic, so they don't bother them.'

'But there are loads of kids left and there are more coming in all the time and half of them have real families already that are locked up in that camp. And Holdstone's just the beginning, they're planning to build more,' I said.

'How do you know that?'

'I overheard a conversation between Grist and Rainer when I was in the Lodge. Ashanti, please don't bite my head off, but this isn't like water voles. This isn't something you can do on your own. This is bigger than you. This is bigger than all of us. This is probably bigger than Britain. There are millions of climate refugees.'

'You mean leave it to the politicians, or the United-Do-Nothing-Nations, Brilliant!'

'No!' I said.

'What then?'

'People don't know what's happening here, right? It's hidden, it's secret, the press aren't allowed near the place, and so long as the refugees disappear and don't clutter up our towns and cities, nobody asks any questions.'

'Yeah. And?'

'We can use the GRID.'

'There is no GRID here, in case you've forgotten. Anyway, aren't there filters to block subversive information?'

'Not if it comes from the centre. Not if it comes from the Global Building. Ashanti, I want you to get me into Holdstone. I've already got a recording of the conversation between Grist and Rainer. If I can video what's happening in the camp, and we can get it all up on the GRID, the whole world will know! We can blow this thing open! We can get people asking questions. We can get a movement going to stop it!'

'No.'

'What?'

'No. You are not going to put at risk what Ruby and I have spent ages building up. FIST already suspect Ruby. They've started following her.'

'Then it's never going to stop! It's just going to get worse and worse and worse and more and more kids are going to have their lives ruined.'

'Mark, you're like your dad. You think you can change the world. I can only deal with my corner of it.'

So, we're back here again, I thought. *I'm like my dad, and he's an evil megalomaniac.*

Owando was out of sight. I guessed he'd use the anchor chain again to get on to the ship. I noticed the breakers were covering more and more of the rocks. The tide must have been coming in, and I wondered how he would get back.

I thought the sound of the first explosion was just a very big wave hitting the shore, but then Ashanti grabbed my arm.

'Oh God! Look!'

She was pointing to a plume of dust and smoke that was rising from the centre of the town.

'What the hell's that?' I said.

The noise of the helicopter had been drowned out by the sound of the surf, but now we both saw it as it swooped in to attack again. Another plume rose, this time nearer to the ship, and we felt as much as heard the wham of the explosion. Little figures appeared on top of the ruined building by the ship. Some stopped to point guns at the sky, others scrambled up the ladder. We saw the missile leave the helicopter. Seconds later, the building sank down into the rising dust.

'Oh no! Oh no! Casablanca! Look what he's done!'

'Owando's out there!' I said. And I started sliding down to the cave mouth, but Ashanti caught me by the sleeve.

'You can't get through!'

I pulled myself free and crawled out. But she was right; the way to the town was now cut off by the tide and fierce surf, and I was forced to return and watch beside Ashanti.

A second helicopter was now hovering just above the ship, and armed officers dropped from its open door on to the deck. It was obvious that, with so few of Casablanca's fighters left, any resistance on the ship would be short lived, and soon we saw heads and shoulders appearing above the railing as the children were lined up along the side deck. Ashanti buried her face in her hands, but I searched the growing line, trying to spot a yellow sweatshirt.

As I watched, a movement at the edge of the town, down by the shore, caught my eye. Three figures were running towards us. Without taking my eyes off them, I shook Ashanti to make her look up. The tallest held the hand of the smallest and pulled him along as fast as he could go. Two more figures appeared from the buildings behind them, bigger, heavier, carrying guns. The three in the lead jumped from the broken seawall on to the weed-covered rock shelf that led to the cave, but a great wave swept in front of them sending them staggering back. Now their pursuers jumped down after them. I saw Owando seize Sarayova's hand and drag them all forward, but they had only gone a few metres when the next swell rolled over the shelf, and they were struggling, out of their depth, in deep water. If one of the officers hadn't plunged in after them and grabbed hold of Abuja's collar, they would have been carried by the retreating wave into the churning sea.

My first reaction was relief that they were safe, but then my gut twisted with the realisation that they had been saved from the sea to be thrown back into Holdstone, and we watched in miserable silence as they were led along the shore and over the harbour wall. As they reached the buildings, Sarayova half turned and looked in our direction. Then they were gone, and Ashanti let out an anguished howl. I put my arm round her. 'We'll get them out. I promise we'll get them out!' I said. But she pulled away and wouldn't look at me. I bit my lip and fought back the angry tears.

When I looked out again, the helicopters were already ferrying children from the ship to some place on the ground, hidden by the buildings, where they would presumably be loaded into vans and taken back to the camp.

We had to wait until the tide had gone down enough to let us leave the cave. By then, all activity in the town had finished, and we decided it would be safe to get out of Combe Martin by the valley rather than climbing back up the cliff.

The crater in the middle of town where the first missile had hit was already half full of muddy rainwater. Beside it a minibus lay on its side, its windows blown out be the blast. Perhaps Casablanca's gang had run into a FIST patrol when they left the Lodge and had used the minibus to try to reach the ship.

Back at the caravan, Yongjo Ma and Yongjo Pa listened in silence as we told them what had happened. When we had finished, Yongjo Pa asked if we knew how many were hurt or killed in the attack. I said I thought there were three left on the building when it was hit, but I didn't know what had happened to them.

'We mustn't stay here any longer,' he said. 'FIST will be searching the whole area. We should move tonight.'

'How can we move, with you like this?' his sister asked.

'You and Dr London better strap me up,' he said.

'But where can we go?'

'Harlan's cottage,' Ashanti said. 'With all the action up here, they won't expect you to be down there, and it's my home, so Mark and me being there will seem like normal.'

So, after we had eaten, packed food and water for the journey, and strapped up Yongjo Pa's ribs, we left the caravan. We only moved at night and hid during the daytime. Ashanti, Yongjo Pa, and Yongjo Ma knew the forest as well as anyone. They knew which of the old roads the patrols tended to use and which were fairly safe, and they knew where there were isolated, abandoned buildings with their own wells or spring water where we could hide during the day.

All the way back to the farm, I worked on my plan. But I decided not say anything to anyone until I was satisfied with all the details.

CHAPTER 29

As we came out of the trees near the cairn on the hill overlooking the farm early on the third morning, the mist in the valley was lifting and breaking, the upper layers catching the low morning light. We expected the farmyard to be deserted, or, if there were anyone about that, it would only be Harlan getting the cows in for milking. So we were surprised to hear shouts, dogs barking, cows bellowing, and the distressed bleating of goats. As the mist cleared, we could see that there were cattle trucks parked in the yard and a horsebox by the stables.

'What do you think's going on?' I asked Ashanti.

'Look,' she said, pointing. The white bonnet of a patrol car with 'FIST' printed across it protruded from behind the farmhouse. 'FIST! They're taking our animals!' As she spoke, we could see two men bringing Starlight out of the stables. The pony tossed her head back, jerking the lead rope, but the man behind her caught her a sharp blow across the flanks with a stick, making her whinny and leap forward. I saw Ashanti flinch as if she herself had been hit. The pony's hooves danced and clattered as the two men forced her up the ramp and into the horsebox.

'Where's Harlan? They can't do this!' Ashanti was ready to charge down the hill. She was pale with anger, and her fists were clenched. But Yongjo Ma and I kept a tight hold on her.

'We can't do anything. We mustn't show ourselves,' I said.

'This is my farm! I have every right to be here!' she said.

'Maybe you don't any longer. Maybe your parents lost. We don't know what's happened,' I said.

The last of the animals were loaded into the trucks, the tailgates were shut and the convoy moved off. When it had gone, we saw Harlan followed by the two dogs moving slowly around the empty farmyard. He stopped in front of each building as if studying something.

'Come on,' said Ashanti.

We climbed the stile over the wall that I had repaired in what seemed to be another lifetime and made our way down the hill.

Harlan had already gone by the time we reached the yard, but we found the signs. They were taped to the doors of each building including the farmhouse; "Property of The Force for Internal Security and Counter Terrorism. Entry strictly forbidden." Ashanti went into the stables anyway. Yongjo Pa rested on the bench by the water trough, and Yongjo Ma sat beside him. After standing about for a few long minutes, I went to see what Ashanti was doing. The air in the stables was still full of the warm smell of the pony. Ashanti was standing with her back to me; she had her arm over her saddle that was hung over one of the railings, and her head was resting on it as if it were a pillow. I left quietly and told Yongjo Pa and Yongjo Ma that Ashanti would join us later, then took them down to Harlan's cottage.

We were met half way down the path by the two dogs. Old Tess gave two woofs and then walked beside us wagging her tail and looking up at me. Scat ran around barking and jumping and generally getting in the way.

Harlan must have heard the dogs because he was standing in the doorway with the door open when we got to the cottage. I thought he must have been ill while I was away; he looked much older than he had just a few days earlier. When he saw who it was, he straightened up, and his eyes brightened, but the worried look returned when he saw Ashanti wasn't with us.

'Her's not with you?' he asked, trying to see behind us.

'She's in the stables,' I said.

He nodded and I saw his shoulders sag. 'You've seen, then.'

'We were on the hill when they took Starlight. But at least, you've still got your cottage.'

'They've given me three weeks to be out,' and he stood aside to let us pass.

It didn't surprise me to discover that Harlan knew the two Koreans. He showed us into the small living room and then said, 'You'll no doubt be hungry,' and went to prepare something for us to eat.

Ashanti joined us while we were eating. She was silent, and her eyes were red and puffy. When we were little, I might have gone to sit with her, but I felt like I wasn't allowed to now, and it was Harlan who drew up a chair next to her and said, 'I know... I know,' and patted her hand. She rested her head against his shoulder and wept, her other hand clenched on top of his.

'When did they take Big Red and Dora-Bella?' she asked him after a little. And I could hear she was fighting to keep her voice steady.

'Yesterday.'

'Where have they taken them?'

'I don't rightly know. But Ruby'll track 'em down. Don't you worry.'

She withdrew her hands from his and squeezed them into a tight ball and then she got up and left the room. Yongjo Ma followed her out.

I mostly slept for the rest of the day. Harlan called Ruby to let her know that we had come back, and she told him that she would be over that evening. The one thing I did do was recharge my G-Port and check to see if, after all the submersions, it was still working. It was as good as Abbie had promised and, most importantly, the recording I had made at the Hunting Lodge was still there.

That evening, Harlan's living room was full to bursting. Besides Harlan, Ashanti, Yongjo Pa, Yongjo Ma, and me, there were Ruby and three members of Ruby's Truckers, Cara and Tony (the forester twins) and Bethan, the techie.

All listened intently as I told them about the events in Combe Martin. From time to time, I turned to Ashanti to check details or for extra information, but she never said much more than 'yes' or 'no'. When I had finished, Ruby looked around the serious faces in the room. 'Well kiddos? What's the plan?' she asked.

'Somehow we must get them all out again,' said Yongjo Pa.

'What do you think, Ashanti?' Ruby asked.

Ashanti was staring at the floor. She looked up slowly. 'I think it's pointless,' she said. There was a brief, stunned silence, and then she added, 'I mean it's pointless to go on doing what we have been doing.'

'And instead?' asked Ruby.

Ashanti looked across at me, 'Mark has a plan.'

CHAPTER 30

The parts of my plan that worried me most were getting in and out of Holdstone. According to Ruby, FIST had taken to searching vehicles as they came in and following them after they left.

'They haven't found the compartment in the timber truck yet,' she said. 'But it's only a matter of time and there's no timber to deliver for a couple of days.'

'What about Pete and Monkey with the skip truck? We've used that before,' said Ashanti.

'There's no hidden compartment on that one for getting you in, and when it leaves, they escort it all the way to the depot.'

'Pity FIST found the tunnel,' said Cara.

'There is another possible way of getting in', said Tony, 'if you don't mind getting wet. There's a reservoir inside the boundary, and it's fed by a canal at the top of the valley outside the fence. There's a grating over the inlet, but I dare say we could remove that one dark night.'

I remembered seeing the reservoir when I had been on hill overlooking the camp with Owando.

Cara shook her head. 'The water goes into a pipe under the perimeter fence. That pipe's got to be over twenty metres long. You'd drown before you ever got to the other end.'

'Couldn't we block the canal – Just for a bit?' asked Tony. 'Dump a load of rubble into it? We could happen to leave one of the Forestry lorries parked up there full of earth. Dump it into the canal just before Mark goes through.'

'I'm going in with Mark,' said Ashanti.

I was about to object. That hadn't been part of my plan. But she seemed to sense my reluctance to have a companion because she went on quickly. 'I've been in before, remember – I know my way around and you don't.'

She had a point, and if I was going to try to video the place and find Sarayova and Owando, I could use some help.

'Well?' said Tony. 'What do you reckon?'

'Yeah. I reckon we could hold the water back long enough for them to get through... ,' said Cara. '. . . Probably... So long as we don't have another storm.'

'Could we come back out the same way?' I asked.

'No,' said Tony. 'There'd be no way for us to know when you were coming through. And, anyhow, if we hang about up there too long, FIST are bound to get suspicious.'

'Pete and Monkey could get you out in the skip truck. The problem would be losing the FIST escort once they're are out of Holdstone,' said Ruby.

'Well, there is the tractor, I 'spose,' said Harlan, slowly.

We all looked at him. There was a twinkle in his old eyes.

'If that tractor was to break down in the middle of the road, just after the skip truck went by, it might hold things up for a good while, I reckon. Specially if I was comin' in from a side road towin' a muck spreader.'

We all laughed.

'Brilliant!' said Ruby. 'But then what, Mark? Let's say you've got your film of what's going on in Holdstone. How do you get it up to London?'

'Jerzy, my dad's driver,' I said. 'We tell my dad that Ashanti and I have been chucked off the farm, and we want to join Aunt Megan and Umi up in London. We ask him to send Jerzy with the Mercedes Estate. Say we've got loads of luggage. We just don't tell him we need a get-away driver and that the luggage is human.'

'Why involve Jerzy?' asked Ashanti.

'Because we need a car with a Transceiver that will open the London Ring and also get us into the garage under the Global Building. Plus, Jerzy is the fastest driver I know,' I said.

'That's settled, then,' said Ruby. 'Tony and Cara get you in and Pete and Monkey get you out. Harlan blocks the road with the tractor while we hand you over to Jerzy.'

'Will Pete and Monkey be up for it?' I asked.

'Yeah, no problem. Only reason they're not here is they're gigging tonight with Trigger,' said Tony.

'How's the map coming on?' Ruby asked.

'We're almost done,' said Bethan. She, Yongjo Pa, and Yongjo Ma had been drawing a map of Holdstone on Bethan's touch screen, marking the positions of all the security cameras. 'There you go.' She tapped the screen with her stylus. 'Hand us your G-Port, and I'll download it so that you can take it with you.'

'While you've got my port linked to your screen, I'd like to show you all something,' I said.

She handed the G-Port back to me and propped her touch-screen up on the mantelpiece so that everyone could see it. I found the file of the recording I'd made at the Lodge and clicked 'play'. There were grunts of disgust when the people in the room recognised Rainer and Grist but, as they began to take in what Rainer was proposing, they edged forward in their seats so as not to miss a single word. There was a low growl when Rainer explained his plan to take over the policing of the whole country and a howl when he suggested Grist would be president, but otherwise, they watched in silence until the end.

'Isn't that enough?' asked Bethan. 'Do we need to show people what's happening in Holdstone? They're talking about turning the country into a dictatorship! Just stick that on the GRID, and there'll be a revolution!'

'No,' I said. 'Rainer will say that it's a fake, that we dubbed it. We need evidence.'

'Mark's right,' said Ruby. 'It wouldn't be enough on its own. And some folk might actually think that having those two evil slime-balls running the country would be a good thing!'

'What will happen if Mark and Ashanti get caught? Have we thought about that?' asked Cara.

'I've thought about it,' I said. 'And I'm sure Ashanti has, and we're prepared to take the chance.'

'Yeah, but are the rest of us prepared to let you?' asked Cara. 'FIST will stop at nothing. We know that. Once you're inside that fence, there's nothing that any of us can do to help you.'

'Considering what these two kids have done already, I don't reckon they need too much help from us,' Ruby said.

'I should go,' said Yongjo Pa. 'You have lost too much already helping us.'

'With a chest full of broken ribs? I don't think so,' I said. 'And anyway, this is no longer just about Holdstone.'

'I've lost too much already *not* to do this,' said Ashanti.

'How soon can we be ready?' I asked.

'No reason why we couldn't block the canal tomorrow night,' said Tony.

'Pete and Monkey pick up a skip full of tree bark from Holdstone every morning around five thirty,' said Ruby. 'Will you be ready to come out by then?'

'Should be,' I said, although I really had no idea. 'I'll just need to make sure that Jerzy can be here by then with the car.'

'Anything we haven't thought of?' Ruby asked.

'We'll need Holdstone uniforms – like they put all the kids in,' I said.

'No problem,' said Ruby. 'We get the kids out of them as soon as we smuggle them out of the camp, so I know where there are plenty.'

'You'll need to be microchipped. I'll look after that. I'll see whose we've got,' said Bethan.

'Anything else?' asked Ruby.

No one could think of anything else. So the meeting broke up.

After Ruby and her team had gone, I called my dad on Harlan's landline. It was so weird to hear his voice sounding just the same as it always did. Like the whole world had changed, and he hadn't. He managed to seem genuinely upset when I told him about FIST taking all the animals and sealing the farm buildings. He said he didn't think they could do that while Aunt Megan and Umi were still fighting the eviction, but he'd have to speak to his legal advisers.

'Yeah, well – FIST have gone and done it, whatever your smart lawyers might say,' I said.

'Listen – Mark,' he said, 'I can hear you're angry, but honestly, I never imagined this would happen. I trusted Rainer. And I'm doing everything I can.'

'I just can't believe you trusted that guy,' I said. But what I was actually thinking was, *How much do you really know?*

The main thing was that he said there was no problem borrowing Jerzy and the Merc and I should just call Jerzy myself and arrange all the details. That suited me fine as I didn't want to tell my dad more than I had to since I no longer knew which side he was on. He said, if I wanted to speak to Mum, I should call her GRID, but I said it was OK, I'd see them both in a couple of days.

Next I called Jerzy. When he answered, there was so much background noise I could hardly hear him.

'Hello?... Hello? Who speaks please?'

'It's Mark.'

'Hello?'

'Jerzy! It's Mark!' I screamed.

'Ah! Mark! Much noise!'

'Are you in a pub?'

'Kto pije i pali ten nie ma robali.'

'What?'

'Old Polish saying: He who smokes and drinks don't get no worms!'

'You what?'

'I go outside.'

After a pause, the pub noises changed to street noises.

'Hey, Mark. What happens?'

'I'd like you to bring the Merc, pick up me and Ashanti, and drive us up to London. Dad says it's OK.'

'Yeah, well – Dad says is OK, then is OK. When we do this?'

'Tomorrow night.'

'So, OK. Tomorrow night I come to the farm.'

'No, not the farm.' I gave him Ruby's address and told him he could stay the night there. Ruby would guide him to the rendezvous with the skip truck, but I didn't tell Jerzy about that part of the plan. I got him to repeat the address to make sure he had it and reminded him that there was no GRID, so he wouldn't be able to contact me and made him promise to be at Ruby's by midnight.

'No worries. Midnight. I will be there.'

I let him get back to his mates in the pub and prayed I could rely on him. How would he react when he discovered what he was really being asked to do? He hated FIST, I knew that. *He's cool*, I told myself. *Jerzy will be fine – Jerzy is the least of your problems.*

CHAPTER 31

'That's The Chiller – the punishment block,' Ashanti said, pointing to a building set apart from the others.

'What happens there?' I asked.

'Solitary confinement, usually. There are loads of little concrete cells – like cupboards. You get locked up on your own for days, weeks – months, sometimes the kids say, if you refuse to work or break a rule or just get on the wrong side of one of the guards. No furniture, no bedding, even in winter.'

It was almost eight in the evening, and we were up on the tor above Holdstone. Bethan had printed me a copy of the map of the camp, and it was now spread out on the rock between us, its corners weighted down with pebbles to stop it blowing away, while we matched the features marked on it with the buildings in the valley below us. We'd brought the binoculars that I had used to watch the rooks during my first days on the farm. I focused them on the punishment block. It was getting a little too dark to make out much detail, but I could see that there were no windows and only one entrance.

'That big building with the chimneys is the woodchip plant. That's where Pete and Monkey pick up the waste skip tomorrow morning around five thirty. The long, low, wooden buildings are the sleeping huts, girls on the right and boys on the left. The camp for the adults is on the other side of the factory buildings.'

'Can you get from one camp to the other?'

'No. Kids and adults work in separate parts of the factory. They're not allowed to meet. Only the kids not old enough to do useful work are left with their mothers.'

A siren sounded down in the valley.

As I examined the factory buildings through the binoculars, a large group emerged and jogged to the parade ground-like space in the centre of the camp, accompanied by four guards. As the group arrived, a similar-sized group with its own guards set off from the parade ground towards the factory.

'Change of shift,' Ashanti said. 'They change every four hours in the children's camp. Four hours on, four hours off, day and night.'

'What do they make in the factory?'

'The boys work in the woodchip plant making building materials, the girls work in that grey building making electronic equipment. Stuff for the GRID mostly. Your G-Port would have been made there.'

'You're kidding!'

'How do you think they can make them so cheap? How do you think they can afford to give you a new one every year? Slave labour. And kids have good eyes; they can put all those little bits together much quicker than adults can.'

I took my G-Port out of my pocket and examined it.

'It says made in Yemen.'

'Yeah, and some say made in Senegal and some say made in East Timor. The whole thing's a lie.'

'Ashanti...' I had to ask – even though I didn't want to hear the answer, '. . . Do you think my dad knows?'

She looked me squarely in the eyes, 'What do you think?'

'He must do, mustn't he?'

'Does it make a difference that what he does exploits kids here rather than in the countries where you thought they made that stuff?'

I put the portal back in my pocket. To be honest, I'd never given any thought to where these things came from. They were just things everybody had.

'That black building – that's new. Built since the last time Ruby managed to smuggle me in.'

I took a look at it through the binoculars. It was made out of some sort of shiny material like darkened glass. As I watched, the image of a desert landscape spread across the walls – hazy at first, and then clearer – in sharper focus. The landscape faded and was replaced by faces – gaunt African faces. The walls were actually giant screens. But why these pictures? Was FIST trying to remind the kids of what they left behind? And why would they do that? Now all but one of the faces faded. The one that was left was the face of a young woman. Despite the hollow cheeks and the sunken eyes, she smiled tenderly.

'What on earth goes on in there?'

'I don't know, but the kids are all scared of it because whatever happens in there messes your brain up.'

'How do you mean?'

'The ones who have been taken in there have lost their memories. They don't even know who they are. FIST calls it Q Block. The kids call it The Eraser. It's got to be some sort of laboratory.'

'Are you saying they're using the kids as guinea pigs?!'

'Must be.'

The screens all went black; then images of multicoloured butterflies fluttered across the glossy walls.

'Come on, time we got going. Should be dark by the time we get up to the top of the valley,' Ashanti said.

I took a final look at our destination. There was the canal that supplied the camp with water. The water entered a pipe that ran under the perimeter fence. We were going to crawl through that pipe when Tony and Cara blocked the canal. Inside the fence, the reservoir glittered in the evening light. A tall watchtower stood close to the entrance to the pipe. I guess we all knew it was a crazy plan. I put away the binoculars and followed Ashanti around behind the tor.

We came out of the trees an hour later on an unsealed forestry service road. A dump-truck was parked a few metres down the track. Keeping to the side, we headed towards it and, as we approached, two stocky figures of identical height stepped from behind it.

'Spot on time,' said Cara.

'Can you get the truck to the canal without being seen from Holdstone?' Ashanti asked.

'The track's still in the trees where it meets the canal,' said Tony.

'What about noise?' I asked 'That watchtower's awfully close.'

'Chainsaw,' said Cara. 'I'll rev one up while Tony dumps the rubble in the canal. They're used to us doing forestry work around the place. They'll just think we're doing a spot of clearing.'

'Hop in,' said Tony.

We all squeezed into the cab. Tony started the engine, and we bumped down the track to a turning place by the canal.

'Here are your uniforms.' Cara handed each of us a sealed, black bag. 'If you change when you're through the pipe, they'll stay dry. Also, you don't want to be creeping around outside the fence in a yellow jumpsuit. We've stitched a microchip into the sleeve of each uniform. Of course, they should be imbedded in your arms, but we figured you wouldn't fancy that. Bethan's done the electronic wizardry. Mark, you've got Owando's details on your chip. That way, you can take his place on his work shift. You don't look anything like him, but the computer will clock you in regardless. There's a sensor in the doorway of every building. Every time you enter or leave a building, the computer knows about it. Enter a building you're not meant to be in, and it'll set the alarms off. Ashanti, we've given you Chittagong's details. You know her, don't you?'

'Yeah, sure.'

'So you swap with her. Here's a G-Port to film with. It's not as flash as Mark's, but it's small and waterproof, and Bethan says it's got a good camera. Right... That's it, I guess. – I'm still not happy about this.'

'Can you think of a better plan?' Ashanti asked.

'No... but... No, I can't. Just... For God's sake, be careful.' She hugged Ashanti tightly.

'We'll give you five minutes to get down to the pipe,' said Tony. 'We removed the grill from the end after we left you last night, and I can tell you, the water's bloody cold. When you hear the chainsaw start up, you'll know we're about to dump the rubble into the canal. As soon as the water level drops, get through the pipe. I don't know how long the dam will hold, so don't hang about.'

I couldn't trust my voice not to give away how scared I was, so I just nodded, then opened the passenger-side door, and jumped down from the cab. Ashanti followed, and we were on our way.

A coil of razor wire, like a big stretched-out spring, ran along the top of the high chain-link fence. Inside the fence, there was a gap of perhaps eight metres and then a second fence.

'When we get to the other side, don't touch the inner fence. It's electrified,' whispered Ashanti.

'If we get to the other side,' I couldn't help muttering.

'Glad you're being positive.'

We were crouching behind a bush at the edge of the canal. Black water swirled past and disappeared into the mouth of the large concrete pipe that took it under the fence. Looking up through the branches, I could see the spindly structure of the watchtower. In the little cabin that was perched on top, two guards were leaning against the railing, chatting. I could hear their voices but not make out any words.

The sudden stutter of the chainsaw made the guards straighten up. A searchlight flicked on throwing a bright circle of light on to the trees at the edge of the forest. The beam probed the foliage and then dropped to scan the open ground between our bush and the forest verge. We pressed further under the bush, keeping our faces down and tucking our hands out of sight. The searchlight snapped off. The guards went back to lounging against the railing.

I watched the water. The level was already dropping. Now it only half filled the pipe. I glanced up at the guards. They had their backs to us.

'Let's go!' I said.

After tucking the bags that held our uniforms up our shirts, we slid down the concrete side of the canal into the water. It wasn't deep, but Tony was right about it being bloody freezing, and I was shocked to see how small the entrance to the pipe was, only just high enough to crawl through. At that moment, the water level was still falling, but I imagined it rising while we were in the pipe and being unable to lift my nose and mouth above the water.

I started down the pipe, Ashanti just behind me. In no time, my knees were raw from the rough surface, and the back of my head was scraped. The flow was down to a trickle, but I was terrified that the dam would break at any moment, and we would be inundated by a surging mass of mud and water. I hurried forward in the total darkness, head down like an old dog.

'Mark!' Ashanti called, urgently. 'The water's coming back!'

She was right. The water was over my hands; it was rising again. It must have topped the dam but not broken it yet. Hurry! Hurry! How much further? There was a new sound, the echo-y sound of water cascading down a slope. *Can't be far now,* I thought. *But what if there is a grate at the other end? Had anyone checked that?* I was about to call back to Ashanti when there was a roar, and she was flung against me as water full of bits of rubble and clods of earth surged past us, then filled the pipe and carried us with it. I fought to hold my breath. The pipe suddenly sloped steeply downwards. One moment I was dropping headfirst, the next, I was out of the pipe and under water, tumbling, disorientated, not knowing which way was up, kicking wildly. Then my head broke the surface, and there was air!

Where was Ashanti? I trod water and twisted this way and that. Had she got out of the pipe? Had she got stuck? It was so dark.

I heard the gasp and the cough. There! She was there! Two strokes and I was beside her. She held on to me as she took choking breaths.

'Tony… and his… great ideas! I'll bloody kill him!' she spluttered.

'Let's get to the side,' I said.

We swam together to the edge of the reservoir and pulled ourselves out. The reservoir was surrounded by a low bank. I was anxious to get out of sight of the watchtower, so I crawled over the bank and rolled down the other side where I lay getting my breath. Ashanti rolled against me.

'Uniforms,' she said. 'Still got yours?'

'Yeah. Do we change here?'

'No. They practically glow in the dark. Change under the sleeping huts.'

Each hut had a patch of loose floorboards that the kids used as a way of getting in and out at night without attracting the attention of the guards. The plan was that I would get into Owando's hut and Ashanti would get into Chittagong's hut using these secret entrances.

'Right. I know the way. I better lead,' she said. 'Ready?'

'Ready as I'll ever be.'

Ashanti squeezed my hand. 'Wish us luck.'

'Yeah. Good luck us,' I said.

CHAPTER 32

The wooden sleeping huts were raised off the ground on short brick piles. Lying on my back in the dark under Hut 5, with the floorboards only inches above my nose, I began wriggling out of my jeans and jacket. They were wet and clung to my arms and legs making them almost impossible to remove. Idiot! Why didn't I at least take my jacket off before going under the hut? At last, they were off, and I pulled the yellow Holdstone jumpsuit out of its sealed bag and squirmed my way into it. Ashanti would be doing the same under Hut 2.

Something scuttled amongst the litter that had collected under the hut. Mice? Maybe a rat. I lay still, listening. Whatever it was, it was also staying still.

I took my G-Port out of my jacket pocket and checked the time. It was 11.30, half an hour before the midnight-shift change. I transferred the port to the hidden pocket that Cara had sewn inside the jumpsuit, stuffed my clothes into the black bag, and tucked it in amongst the litter.

I counted the floor joists from the back of the hut. The loose boards should be between the fourth and fifth joists and near to the third brick pile from the left side of the hut. Pushing with my feet and kind of walking with my shoulders, I got myself under what I hoped was the right spot. My hair, by now, was full of spiderwebs and a good deal of dirt had gone down my neck. The first couple of boards I tried didn't move, but then I pushed a board a little further to the left, and a small, roughly square section lifted. The boards had been cut and joined together to make a trapdoor. Carefully, I eased it up. It struck something and wouldn't go any further. I found that it wasn't hinged, like I first thought, but that I could push the whole thing up and slide it aside. I got my head and arms through the hole, but I was under something. Then the something began to move, and I saw that there were faces peering at me down on my level. I could see now that the thing I had come up under was a bed that must have been placed there to hide the trapdoor.

'Hey! Who is it?' someone asked.

'It's a new one.'

'No. He been on the ship. Casablanca almost kill him!'

'It's the English.'

'It's rich boy!'

'What you doing here, rich boy?'

Then Owando pushed his way through to kneel beside me.

'Dr London! You here! What happens?'

I got the rest of myself up through the hole in the floor and sat on the edge of the bed. A little light came in through the bare windows from the security lights outside. There was a row of wooden bunk beds down each side of the long hut, and by each bunk, there was a small steel locker that the kid on the upper and the lower bunk must have had to share. There was no other furniture. All the kids in the hut crowded round me, climbing on to the bunk above where I sat and on to the bunks opposite.

'I've come to take your place on tonight's work shift,' I said.

'Why? How? You have no chip in the arm. The computer, it knows who comes.'

'It's OK. I have a chip. Here – feel.' I guided his hand to the tiny lump in my sleeve. 'It has your details on it. The computer won't know. Do the guards ever bother to check who is there?'

'No, they are lazy pigs.'

'Good.' I took out my G-Port. 'I need to film everything. We are going to show the world what is happening here. Ashanti is here too. She will film in the electronics factory.'

'Why should the world care?' an older boy asked.

'People will care. I promise,' I said. 'There are lots of decent people in this country.'

'Where they live? How come I never meet them?' the boy said.

'Hey! Shut up, you! Dr London try to help us! Sorry, Dr London,' Owando said, 'some very ignorant persons.'

I wanted to tell Owando that my plan included getting him out with us, but I couldn't tell him in front of the others. Somehow I'd have to get him on his own. Then I noticed that one of the kids on the bunk opposite me was Abuja, but rather than looking at me, he seemed to stare through me at something much further away.

'Hi, Abuja,' I said. There was not even a flicker of recognition. His little face continued to stare with the same vacant expression.

'No good, Dr London. They take Abuja to the Eraser. There is nothing left in his head.'

I saw that all the other kids' faces change; now they looked at me with a mixture of fear and challenge.

'This is going to stop,' I said. 'I promise this is going to stop. But you must all help me.'

'We help you, Dr London. Don't we!' Owando said, looking around fiercely, and there was a murmur of agreement.

'Good. You have to show me what I'm meant to be doing when I take Owando's place tonight and don't let the guards suspect anything. If some of you can get between me and the guards, then I can film without them seeing.'

'One problem,' said Owando.

'What's that?'

'Salamandaga, he is in the same work shift.'

'You think he will make trouble?'

'Maybe. He don't know it was me jumped on him, but he know you.'

'What about Casablanca? Is he on the shift?'

'Casablanca, they put him in the Chiller for good after what he do.'

Just then, the siren sounded for the change of shift. All the kids except Abuja and Owando jumped down off the bunks to line up at the door. One of the bigger boys grabbed Abuja and made him line up with the others.

'Sarayova? What hut's she in?' I whispered when the others were out of earshot.

'Hut 2. But I don't see her yesterday.'

'Ashanti will see her. She's gone to Hut 2. We're going to get you two out. We all go out in the skip truck in the morning.'

'We talk when shift end,' Owando said. 'You got hat?' I noticed all the others were now wearing peaked cloth caps.

'No, I don't.' Perhaps there was one in the bag that I hadn't noticed.

'Here,' Owando handed me his. 'You wear this.'

'Thanks.'

'Quick! Before guards come, I must hide.' Owando dropped down through the hole in the floor, only to pop up again. 'Take care of the conveyer – He ate my fingers!' He gave a cheery wave of his fingerless hand and disappeared. I'd always thought he'd lost his fingers in some brutal African conflict. But no, it was here. I closed the hatch and pushed the bunk back over it, then hurried to join the line by the door, pulling the cap down low on my forehead. A boy my own height made room for me and indicated with a little flick of his head that I should stand with him and the other older kids. I felt very conspicuous, but hoped I didn't look it. A moment later, when the door was thrown open and the lights came on, I felt even more conspicuous. In the doorway stood a FIST officer. He looked massive in his black uniform, stabvest and steel-capped boots. In his leather-gloved right hand, he carried a long baton that he beat rhythmically against his trouser leg. I could feel the fear rise in the group around me.

'OK, kiddies! It's playtime again,' he said, smiling and stepped aside to let us out.

We filed out through the door. As each boy passed it, a little box in the entranceway gave a loud bleep, and an orange light flashed. Bethan was supposed to be a technical whizz-kid; I was about to find out if that was true. The line shortened in front of me. The boy ahead passed the detector, and the bleep sounded. Now it was my turn. I stepped forward, trying to look unconcerned, but I wasn't actually breathing. I must have hesitated because the boy behind me gave me a small shove. Then – what relief! There was a bleep, and I was standing with the others outside the hut.

'Get in line, you!'

Before I realised I was being spoken to, I felt the guard's baton poke me hard in the ribs, and I staggered into my place. Three other guards stood watching us: a woman and two more men. All had the same long batons that they swung by their wrist straps or tapped against their legs like the first guard.

'Right! Move it! Come on! Quick time, you horrible little foreigners!'

Flanked by the guards, we jogged down a path and on to the floodlit parade ground in the middle of the camp. Other groups with their own guards were arriving from other huts. I searched the girls' group and found Ashanti. Like me, she was standing with kids her own age and height, and her African features and wiry build helped her blend in with the mixed bunch of skinny girls around her. But I was looking for another face and couldn't find it. Where was Sarayova? She should be in the same work shift as Ashanti. Why wasn't she there? Dread gripped my stomach. What if we couldn't find her? What had they done to her? If they'd put her in the Chiller... No, there was no way of getting her out of the Chiller, with its one door and no windows. Where was she?

'Oy!'

I'd failed to move as the others began to move and a baton caught me hard across the shoulder. I closed up the gap between me and the boy in front of me and told myself to stay on the ball.

We were heading for the woodchip plant behind another group of boys, with four more guards. Good, that would be Salamandaga's group. If he arrived at the plant first, maybe I could keep out of his way.

We jogged rounded the corner of the electronics factory, that had now swallowed Ashanti's group, and there, ahead of us were the glistening walls of The Eraser. The screens were showing images that must have been coming from the CCTV cameras around the camp. High up on the wall, facing us, I could see a mirror image of our own group as we approached the camera mounted on the corner of the building, and a small boy at the front earned himself a viscous blow across the head for being stupid enough to wave at the camera. He cried out and stumbled but was hauled up and carried forward by the kids around him who hardly dropped their pace.

As we passed them, the screens went to black and then a single image spread across the entire side wall: a beautiful, peaceful scene, like something out of a travelogue. A quiet, country road led down a mountain between forests and fields. There was a stream and a stone bridge and people picnicking by the stream. The sun shone and the water in the stream sparkled. We couldn't help slowing down to look, and a sound somewhere between a sigh and a groan escaped from the group. In the concrete and barbed wire surroundings of the camp, it was like a glimpse of paradise. 'Stop gawping and get moving!' the guards screamed at us. And so we looked away and moved quickly on.

I needn't have worried about not knowing what I was supposed to do in the woodchip plant. Our job was simple enough. We were taken to a building the size of an aircraft hangar in which there was a mountain of pieces of timber that were too small or too knotted for the sawmill. These had to be carried to the conveyer belt that fed them into the teeth of the chipping machinery. A number of boys were positioned along the edge of the mountain as 'loaders'; the rest of us were 'carriers'. The loaders piled as much timber on to our arms as we could hold. We then ran to the conveyer, dumped the timber on to it and ran back to the loaders. Soon my hands were full of splinters, and my arms were raw, but anyone not running, not carrying enough or dropping a piece of wood, earned a kick or a blow from the guards.

As I ran between the conveyer and the timber mountain that never seemed to get smaller, the image on the screens of the Eraser kept coming back to me. That road and the stream, it was like somewhere I remembered but couldn't place, or maybe a dream I had had. Why was it so familiar? Had I really been there? I saw it over and over, like a little piece of film in my mind. *Sarayova! It's her road! Her stream!* I was sure. I was absolutely certain. *No. That's crazy,* I told myself. *That road, that stream could be anywhere.* But if I were right, what would that mean? How could a place that she had described to me, a place that no longer even looked like that, be there, projected on the screens of the Eraser? And where was Sarayova? Why wasn't she in the work detail with the rest of her hut?

I had to remind myself what I was here for. I was collecting evidence. Whenever I found myself hidden in the middle of a pack of kids waiting for the loaders, I would get out my G-Port and photograph the torn and bleeding hands of my companions or film them staggering under their loads, weaving between the eight guards, dodging the kicks and blows.

A few boys were detailed to work in pairs and carry pieces too heavy for one boy to lift alone. I managed for the first half of the shift to time my journeys to and from the conveyer so that my path never crossed Salamandaga's, but when a guard noticed a large log that everyone had been avoiding, he beckoned me over and then, to my horror, pointed at Salamandaga and shouted for him to come and help me.

I tugged my cap even lower and kept my face down as if looking at the log. Together we lugged it across the yard without him noticing who I was, but as I turned from dropping the log on to the belt, he caught sight of my face, and in a flash, he had grabbed hold of the front of my overall, and he was forcing me back against the moving conveyer.

From the corner of my eye, I could see the pieces of timber falling from the end of the belt into the spinning teeth of the woodchip machine. If I lost my balance, the conveyer would carry me into the hopper and drop me down that smooth metal shoot into the rotating blades.

I twisted to the side, throwing my weight away from the machinery. But he was bigger and stronger and forced me back against the rollers. I seized two fistfuls of his overall; if I fell, he'd fall with me. He tried to shake me loose, but I hung on. My overall tore open, and I saw something small and black drop amongst the timber on the conveyer. It was my G-Port! The evidence! The recordings! It was all about to be destroyed by the chipping machine! But just before it dropped into the hopper, a hand shot over and picked it up. I had no time to see whose it was. Salamandaga's head connected with mine, and we topped sideways, still locked together, to roll over and over on the ground. Neither of us had spoken a word, and we continued to struggle in grim, determined silence until the guards stepped in and hauled us apart giving us each a few strokes with their batons for good measure.

'If you want a beating, just ask one of us!' the guard who had my arm twisted up behind my back shouted. 'Now, what's your problem?'

Salamandaga looked at me, then spat on the floor. 'A spy. I know him. He betray us.'

'Don't you spit at me, or I'll beat your black skin off your back!' the guard growled.

'Right! Who've we got here?' The big man who had let us out of the sleeping hut and seemed to be in charge, strode over. He unhooked a device like an ID card reader from his belt and ran it down beside Salamandaga's arm, then looked at the screen. 'Might have known. You lot from Mali spend more time in the Chiller than out of it! Get him out of here, he obviously wants another dose.' Salamandaga managed to turn and glare at me one last time as he was marched away.

'And who are you?' He ran the reader down my arm. 'The Congo! You don't look like you come from the Congo! So who the hell are you?' He took hold of my collar and yanked open the front of my jumpsuit, pulling it off my shoulder. I knew what he was looking for. The telltale scar left when the chip was inserted. 'Have a look at this!' he called to the woman guard who came over to see what was interesting him. 'The chip, it's sewn into the bloody suit.' He took a multi-tool out of its little leather pouch, opened the blade and cut the stitching, then removed the chip and, after they had both examined it, he put it in his pocket.

All work had stopped. The other kids, round-eyed with expectation, watched to see what would happen next.

'No one told you to stop working!' the big guard bellowed. The movement back and forward to the conveyer started up again, but heads turned as they passed.

'So... who are you, and what are you doing here?'

I stared straight ahead. The woman swung her baton back and brought it cracking across the side of my head, making my ear sing and an explosion of dots burst before my eyes.

'He asked you a question!'

I had to give them something. But what could I say? My head whirled and throbbed. The next blow was to my lower back and the pain was deep and ugly. They knew just where to hit you, these people. I could feel the blood trickling from my ear, down my neck and into my overalls.

'OK! OK! I was sent by Get Real Magazine!'

'Never heard of it.'

'It's a kids' magazine. They're doing a story on climate refugees.'

'So how did you get in here?'

'They paid one of the guards.'

'The little shit's lying!' The woman swung back her baton.

'Hang on, Mary,' the big guard said. 'We'll take him up to Q Block. He's perfect for them. Soon find out if he's telling the truth.'

'Quicker to beat it out of him.'

'What if he really is from a magazine?'

'Na!'

'He could be. He's sort-a geeky looking.'

'Na! He'd have a camera, wouldn't he, or som'in'.'

The one who had been twisting my arm let it go and frisked me quickly. 'Not carrying anything.'

'You stay here and keep an eye on this lot, Mary. I'm taking him up to Q Block. If we beat him up, and some magazine gets hold of it… You know what those bleeding-heart reporters are like.'

'What's it matter? When he comes out of Q Block, his brain will be fried – he won't remember anything anyway!'

'Yeah, well. I'm taking him up there. Come on you! Or I'll let Mary do what she likes with you.'

As we left, I glanced around all the kids, wondering who had the G-Port, but there was no way of telling. Would they give it to Ashanti? It was all up to her now; there was no way I was going to get to the rendezvous in the morning.

CHAPTER 33

The same scene of the mountain road, the stream, and the bridge was playing on the screens on the side of the Eraser as we passed them. The guard took an electronic key from a pouch on his belt and squeezed it. The doors to the sleek, black building slid open.

'Don't try anything in here,' he said and prodded me in with the end of his baton.

In the building, it was dark. It was like walking into a cinema when the film has already started because the insides of the walls, like the outsides, were giant screens, and they were lit up with the pictures of the road and the stream, only now we were closer to the picnickers, and I could see that there were about a dozen adults sitting on the bank and lots of children playing in the water.

All the surfaces in the building that weren't glass or brushed steel were black. The floor was tiled with black polished stone that reflected the flickering images on the screens.

Another guard sat behind a desk made of the same black material. The guards nodded to each other, and the one at the desk indicated that we should be quiet. Ahead of us was a glass barrier, about waist-height, and as we came closer to it, I saw that the floor we had entered on ended and beyond the barrier, it dropped down to a lower level so that we were looking down on the main floor of the Eraser which was below ground. There were workstations with consoles and monitors and, in the centre, in a bright pool of light, a machine of some sort, like a long, horizontal tube.

Five people in white, laboratory coveralls stood by the machine. One I recognised immediately: Tristram Rainer. But who was the short, fat man he was talking to? Then he turned slightly, and I saw his face – Ronald Parker – Roll-over-Ron! The Mayor of London. So he was in this too!

'This is only a proto-type,' Rainer was saying. 'Eventually, we will be able to make small units that can be sited anywhere. People will only need to walk past them; like CCTV cameras, they will be all over every city, every building, only we won't just be able to see what people are doing, we will be able to see what they are thinking. Imagine the security implications for London, Ronald! Anyone thinking of planting a bomb, starting a demonstration, committing a crime, causing any sort of disruption, and we will be able to see it. We will be able to use people's own thoughts as evidence against them.'

'And does it work?' Parker asked.

'It's improving, eh, Doctor?'

'Still the problem with amnesia.'

'Meaning?' asked Parker.

'It wipes our subjects' memories,' said the doctor.

'Turns 'em into zombies,' Rainer laughed.

'We don't know how permanently,' the doctor added. 'And like this girl, some subjects have learnt to block the machine from accessing their thoughts by concentrating on an image that possesses particularly strong emotional associations.'

They all looked up at the screens where the children still played happily in the stream while their parents watched and chatted.

'This girl,' the doctor had said, 'This girl!' – He was talking about Sarayova – I knew it was Sarayova! And what we were seeing were her thoughts, her beautiful memories of her home, her mountain, her stream before her neighbours killed her parents. But where was she? What were they doing to her? Was she in that machine? I wanted to run down the steps and throttle the doctor! I wanted to scream in his face, 'That girl is not a subject! She's not a thing to stick in a test tube! You know nothing about her! That girl is the bravest, most incredible person on the planet!' What could I do? I felt useless, helpless. I'd let them catch me, and now all I could do was watch while these monsters destroyed Sarayova's mind.

'We think that if we increase the power of the magnetic resonator, we can get past these blocking techniques, but it means shutting down and adding more circuits.'

'How soon can you be ready?' asked Rainer.

'We'll need a couple of hours.'

'Get them to call me as soon as you've cracked the problem,' said Rainer. 'Luckily we're not short of guinea-pigs,' he remarked to Parker as they turned to go, and they both chuckled.

I thought they would come up the steps to our level, and I knew both Rainer and Parker would recognise me. But they came up by the lift near the main doors, so they didn't pass me on their way out.

'Hey, Doc! I've got you a really good one!' my guard called down.

The doctor looked up at us. 'We're making some improvements. Bring him back in a couple of hours.'

'Right you are,' the guard said, and then, 'Well, son, looks like we'll have to show you some of our other facilities before they fry your brains.' He took me by the arm, but I pulled back.

'Wait!'

A body was sliding out of the machine on a rolling bed. When I saw her face, the skin was white and the lips were blue, as if she had been drained of blood, and when the two assistants got her sitting up her head lolled forward.

'Get her back to her hut,' the doctor said without looking at her. He was already busy with something inside the machine.

'Don't worry, it'll be your turn soon,' the guard said. But as he propelled me towards the doors, all I could think of was Sarayova's corpse-like body sliding out of the machine. Was it already too late? Would she know me if she saw me? A hopeless desperation flooded up through my chest, and I dug my fingernails into my palms as the tears stung my eyes.

'We're full,' the guard on duty at the Chiller said. 'Got two in each cell as it is, what with all them troublemakers they caught.'

'What about the Moroccan?'

'Na, we've not got anyone in with him. He's got to be kept strictly solitary. That's the orders. After what he's done, I reckon he'll spend the rest of his life in solitary.'

'It's just for a couple of hours. Then I take him back to Q Block.'

'Well? And what am I meant to do with him?'

'Put him in with the Moroccan.'

''Gainst orders. I told you.'

'Ah, for Pete's sake! Two hours! Who's going to know? Otherwise, I have to look after him, and I miss my break. Go on. Be a pal.'

'Well…'

'Go on. Two hours. No more.'

'All right. Bring him in. But two hours, and no more!'

'Scouts' honour.'

'You was never a scout.'

'What do you know?'

'I know you was never a scout!'

The Chiller guard sorted through a number of electronic keys on a large ring, pressed one, the barred inner door swung open, and he shoved me through.

'Thanks, mate.'

'Yeah, yeah. Just make sure you're back in two hours.' The door swung shut with a heavy clang behind us, and he pushed me along a narrow, windowless passage lined on one side by the locked doors of the cells. The place stank like a zoo.

'Stop there,' he said. He flicked through his keys again and then the door of the nearest cell opened.

'Brought you some company!' The boot in the backside sent me flying into the cell before the door slammed. I tripped over a pair of legs and crashed into the back wall. When I turned, Casablanca's furious face was staring up at me. He was sitting with his back against the side wall and his legs stretched out. The cell was no more than two metres long and a metre and half wide and brightly lit. The walls had been white but were now a filthy grey to shoulder height. There was a foul-smelling bucket at the end opposite the door, otherwise the cell was bare.

'You! Everywhere you come to spy on me!'

He got to his feet and with one hand on my throat, pinned me to the wall.

'No,' I croaked, 'no, you have it all wrong.'

'I don't think so.'

'Why would I be in here if I were a spy?'

'You come to the house in the woods, then FIST come. You come to the ship, then FIST come. Now you come here. It was a mistake I don't shoot you. This time I really kill you.'

'I'm your chance to get out of here. You kill me, you'll never get out.'

'You get me out? Ha! How you get me out? Oh, I see it's a trick. They send you in here. You promise me things, get me to talk – where I hide the guns, things like that – then you tell FIST. No!' He slammed me back against the wall. 'No deal!'

'No! I hate FIST! I have nothing to do with them.'

'Then why are you here, rich boy?'

He was crushing my windpipe. What could I tell him? What would he believe? Particularly now that everything had gone so terribly wrong. I searched, desperately in my mind for something, anything, a crumb to throw to him – 'Help me... and I'll teach you to play the saxophone!' Don't ask me how or why I came up with that, it just sort of fell out of my mouth.

'What?!'

'The saxophone... you know...' It sounded ridiculous. What was I saying?!

'You teach me?' The anger in his face changed to bafflement.

'Yes.'

He started to laugh. 'The saxophone!' He eased the pressure on my throat. 'You teach me saxophone!'

'Yes. Would you like that?'

'You're crazy!'

'No. Really. You could learn, I'm certain – really – believe me. In the forest... when you hijacked our car, when you picked it up, when you played a note – I knew – You can always tell – I could see that you could learn.' I didn't care what I was saying, if I could keep talking, if I could get him to talk to me about anything other than killing. 'Of course, we'd have to start with easy tunes. Not, you know, not nursery rhymes of course, but... You'd soon pick it up.'

'Easy tunes?' He snorted with laughter.

'Yes.'

'So, you come to Holdstone to teach me music?!' His expression darkened and his grip tightened.

'No – No, of course not.'

'Why then?'

'To find out what is happening here. Listen, I have a plan – Maybe it's not a good plan, but I think that if people knew what was happening here, then this place would be shut down. Ashanti is here too, and FIST haven't caught her yet. We are taking pictures. We are going to show the world what FIST are doing here.'

'No one cares.'

'They will.'

'Who will?'

'Young people – decent people. Think of Ashanti, think of Ruby – Bethan, Tony, Cara. They've risked their lives for you.'

He let go of my throat. 'Ashanti is here?'

'Yes.'

'How did you get in?'

'The reservoir. We came through the pipe.'

'How do you get out?'

'In the skip truck in the morning.'

He turned my face to inspect my split ear and swollen cheek. 'They beat you?'

'Yes.'

'So... I don't understand – if this is true – why do you do this?'

'I don't know. Really, I don't know. I didn't mean to get mixed up in this, it just happened.'

He looked at me steadily, and then smiled knowingly. 'And now there is the Turkish girl, Mm? Sarayova – or do you call her Rana?'

I saw her white face again, her lifeless body emerging from the machine, and the helpless desperation flooded back. 'Get me out. You have to help me get out of here,' I begged. 'Please.'

'Oh dear,' he mimed patting his pockets, 'I lost my keys.'

'There are two of us. We could overpower the guard.'

'Oh yes! Simple! Of course!' He was angry again. His face in my face. 'You think I don't think of that before? The chip – as soon as I leave the cell, it sets off the alarm and a hundred guards come running.'

'I don't have a chip.' I pulled down my collar. He looked at my arm.

'OK for you! You know what they do to me for attacking a guard? Eh? You think that little bruise on your face is something? That little bruise is nothing!'

I could imagine what they would do. I could imagine it very well, but I needed him to help me, so I pushed on. I looked him in the eye. 'You remember what you said to me on the ship? "Better be dead than a slave. Better be dead than live without honour." Think of Hatiya! You want her to have a chance of freedom? You want her to have a life? You going to let them put her in the Eraser because you're scared of what the guards might do to you? What about respect? What about honour? If I get out, there's hope. Maybe I can do something.'

'Or maybe the guards beat us both to death.'

'Maybe.'

We stared at each other. I'd challenged him; I'd very nearly called him a coward. The thick, stinking air in the tiny cell pulsed under the bright strip light. He took a deep breath like a diver about to plunge into the water. 'OK... OK,' he said at last, 'This is what we do – We beat on the door, OK? We shout, we scream, we make a big noise until the guard open the door. Understand?'

I nodded.

'As soon as he open the door, we grab him, and we run fast at that wall.' He pointed to the back of the cell.

'Right.'

'You take the key. You lock the cell. You go. I stay and watch the guard.'

I nodded again.

'Now!' he shouted.

We threw ourselves at the door, kicking it, hammering it with our fists and screaming at the top of our voices. After a just a few minutes, the viewing window slid open.

'Hey!' the guard outside screamed. 'Hey! Cut that out!' But we kept it up. 'Hey! If you don't cut that out you're going to regret it!' We got even louder. 'Hey! I warned you!'

Finally, the door began to open. Casablanca's arm shot through the gap, grabbed the guard's uniform, and pulled. As the guard, caught off balance, almost fell through the doorway, I seized him on the other side, and we launch ourselves at the back wall. There was a sickening crunch as the guard hit the wall and he slid to the floor. Casablanca was on top of him immediately, pulling the guard's arms behind his back and handcuffing them with his own handcuffs. Then he used the guard's belt to tie his legs together.

'Keys, keys, keys!' Casablanca yelled at me. I realised I had been standing, stunned, watching like an idiot. I picked up the ring of keys as Casablanca finished trussing and gagging the guard.

'Here!' Casablanca took the guard's pistol out of its holster and handed it to me. It was black and heavy.

'No,' I said.

'Take it!'

'No.' I laid it on the floor beside Casablanca. I was scared of it, scared to even hold it.

'Go!' He kicked the pistol well away from the guard.

I stopped in the doorway. 'Thank you.'

He gave a scornful snort.

'I don't know your name.'

'Amal.'

'Thank you, Amal.'

'Go!'

I stepped through the door and pulled it shut. Then I heard the *click* as it locked.

I hurried down the passage, and as I passed the other cells, I could hear kids inside calling out. I wanted to free them all, but their chips would trigger the alarm. I kept going. Luckily the electronic keys were labelled. I found the one for the main door and unlocked it. The guard's lobby was empty. The sports pages of a newspaper were open on the desk and steam still rose from a half drunk cup of coffee.

The clock on the wall said 04.45. That meant the skip truck would be leaving in three-quarters of an hour. I had to find Ashanti, Owando, and Sarayova. I checked the image on the CCTV screen in the lobby to see which way the camera outside the door pointed. It pointed down the path. If I hugged the wall, I should slip under it.

Outside the Chiller, it was still dark except where floodlights on sides of buildings and on posts around the parade ground created pools of brightness. I mapped out a route in my head that would keep me in the shadows and avoid the cameras, then set off.

At every corner, I expected to walk into a guard, every sound made me freeze, and it was a relief when at last I was back under the sleeping hut. But how long before they discovered what had happened in the Chiller? The guard who had taken me there had said he would be back in two hours. The problem was that I didn't know how long ago that had been.

'Owando!' I called softly. There was rustling in the litter. 'Owando,' I tried again. The rustling continued, but it must have been rats. I pushed up the trapdoor in the floorboards.

'Dr London?'

'Owando! Thank goodness.'

There was the scraping of the bed being moved aside and hands reached down to help me up, faces crowded around.

'Mark, what happened? Your face!' Ashanti was beside me as I climbed out of the hole. 'We heard they took you away.'

'Sarayova, is she with you?' I asked.

I saw the look that passed between Ashanti and Owando.

'What? I know she was in the Eraser, but she was fighting it – She wouldn't let them into her head. I saw her.'

'How did you see?' Ashanti asked.

'It doesn't matter how! Where is she?'

'She's in the girls' hut. They brought her back... Mark... It's not good. We can't help her.'

'It's not permanent! The doctor – I heard him say – She could recover – We have to get her out.'

'It's too risky, Mark. She doesn't know what she's doing. She'll give us away.'

'Listen, Ashanti,' I gripped her arms and made her look at me, 'you do what you like, I'm not leaving without her.'

'You're risking everything!'

'I know. And she risked everything for you.'

That got through. Ashanti sat down on the bunk. 'OK,' she said, 'But I don't know how we're going to do this – and we're running out of time.'

I heard whispering in the crowd of kids around us; then Owando said, 'Dr London, we can help.'

We both looked at him, his face so serious and determined. 'We all go out – everyone – from all the huts. We make big trouble for the guards. They chase us while you take Sarayova and go.'

'But will she come with us?' Ashanti asked. 'She didn't recognise me.'

'Take Abuja,' Owando said, 'he is special to her. Perhaps she still know him. In five minutes we start the trouble. We lead the guards away, then you go.'

'Can you do something else for me?'

'Yes, Dr London.'

'These are the keys to the Chiller. Can you get there without being caught?'

'Of course.'

'Unlock all the cells. Casablanca is in cell eight. Let him out too.'

'Casablanca!' Ashanti looked shocked.

'Casablanca – yes. They'll beat him to a pulp if we leave him there.'

'But...'

'He helped me.'

'OK, Dr London,' said Owando, 'but the alarm?'

'Set all the alarms off. The more confusion the better. The guards won't know where to go first. When you're finished at the Chiller, meet us at the skip bay.'

One by one the boys dropped down through the hole. As one of them passed me, he handed me my G-Port. 'I catch it for you,' he said and grinned. Owando brought Abuja over to Ashanti. The little boy seemed happy enough to be led around, but he was like a sleepwalker.

'Five minutes,' Owando said and disappeared.

I watched through one of the windows. It was still dark, but the darkness was thinner, the pools of light from the floodlights less bright. From under our hut, boys crept quickly to vanish under each of the occupied huts, spreading Owando's instructions. Minutes later, it was as if a cork had been pulled as yellow bodies flooded out from beneath the huts, joined into one mass, and poured across the parade ground.

'Let's go,' I said.

We bundled Abuja down through the floor, dropped down after him, crawled out into the open, and with him between us dashed across to dive under Hut 2. On hands and knees, Ashanti led the way to the hole in Hut 2's floor. Except for one figure sitting absolutely still on a bunk, the hut was empty.

'Sarayova! Rana, it's me, Mark!' I took her hands and tried to pull her to her feet, but she turned her face away and wouldn't move. 'We have to go! Come on, please, Rana, we have to go!' I begged.

'Mark, wait.' Ashanti pushed me aside and guided Abuja to stand beside her. He gazed at Sarayova, then reached out and touched her as if checking she was real. At first, she didn't stir, but then she turned and looked at him, and something in her face changed, as if she had come back from a long way away. Abuja took her hand and held it.

'What do we do?' I was desperate to go. I could hear alarms going off and whistles and shouts outside.

Gently, Ashanti took Abuja by the hand and, as she drew him back towards the trapdoor, Sarayova got to her feet and followed. Once outside, I could see that Owando's diversion was working. Guards were pursuing crowds of darting yellow figures in the early pre-dawn greyness way down at the far end of the camp, and the area around the huts was completely deserted. Ashanti steered us around the backs of the buildings, towing Abuja who held on tightly to Sarayova's hand. Every second I expected to hear a shouted challenge, but we reached the skip bay behind the woodchip factory without meeting a single guard. As we got there, Pete and Monkey were hooking the chains to the skip, ready to lift it on to the back of the skip truck.

'Bloody hell!' said Monkey. 'We thought they must have got you when we heard all the alarms going off. You cut it fine, didn't you?'

'Just get 'em in before some bastard sees 'em!' said Pete.

'What about microchips? They'll sweep for chips when we go through the gate.'

'There's a kit in the cab. Ashanti, can you do them?' asked Pete.

Ashanti bit her lip and nodded. Pete dived into the cab.

'These two look like they're away with the fairies,' said Monkey, looking quizzically Sarayova and Abuja.

'Just leave it,' said Ashanti.

Pete came back with a plastic box that he handed to Ashanti; then it was time to get us into the skip, but this wasn't one of your little domestic skips, this was big square industrial monster, and we had to climb up the side and over the top. Somehow, with Pete and Monkey pushing from below, we got Abuja and Sarayova up and in, and then we dropped down beside them. The skip was three-quarters full of tree bark, so it was a soft landing, but we raised a cloud of choking dust. As soon as we were in, Pete and Monkey started to pull the heavy tarp over the top of the skip.

'When you've done the chips, bury yourselves in the bark until we're through the gates in case anyone looks in,' said Pete.

'There's one more to come,' I said.

'No way. We can't wait. They'll cop us for sure,' said Pete, and they continued with the tarp.

'You'll have to help me,' Ashanti said. She had the plastic box open, and it now dawned on me what it was we had to do; we had to cut the microchips out of Sarayova and Abuja's arms. The box contained disposable scalpels, tweezers, anesthetising spray, and plasters.

'I've had to do it before,' Ashanti said, but she looked pale. 'Abuja, first. Left arm, just below the shoulder. You hold him.'

Perhaps it was as well that Abuja and Sarayova were off in their own worlds somewhere; they put up no resistance as I held each in turn, pulling their uniforms off their left shoulders while Ashanti sprayed, made a small cut, tweezed the chip out from under the skin, and covered the wound with a plaster. She was quick, and there wasn't much blood. She dropped the chips into a little plastic bottle. Then I cut the chip out of Ashanti's uniform and added it to the others.

'I'm going to chuck these chips out of the skip. I don't think Owando's going to make it,' Ashanti said.

'Wait! Just wait,' I said.

Standing on the bark, I could look over the edge of the skip. *Come on, Owando! Come on!* I stared out at the empty bay in gathering daylight, willing him to come sprinting around the corner. *I shouldn't have sent him to the Chiller.*

Pete and Monkey had finished tying down the front and were starting on the back when Casablanca and Salamandaga, with Owando between them, skidded into the skip bay. Casablanca and Salamandaga lifted Owando and tossed him over the edge and into the skip where he landed, laughing, next to Ashanti.

'Don't forget saxophone lesson!' Casablanca shouted and waved. In his hand was the guard's pistol that I had refused to take. Then he and Salamandaga turned and ran out of the bay. The gun. Of course, I should have known that he would take it and now, for certain, he was going to use it.

'You do his chip,' Ashanti commanded. She was busy covering Abuja and Sarayova with tree bark.

'OK, Dr London, I'm ready,' said Owando, and he presented me with his left shoulder. It's one thing to dress a wound, it's quite another to cut someone else's skin, but I did it, and as soon as Owando's chip was with the others in the little bottle, I threw it out of the skip; then Pete and Monkey pulled the last corner of the tarp across, and we were in darkness.

'Dig yourself under the bark,' I said to Owando. And down we burrowed as the skip swung into the air to land with a heavy jolt on the back of the lorry.

CHAPTER 34

The truck's breaks hissed and we came to a juddering halt. *Must be the gates*, I thought, and held my breath, certain they would want to search the skip.

'You seem to be having a bit of trouble.' Pete called, cheerily.

'Soon round the little bleeders up,' the guard replied.

'Want to take a look inside?'

'Too right I do.'

'Aw, for crying out loud! Just finished tying the blessed thing down,' Pete complained.

I burrowed even deeper. The dust from the bark filled my nose and throat, and I had to fight against the urge to cough. I could hear the banging of Pete and the guard's boots against the side as they climbed the skip and then the rasping of the corner of the tarp being dragged back.

'Yeah, OK,' the guard said. 'Any road, if some of the little toerags are hiding in that stuff, your escort will catch 'em when you unload.'

The cover was pulled back over, and there was the scrunching of boots on gravel as the two men jumped down.

'OK, mate – On you go. Your escort vehicle will be right behind you. If for any reason you get separated, you are to wait until the escort catches up with you.'

'Yeah, we know the drill,' Pete said and the truck lurched forward, changed gear, and, as it picked up speed, we all emerged from under the bark, coughing and spitting. The wind lifted the tarp, making it billow and flap.

'Where we get out?' Owando asked.

'First we lose the escort,' I said.

I crawled to the back of the skip, and steadying myself against its side, I got to my feet. Every time the wind got under the tarp, it opened up a small gap that I could see through. The FIST patrol car was about thirty metres behind us. Its lights were on, and I couldn't see through their dazzle to know how many officers were in the car. My head ached, and my ear throbbed. From the inside, one side of my face felt like it was swollen to twice its normal size.

We had been going for about fifteen minutes, and we'd turned off from the main road leading to Holdstone into a minor road, when the growl of the truck's engine grew suddenly louder, and the gap between us and the patrol car opened up. Out of a small side lane and into the gap rolled a large green tractor towing a big, rusty muck spreader. The patrol car's horn blared, and there was a squeal of tyres as the car braked hard so as not to hit the tractor that had now come to a halt completely blocking the road. The car's doors flew open, and two irate officers leapt out waving their arms.

'Quick Ashanti! It's Harlan!' I yelled.

Ashanti scrambled up beside me just as the tractor driver turned on the muck spreader, sending a volley of stinking brown slurry flying high in the air to cascade down on the advancing FIST officers, their patrol car, and the road around them. Slipping and sliding in the muck, the two men turned and fled to the safety of their vehicle; the doors slammed, and the car began to reverse rapidly away from the flying manure, but it hadn't travelled far before a gaily-painted double-decker bus pulled out of a second side lane, cutting off its retreat. The reversing patrol car veered wildly before slewing off the road and into the roadside ditch. No sooner had it come to rest, than it was set upon by a crowd of travellers that burst from the bus. Seconds later, the whole scene was lost to view as the skip truck swung round a sharp bend in the road and juddered to a standstill. The corner of the tarp was pulled back and Pete's face appeared. 'Out! Quick! This is as far as we take you.'

We scrambled out of the skip and down on to the road beside Monkey, who was laughing so much that he was no help at all.

'Harlan!' roared Monkey. 'Harlan! And the muck spreader! That wasn't in the script, was it?'

'Bloody funny though!' said Pete, 'And I only saw it in my mirrors.'

'Over here!' came a shout. Bethan and Jerzy were waiting in the trees, signalling madly for us to hurry and, as soon as we reached the other side of the road, they set off at a dodging run through the forest, expecting us to follow. Owando soon caught them up, but Abuja and Sarayova had to be dragged with me on one side and Ashanti on the other.

The big Mercedes estate and Ruby's old electric pickup were tucked out of sight under some scrubby trees in a disused quarry ten minutes from where we had left the road. Ruby and Yongjo Ma were standing by the pickup, but as soon as Yongjo Ma saw Sarayova, she ran to meet us and threw her arms around her friend. 'Sarayova, I heard what you did on the ship! You are so brave! Thank God, you're safe!' But when she got no response, she stepped back, holding Sarayova at arm's length, and her delighted smile faded as she studied Sarayova's expressionless face. 'What is it? What did they do to you?'

Ruby strode over, hands in pockets, 'I wasn't expecting so many,' she said, and then she noticed my bruised and swollen cheek and bloody ear. 'Oo, boy! You OK, kiddo?'

'Yeah, I'm OK. It's these two.'

'Why? What have those freaks done to them?'

'Rana?... Rana?' Yongjo Ma was holding Sarayova'a face between her two hands. 'Rana, what have they done to you? Oh God – speak to me!'

Sarayova pushed the other girl's hands away and looked from one to other of us; then she spoke for the first time, 'I want to go home now. Can I go home now?' she said, like a tired child kept out too late. 'Please... Can I go home now... Please? I want to go home.'

I tried to speak, but the words wouldn't come out.

'They've been running experiments,' Ashanti said.

Ruby took Sarayova's hand, 'We'll take you home, Rana, don't you worry. We'll take you home.' She led her over and sat her in the front of the pickup. Abuja followed after them and, as soon as Sarayova was seated, he climbed on to her lap and curled into her. She wrapped her arms around him and let her face rest on his hair.

Ruby came back to us. There were tears in her eyes, but they glittered with anger. 'We'll get them! Mark, tell me we're going to get them. We are going to get the bastards for this, aren't we?'

'Yes,' I said. 'We're going to get them.'

Jerzy had been watching. Now he came across to us. 'We should go. Soon FIST will be looking for you. What about the clothing?'

'Who are you taking, Mark?' Ruby asked.

'Ashanti and Bethan. Owando and Yongjo Ma, if they'll come.'

'Yes, Dr London, I come,' said Owando.

'Of course, we will come,' said Yongjo Ma.

'Change of clothes for you in the back of the pickup,' said Ruby. 'Mark and Ashanti, your ID cards are in your pockets.'

As soon as Ashanti, Owando, and I had changed out of our very conspicuous Holdstone uniforms, we piled into the Merc, where Jerzy was waiting with the engine running. Jerzy had set up the two extra seats in the very back of the estate for Ashanti and Yongjo Ma. Bethan and I sat together in the middle so that we could download all the images from the two G-Ports to Bethan's touch screen, and Owando got in the front with Jerzy.

'Here,' Ruby handed a first-aid kit through the window to Bethan. 'See if you can patch up the boy's ear.' Then she wished us luck, and we were on our way.

'We need to get out before FIST set up checkpoints,' said Jerzy. 'Maybe they do it already, so we take small roads. You know left and right?' he asked Owando.

'Of course,' Owando said.

'Good. You navigate. Each junction you shout "left", "right" or "straight". You understand? Ruby makes us a map.' He fished a sheet of paper out of the pocket on the door and passed it to Owando.

There was no chance of Bethan doing any first aid or anything else for the next hour; all we could do was cling on as Jerzy threw the big car around the sharp bends, and we bounced and bucked over the potholed lanes. Early on, Owando missed a couple of turns, and Jerzy had to reverse, making the tyres scream and muttering angrily in Polish, but soon they were working together like a true rally team, with Owando counting down to each junction, 'Left – five, four, three, two, one – Now!... Right – five, four, three, two, one – Now!' and Jerzy shouting 'Yee-Ha!' as he spun the steering wheel.

Ruby's route kept us off the link road and beneath the cover of the forest canopy for as long as possible, since FIST were almost certain to send out helicopters or drones to scan the countryside for suspicious movements around Holdstone as soon as they'd restored enough order to discover that we were missing. Of course, they hadn't found out who I was, so there was no reason for them to look for us on the road to London – I hoped.

Seemed like Ruby had done a good job of explaining to Jerzy what was going on; he never questioned why we were doing what we were doing, but once we were out on the main road, and he no longer had to concentrate on Owando's shouted directions, he wanted to know everything about what had happened to us in Holdstone, about FIST's experiments with the Eraser, and about Rainer. 'I never, never like him. Now I know I am right,' he said. 'I think he make bad trouble for your father, Mark.'

'He's going to make bad trouble for the whole country, if we don't stop him,' I said. And when Bethan had finished patching up my ear, we got down to editing the material for the GRID.

After the New Bridgewater turnoff, there was a bit more traffic, and we began to feel less conspicuous, but we kept scanning the sky for drones, and the car went very quiet when three FIST patrol cars sped past in the opposite direction.

Owando, freed of navigation duty, explored all the controls on the Merc's dashboard, bombarding Jerzy with questions. Jerzy, in his typically subtle way, nicknamed Owando 'Fingers', so Owando retaliated by calling Jerzy 'Pole-Driver', and they became instant best friends. When he had finally exhausted the wonders of the GRIDscreen, Owando turned his attention to the glove box where he found Jerzy's pistol.

'Hey! You remember this, Yongjo Ma?' he held it up for her to see. 'You make Casablanca give it back to Mr Pole-Driver.'

'OK, Fingers – You want the driver of that lorry to see we got a gun?' Jerzy said, and Owando hurriedly lowered the pistol.

'And where does a beauty queen learn so much about guns?' Jerzy asked Yongjo Ma, tilting his head so that he could see her in his rear-vision mirror.

'North Korean army – national service – captain of the pistol shooting team,' she said, matter-of-factly.

Jerzy gave an 'I'm-impressed' whistle.

'Then the famine came and the uprising, and they ordered us to shoot civilians. That's when my brother and I left.'

'Fingers, put the gun away,' Jerzy said, and Owando returned the pistol to the glove box.

As we approached the outskirts of London, Jerzy tuned the car's GRID to a news and traffic channel to see if there were reports of any major hold-ups to avoid in and around the city. There was a list of road works and tailbacks and diversions around the flood damage, and then silence, after which a new voice cut in: –

We interrupt the traffic report to bring you a major item of breaking news – The Force for Internal Security and Counter Terrorism has conclusive evidence that the flooding of London was due to an act of terrorism and not to a natural disaster, as previously thought. A state of emergency has been declared. Special powers have been granted to FIST to make arrests. A number of senior figures in the opposition, thought to have been involved in the plot that drowned thousands of Londoners, have already been detained – More arrests are expected to follow. From twelve o'clock tonight everyone will be required to carry identity cards at all times. The Prime Minister will speak to the nation this afternoon on GRIDnews at One.

'It's started!' Ashanti said. 'We may already be too late.'

'Do you think we'll still be able to get into the City?' I asked Jerzy.

'Maybe. Or maybe they seal the Ring.'

'I'll bet the GRID's going wild.' I got out my portal to see what everyone was saying.

'Don't!' said Bethan. 'Don't connect to the GRID. If they're looking for you and you connect your port to the GRID, they'll know within seconds where you are.'

'But we've had the car's GRID connection on!'

'So, at least we know they're not looking for this car.'

'They didn't mention the police,' said Ashanti. 'They said FIST was making arrests.'

'Sounds like Mrs Grist doesn't know if she can trust the police to back her,' said Bethan.

'More likely, Rainer is running the show. The Prime Minister is just doing what she's told,' I said.

'Yeah,' said Jerzy. 'This is Rainer for certain.'

'But surely people don't believe this stuff about terrorists causing the flood,' I said.

'Oh yes, they do,' said Jerzy. 'You haven't been here, Mark. Ever since FIST made that report, people start blaming foreigners. You have an accent like mine, everyone think you got a bomb up your jumper. And you don't know how big the damage. You wait till you see. Everyone wants someone to blame.'

Jerzy was right; I hadn't been prepared for the extent of the devastation left by the flood. As we came over Shepherd's Bush flyover, I could see mile upon mile of abandoned houses, many of their roads still choked with silt and debris, and that stench of rotting cabbage that had hit us when we left the Global Building on the night of the flood still hung in the air. Whole blocks of terraced houses were being demolished. Yellow earthmoving equipment crawled through the dead suburbs, shovelling rubble mixed with people's possessions into the backs of lorries: fridges, cookers, toys, wardrobes spilling clothes. Not surprising people wanted scapegoats.

It seemed like every Metropolitan Police car in London was out on patrol and minibuses packed with officers in riot gear lurked in the side streets. There were FIST patrols out too, but the two forces didn't appear to be working together. We passed a FIST armoured car parked at an intersection, its driver embroiled in a heated argument with a pair of regular police officers.

'Turf war,' said Jerzy.

'How do you mean?' I asked.

'The Met don't want FIST on their patch.'

Then I remembered the other part of Rainer's plan; if he got his way, FIST would take over the policing of the whole country. Had the

Met already got wind of it? Were they getting ready for a showdown with FIST?

Jerzy chose to bring us into the City via the Ring at Moorgate. It was one of the busier openings and so there was less likelihood of being stopped but, before we reached the gate, he turned off into a quiet side road.

'Just in case they check for ID cards, we hide Fingers and the Beauty Queen,' he said. He folded down the two rear-most seats and pulled the cover over the luggage compartment. Owando and Yongjo Ma crawled underneath. I got into the front, and Ashanti joined Bethan in the back.

'All cosy?' Jerzy asked before closing the tailgate and getting back in the car.

At the opening in the Ring, we are the sixth car in the queue. Normally you just drive up to the gate and the car's transceiver triggers the gate to open it, but today it resembles a border crossing between two countries with the police guarding one side, and FIST officers on the other. Some cars the police wave through, others they stop and inspect the occupants' ID cards; some are stopped again by the FIST officers on the other side. As we edge forward, a car at a time, we dig out our cards and wait. My hands grow sweaty, and I have to rub them on my trouser legs to dry them. The great, bomb-proof glass gates slide shut after the car ahead of us has passed through, and it is our turn. Should I look straight ahead, or should I smile at the police officer? I am quite certain whatever I do I'm going to look shifty and how do I explain my battered face? He's bending down to look in the car. He looks at each of us, Jerzy, then at me, then Ashanti and Bethan. Then he takes another long look at Ashanti. Is it her dark skin that makes him suspicious? *It doesn't matter*, I tell myself – she's OK, she's got an ID card – just so long as he doesn't ask to look in the boot. He's straightening. What's he going to do? He's waving us through! He's waving us through! The glass gates slide apart... And then I see that they've got dogs on the other side – sniffer dogs! If FIST stop us and the dogs smell the two in the back, we're done for. What's Jerzy doing? Why's he slowing down? Keep going, Jerzy! Keep going! Oh no! He's waving to them! He's crazy! At any moment, I expect to hear a whistle, a shout, a shot even, but nothing happens! We drive on.

'They didn't stop us!' I almost scream.

'No,' says Jerzy. 'That one with dog, I know him. Sometimes I even buy him a drink.'

'You pick the sweetest friends,' I say, but I'm that relieved I could hug him.

Next hurdle is the Global Building itself. As we come around the corner and I see its great leaf form rising, shimmering above the surrounding office buildings, I also see that there is a cordon of FIST officers right across the front entrance.

'Everyone down,' says Jerzy.

We slide off our seats, and I huddle under the dashboard. Now what? Why have FIST staked out the building? I try to picture what is happening outside the car. We must be driving round to the back, to the entrance to the underground car park. Will that be guarded too? Then I feel the bump-bump as the wheels pass over the gutter and on to the down ramp. The car tilts downward. We're going in. We stop. This is the gate. I hear the whine of the gate opening, and we're on the move again. The tyres squeak on the smooth cement surface as we level out in the garage, and Jerzy manoeuvres us into the parking bay. Then he turns off the engine.

'So – we are in. What now, Mark? How do you get into your daddy's office?' Jerzy says.

'We take my dad's private lift. I'm hoping the system still recognises my handprint,' I say, slipping back on to my seat.

'Everyone out the driver door and keep low. That way, the camera doesn't see you,' Jerzy says. 'Ashanti, please open the cover over the luggage.'

Jerzy gets out first while Ashanti reaches back and releases the cover over the luggage compartment; then Jerzy busies himself cleaning the car's windscreen while the rest of us climb over the seats and one by one slide out the driver's door and crouch behind the car.

Owando is the last out. Jerzy has parked the car right next to the lifts so that, if we stay low, we can reach them unseen.

'Jerzy,' I whisper, 'go and stand by the lifts. It'll look odd if the door opens, and no one gets it.'

He puts his cleaning things away, closes the car door, and crosses to the lifts. I'm hoping that the security guard, if he's watching, won't notice which lift Jerzy gets into.

'OK, when the lift door opens, everyone in but stay down.' I scuttle over and crouch by Jerzy's knees. He sees what I mean to do and mimes pushing the button for the general lifts just as I reach up and place my hand on the print-recognition screen for the private lift. I hold my breath. There's a soft 'ping!' and the doors open. Quickly, we all get in, and Jerzy steps in after us as the doors close. There's no camera in this lift, and I quietly thank my dad for insisting on that when they designed the building. We all get to our feet, and our reflections look back at us from the lift's mirrored walls: Jerzy, Ashanti, Bethan, little Owando, with his missing fingers, tall, beautiful Yongjo Ma, and me, with my left cheek and eye a nasty swollen mix of black, yellow, and red and my left ear taped up and bloody. Our feet press into the floor as the lift begins its rapid journey. What will my dad do when we walk into his office? It is only now that it occurs to me that I haven't prepared what I am going to say to him. He's my dad, right? I've just been assuming he'll help us, but maybe he won't, maybe he's not on our side, maybe... He must know about Holdstone because he must have given the OK to switching off the GRID over the forest. What am I leading my friends into?

We are momentarily weightless as the lift slows and stops at my dad's floor; the doors open, and we step out into the lobby. All eyes look at me.

'I better go in first. Wait here, and I'll call you in when it's OK,' I say.

I'm just going to have to busk it. I try to picture my father in a really good mood, relaxed, smiling, like when we do stuff together on holiday; then I put my hand on the screen. The door opens, and I walk into his office.

Seated at a glass-topped conference table in the middle of the room are Rainer, Mrs Grist, and Ronald Parker, the fat mayor of London; Rainer looks surprised to see me, the Prime Minister looks furious, and the Mayor looks confused. My father isn't in the room. Rainer's expression quickly changes to what is supposed to be a friendly smile as he gets to his feet.

'Mark! Well, well, this is a surprise! Thought you were off, mucking about in the country.'

'Where's my father?'

'Dear me, you seem to have been in the wars. What have you done to your face? I'll call Abbie and get her to look after you.'

'Where is my father?!'

Rainer pushes the button on my father's desk that will summon Abbie.

'Your dad's in a bit of trouble, I'm afraid. He was arrested this morning,' he says, smoothly. He picks up my father's fountain pen and twiddles it between his fingers.

'Arrested?' My head is beginning to spin, and I feel cold and sweaty. Abbie enters the room, the door closing behind her; her mouth drops open slightly when she sees me, and she looks to Rainer for an explanation.

'Why was my father arrested?' I hear myself ask, but my voice sounds thin and distant.

'It's a little complicated, Mark, but there was honestly nothing I could do to stop it.'

I know this is a lie, and I see Abbie's eyes narrow and her mouth harden. Perhaps I have one ally in the room. The Mayor is whispering to the Prime Minister.

'How on earth did the wretched boy get into the building?' Mrs Grist demands to know.

Rainer turns to Abbie, 'Take him to security. Find out how he got access to the lift.'

'You better come with me,' Abbie says, and she begins to walk towards me to lead me out of the room, but she stops and her eyes widen as she stares in astonishment over my shoulder. Mrs Grist gasps, and the Mayor lets out a little squeak. Rainer, who has been looking at Abbie, turns to see what she has seen.

'Step away from the desk and keep your hands where they are.' The voice is ice cold and steady. When I look, I find Yongjo Ma standing in the doorway to the lobby; she is aiming down the barrel of Jerzy's pistol that she holds, arms almost straight, left hand supporting the right. There is not a tremor of movement in her hand or arm. She is like a statue.

'Don't be crazy! Put that gun down!' Rainer takes a step towards her, brandishing the fountain pen. The next second, there is a 'crack!' that makes my ears ring; the fountain pen disappears, and little blue freckles of ink appear all over Rainer's face.

'The next bullet will be between the eyes of the first person who does not do what I tell them. You two, keep your hands on the table where I can see them. You, Mr Rainer, hands against the wall and spread your legs.'

'You'll never get out of here. You know that!' Rainer says, but he does what he's told. Mrs Gist is completely rigid; the Mayor is shaking so much, his fat cheeks are wobbling and he's whimpering.

'Jerzy, see if he has a gun.'

Jerzy, keeping the line of fire clear between Yongjo Ma and Rainer, expertly frisks him and removes his G-Port and a pistol from under his jacket.

'Good. Now you sit with the others and keep your hands on the table.'

Rainer, obediently, returns to his place.

Suddenly Mrs Grist explodes, 'This is outrageous! How did this happen? These are terrorists! Your people have let terrorists into the building! They're terrorists! They're terrorists, Rainer! I'm not going to stay here! I can't stay here. I'm the Prime Minister!' and she gets to her feet.

'Sit down! And shut up!' Yongjo Ma commands.

Mrs Grist's mouth slowly closes, and she sinks back down into her seat. So far, Abbie hasn't moved, but I'm watching her, and I notice that Jerzy's eyes keep flicking in her direction. Is she with us, or might she try to alert security?

'Listen, Mark,' Rainer says, 'I don't know what you and your criminal friends hope to achieve, but this is only going to make it worse for your father. Be sensible and perhaps we can make it easier for him. You should know that he is facing very serious charges connected with covering up the sabotaging of the Thames Barrier, and the government is considering reintroducing the death penalty for terrorism.'

'Don't listen to him, Mark,' Abbie says. 'I know your father. He would never do what these people say he's done. If you have an idea – if you have some way of stopping these... these lunatics, then do it for God's sake!'

For the last few minutes, things have been happening all around and I have done nothing; now I know everyone is waiting for me to say what happens next.

'We need an unfiltered connection to the GRID, and we need the camera on so that we can mix live and pre-recorded images,' I say.

'You can connect direct from your father's desk', Abbie says, 'and the camera is already programmed for Mrs Grist's one o'clock broadcast – that's in five minutes.'

'Great. Lock down the office so we're not disturbed.'

Bethan doesn't need me to tell her anything; she is already plugging her touch screen up to the connection, and within a few seconds, the conversation between Mrs Grist and Rainer that I recorded in the Lodge appears on the big screens on the office wall. Mrs Grist spins round at the sound of her own voice and stares in disbelief at the magnified image of herself plotting with Rainer to take over the country.

'How did they get hold of this?!' she asks, eyes popping.

'I've no idea. But don't worry, no one will believe it,' says Rainer, but I can hear that even he is rattled.

'Turn that off! Turn that off!' screams Mrs Grist, standing and pointing at the screen.

'I won't warn you again,' Yongjo Ma says, taking a step towards her.

'Sit down, Angela. Please sit down. For God's sake, woman, sit down before they shoot us all,' whimpers the Mayor.

'I will not be told to sit by you, you fat worm!'

Yongjo Ma takes careful aim, and I really do think she is about to shoot the Prime Minsiter. 'One… two…' she begins.

'*Sit!*' Rainer grabs Mrs Grist's arm and thrusts her into her chair.

'Now, look,' says Rainer, 'just tell us what you want. Promise you won't broadcast what you've got there, and we can do a deal. We can drop the charges against your father – If your friends here need passports, that can be arranged. And, Mark, you have my word that you will walk from this building, and no one will touch you.'

'I'll speak to you in a minute,' I say to Rainer, and I can see that he is seething, but he's playing at being reasonable, so he says nothing.

'How long have we got?' I ask Abbie.

'Three minutes, until the one o'clock broadcast.'

I call Owando and Ashanti over and explain to them what I want them to do and show them where to stand on the little platform in front of the screens for the broadcast camera. Ashanti nods, Owando says, 'No problem, Dr London.' Then I turn to Rainer. 'Here's the deal. We do our show, then we give ourselves up. But not to FIST. We give ourselves up to the real police.'

'My force won't let the police into the City.'

'You forget, the building has a helipad.'

'It's guarded.'

'Abbie,' I say, 'as soon as we begin the broadcast, please call Sir Patrick Kelly. Explain the situation and then go up to the helipad and tell Rainer's thugs that the Prime Minister has asked for a meeting with the Chief of the Metropolitan Police.'

'Certainly,' she says.

Mrs Grist opens her mouth to speak, but I cut her off. 'I am going to have to ask you all to be quiet for the next five minutes.'

Abbie says, 'One minute to go.'

I signal to Ashanti who steps on to the platform in front of the broadcast camera. Suddenly, Mrs Grist is on her feet again. 'No! No! No!' she is shouting. Yongjo Ma swings to aim at her, but Rainer sees his chance to move and leaps at Ashanti. Almost at the same instant,

Jerzy throws himself at Rainer and brings him crashing to the floor where the two men roll, locked together. Yongjo Ma has forced Mrs Grist into her seat and has the gun at her head, but Rainer is on top of Jerzy and has wrestled his pistol out of Jerzy's grasp. A small body rockets past me – it's Owando, and in his raised left hand is the heavy glass paperweight from my father's desk, which he brings down, hard, on Rainer's head, who slumps on to the carpet beside Jerzy. For a few seconds nobody moves; then Jerzy gets to his feet. 'Thanks Fingers,' he says. He drags Rainer across the room and props him against the wall.

'Ten seconds,' says Abbie – 'Five... Four... Three... Two... One.'

The red light on the camera comes on to show that the moment for the Prime Minister's speech has arrived. Ashanti says, 'Good afternoon. Mrs Grist, the prime minister, will not be speaking to you today. Instead, we are showing a recent meeting between the Prime Minister and Tristram Rainer, the head of FIST. We hope you find it interesting. It will be followed by a short film. Thank you.' Bethan cues the video, and now the whole country can see just what Rainer and Grist have been planning. As the video finishes, I nod to Owando who stands where Ashanti had stood. Bethan begins showing the video we filmed in the camp as Owando speaks, and his image is superimposed on the images of children whose eyes are blank, who look like half-starved sleep-walkers, of boys with bleeding hands carrying logs running the gauntlet between the laughing guards with their vicious batons, of little girls bent double soldering tiny circuits on the production line and of the barren sleeping quarters.

'My name is Kitwana Dibala. I come from the town of Owando in West Africa. I am ten years old. I want to show you the prison where I live. Many, many children live here, girls and also boys. Some are only five years old. Maybe we are not prisoners; maybe we are slaves. We work twelve hours every day, but we never get money, only a little food. We make furniture for your houses. We make portals for the GRID, we make your computers. The machinery is dangerous, it stole my fingers; sometimes it kills us. If we disobey the guards, they beat us. If we try to escape, they hunt us with dogs. Maybe you think our prison is in Africa. Maybe you think it is in China. No, it is here in your England, it is in the great forest. They tell you the forest is for the climate – it is a lie – the forest is to hide our prison. Our prison is called Holdstone.' He looks at me, and I give him the thumbs-up; I expect him to step down from the platform, but he looks back at the camera – 'I come to your England to look for my mother, but I do not find her. I come with my sister, but the smugglers throw her from the boat, and she is drowned. If anyone knows Adila Dibala, please tell her that her son is looking for her.' He stands looking at the camera, and the tears run down his face.

'Can you turn off the camera please?' I ask Abbie.

She taps the touch screen on my father's desk; the red light goes out, and camera rises up and disappears into its housing in the ceiling. Another little tap and the big screen on the wall breaks into multiple images, showing an array of news channels and chat channels, all of which are showing and re-showing our video of Rainer and Mrs Grist. Ashanti puts her arms around Owando.

'I'll go to meet Sir Patrick,' Abbie says and goes off to the private lift.

The next quarter of an hour passes like a strange dream. All the fight has gone out of Mrs Grist; she stares at the screens as commentators on the news channels begin to speculate about whether our video is genuine and, if it is, what that means for the country. The Mayor, with his head in his pudgy hands, keeps repeating, 'We're ruined... we're ruined... we're ruined.' Rainer begins to revive but remains propped against the wall with Jerzy standing over him. I expect, at any moment, for FIST to mount an assault on the locked doors of the office, but all remains weirdly quiet. Perhaps they are waiting for orders from their leader. At last, the door to the lobby opens, and the Chief of Police strides into the room accompanied by four officers in body armour, clutching automatic weapons, which all snap towards Yongjo Ma as if their muzzles are drawn to her by a magnet.

'OK, Miss, let's have the gun,' Sir Patrick says crisply.

Yongjo Ma slowly lowers her weapon, puts on the safety catch, and hands it to Sir Patrick. 'Thank you,' he says. Yongjo Ma closes her eyes and breaths out a long breath. She looks completely drained. Jerzy holds out Rainer's gun, and Sir Patrick takes it and hands it to one of the other officers. With the threat of the guns removed, Mrs Grist springs to life as if an invisible hand has just switched her back on – 'You took your time getting here! Thank God the safety of this country does not depend on the Metropolitan Police! Arrest this filth and get us out of here immediately!' she commands shrilly, glaring at Sir Patrick.

Sir Patrick looks at each of us, and when his eyes meet mine he appears to be trying not to smile. He turns back towards the table. 'Angela Grist and Ronald Parker, I am arresting you on suspicion of conspiring to commit misconduct while in public office. You do not have to say anything, but it may harm your defence if you do not mention, when questioned, something which you later rely on in court. Anything you do say may be given in evidence.' Mrs Grist's jaw drops open; the Mayor who had just sat up, slumps back on to the table. 'As Mr Rainer appears a little... indisposed,' continues Sir Patrick, 'we will caution him at the station. You can take them away.'

Two officers haul Rainer to his feet while the other two take hold of Mrs Grist and the Mayor and they march the three of them off to the lift.

'Thank you, Mark,' says Sir Patrick. 'I have to confess I rather enjoyed doing that.'

CHAPTER 35

'What do you think you'll do now?' Ashanti asked. We were sitting by the cairn, looking down at the farm. Tess was lying with her head on my legs so I could scratch her behind the ear, while Scat was off hunting amongst the gorse bushes.

'Dunno really. Don't fancy going back to London much… or school. Maybe they'll let me go to college. I'd like to stay here.'

'It's your life. Why don't you just tell them that's what you want to do?'

'What about your parents?'

'They wouldn't mind. They've already got Rana and Abuja. We've always taken in strays.'

'Well, my parents will be here tomorrow.' Aunt Megan had asked my dad and mum to come and stay after my dad was released and the charges against him were dropped. I'd seen my mum before I came back to the farm with Ashanti and her family, but I still hadn't seen my dad, and I didn't know how I felt about him. If Aunt Megan was giving him another chance, I supposed I ought to. 'Do you think they'll fight?' I said.

'Who?'

'Your mum and my dad.'

'They might.'

'Let's run away if they do. Go camping, or something.'

'I'd be up for that.'

Down in the valley the workhorses, Big Red and Dora-Bella, were pulling the seed drill up and down the field that Harlan had prepared before the eviction. Harlan was teaching Rana to drive the horses, and Abuja was riding on the back of Dora-Bella with Dilly.

Rana spent most of her time with the horses. It was Harlan's idea to get her grooming them. 'Horses lets you talk to them, and they don't give you their opinion,' Harlan explained.

'She smiled at me yesterday,' I said. 'Well, she smiled, I'm not sure if it was at me.'

'You can talk about her if you want. I won't be jealous,' Ashanti said.

'Why would you be jealous?' I asked.

'Just kidding.' And Ashanti seemed to become very interested in a small beetle that was on its back and trying to get itself the right way up.

'What's Abuja's real name?' I asked.

'I don't know. He never told me.'

'Have you thought about going with the Yongjos to Scotland?' – Yongjo Pa and Yongjo Ma were going to Edinburgh to speak to the Scottish Parliament about climate refugees, and they'd asked Ashanti to go with them.

'I don't think public speaking is really my thing.'

'You're joking! You were amazing at those rallies in London! You got up in front of one and half million people in Hyde Park!'

'That was different. Those were people, and these will be politicians. Besides...'

'Besides what?'

She looked at me, and her eyes sparkled. 'Tony and Cara say they've seen water vole.'

'Where?'

'Wislanpound reservoir. You want to come?'

'Yeah, definitely!'

'We'd have to go for a few days. We mightn't find them straight away.'

'Fine by me.'

'And there's another big Atlantic storm coming through.'

'I bet you know plenty of places we can shelter.'

'OK, we'll talk about it when you get back this evening.'

My SoftPortal gently squeezed my wrist to let me know I had a message. It was Ruby to say she was just turning into the lane.

'You should get one of these,' I said.

'You're such a boy!'

'What? There's loads of nature stuff on the GRID.'

'Let's just say I prefer the real thing.'

'I better go. You coming down?'

'No. I'll stay up here a bit longer.'

The dogs decided to stay with Ashanti, so I walked back to the farm on my own. By the time I got there, Ruby had already driven into the yard in the pickup and was talking to Umi.

'Ready to go, kiddo?' she asked when she saw me.

'Just get the sax.'

I got my saxophone from the farmhouse and climbed into the pickup.

When we reached Holdstone, it seemed strange to be able to simply drive in; there were two police officers at the gate, but they just waved to Ruby and continued chatting to a group of kids who were showing them a large toad that they'd caught, probably up by the reservoir.

The camp didn't look so very different. What had I expected? That it would disappear? That all the kids would magically find families to adopt them? That the adults would be given jobs, houses, citizenship? Of course, families had been reunited; kids who had parents in the camp could now live with them; the living quarters were being improved, the punishment block had been demolished; there was a playground, and they were building a school, and those adults who chose to work in the factory got paid, but they were still living in a refugee camp – and there'd be more refugees and there'd have to be more camps. After all the rallies and speeches and brave words about 'standing together with those who had lost their countries', how much had we achieved?

'You look a bit down, kiddo,' said Ruby.

'I'm fine,' I said.

'It'll take time.'

'I know.'

'There's going to be a conference in Oslo next month, you know.'

'Yeah, I heard.'

We drove past the hoardings that hid the Eraser and pulled up beside the parade ground that had been turned into a basketball court and an all-weather football pitch, where a twenty-five-a-side game in a dozen languages was loudly in progress.

'You want me to come?' Ruby asked.

'No, I'd rather go on my own.'

'OK. I'll pick you up in half an hour.'

Of course, I wasn't on my own for more than a few seconds; soon there was a large crowd of kids, all wanting to talk to me, show me things, ask me where I was going, and what I was going to do. Shahana came to meet me, and I remembered not to call her Hatiya. She shooed the other kids away, but they followed us anyway as we walked together to the camp's cemetery, and there she showed me where Casablanca was buried. I got the saxophone out of its case and fitted the mouthpiece. I hadn't imagined doing this with an audience, but it couldn't be helped, so I composed myself and then said, 'This is for you, Amal. I hope you like it,' and I started to play. At first, I played badly because all the kids were watching and because I was thinking *If I'd taken the gun, he wouldn't have had it and then they wouldn't have killed him,* but in the end, I let the music get into me, and I think it was OK.

Shahana said, 'Thank you. Amal would like that.' And I couldn't think what to say to her, so I just said, 'I hope so,' and she stayed while I walked back to the centre of the camp with my band of followers. They'd remained quiet while we were in the cemetery, but as soon as we were past the factory, a little girl said, 'How do you play that music?' and in no time, I was besieged with questions and demands from kids to let them have a go.

'All right,' I said, 'OK, anyone that wants can have a go, *but* it will have to be one at a time.' The older kids took charge and, half an hour later, when Ruby came to find me, I'd only got half way down the queue.

'I see you're giving music lessons,' she said.

'Yeah, but I could do with more teachers!'

'I'll tell the Truckers,' she said, and it didn't sound as if she was joking.

'Are you serious?' It was like a door opening – Something we could do, something I could do.

'Completely.'

'But what about instruments? We'll need more instruments.'

'No problem. We'll get them. Beg them, borrow them, hijack 'em if we have to. We'll have a benefit, we'll hassle the government.'

'We could start a band! An orchestra! Let's get names!'

'OK, kiddo, OK! Slow down. We'll get the names today of all those who want to join your orchestra, and we'll get instruments. We'll make them find us a space, and there are sure to be adults, kids even who play already who can help us. But... right now, somebody has something really important they want to tell you.'

'Who?' I searched the wall of faces surrounding us.

There was some pushing and shuffling and a gap opened, and Owando was standing there in the gap, grinning his biggest grin, and beside him, with an arm around his shoulder, stood a woman with a perfectly matching smile.

'Dr London,' Owando said. 'I'd like you to meet my mum.'

THANKS

Thanks to friends and family for your wonderful support.

Special thanks to Grace Barnes for her thoughtful comments, to David and Katie Bond for always being there when I needed help and to my wife Katherine for everything.

BIOGRAPHY

Chris Speyer was born in China and grew up in Sydney, where he trained at the National Institute of Dramatic Art before moving to England.

Chris has worked as a theatre designer, director and playwright. His many plays and musicals have been performed all over the UK by theatres and touring theatre companies.

Chris's first novel for young people, DEVIL'S ROCK, was published by Bloomsbury in 2009.

Chris lives with his wife and daughter in Devon where he runs creative writing projects for schools and communities through Music & Words.

To find out more about Chris Speyer's books, to keep up with all the latest news and to join Chris's mailing list, visit www.chrisspeyer.com.

More by Chris Speyer:

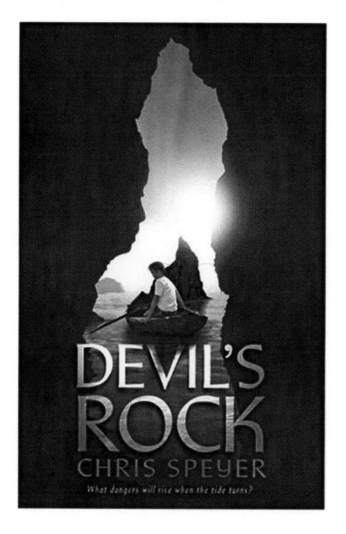

Paperback: 288 pages

Bloomsbury Publishing PLC
ISBN-10: 0747597529

Lightning Source UK Ltd.
Milton Keynes UK
UKOW05f0520111013

218871UK00001B/1/P